HOMELAND SECURITY

HOMELAND
SECURITY

A L E X A   H U N T

A TOM DOHERTY ASSOCIATES BOOK

NEW YORK

HOMELAND SECURITY

Copyright © 2007 by Alexa Hunt

This book is printed on acid-free paper.

A Forge Book
Published by Tom Doherty Associates, LLC
175 Fifth Avenue
New York, NY 10010

www.tor.com

Forge® is a registered trademark of Tom Doherty Associates, LLC.

Library of Congress Cataloging-in-Publication Data

Hunt, Alexa.
    Homeland security / Alexa Hunt.—1st hardcover ed.
      p. cm.
    "A Tom Doherty Associates Book."
    ISBN-13: 978-0-765-31150-4
    ISBN-10: 0-765-31150-X
  1. Bombs—Fiction. 2. Journalists—Fiction. 3. Assassins—Fiction. I. Title.
    PS3608.U57H66   2007
    813'.6—dc22

                                          2006036536

First Edition: March 2007

Printed in the United States of America

0 9 8 7 6 5 4 3 2 1

*For the Law Enforcement Officers of the United States
who make our homeland secure*

ACKNOWLEDGMENTS

The idea for this book came when my editor asked, "Do you plan a sequel to *Corrupts Absolutely*?" I hadn't, but once Natalia Aponte sowed that seed, it took root. I committed to continuing the world I'd built in a frightening near-future America. ChiChi Bernal's character gave me the thread with which to weave together the story of two deadly nukes on a cross-country race.

After that, I began research with a great deal of help, most especially from my husband, Jim, who spent hours (and sacrificed one computer to Internet viruses) searching for details on how experimental "suitcase nuclear devices" work. I am culpable for any literary license with the hardware.

For the Miami sequences, I owe special thanks to Detective Juan Delcastillo, Miami-Dade PD, who gave me an ideal setting for the takedown of Miguel Lopez. Calle Ocho is a beautiful and tourist-friendly neighborhood, not the brutal run-down one I painted in the book. For the St. Louis sequences, I wish to thank the St. Louis PD, the local FBI, and all the wonderful personnel at the Jefferson National Expansion Memorial. As a native St. Louisan, I still get a thrill every time I see Eero Saarinen's diamond bright Arch. Adrian, Michigan, is a real town where I've spent many weeks during the past twenty years while visiting Carol and Ken Reynard, lifetime friends. Although the town does have a large Mexican-American population, none in any way resemble ChiChi Bernal. And my apologies, too, for taking literary license with the landscape in Manhattan and the

Bronx. For those who've missed the opportunity to visit America's number one city, don't let this stop you.

In the middle of writing this book, I called upon a close circle of author friends who gave unstintingly of their time and expertise to brainstorm with me over characterizations and plot twists. Julie Beard, Eileen Dreyer, Carol Monk, Ginny Schweiss, and Karyn Witmer-Gow—you gals are the greatest.

No book sees the light of day without many people being involved in the process. I want to thank not only my outstanding editor, Natalia Aponte, but the whole Tor/Forge family. My publisher, Tom Doherty, brainstormed with me about a very credible and fascinating Middle East scenario that I've filed away. If I ever write that one, I'll give you full credit, Tom.

And last but certainly not least, I owe this book, and many others, to my outstanding agents, Nancy Yost and Julie Culver, who even got the Japanese interested in my post-apocalypse America. I hope everyone enjoys the action as Leah and Del face off against the bad guys once more. Hang on for the ride!

HOMELAND SECURITY

MARTIAL LAW ACT REPEALED! BISC TO BE DISMANTLED

SAMSON CONVENES SPECIAL SESSION OF CONGRESS TO DEAL WITH CRISIS

July 23

WASHINGTON—President Wade Samson spoke for the second time before a joint session of Congress, applauding the repeal of the Martial Law Act, admitting that it was a mistake for which his administration must share the blame. The act created the Bureau of Illegal Substance Control in response to the Slaughter, coordinated Colombian Cartel terrorist attacks across the nation eight years ago. BISC's secret agents were empowered to terminate anyone found guilty of drug trafficking, which the Martial Law Act defined as treason. . . .

SECRECY OF TRIBUNAL CREATED "FERTILE GROUND FOR ATTEMPTED COUP" SAYS FORMER SENATOR

July 23

MACIAS PORT, ME—Former senator Adam Manchester, one of only three senators to vote against the Martial Law Act, spoke at a press conference in his hometown today, condemning the president and Congress for turning loose what he then and now termed "a

secret society of assassins, providing fertile ground for the overthrow of constitutional government in this country."

Manchester, now considered the top contender for the GOP nomination for president, has emerged as a bipartisan spokesman for a
wide spectrum of human rights groups. . . .

SAUDIS OVERTHROWN! ISLAMIC STATE OF "HOLY ARABIA" CREATED

RELIGIOUS LEADERS HOLD REMAINDER OF ROYAL FAMILY HOSTAGE; DEMAND RECOGNITION

August 1

RIYADH—The nation of Saudi Arabia, ruled with an iron fist by the
House of Saud since 1932, is no more. The royal family, which
boasted more than 5,000 princes, has now been decimated, leaving
only a handful of members, mostly women and children, still alive.
King Mishaal bin Abdul al-Saud, who assumed control of the oil-rich
nation only last year, is known to have been assassinated along with
his younger brother Abdullah.

The bloody uprising appears well planned and was swiftly executed. Well-armed Islamic revolutionaries captured Mecca and Med-
ina, the two most holy cities revered worldwide by Muslims. Within
hours key port cities Jidda on the Red Sea and Ad-Dammam,
Dhahran, and Al-Khubar on the Persian Gulf were in the hands of
anti-Saud forces.

Immediately following prayers at daybreak, mobs rioted in the
streets of Riyadh, led by militants who condemned the Sauds for cor-
rupting the strict Wahhabi interpretation of Islam with Western

influences. An unknown number of high-ranking officers in the Saudi military appear to have been in collusion with the revolutionaries as key government offices and royal residences were overrun with little or no defense. . . .

1.

ChiChi Bernal always beat the odds. That's why he'd lived this long. But right now things weren't looking too good. He felt the pull of two innocuous suitcases, one gripped in each meaty fist. They were heavy mothers, but he held them easily. He was a stocky man whose squat, round body hid hard muscle beneath a genial layer of belly flab.

He was late but dared not rush, running the risk of unwelcome attention. San Carlos was a quiet seaside resort that attracted tourists like yellow drew bees. They moved with the languid ease of the balmy weather, gawking at the sky, sipping umbrella-topped alcoholic drinks, and fending off persistent vendors who offered everything from handwoven blankets to plaster statuettes of the Virgin.

A soft hum of conversation surrounded Bernal, English and Spanish blended with German and Japanese. Being a seasoned traveler, he understood snatches of it as he moved through the crowds with watchful eyes.

The aquamarine bay glimmered in evening sunlight, hinting that the tropics extended to northern Mexico. ChiChi walked through the maze of dissecting piers that comprised the big marina, hard black eyes searching out the longest one—his rendezvous site was at the end of it. A maze of sailing masts and power antennae jutted against the orange-gold of the sky as hundreds of yachts bobbed on the incoming tide, obscuring his view. He cursed silently and kept walking.

He'd dressed like a tourist, in a floral print shirt and linen slacks, but his casual jacket concealed the .25-caliber pistol strapped beneath his arm. If anyone wondered why a heavyset man perspired in a linen coat, Bernal saw no evidence of it. He'd made a life's work of blending in. As he neared his destination, the sun sank slowly into the bay, gilding the jagged twin spikes of old Tetakawi, the highest landmark in the coastal range.

From halfway down the pier, Bernal could at last see the opening from the bay to the ocean beyond. "No boat coming in," he muttered to himself. His gut clenched.

Cabril's man, Felix Ortiz, had spotted him in Ciudad Obregon that afternoon and smelled a rat. ChiChi was supposed to be in Culiacán, two hundred kilometers to the south. Had Felix intended to cut himself in on Bernal's action, or had he reported Bernal's whereabouts to Cabril? He'd had no time to find out.

Ortiz and two of his men lay dead near a rest stop forty kilometers south on Highway 15. That had added an hour to this leg of Bernal's trip. It took time to dispose of the bodies, wash away the blood, and change clothes. If Ortiz had told Cabril ChiChi's destination before he died, ChiChi was screwed. He set one case down on the dock and looked around, feeling the weight of the Colt under his jacket. In spite of the cool breeze off the ocean he was now sweating profusely.

Cabril must be the reason the damn boat wasn't here. Bernal looked around the marina crowded with pleasure crafts. Maybe he could steal one, but even after serving three years in the U.S. Navy and seven in its Mexican counterpart, he'd never learned to operate so much as a dingy. He was a cook by trade, not a boatswain mate. His only option would be to kidnap an owner and force him to head out to sea. Bernal didn't like the odds on that. Cabril's outfit had spy planes patrolling the coast regularly.

Scanning the crowd of tourists and vendors, he saw no one suspicious until two big, blond Anglo types approached him, splitting up casually as they drew nearer. The hair on the back of his thick neck prickled. Like him, they wore jackets on this warm night when most men dressed in short-sleeved shirts.

Shit! He picked up the cases and walked as fast as his short legs would carry him, heading to the end of the crowded pier. He knew without looking that the gringos were closing the distance between them. Still no sign of his contact entering the narrow neck of the harbor.

Much as he disliked using some frightened hostage as a pilot, he might not have another choice. The pier he was on ran parallel to three others, all crowded with boats of various sizes. He glanced into each cabin as he walked past, looking for one that was occupied, but quickly abandoned the idea. It would take far too long to ease a boat from its berth.

Decision time.

Bernal went with his gut and jumped onto the small Sea Ray directly beside him. He landed with surprising agility for a stocky man carrying such a heavy load. He could hear his pursuers' footsteps break into a run as he regained his footing on the rocking deck and flattened himself behind the cover of the cabin. The soft ping of a silenced bullet ricocheted off the metal rail to his right as he moved to the stern of the boat. He held his breath and threw the cases onto the bow of a large Bayliner moored beside it.

The next shot missed his head by an inch. One of the men fired from the stability of the pier while the other jumped onto the boat, causing it to rock violently under his weight. A tall man with a high center of gravity, he lost his balance and pitched forward. When he seized hold of the rail, ChiChi fired a single shot. The gringo tumbled over the edge and dropped with a loud splash into the water.

Down the pier a woman screamed. Bernal swore as he sighted in on the second man who dived behind the gate of the Bayliner. He fired when the blond head appeared over the edge of the stern, then jumped to the bow of the Bayliner, flattening himself at another popping sound. It was a standoff now. Both men were pinned down on the same boat, but Bernal once more held the suitcases.

At the opposite end of the pier a crowd gathered for the impromptu entertainment. He could hear the sound of angry voices and women's hysteria. Soon the police would arrive. In a rich tourist area like this they were uncharacteristically prompt. ChiChi looked at the alloy metal cases and went with his gut again.

Using them as a shield was his only option. Would his enemy fire and risk hitting one? He had no time to consider because the man he'd sent into the drink surfaced, bloody but decidedly alive. And still armed. He climbed over the bow of the Sea Ray with the business end of a Browning pointed directly at Bernal.

ChiChi could see his finger, glistening with water, tighten on the trigger. "Son of a bitch, die!" He raised the suitcase to his chest and fired his Colt at the same time. The gringo's slug hit the metal case and knocked the air from his lungs. His ears rang. He shook his head, rolling with the case clutched to his chest, ready to fire again, but his target went down, this time falling across the narrow bow of the Sea Ray.

The big man didn't move but his companion did. Bernal could hear him climbing around the far side of the cabin. He could also hear the clump of police boots running down the wooden pier. Lots of them. He shoved the Colt into his belt and seized both cases, then jumped to the next boat, a two-story yacht bigger than the house in Detroit where he'd grown up. It provided him enough cover to clear another craft before Blondie followed.

Now they were playing the same game. Elude the cops first, then settle who got the cases. To keep the police from outrunning them to the end of the pier, both antagonists fired at them. Brown uniforms hit the ground like cow shit plopping on a flat rock. The harbor cops found cover on the boats just as the gunmen had done.

Bernal stayed a couple of boats ahead of Blondie as they continued the deadly game of leapfrog. He watched the bay and prayed for a miracle. Then he saw it. A small fishing boat cut like a knife across the calm water. His ride had made it! All he had to do was reach the old shrimper alive with the suitcases. He considered throwing one to his pursuer.

"Five million bucks. Fuck him," he muttered and held on to both of them as he made another leap, this time almost missing his footing between decks. The big Anglo was gaining on him when he landed on the last boat at the end of the pier, a small Monterey providing little cover. The shrimper was close now. He just might make it—unless the Harbor Patrol boats got in on the act. Or Blondie got lucky. He crouched and waited, peering out from behind one of the cases.

He could hear the roar of the powerful engine concealed beneath the beat-up old boat's weathered hull. So close. Sounds of orders barked sharply in Spanish led the more foolhardy of the police to dash down the pier. Blondie had finally calculated the odds and knew there was no way he was going to recover the suitcases and elude the authorities with them. The big man dove into the water and vanished in the gathering darkness.

Bernal watched for him to surface at the next pier. "Come on . . . come on." Then he grinned. His target slid over the side of a small powerboat. ChiChi took careful aim. In spite of the wake created by his approaching rescuer, he hit the mark. As the man went down, he fired again, knocking him back into the water.

One piece of business finished. He couldn't have anyone reporting back to Cabril, who would recognize a description of the shrimper and know its captain—that was, if the big blond worked for Cabril. He might have worked for the buyer. There was too much money involved not to anticipate a double-cross. After all, he was considering one himself.

ChiChi never left loose ends. He took the last ammo clip from his pocket and shoved it into the Colt. When a young cop dashed a few meters closer he fired. The bullet hit the dumb kid in the thigh and he went down.

"*ChiChi, como estas, mi hijo?*" a gray-haired man wearing a battered straw hat called out as he swung his craft neatly alongside the Monterey.

"Sandoval, you old fart, what the fuck took you so long?" he replied as he pitched the cases onto the shrimper's deck and jumped after them.

"A small delay." The old man shrugged as his gnarled hands clutched the wheel expertly. "It seems Hernan, he wanted to discuss a certain matter with me," Enrico Sandoval replied in Spanish. Although the old man's English was serviceable, he refused to use it unless he had to.

As they swung clear of the pier, Bernal was relieved to know the

gringos had been Cabril's men. The alternative would have complicated matters. He shoved the cases against the side of the deck, taking
cover as the police fired after them. San Carlos's finest were lousy
shots. Quickly the shrimper slipped out of range. Still, ChiChi scanned
the harbor, looking for signs of patrol boats. He was in too deep to
get caught now.

The old man continued speaking. His voice was as rusty as the hull
of his boat. "Hernan Cabril is not a man to cross. Did I know about
certain stolen merchandise, he asks. . . ." He let his words trail away
and grinned toothlessly at Bernal.

"Of course, you assured him you knew nothing," ChiChi replied.
Sandoval was his father's cousin. The two men had grown up together working the shrimp trade along the south Sonoran coast before the elder Bernal and his family emigrated to Detroit. ChiChi had
spent many summers in Guaymas as a boy. Old Enrico had been like
a second father to him. He grinned back sharkishly.

"I swore I had not heard a word from you for months. But they
know you are the one who took the suitcases. You have made some
very powerful enemies, my son."

"For ten million American, I'll take my chances."

The old man shrugged again and returned his attention to piloting
the boat.

"Did you see any Harbor Patrol when you came in?" Bernal asked.

"Them we can outrun. It is the skies you need to watch."

ChiChi knew Sandoval was right. If the drug lord's planes spotted
them before they could reach the inlet where he'd hidden his all-terrain
vehicle, they were dead men. They made it to the open sea easily. When
the police contacted the Harbor Patrol, no boats must have been in
range. Good. That way they couldn't report which direction the fugi-
tives were headed for a spy plane to pick up and relay to Cabril, whose
boss had much better equipment than the Mexican government.

The night grew overcast. Another favorable omen. ChiChi started
to relax, then reminded himself the journey had barely begun. Enrico
Sandoval's boat, often employed in the local drug trade, plowed
through the coastal water headed for an obscure destination known
only to the old man and his passenger.

After an hour heading due south, the opposite direction from which his enemies would think to look, his companion's boat pulled into a small inlet overgrown with mangroves, one of a myriad known to the old drug runner like the palm of his creased hand. "We are here, my son," he announced proudly. Sandoval had known it was dangerous to cross his employers, but he was an old man who wanted to retire. When ChiChi had approached him, he'd asked for only enough money to allow him and his aged wife to live modestly.

Bernal understood that Enrico was trustworthy. But like the two gringos, his old companion could tell Cabril about his escape route. Not willingly, ChiChi granted. But tell them he would if the drug lord learned that an old shrimp boat with a powerful engine had rescued him. He watched as Sandoval pulled his boat up to the shoreline, concealing it between dense mangroves.

The old man cut the engine and peered up the hillside into the darkness. "You have a Jeep hidden there?" he asked dubiously.

"An all-terrain vehicle. It could travel on the moon," ChiChi replied with a grin. By the time Cabril found the boat, he would be thousands of miles away on the next leg of his journey. He pulled the Colt from his belt and shot Enrico Sandoval between his eyes.

ChiChi Bernal never left loose ends.

2:00 A.M. PST, SATURDAY, NOVEMBER 8
LOS ANGELES, CALIFORNIA

Leah sat in the window of the old deserted warehouse smelling the coppery stench of fresh blood. Far below, a fat man lay on the floor with a single hole in his bulging forehead, directly between his eyes. She never missed.

For some reason she felt compelled to climb down to where Big Frankie Dittmeier lay. The second-story window made that impractical but she was lithe and athletic. Holding on to the edge of the sill, she lowered herself, using her feet on the rough cinder-block wall for purchase. Then she jumped the last several meters onto a pile of boxes. Before they could topple over, she leaped clear, approached the corpse.

Suddenly the "Big" sat up. But it no longer was Frankie, the obese drug kingpin. His whole body melted before her horrified eyes. "Zig-Zag!" she gasped, standing frozen as she looked at the skinny fifteen-year-old named Rob Zigler, a boy she was trying to save. A boy who reminded her of Kevin . . .

Then she was in the car with Griffin, her trainer. He drove down the spiraling exit ramp from the parking deck where she'd made her first "cancellation." Only this time the ramp went down instead of up. Down and down, circling . . .

"Stop! Please, stop the car. I'm going to be sick," she gasped as the dark concrete walls sped past her window like a grainy old black and white film.

He kept on driving, his harsh profile focused straight ahead. Not saying anything.

"Didn't you hear me, Griff?" She felt the icy cold of the metal door handle and yanked on it. It wouldn't move.

But then he broke his silence. Leah swiveled her head to look at him. A middle-aged white man morphed into a fourteen-year-old black kid named Danny Taylor, Danny T, Zig-Zag's friend. "It get easier, Sista. Word," he mouthed, grinning at her.

"No! This is crazy! This can't be happening. I'm going to throw up! Stop the car! Stop the fucking car!" she screamed, but the black youth, his eyes barely able to see over the steering wheel, kept driving intently in downward circles.

They spiraled into oblivion, picking up speed. She rolled down the window and vomited over the faded gray paint on the government-issue electric vehicle. Then a new voice brought her wheeling around in her seat.

"Murderer! You're a killer. A natural-born killer!"

A child's voice but not Danny Taylor's or Rob Zigler's. It was Mike Delgado who accused her. Mike, the twelve-year-old son of her lover . . . Mike who then raised a Smith & Wesson .50-caliber handgun far too big for his hands.

"You killed my father," he cried. And fired point-blank at her. . . .

But the explosion never came. Instead, a soft buzz jarred her consciousness. The sickening downward spiraling slowed as she rolled to the side of the bed, sweat-soaked and trembling. Swallowing the acid taste of bile, she picked up the beeping link and opened it. "Berglund here," was all she could manage. Her throat felt as raw as if she had really vomited.

A hesitant voice on the other end of the link said, "Ms. Berglund, I'm so sorry to be wakin' you, but Joey . . ." Her voice choked.

Leah came fully awake now, peering around in the dark. She was in her modest Long Beach apartment. "Mrs. Buccoli?" It was Joey's mother. He was one of the kids she was trying to rescue from a nasty street gang whose members sold Elevator, the lethal drug that had turned most of America's cities into free-fire zones for dealers and addicts. And her into a government assassin.

In this rare instance, the boy Joey had a parent who gave a damn what happened to her kid. "Where's Joey, Mrs. Buccoli?" she asked, praying he wasn't lying in the morgue.

3 A.M. PST, SATURDAY, NOVEMBER 8
SAN PEDRO WATERFRONT, CALIFORNIA

Social work wasn't supposed to be a life-threatening occupation. At least, in theory. Leah Berglund knew theory was usually crap. She walked along the deserted wharf, a tall woman with white-blond hair and an easy, self-confident stride. But tonight she walked with a wary step.

San Pedro Harbor had once been the site for scenic cruises and whale watching. Now it was a drug-infested hellhole, thanks to the "Elevator epidemic." The deadly cocaine-Viagra combo sent users on a fast high that sometimes cost their lives. But there was serious money for the Elevator Operators, or El-Ops, as they were called. They'd taken over what had once been a prosperous scenic bay. Tourists had been replaced by thugs carrying automatic weapons.

"Even drug dealers have to sleep sometime," she muttered as she listened to the wheeze of tug engines in the darkness, not wanting to think of what else was out there. The fog-laden air was heavy with the smell of diesel fuel, a rare occurrence since the Fossil Fuels Prohibition Act. It burned her nose and swirled around her body like a slimy gray raincoat.

She suppressed a shiver of apprehension and focused on what she had to do. Becoming a caseworker for a drug rehab project was her atonement for joining BISC. She'd thrown herself into the job with desperate intensity, hoping she could redeem her soul . . . and stop the nightmares. So far it hadn't worked.

Leah scanned the dark warehouse windows with the practiced eye of an assassin. *From government sanctioned killer to savior of lost youth.* Just then a soft rustling sound, barely audible over the lap of water, caused her to freeze. "Joey?"

No answer.

Her hand automatically went for the needle gun she'd carried for over three years, but the personalized weapons were unavailable since the agency that created them had been disbanded. She was unarmed now. And crazy to be here alone, but it was the only way Joey Buccoli would meet her. He'd picked the time and place. His mother relayed the message but Leah had heard the unspoken warning under the old woman's desperate plea.

Another noise. Leah tensed, glad she'd opted for hard-toed boots and loose slacks since she was now certain there were two people in the darkness, one ahead and one behind her. Joey's friends didn't want him leaving the gang. He'd been one of their most successful "El-Ops."

At age fourteen. *Like Danny T. Don't go there.*

Had Joey sold her out? She continued toward the opening between the two warehouses where the first member of the welcoming committee waited, listening for the inevitable footsteps behind her.

He came up quick and clean, but not as well as she'd have done it in her other life. Years of conditioning switched on. A split second before the blade could slash her throat she pivoted, seizing its owner's arm as she bent forward, pulling him off balance, causing him to tumble onto her back for the throw. He sailed over her head and hit the filthy wooden boards with a nasty thump.

Leah followed through with the toe of her boot, kicking the soft flesh beneath his chin. She felt the jawbone snap and he flopped backward on the pier like a tuna tossed from a fishing boat. His knife slithered out of her reach as the second attacker materialized directly ahead. He raised an old snub-nosed revolver and fired.

"Cunt!"

The shot whizzed past her ear, missing by several inches. Before he could get off another round she tackled him head-on. They went down with her on top, smashing his gun arm hard against the splintery wood of the wharf. A second shot cracked, sending a spray of brick dust flying from the warehouse nearby as she punched his throat. Twice.

The whole thing took less than a minute. Both men lay unconscious in the fog. "I may be a cunt, but you shoot like a pussy," she muttered as she stood up, brushing splinters and brick dust from her now filthy sweater and slacks. When she heard footsteps running down the gangway between the warehouses, Leah scooped up the .357 from the pier, spun around, and aimed.

"For Christ sake, don't shoot! Fuck, don't shoot me! I didn't know they'd be here, I swear." Joey, panting, with hands above his head, emerged into the dim glow cast by a pole light a dozen meters down the wharf.

She lowered the piece. He had trouble keeping his hands in the air and maintaining his balance at the same time. He was a skinny kid with near terminal acne and long, greasy brown hair. Crumpled against the wall of the warehouse, he looked very young and even more frightened.

"I believe you, Joey," she said, resigned, pocketing the gun. He'd probably been so hopped up on Elevator he didn't know what he'd said to anyone all night. "Put your hands down. If I intended to shoot you, you'd be lying there with your two pals."

"Fuck, you're one mean mama for a social worker," he said with a nervous hiccup, lowering his arms to hug himself, still using the wall for support. "How'd you learn to fight like that?"

Youthful curiosity trumped fear, even drug-induced confusion, for a fourteen-year-old kid. "It's a long story, Joey. How about I explain to you on the way to the rehab center?"

He hesitated, shivering in the damp fog as the high began to wear off. "I dunno . . . Marko and Big Jake, they don't want me messin' with no rehab workers."

"But you came to meet me anyway, didn't you?" *Even if it took getting high to work up the nerve.* She didn't say that, just waited.

In the distance a siren wailed.

"It's what your mother wants, Joey. And if I don't get you out of here before the cops arrive to collect these creeps, you'll end up in juvvie. Besides, if you come along I'll tell you about me and Wesley Snipes."

That convinced him. He staggered away from the wall and followed her lead down the wharf to her EV. The electric vehicle was a stripped down gray model, standard issue for caseworkers . . . similar to those used by BISC. Just as they pulled away from the pier the bright flashing lights of a police cruiser illuminated the darkness. Leah's nondescript car rounded the corner and vanished into the maze of the warehouse district as the cop car screeched to a halt.

She'd visit the station and make a report once she had Joey in detox at Clean Ride Clinic. Since starting to work for the program, she'd spent more time talking to cops than she ever had when she was an agent for the Bureau of Illegal Substance Control. In minutes the little EV sped across the Vincent Thomas Bridge and headed up I-110.

"So, you learned street fighting from Wesley Snipes?" Joey asked. "Man, dude's gotta be a hundred years old!" He sounded a lot better now that the sirens were silent.

Before she could frame a reply, her link vibrated. She flipped on the display and recognized the white-haired craggy face instantly. Not often a woman received a middle-of-the-night call from the next president of the United States. She could always gauge Adam Manchester's mood by looking at him. Her grandfather did not have good news.

2.

If he hadn't habitually checked the rear vid he wouldn't have reached his gun in time. Even stalled in gridlock with auto headlights distorting his vision, Elliott Delgado always watched his back. "Get down, Mike!" Knocking his son forward, he pulled the .50-caliber Smith & Wesson from beneath his seat.

Small pellets of glass pinged across the interior of their Buick Turbo Electric as the blast from an old automatic rifle shattered the left rear passenger window. Delgado twisted around to fire at the outline of the man limned in high beams. He missed but so did the Elevator Operator with the M16A1. That didn't stop the thug from spraying the roof of the car with another barrage.

"Dad! Are you hurt?" Mike whispered, his voice fierce with terror.

"I'm fine. Stay down. Curl in a ball on the floor," Delgado whispered, unclipping the seat belt holding his son. His was already off, slipped in the quick move to reach his gun. "There might be more of them around," he replied, scanning the vehicles, large and small surrounding him. Damn fools, some still had on their headlights!

According to the radio, a shoot-out and car crash between rival gangs of Elevator Operators stopped traffic on the freeway for a half-dozen kilometers ahead of them. The San Diego PD had sped by on the berm a quarter hour ago with lights flashing. After an initial exchange of gunfire in the distance, Del hadn't heard any more for several minutes—until now.

He opened the door a crack, trying to keep the fire to his side of the car. He knew better than to place a foot on the ground and get it blown off. Immediately he was rewarded by another burst of fire sparking off the pavement, indicating the shooter was crouched behind the left rear tire.

By now some idiots in vehicles around them were yelling, blowing their horns, and otherwise acting like assholes. A few of the brighter ones jumped out and ran through the bumper-to-bumper traffic on Interstate 5, putting steel between them and the shoot-out that had suddenly come all too close.

Twisting backward, Delgado fired another round, eliciting more automatic fire. He held on to the door frame and swung his upper body out far enough to see part of his target's body. One knee. All he required. Taking careful aim, he squeezed the trigger and was rewarded with a shriek of agony. The El-Op rolled to the ground, trying to straighten out what was left of his leg, but didn't let go of the automatic weapon. A burst of fire went wild, peppering several vehicles around Del's Buick.

A series of screams followed. Collateral damage had become a by-word in the drug wars on America's streets and highways. Those who hadn't been shot or fled had brains enough by now to turn off their headlights and crouch in darkness.

Delgado had to stop the El-Op before more innocents were hurt. He aimed at the man writhing on the ground and placed one bullet dead center in his chest. The gunman's hold on the cut-down M16A1 went slack. Colt had made over four million of these older weapons before the improved burst-fire versions were developed. El-Ops favored the older fully automatic ones, which were cheaper and easier to get.

Del jumped out of the car and in two quick steps kicked the weapon away, making certain their attacker was dead.

"Are you okay, Dad?" Mike's voice was shaky.

"I'm fine." Delgado slid inside the ruined TE to check on his son. "You all right, Tige?"

Mike nodded gamely. Some kids would want to sneak a look at the corpse but Mike didn't show any interest. He'd been through more in twelve years than most people endured in seventy. "Who was that guy?" he asked. "Did you recognize him?"

As they brushed glass pebbles off the seat, Delgado replied, "No. Probably just one of the El-Ops trying to escape from the cops by hijacking a fast car." He knew Mike still feared someone coming after them again. He'd been abducted by BISC only four months ago and held hostage.

"He wanted a TE with flash drive," Mike said, nodding in understanding.

"Yeah, and we're in the outside lane so he could swing on the berm, turn around, and head the other direction." He looked at the ruined car, once his pride and joy. *How the hell am I going to explain this to Diana?*

Intuiting his thoughts, Mike said, "Mom's gonna be mad, isn't she? Maybe we shouldn't tell her."

Delgado gave Mike's arm a reassuring squeeze and forced a grin. "You think we should just drive up with the windows and roof shot out and act like nothing happened?"

Mike's apprehension lessened. Responding to his father's calm good humor, he returned the grin. "Naw, some nosy reporter'll put it on the news before we get home." His dad was a Pulitzer-winning reporter.

Before Delgado could reply, two officers approached, eyeing the corpse spread out on the asphalt. The M16 was hidden behind the Buick where Delgado had kicked it. A round-faced older cop with tired eyes stepped up and looked inside, then said, "Can I ask you to step outside the car and raise your hands, sir?"

His younger partner had already drawn his Glock after seeing the cannon Delgado had placed on the seat. "Leave the weapon where it is," he instructed.

Delgado complied, watching as the young one reached inside and seized the .50-caliber handgun. "I have a permit. And ID." He looked questioningly at the older man before reaching carefully into his back pocket and removing his wallet.

"FBI, huh?" the old guy asked after looking through the various papers inside.

"Retired."

"Suppose you tell us why you shot that man?" the young cop asked.

"Because he was a litterbug. Using an M16 to strew parts of my Buick all over the freeway. Look behind what's left of my car for his piece."

"No need to be a smart-ass," the old cop cautioned.

Delgado forced himself to relax as the kid walked back and kicked the automatic rifle into plain view. The Boy Scout still looked suspicious. Delgado had seen the type before. This could take a while.

"Look, I'd like to get my son out of here before the paramedics come for the casualties," he said to the older guy. Already the sound of ambulances wailed in the distance. Up close they could hear the moans of wounded civilians.

"Sorry, buddy, but I got to call this in. You killed that bozo—not that I mind one iota, but you know the drill if you were a fibbie."

Delgado sighed. "Yeah, I know the drill."

After the officers received confirmation of his identity, Del promised them he'd come to the precinct that afternoon and sign a statement if they'd let him take Mike home. By that time the emergency medics had transported the wounded to nearby trauma centers. Smashed cars were being towed away so traffic could flow again. Apparently all the drug dealers were either dead or in custody.

Delgado slid back into his seat and tried the ignition. When the engine turned over, he breathed a sigh of relief. At least they wouldn't have to wait hours more for a tow, even if it did scare Diana half to death when she saw the condition of the car.

He looked over at Mike. "You want to call your mom?" he asked.

The boy grinned. "Chicken."

"You bet I am." He pulled out his link and punched in the code, grimacing over what he had to tell his ex-wife. Hours ago he'd called her to say they'd be late returning from the Chargers game that had gone into overtime. Of course, he hadn't counted on being involved in a shoot-out on I-5, even though the drug gangs in San Diego were having a jim-dandy new turf war.

After summarizing what had just happened he could see her

normally serene expression grow tense. "We should be exiting the freeway in a few minutes, Diana."

"You're sure Mike's okay?" she asked for what seemed the hundredth time.

"Mike's fine, Diana. Here, I'll let him tell you himself," he said, handing the link to his son.

"Yeah, I'm okay, Mom, honest." He rolled his eyes at his dad as if to say, "Women."

Del suddenly thought of Leah and realized that Mike wouldn't expect her to be upset. Leah, who'd stood the kid up for their last outing. *Don't think about her, Delgado.* He reminded himself that Mike wouldn't be a kid much longer. He had to take advantage of what years he had left while his son was still growing up. If Leah Berglund didn't have time for them, they'd just have to live with it.

Mike handed the small link to him after signing off with his mom. Del turned it off and slid it into his jacket pocket. No more interruptions. He needed to see how much the brush with death had really affected Mike. "How're you feeling, Tige?"

Mike met his eyes calmly. "I'm all right, Dad. Just like I told Mom. I was scared for you."

"Yeah, so was I," Delgado admitted, watching as the boy suppressed a yawn. "You should be really tired. Try to get some sleep."

"I'm not sleepy," the leggy twelve-year-old replied, in spite of another yawn. He had his mother's blue eyes and his father's curly black hair and olive complexion and he'd just started another growth spurt the past few months.

Del was glad he was here to see it after spending so many years a continent away. His work had cost him a lot in Mike's young life. But no more. Since taking the job transfer to *U.S. News-Time*'s San Diego office, he never missed an opportunity for them to spend time together.

"Well, I'm tired. Be good to sleep in tomorrow. Glad it's Saturday," he said, not suppressing his yawn.

"Hey, Dad . . ." Mike's voice faded for a minute. "I was thinking."

"Always dangerous," Del said.

"You could spend the night. Then we could have breakfast

together. Mom'll make that orange French toast you like. I know she will."

"Sorry, Tige, but I have work—"

"Thought you said you were going to sleep in."

Damn. The kid had him. Then he remembered the police report. "I have to sign some papers for San Diego's finest, remember?"

"You told them you'd do that in the afternoon," Mike said.

Trying to divert his attention, Delgado asked, "How's that project of yours going for the Science Fair? We never did finish that conversation before the game."

Mike brightened immediately in spite of the late hour. "I've talked with the head of the zoo's primatology division. Dr. Kelly's really neat and she's sent me enough of their file films to prove my thesis."

He launched into enough Latin phrases and zoological terminology to put his father asleep at the wheel. But if his kid was fascinated by the dietary habits of chimps, well, so was he. Besides, the boy was so damn smart it made his chest swell with pride.

"Because my project passed the state board, I'll get to go to New York City for the national fair. Mom already has plane tickets. It'd be neat if you could come see the exhibition," Mike said hopefully.

Before Del could explain that he'd have to do some pretty fancy juggling on his work schedule to fly to New York, he noticed his son had begun to slump in his seat. In a moment he was dozing in the boneless way children sleep. Delgado began to consider how he could get away to the Big Apple, even if it was only for a day.

4:05 A.M., SATURDAY, NOVEMBER 8
LA JOLLA, CALIFORNIA

"I should go. Have to go downtown to sign that report for the police." Delgado drained the cup of coffee and set it on the smooth marble countertop, scooting his chair back from the breakfast bar in Diana Shrewsbury's lavish kitchen. After they'd put their son to bed, she'd invited him to have a cup of coffee so she could grill him about his and Mike's brush with death. The kid had been right. Before they made it home the story was already on late-breaking news.

"I can't believe you actually killed a man tonight." She shuddered. "He could've killed Mike—or you."

"Thanks for remembering the mitigating circumstances," he said.

"You're absolutely sure that man attacking you had nothing to do with your work? Are you writing another story about drug dealers?" she asked again.

Elliott Delgado raked his hand through his hair and sighed. "No. Right now the most controversial piece I've assigned anyone on staff is researching state legislators who take 'fact-finding trips' to Bermuda. Somehow I don't see any of them in league with thugs dealing Elevator." He was bone-tired and they'd had variations on this argument since he'd been an FBI agent. All he wanted right now was sleep.

She surprised him by suggesting, "Why don't you use one of our spare bedrooms? Mike's right, we have, oh, let's see, about a dozen at last count." She was an elegant honey-blond with a smile that could light up Qualcomm Stadium.

"I don't think that's such a hot idea, Diana. He's already trying to get us back together. No sense getting his hopes up more."

"It's only natural, El, especially since . . ." She paused for a moment to gather her composure. "Since Hugh's gone."

Hugh Shrewsbury had been dead only a few months. Although the marriage had not been great, it was certainly better than the one he and Diana had shared. *Lord knows, he left her better provided for than I could've*, he thought, glancing around the redwood and glass mansion jutting out over the ocean.

He studied her. "I know you miss him. You handling everything okay?"

She shrugged. "I'll be honest, El. The past year or so . . . we really didn't see much of each other, with his career in LA and me busy with the Symphony Society and other social activities that bored rich women do. I suppose I feel more guilty than lonely."

"Tough but understandable. Don't beat yourself up for it."

"I wish he'd been able to be a better father to Mike."

"I wish I'd been a better father. I had the job in the first place and blew it, remember?"

"You're here for Mike now, El. That's what counts."

"If only he hadn't started this stuff about us getting together again. I don't know how to handle it."

Diana seemed to hesitate a moment, then asked, "How's Leah? Mike really seemed to take to her."

He let out a long whistling breath. "I think that may be why he's started to fixate on reuniting us. Her damn job is consuming her, Diana. I hardly see her. She works such crazy hours and it's—"

"Dangerous?" she supplied with a wry smile.

"Sounds just like me when I was with the Bureau, doesn't it?"

"As the old saw goes, if the shoe fits? Looks to me like an eleven E."

"You're entitled to gloating rights."

"What I'd rather have is my son happy. He must miss her, too." She studied him with cool intelligent eyes.

In spite of the differences in their backgrounds and life choices, Diana and Leah were a lot alike. *I always did go for tall leggy blondes,* he remembered blurting out to Leah before he found out she was a BISC agent sent to terminate him. But physical resemblance was unimportant. It was the core of inner toughness and common sense that he most admired in both women.

"Yeah, he misses her." *So do I.*

Before she could frame another question, her phone rang. Glancing at the clock over the stove, she quickly reached for it, but didn't activate the vid. "Hello. Shrewsbury residence," she said in a voice reserved for middle-of-the-night bad news.

Hearing the voice on the other side of the link, Diana's expression altered subtly. "Why, hi . . . No, I wasn't asleep . . . It's perfectly fine, don't worry . . . Doing all right, thanks. It's kind of you to ask . . . Yes, he's here." She handed the link to Delgado.

With a puzzled expression on his face he took the unit and flicked on the vid. Leah's white-blond hair and angular face filled the tiny screen. She looked pale and worried. "Leah. You all right?"

"I just caught the news. Better question is are you?"

"I'm fine but you don't look too hot."

She ignored the comment. "I've been trying your link for the past hour. Sorry to wake up Mike and Diana."

If she felt any jealousy or suspicion, it surely wasn't detectable in her voice or facial expression. That bothered him more than he cared to admit. "I turned the sound off. Mike had fallen asleep and I didn't want to wake him. Must've forgotten to put it on vibrate. What's so serious that it can't wait until morning?"

"If it was up to me, I'd never involve you. But my grandfather threatened to track you down himself. He never bluffs." She rubbed her eyes, tired to the bone.

Del could see that she was upset over whatever Adam Manchester wanted. "What's going on, Leah?"

"Gramps wants us to meet him in Washington immediately. I told him I'd be there, to leave you out of it. I don't know what's going on but it sounds dangerous. You have a son to worry about." She rubbed her eyes again. "He wouldn't take no for an answer."

Leah-Pia, always trying to protect the innocent. Half irritated, he said, "D.C., in case you forgot, is three thousand miles away. We can't get there 'immediately.' "

"That's why Gramps has a private jet warming up at Lindbergh Field. I'm on I-5 passing La Jolla. I could stop and pick you up, but—"

"Hey, who am I to turn down the next president? I'm coming with you, Leah. No argument."

"Is that new bruise a love tap from a client or are you getting sloppy when you work out?" Del asked as she drove down the twisting road from Diana's seaside mansion.

Leah touched her throat. *Damn man never misses a thing!* "I'm used to taking my lumps—besides, I don't have your family responsibilities."

He couldn't keep the irritation out of his voice. "If the senator wants us both, Leah, we go together. Dangerous or not. Besides, you're the one working on the San Pedro docks, not me."

"After icing an El-Op, you're a fine one to talk. You gotta learn to stay out of trouble, Delgado. You or Mike could've been killed."

"So could you. What happened—and no bullshit, okay?"

She sighed, too tired to argue. He'd find out the truth one way or the other, nosy reporter. "One of my client's gang-member pals objected to him going into rehab. The harbor cops'll offer him accommodations—after city hospital gets through putting his jaw back together."

He chuckled grimly. "My Leah, the lean, mean muscle machine. Want to talk about it?"

She glanced over at him. "Why, so we can have another dandy fight?"

"What're you worried about? You always win."

Leah knew he worried about her safety, working in drug rehab around the harbor slums. "Look, Del, it's what I have to do. You were an FBI agent. You risked your life as a reporter, too, but you don't have to anymore."

"I wasn't doing it as penance, Leah. BISC betrayed you. You're not guilty of anything but integrity and dedication."

"I sure picked a great agency to dedicate my life to, didn't I? Canceling the innocent right along with the guilty."

"You never made a wrongful termination," he said flatly.

"Neither one of us will ever know if that's really true, will we, Del? Besides, I love what I'm doing now. You should've seen Joey Buccoli tonight. Poor kid's only fourteen, can't weigh more than a decent-sized border collie. If I hadn't—"

"Okay, okay, I know how important those kids are to you. But Mike misses you. What about him? Last time I checked he was a kid, too—and he doesn't weigh much more than a decent-sized border collie either."

"I'm sorry I missed the zoo trip last week," she said with real regret.

"It was the week before last, but who's counting?" He watched her grip on the wheel tighten and cursed himself. *That's the way to go, Delgado, heap on more guilt as if she isn't eaten up with enough already.*

He tapped his fingers on the leather armrest of the Lincoln Turbo-Electric. It had all the bells and whistles including flash drive that breezed along at 120 kilometers per hour. He thought wistfully about his Buick. "Adam arrange for this fancy transpo?"

"You think I could afford it on a social worker's salary?" she asked.

"Any speculations on why the Grand Old Man wants us in D.C.—or why he's even there himself? Latest word off the wire yesterday said he was still down home."

"It's 'down east,'" she corrected, grateful for the reprieve from what had become a constant tug-of-war between her job and her personal life. "I thought he was in Maine, too. It would take something really serious to lure him to Washington."

He grinned. "An odd aversion for a man who, according to all the polls, is a shoo-in for the Republican nomination next year. How's he expect to withstand the campaign trail?"

"Gramps loves people. It's politicians he can't stand."

That drew a laugh. "A man after my own heart. Too damned bad he'll probably become president."

7:02 A.M. EST, SATURDAY, NOVEMBER 8
WASHINGTON, D.C.

Secretary of Homeland Security Robert Labat had the most thankless job in Wade Samson's cabinet. Everyone inside the Beltway understood the problems inherent in a department charged with keeping agencies as diverse as the Secret Service, Customs, Immigration, the Coast Guard, and FEMA—the Federal Emergency Management Administration—working together. To heighten Labat's frustration quotient, Homeland Security was supposed to keep the FBI and CIA not only talking to each other but also sharing information with him. Fat chance.

FDR would have been hard put to handle the morass in which the department wallowed. Bob Labat was the first to admit he was no Roosevelt. He'd slipped into politics via the back door. After working his way through school, he'd taken a job as project administrator for the Nevada Department of Natural Resources. Typical civil service, low pay, long hours, and all the grief anyone could ask. Then a group of protesters had cornered him on the parking lot after work one day, asking his help stopping the storage of nuclear waste.

At first he thought they were just a bunch of rich kids in Stetsons, but then it occurred to him that they had a good idea. He was assigned to monitor waste transpo. Only the week before his boss had warned him not to say a word about the routes of tankers bringing in radioactive waste. Some of the politicians in Carson City were getting nervous about it. After all, it was an election year.

So he'd quit his job and run for the state legislature on an antistorage platform. Using another disgruntled employee as a source, he'd led protests against the department. He made headlines lying down on the highway in front of hazmat trucks crossing the Nevada state line. Within five years he was a crusading governor.

Now look where that got me.

The tall, emaciated man sighed, combed his fingers through his thinning hair, and flicked the vid on, revealing the very angry face of President Wade Samson. He'd been expecting the call. That was why he was in his office on a weekend at this ungodly hour.

"Good morning, Mr. President."

"You know there's not a damn thing good about it," Samson snapped. "What have your undersecretaries learned?"

"Well"—he swallowed, feeling his shirt collar tighten around his Adam's apple like a noose—"Border Patrol let him in, near as we can tell—"

"Near as you can tell!" Samson echoed. "How the hell could that happen? Globe Net reports every crossing to the National Reconnaissance Office, but this thug coasts in without a trace!"

"I'm certain by the time of the meeting I'll have more information. There was some sort of technical glitch between Border Patrol and the NRO."

"The AG and his FBI director will come after you like junkyard dogs."

Samson's presidential act was too smooth for him to grin at his own lousy pun but Labat knew mentioning dogs after a rabbit wasn't accidental. His French name had been corrupted generations back. Labat was pronounced to rhyme with rabbit. One snotty television news pundit had dubbed him "Labat the Rabbit" when he first arrived in Washington. It stuck.

"I give you my word, sir, I'll get to the bottom of what went wrong in my bailiwick."

"You'd better. This is a major breech in national security and it occurred on our watch, Bob. As I told you yesterday evening, Delgado and Berglund are en route. Manchester's bringing them to the White House." He pronounced his archrival's name as if he'd just swallowed a wad of dirty flannel.

"Are you certain you can trust Manchester—not to question your judgment, Mr. President, but—"

"Hell, no, I don't trust the old goat. But there's no other way to get Delgado and Berglund aboard. Frankly, we need their expertise."

Labat nodded, swallowing nervously. "Do you think those bombs—"

"Don't ever say it, Bob. Don't even think it."

The screen went blank and Bob Labat was left alone as the feeble winter sun cast pale light through the windows of his office. There were days when he'd felt as weak and ineffectual as that sun. He tapped in a number on his PDA and waited until a voice answered. "This is Bob Labat. Let me speak to the undersecretary," he said in his most authoritative voice.

He was put on hold.

5:20 A.M. MST, SATURDAY, NOVEMBER 8
SOMEWHERE OVER NEW MEXICO

The private jet was small and spartan but state-of-the-art in speed. After the night she'd spent with Joey and his ex-pals, Leah should've been bone-tired but adrenaline pounded through her veins like the straight shot of Elevator that had killed her brother and brought her to BISC. She glanced at Delgado, who was fast asleep, his long body stretched over the seat.

He looked years younger when he slept. Only a few gray hairs and the squint lines around his eyes indicated he was pushing forty. Since leaving D.C. and taking the job as San Diego bureau chief for his news magazine, he'd been less driven and cynical, happy to be with his son. But what about her? Leah knew she'd pushed him away. Part of it was her work. But there was more . . . so much more. Ugliness she didn't want to drag out into the light of day and have to face.

Del pushed for her to make a commitment. Leah wasn't sure she knew how. *But Diana does.* That bit. Del had looked homey in her spacious kitchen when she'd seen him on the vid. He'd given his ex-wife an affectionate hug before climbing into the car with her. He and Mike needed someone like his ex. Not a retired assassin.

Besides, she was a lousy risk anyway. Her parents had a shaky marriage. Hell, she'd spent more than one night in a Minneapolis ER after her mother nearly killed herself, overdosing on legals. Since her brother died, the situation had become far worse. The thin ties binding them together had simply snapped. Her grandfather remained the only family member she could rely on.

She'd never had a lasting relationship with a lover until she met Elliott Delgado five months ago. Could she ever leave her past behind?

As the plane hurtled toward sunrise, the approaching light held no answers.

9:30 A.M. EST, SATURDAY, NOVEMBER 8
WASHINGTON, D.C.

A black limo dripping chrome was waiting at the end of the runway as their plane taxied to a stop at National. Adam Manchester's white hair and craggy face were recognizable from fifty meters away even through the drizzling rain. He stood by the car, as impervious to the elements as the granite rocks on his native Maine coastline. The former senator had not sought reelection after the Martial Law Act created what he termed "a police state legalizing assassination." In spite of his granddaughter's decision to become one of those assassins, he had loved her unconditionally even as he condemned BISC's architect, Wade Samson.

GOM, or the "grand old man" as Leah and her brother had always referred to him, walked toward her and Del with the stride of someone half his age. He hugged Leah fondly, then extended his hand to Delgado for a firm shake.

"I appreciate your coming on such short notice. We can talk on the ride." With that, he turned and led the way to the limo, watching the isolated stretch of runway to be certain no one saw them.

Once they were inside the plush interior, Del asked, "All right, Senator, why all the cloak-and-dagger stuff?"

"You look tired, Gramps," Leah said, studying the faint bruising around his eyes. No one but she would notice such slight evidence of fatigue.

He made a dismissive gesture with one hand. "First things first. Tell me about California. How's the job working out? Last time we talked, you were spending a lot of time at that center."

"Working with addicted kids to get them clean sure beats the hell out of killing them," she replied. Leah had always been brutally honest with her grandfather and knew he would accept the bald statement, not judge her. "The El-Ops lose every time I get a kid to Clean Ride for rehab. Our success rate's nearly sixty-five percent. Last night when you called, I'd just brought in a fourteen-year-old boy whose mother helped me talk him into giving our program a try."

"She works too hard. Always did," Manchester said to Delgado.

"Look who's talking," she shot back. "Most men your age are out fishing—for salmon or pike, not votes."

The old man chuckled without mirth. "This whole presidential thing sought me out, not the other way around, Leah-Pia. I could've been happy just returning to the Senate."

"But now you're back inside the Beltway to stay. And something big's made you call us. What?" Del waited, wondering if Manchester would answer now.

"Wade Samson has asked me for help."

Leah blinked in amazement.

Delgado raised his left eyebrow. "He's scared spitless you're going to hammer him next November. Why would he come to you?"

Manchester leaned back as their driver wove into traffic on the George Washington Memorial Parkway. "Oh, he didn't. He summoned me to come to him. We're on our way to the White House."

3.

Once they were inside the heavy iron gates at 1600 Pennsylvania Avenue, the limo glided up the drive, following two school buses filled with elementary students. Good cover for their arrival. Completely underawed in the shadow of the White House, the boisterous children spilled out of the buses talking and laughing.

President Samson's chief of security, Abbie Rutledge, barked at the hapless Secret Service Uniform Division officer assigned the unhappy task of riding herd on forty preteens and four teachers. "You'd better not let one of those little dragons sneak away from the tour and end up in the first lady's bathroom again. She nearly swallowed her tongue when he jumped out of the shower stall."

The uniform officer nodded, shaking in his boots. Then the tall black woman nodded discreetly in the direction of Manchester's limo and walked briskly inside with a self-assured stride. The driver opened the doors for the senator and his guests instantly. No one kept Abbie waiting and he obviously knew it.

Inside, Abbie tapped the toe of a stiletto heel impatiently until they made their way past the children. "Good morning, Senator, Miss Berglund, Special Agent Delgado," she said, turning to lead them through the labyrinth to wherever Samson had ordered.

"I'm not with the Bureau anymore, Abbie," Del said, even though he knew she was well aware of the fact.

"Don't be too sure of that, Delgado." She opened the door to a small conference room with a polished mahogany table in the center. The thick carpet cut a good inch off her Ferragamo heels as they sank into the cream-colored pile. "The president is in the Cement Mixer with key staff right now."

"That's White House lingo for the Situation Room in the West Wing," Del whispered to Leah, who looked puzzled.

Abbie frowned at the interruption as if Del and Leah were schoolkids caught passing notes in third grade. "The president will be here as soon as possible. Please have a seat." She gestured to the three chairs positioned in front of the table, then turned to leave.

"What's this all about, Abbie?" Delgado asked.

She looked at him with hard brown eyes. "That's for President Samson to tell you, not me." She closed the door firmly behind her.

"Her usual charming self," Del said. He'd known her since his days with the FBI. She had been on the podium with him during the assassination attempt on the president last summer. Abbie was tough, the best in the business, and her loyalty to Samson was absolute.

Leah watched her grandfather calmly pour himself a glass of water from the pitcher on the table. *We're in for an interrogation.*

Shortly, the door at the opposite side of the room opened and President Wade Samson walked in, followed by four grim-faced men. Delgado knew one personally from his time with the Bureau, the others only by reputation.

General Howard McKinney was chairman of the Joint Chiefs; Bob Labat, secretary of Homeland Security; John Scarletti, the attorney general; and Paul Oppermann, director of the newly reorganized FBI. *Quite an impressive gathering*, Del thought as he and Leah exchanged glances.

The only major players absent were Breck Souders, Samson's national security advisor, whom they all knew had been hospitalized with a stroke two days ago, and Secretary of State Stuart Kensington and Secretary of Defense Karl Banecek. Both men were currently in Korea for discussions on U.S. withdrawals from the DMZ now that the reunification had been completed.

Wade Samson looked presidential. He was tall with serious hair, a Dick Tracy jaw line, and ice-blue eyes that met you head-on. When he entered a room, he didn't need anyone to play "Hail to the Chief" to become the center of attention. Only today his gravitas wasn't quite working. His appointees fixed their attention on Adam Manchester, who looked pretty damn presidential himself.

Samson quickly took the initiative, walking around the table to grasp the older man's hand in a firm shake. "Good of you to come, Senator."

"Not as if I had a lot of choice, Mr. President," Manchester replied bluntly. "I believe you've met Elliott Delgado."

Samson extended his hand. "I'm not likely to forget the man who knocked me to the ground in front of half a million people."

"That's not counting the live vid audience and the reruns, Mr. President."

Samson's laughter was genuine. "You saved my life and I'll never forget it. And Ms. Berglund gave an able assist," he said, turning to Leah.

She extended her hand. "We were glad to be of service, Mr. President."

Samson gestured to the four men standing around him and made introductions. Leah had never met any of them. From his days on the Hill Manchester knew General McKinney and Del had worked for Paul Oppermann when the FBI director was SAC of New York City. All three had heard rumors about Homeland Security secretary Bob Labat, a Washington outsider caught in the middle of turf wars between CIA, FBI, Treasury, and just about every other federal department or agency.

Scarletti, a small, swarthy man wearing wire-rimmed glasses, was the most mysterious, a deputy AG appointed to head the Justice Department during the era when BISC made it virtually superfluous. Now, with a mandate from Congress to expand his department, he might become the most powerful man in Samson's Cabinet.

Adam Manchester studied the younger man, searching for any trace of Annie in him . . . found none. *His father's son all the way. . . .*

Samson finished the stilted amenities, then took his seat at the center of the table, and the rest of them sat in their designated places, the three guests facing them. *The hot seats,* Leah thought grimly, feeling the tension already humming between her grandfather and the chief executive. She'd also noted the way Adam had stared at the AG for a moment, as if he should know him. As far as she was aware, they'd never met.

"First, let me preface this by saying that absolutely nothing discussed in this room is for public consumption." Samson's gaze moved from Manchester to his granddaughter, then settled on Delgado, the reporter.

"You told me this concerned national security, Mr. President. Of course none of us would breech such a confidence," Manchester replied.

"To make certain that Mr. Delgado and Ms. Berglund can act with official sanction, the president has issued an executive order," the attorney general said in a soft sandpapery voice. He shoved two documents across the table. "For the duration of this investigation, you will be special agents under Director Oppermann's supervision."

Leah Berglund paled but said nothing. After BISC betrayed her, she had sworn never again to work for the government. In fact, she'd refused a job offer from the last director of the FBI, Cal Putnam.

Elliott Delgado looked cynically amused. "I was retired on full disability. This mean you guys take away my pension?"

"This is for your own protection as well as ours, Mr. Delgado." Scarletti's soft murmur had steel beneath it.

"You didn't mention this when you called me, Mr. President," Adam Manchester said. "Are you quite certain I shouldn't be inducted into the Bureau as well? Or am I too old?"

But not too old to be president. The possibility hung in the air between the two men. "I think we can dispense with that, Senator," Samson snapped. Then he looked at the two young people. "I'm asking you to do this for your country. If, after the briefing, you decline to help, you'll be free to leave as long as you swear not to divulge anything discussed. The status as special agents is only temporary."

"Tell us what's so urgent. Then we'll decide if we want to re-up, sir," Delgado said.

"I'll listen." Leah's voice was flat.

Samson nodded, satisfied, and began. "As you know, during last summer's attempted coup General Sommerville's forces intended to invade Colombia. With nuclear hardware." Samson paused for effect. "That invasion was thwarted and the nuclear devices recovered. Your cousins, Mr. Delgado, both members of Mexican Special Forces, led the team that recaptured the nukes."

He glanced down at his notes. "Raoul and Ernesto Mulcahey. Grandsons of your great-uncle, Francisco Mulcahey, whose brother-in-law is the Pacific coast drug lord Inocensio Ramirez."

Del felt the hair on the back of his neck stand straight out. *No wonder Adam was kept in the dark.* "I only learned about my uncle's relationship by marriage to Ramirez last summer. But my aunt is long dead. Uncle Mac and his family have nothing to do with the drug trade. Never did," Del said. He resented being handled this way.

Samson shook his head. "Please, no one's accusing them of being involved in drug dealing."

"Then why spring this on us?" Manchester asked.

"It isn't drugs we're worried about. It's the nuclear devices."

"But they were returned to the U.S.," Leah said.

"Apparently not all of them," Samson replied.

"It seems this administration has a less than sterling record keeping track of their arsenal," Manchester said.

Samson bristled but Delgado interrupted before the president could reply to the comment. "You think my cousins are involved in stealing nuclear weapons?"

Regaining his composure, Samson nodded for his secretary of Homeland Security to answer the loaded question. Labat equivocated nervously by asking, "Does the name ChiChi Bernal mean anything to you?"

Tall and lanky, Labat looked a little like Jimmy Stewart—without the charisma, Del thought. "No. Is it supposed to?"

"We have reason to believe he may have the stolen devices," General McKinney said in a soft Carolina drawl.

"Let me guess. This Bernal character works for Inocensio," Del replied.

McKinney and Labat both nodded. Oppermann looked irritated, but his boss Scarletti's face remained impassive as Samson said, "You can see that your family's connection to Ramirez is the starting place."

"With all respect, Mr. President, I disagree," Manchester said. "The first question is why it took five months for the government to figure out nuclear weapons had gone missing." He had to admire Samson's devious political mind. By bringing him into the loop on this, the president had neutralized his opponent's ability to cast blame on the administration during the campaign.

The president read the senator's shrewd expression. *The cagey old bastard's figured it out.* "Washington has been in chaos dealing with a conspiracy to topple the government. That's kept me and the Pentagon occupied for a while. But Justice and Homeland Security have been investigating." Samson turned to Scarletti and Labat.

Before Labat could finish clearing his throat, the acne-scarred attorney general said impassively, "Mr. Oppermann will brief you on what we've learned."

The new FBI director was short and bald with an in-your-face Brooklyn attitude. "Two special alloy suitcases weighing approximately twenty-one-and-a-half kilos each and both carrying as much as ten-kiloton payloads were stolen in the confusion after Sommerville's aborted attack on Colombia. The Bureau's found out these little honeys weren't made in America. They came from the Arzamov-16 Laboratories—in Russia. Apparently, we got a dozen of 'em in a CIA black op several years ago."

General McKinney sat tight-lipped. Delgado surmised that the Pentagon didn't have a clue how or why the CIA obtained the devices. He looked over at Leah. She nodded. *The chairman of the Joint Chiefs is seriously pissed.*

Oppermann continued. "From what we've been able to figure, each device packs enough juice to level more than a square kilometer. Depending on population density, one bomb could translate into a quarter of a million to half a million deaths, and that doesn't account for fallout. Our people think they're dirty enough to do lots of long-term damage."

"Dear God," Manchester muttered beneath his breath.

"We think someone snagged the two nukes before they were

returned from Mexico, but since no one in the Pentagon or Home-land Security was minding the store for nearly four months, the trail's cold as gefilte fish on Saturday morning."

If the AG objected to his FBI chief's accusation, he gave no indication, just observed with detachment.

General McKinney sat rigidly in absolute silence, but the secretary of Homeland Security's face reddened. Labat looked over at Samson, but when the president gave him no encouragement for a rebuttal, he said nothing.

"Care to speculate on why 'no one was minding the store,' General?" Manchester asked the chairman of the Joint Chiefs.

McKinney was tall and slim but there the resemblance between him and Labat ended. A much decorated soldier, he was highly respected inside the Beltway. "The weapons were procured by General Sommerville working with several other renegade officers from the Fort Leonard Wood Annex in southern Missouri. Little Lennie, as it's called, is the Army's central storage unit for certain nuclear devices. The records on base were tampered with and the misappropriation never reported. We all know the extent of the conspiracy that nearly toppled the government last summer."

He paused and looked pointedly at Delgado, who had broken the story for *U.S. News-Time,* then continued. "The devices were turned over by the Mexican military to the newly appointed CO for Little Lennie, Colonel Warren Thompkinson. The colonel returned ten devices to the annex. Unfortunately, because of the . . . irregular way they were acquired"—he paused and met Samson's level stare, then resumed speaking—"we had no idea how many there actually were in the first place.

"Colonel Thompkinson was killed in a car crash on a rural Missouri highway less than a month later. He had no time to complete the inventory of weapons before his death. The new CO, Colonel Byrne Taylor, recently discovered that originally there had been a dozen of those Russian bombs removed from the annex by Sommerville. Colonel Taylor alerted the Pentagon regarding the discrepancy." Having given as much as he felt required to share, he ran one big hand over his silver widow's peak and sat back stiffly in his chair.

The president took over again. "The bottom line is that we now know twelve devices left the annex but only ten returned. Colonel Raoul Mulcahey handed the devices over to Colonel Thompkinson whose report listed ten devices. Until recent events, we assumed that's all there were."

"I've known Warren Thompkinson for seven years and appointed him CO of the arsenal because I knew he could be trusted to straighten out the mess Sommerville had created," the chairman replied, icy calm.

"Well, I've known Raoul Mulcahey all my life and I know he can be trusted. Implicitly." Delgado's voice was deadly as he looked at Samson. *The bastard wants to hang this on my family!*

Adam Manchester's expression was thunderous. "Mr. Delgado's cousins risked their lives to disarm those weapons and capture a multinational force led by *American* traitors. The Mexican Special Forces team was hopelessly outnumbered yet they performed their duty with distinction." His gaze swept the men surrounding the president, then fixed directly on Samson. "Now, I strongly suggest we stop casting aspersions and start looking at the chain of evidence."

"Where does ChiChi Bernal fit in?" Del asked Paul Oppermann. Having served under the new FBI chief, he knew the man was a straight shooter.

"We've had contacts in Mexico watching Ramirez for years. The *mamzer*'s a real shark. ChiChi's a minnow. A cook in the Mexican Navy. He was assigned to help your cousins stop Sommerville's invasion flotilla."

"Your uncle, Mr. Delgado, was able to convince Inocensio Ramirez to lend him ChiChi Bernal and several dozen other of his thugs for the operation," Samson said.

Manchester snorted. "Hardly a nefarious mystery there. If Sommerville had attacked the Cartel, Benito Zuloaga would've left all Central America glowing in the dark. You were glad enough for Ramirez's help at the time."

"That does not mean that we can ignore this connection between Mr. Delgado's family and the missing devices now," Samson snapped. "This Bernal was aboard ship when Colonel Mulcahey's forces disarmed the nuclear devices. Wasn't he, Mr. Oppermann?"

The FBI director nodded. "As soon as we were notified about the missing nukes, we started checking everybody connected to Sommerville's takedown. ChiChi was the Mulcaheys' guide aboard the *Cárdenas*. Less than a month after the mission was over Bernal dropped off the edge of the earth. Then we caught a break.

"A week ago, a light aircraft with a murdered pilot was found by authorities on the Papago Indian Reservation in Arizona, near the Mexican border. The dead man was shot in back of the head with a .25-caliber bullet, execution style. The newspapers speculated about a drug-smuggling deal gone bad but there was no evidence.

"The whole thing felt hinkey, so the rez cops called the Bureau's Tucson office. My agents found a faint radioactive signature in the plane and reported it. Now, if that Cessna pilot was wasted by ChiChi—and I'd bet the farm on it—our boy's here to set up a deal."

"Any leads on Bernal in the U.S.?" Manchester asked.

Samson nodded to Labat again. This had happened on his watch since Border Protection fell under the Homeland Security umbrella. Obviously unhappy to be on the hot seat, he cleared his throat before saying, "We have more questions than answers right now, but it's obvious that he's here with the weapons."

McKinney leaned forward, waiting for Labat's explanation. Scarletti remained motionless, observing without a word.

"I checked with the NRO, which monitors all Globe Net activity, to see if that plane crossed the border recently," Labat began. "They have no record of it. FAA has no record of U.S. registration. No Mexican registration either, er, that we've been able to determine—but we're still working on that. The Bureau's forensics people are going over the plane. Cooperating, we'll get to the bottom of this." Labat looked to Oppermann for assurance, but the director was reading a note the AG had just handed him and failed to notice.

"What about the murdered pilot?" Berglund asked Oppermann.

"*Bobkes*. No ID in any data bank." Oppermann glanced from her to Delgado before adding, "Like he never existed, but he had fingerprints."

Everyone in the room knew BISC agents had their removed. Leah remained perfectly still but her mouth tightened imperceptibly.

"The threat is obvious, then," Manchester said. "These devices

could end up in the hands of terrorists and be used on Americans."
Samson, McKinney, Labat, and Oppermann nodded. Scarletti just
studied Berglund and Delgado. The senator was pleased that "the
Scar's" scrutiny had not unnerved them. "Now we understand why
you require Mr. Delgado's assistance. He has sources inside Mexico
you'd never be able to access."

"Whatever this Bernal plans in no way involves my family," Del
said, looking straight at Samson.

"Then I imagine it would be in their interest for you to prove that,
wouldn't you agree, Mr. Delgado?" Samson's expression was carefully
neutral.

"Yeah. I imagine it would." Delgado couldn't keep the sarcasm
from his voice.

"Where do I come in?" Leah's cool question cut through the tension in the room.

Samson gave her one of his famous megawatt smiles. She wasn't
buying and he knew it. Shrugging, he said, "You worked closely with
Mr. Delgado in uncovering the conspiracy."

"And I may still have contacts with some BISC agents forced into
early retirement," she replied cynically. *This stinks.* The spin-doctored
SOB was using Del's family as hostage and he'd dragged her grandfather in to cover his butt if this mess erupted during the campaign.

"ChiChi Bernal is trying to sell nuclear weapons on the black market. We have to stop him before this ends in another Slaughter," Samson replied, reminding her of the first terrorist attack on American
soil launched by the Colombian Cartel nearly a decade ago. It had re-
sulted in the creation of BISC . . . and made her an assassin. "Who
better to track Bernal down than you?"

"The CIA? After all, they're responsible for bringing these damnable
weapons here in the first place," Manchester said with a nasty smile.

Samson's face reddened. "You're surely aware, Senator, that we have
reasons for concern about the Agency during its . . . restructuring."

Scandal had plagued the Central Intelligence Agency even before
the House of Saud had been overthrown. Samson had been forced to
dismiss Director Ralph Whitherspoon and a number of his Middle
East specialists. Desperate to recoup his flagging poll numbers, the

president had made diplomatic overtures to the militants in Riyadh, hoping to defuse the crisis and better his own image both at home and abroad.

"So, we can't trust the CIA. The FBI and Homeland Security have no leads on Bernal or even how the hell he got in the country. But he's here rendezvousing with a buyer. You need to keep this under wraps while we find Bernal or whoever's got those nukes," Delgado said. "That about sum it up, Mr. President?"

Samson fixed a camera-ready earnest expression on his face. "I'm afraid so. Please forgive me for dragging you into this mess, but after last summer, I can't think of anyone better qualified."

"And you get my granddaughter's expertise thrown in to sweeten the bargain . . . if either she or Mr. Delgado chooses to help," Manchester said.

Samson spread his hands in a gesture that was part concession, part admonition. "Their country needs them. I sincerely hope they'll agree." He looked from the senator to Delgado and Berglund.

They exchanged glances for a moment. She did not look happy but she nodded to Del.

"Mr. President, I think you just made us an offer we can't refuse," Delgado said ironically.

4.

"Give me everything you got, Paul," Delgado said, trying to pull out a seat for Leah in the small cubicle. As usual, she beat him to it, dropping into the battered gray chair, cat-quick.

Paul Oppermann perched on the edge of a dented steel desk, riffling through a bunch of papers stamped with the highest security clearances. "Sorry about the digs, but if we used my office there'd be questions about your special assignment with the Bureau."

"And we all know the president doesn't want questions," Del said with a hard smile.

"Neither do I. I've only been here a couple of months and I don't know *mentsh* from *meshugener* . . . yet."

"Which is John Scarletti?" Delgado asked.

"Before the Martial Law Act was repealed he was a toothless tiger. Now . . . I peg him for a *mentsh*."

"He creeped me out," Leah said. "He always watch people like a coiled snake ready to strike?"

Oppermann laughed. "Interesting analogy. He creeps lots of people out, but during twenty years in Justice his conviction rate was top drawer." He let the topic of his boss drop and handed several of the reports to Del and Leah. "Even though you're on the payroll, this stuff can't leave here. My short list of possible players. Read fast."

After scanning one sheet, Leah said, "Samson doesn't know you suspect General McKinney?"

"If he did, he'd skin me like lox." The chairman of the Joint Chiefs was powerful and popular. Crossing him was political suicide. "Some *makher* had to cover up those missing nukes. Someone with ties to the CIA . . . or the Pentagon."

"Banecek used to be CIA director before he became secretary of defense," Delgado suggested.

"Yes, but he backs Samson's plan to negotiate with Holy Arabia. Last thing he'd want would be to have their terrorists buying nukes inside the U.S.," Leah said.

"Maybe so." Oppermann nodded. "But you can't leave him off the list. He was a spook, and at Defense he's in a position to cover up the stolen nukes. My gut tells me someone intends to sell to Holy Arabia and everyone's a suspect, even our much revered ex general cum secretary of state, Kensington."

"I agree with Paul," Del said to Leah. "Stuart Kensington's foursquare against negotiating with those Holy Arabian nuts. I can see why he made the short list."

"He and McKinney both hate Samson's guts and oppose his military and political goals," Oppermann said.

"So does my grandfather. Why didn't he make your list?" Leah asked.

"He wasn't inside the Beltway loop enough the past couple of years."

"Don't count on it," she said. "Gramps keeps pretty close tabs on what's happening in D.C. He's mentioned that Kensington never got along with McKinney—old rivalry when they served together in the war."

"Your grandfather's right about that," Oppermann said. "Now Kensington has zilch influence inside the Pentagon. No ties with the CIA that we've uncovered. He's from old money. Isolated in this administration."

"So you'll keep digging on him," Del said with a chuckle.

Oppermann shrugged. "Hell, I'm even open to investigating the Rabbit."

Del laughed. "Labat's a long shot. But the truth is, someone high up kept the theft of two nukes under wraps for months. We can't rule him out either."

"I don't see McKinney involved. Gramps worked with him when he served on the Senate Armed Services Committee," Leah said.

Del played devil's advocate. "But he'd love nothing better than to see Samson and Banecek with egg on their faces if this went public. It'd sink their whole plan for downsizing the military, besides wrecking any hope for negotiating with al Ibrim and his pals in Riyadh."

"Same's true of Kensington," she argued.

"Yeah, but McKinney's in a better position for a cover-up. Remember, he sent Tompkinson to pick up those nukes from my cousins. I know damn sure they gave him every last one."

Leah had worked with Raoul and Ernesto Mulcahey. "Gramps and I know your family had nothing to do with it. We'll find out who the *makhers* and *k'nockers* are."

Oppermann grinned. "She knows Yiddish. Already I like her." He measured her with shrewd brown eyes. "What about your contacts in BISC? Some of those *mamzarim* are doing real well in the information technology business now."

Delgado could almost see her flinch.

"I'll make some inquiries," she replied quietly, then went back to skimming documents.

"You want me to go to Mexico, of course."

"Vat den?" Oppermann said in the exaggerated accent of his grandmother. "You have an inside track through your uncle." He scrubbed his shiny head with one meaty hand. "For what it's worth, I didn't like the way Samson handled that."

"Neither did I. Don't think I'll vote for him."

Leah couldn't suppress a snort. "This report indicates possible Cartel involvement. Maybe we should talk with Benito Zuloaga, if we can."

"If he ordered the theft, he had to use Mexican assets," Oppermann said.

"Someone inside Ramirez's organization—Bernal," Del agreed.

"You start in Mexico. I'll work my BISC contacts," she said.

"Sounds like we got a plan. Oh, I have a few items for you." He gave each of them a badge, the photo IDs on them obviously lifted from old records.

"I was a handsome devil in my youth," Del said.

Leah looked at her BISC photo on the FBI badge and swallowed hard. She quickly slipped it into her handbag.

"Use these when you call me." Oppermann handed each of them a small link without vid. "The latest in Bureau technology. Nobody can break the encryption."

Delgado and Berglund exchanged glances. Paul Oppermann had never met Gracie Kell. When it came to breaking codes, she was definitely a *makher*.

12:20 P.M. CST, SATURDAY, NOVEMBER 8
TERRELL COUNTY, TEXAS

ChiChi Bernal stared out the cell window at the bleakest stretch of nothing this side of the Sonoran desert. Just his luck to spend the past week in a Podunk jail while a cool ten mil waited in a locker at the local Greyhound station. At least the sheriff and his deputy dawgs had not seen him jam the locker key in the potted cactus before they arrested him in Lu Lu's Saloon.

After riding buses and stolen cars across Arizona and half of Texas, he felt beat down to his socks. He hadn't had more than four hours of sleep since he stole the nukes. He'd checked into a fleabag hotel in this burg, slept around the clock, then headed to the nearest watering hole for some beer and a steak. How the hell could his luck turn so rotten now?

Nothing more than gila monsters for customers but some shit dumb El-Op had shown up. Bernal got caught in the middle of a bust when the buyer tossed a bean bag over the back of his booth during the scuffle. One of the deputies spotted the packet of Elevator and the sheriff arrested him before he could scoot out of the joint. Of course, he had no ID and carried only an unregistered .25-caliber Colt and some cash. A sizable amount that they confiscated. He didn't expect to see it again. Lucky at least, he'd left much more with the suitcases.

He muttered an obscenity and took a drag on his cigarette. Fortunately, no one in the Greatest State took unlicensed weapons seriously.

But they held him on suspicion of drug trafficking until the judge cleared his docket at the county seat to hear the sorry mess. Even after repeal of the Martial Law Act, he could be looking at serious prison time.

ChiChi had to escape before the judge got back to work. Or some nosy public defender came riding into town on his white horse and screwed things up even more. He'd been studying the jailhouse routine for the past week. The pitiful joint had one surveillance camera but no one manned it while the lone deputy made his patrol. And it had no night-vision lens on it. Unobserved last night, he finished filing the spoon he'd stolen from a meal tray. It wasn't much, but sharp enough to do the job.

He'd have preferred to move after dark, but the night guard was a burley sucker who kept his distance from the prisoners. He had watchful soldier's eyes. The afternoon guard was a Barney Fife clone, garrulous and scrawny. This would not be his lucky afternoon. Bernal's cell was hidden around a corner in the makeshift jail, which was a hodgepodge of cinder-block additions. The problem wouldn't be the guard; it would be the El-Op and his customer. They'd want him to free them or raise hell and prevent his getaway.

That he couldn't risk. Stupid amateurs would get them all recaptured in minutes. Besides, he owed the one who tossed the pills at him. Smiling, he waited as the guard made his afternoon rounds. "Howdy, Deputy. Hey, you mind moving that fan a little closer? Air's stuffy as hell in this corner." He gestured to the small floor fan oscillating fecklessly.

The deputy bent over to pick up the fan and move it nearer to the cot where ChiChi sat. "Sorry about—"

The instant the deputy stooped to move the fan Bernal lunged, seizing hold of his belt and slamming his head against the hard steel lock. He plunged the shiv neatly into his back between the ribs, going directly for the heart. Piece of cake with a guy this thin. ChiChi carefully lowered the gurgling body to the concrete floor, reaching for his gun first. Once he had that, he pulled the keys off his belt and unlocked the cell door, shaking his head at the stupid operation. Who used cell keys nowadays—much less carried them on a belt? It was like a B-movie from way back in the last century. Hell, whoever heard of cell keys nowadays, even in Mexico?

Working quickly, he snatched the lumpy pillow from his cot. He jammed the muzzle of the deputy's .40-caliber Smith & Wesson against the sack of soggy cotton. It would serve as a decent silencer—providing the bikers arrived soon.

Within ten minutes—ChiChi had been timing them every day for the past seven—half a dozen homegrown Hell's Angels came roaring down the street for their afternoon libation at Lu Lu's. With silent grace, he moved over the cracked concrete, rounding the corner to where the two other prisoners slept. After days of routine, they had learned to ignore the bikers. ChiChi fired through the bars. The El-Op twitched and his head rolled to one side as a red stain widened on his forehead. Bernal shifted the muzzle of the gun to an unscorched portion of the pillow.

"Hey, what the fuck—" the buyer said, rolling off his cot after the muffled shot reverberated over the din of bikes passing by.

He got nothing more out before Bernal fired again, dropping him.

ChiChi tossed aside the smoldering pillow and shoved the automatic into the waist of his jeans. He walked quickly through the door into the main office where the antique surveillance camera rolled. No use leaving evidence. He smashed it with a heavy stapler from the sheriff's desk, then headed for the door marked "Private," the officer's john. It faced the back of the building and had a window that opened. *Mil gracias,* Barney Fife.

Bernal's hand gripped the worn knob when the front door opened. "What's going on here?"

The sheriff reached for his holstered weapon but the catch caught, slowing him. ChiChi pulled his gun out, cursing his incredibly bad luck. But the instant before he fired and alerted passersby, the sheriff stumbled forward and collapsed on the floor. It happened so quickly all Bernal saw was the blur of a man's hand slamming into the back of the sheriff's neck. A shabbily dressed stranger wearing jeans and a dirty T-shirt with a ball cap pulled down shadowing his face stepped inside and closed the door.

"I'm here to help you," he said, motioning toward the rear escape route.

Bernal didn't waste time. He'd figure this one out later. Replacing the gun in his waistband, he yanked open the door to the head and climbed out the window.

2:35 P.M. EST, SATURDAY, NOVEMBER 8
WASHINGTON, D.C.

The office was paneled in rich walnut and the paintings on the walls were originals, all by famous American artists of the past two centuries. Thick dark blue carpet muffled sound as the man in residence walked across the room to pour himself a drink. He took an experimental sip, then returned to his desk and opened a secured link. In a moment the connection was made and the voiceprint identified. He opened the vid.

"Give me the details," he said.

The man on screen replied, "He was in jail in Texas. Fool was mixed up in some drug bust. My man got him out. . . ."

"And?" His boss took an impatient swallow and felt the mellow burn of top shelf liquor.

"Rizzo's dead. Bernal cut his throat and left him in a drainage ditch. Stole his car but ditched it a few miles away. He's smart. Figured we'd track the car."

"You are certain he still has the cases?"

"No way he'd leave them behind. If those hicks who arrested him had found them, it'd be all over the media by now."

"Do you think your man talked before Bernal killed him?"

"Wouldn't have had time to waste and Rizzo was a pro. No way he'd give up without it taking time."

"Then you believe he's still headed in the anticipated direction?"

"I've had my source position his men. It should take Bernal several hours at best to get there. We have his wife's house and the bar where she works under surveillance. He'll show. When he does, our source will pass along the information."

"I don't want any more blunders. Report when Bernal's located. Our boy has to retrieve those cases and dispose of the Mexican—for your sake."

"I know ChiChi could ID me. He should live so long." His chuckle brought on a harsh cough that he quickly suppressed.

"I want to know the minute this situation's back on track." He closed the link and turned his attention to the classified papers he'd taken out of his briefcase moments before.

The frown marring his face vanished as he read. On the fifteenth of last month the subject had flown to Guantanamo where Aziz al Ambas was being held. Said subject interrogated the terrorist prisoner without any guards present. "So, you made contact with Holy Arabia's point man, did you? Perfect."

He smiled and polished off his drink. A temporary glitch with Bernal but everything else was falling into place beautifully. A discreet knock on the door caused him to slide the dossier back into his briefcase and place the empty glass out of sight before he said, "Come in, Louise."

"I'm sorry to interrupt you, Mr. Secretary, but your three o'clock is a bit early and you know how a four-star general hates to be kept waiting."

4:37 P.M. EST, SATURDAY, NOVEMBER 8
WASHINGTON, D.C.

The hotel lobby looked like hundreds of others in the nation's capital, large with pseudo-classical columns and statuary, cluttered with potted ferns, but the once-wide glass windows fronting the building had been removed and a frescoed wall replaced them. Even this near the seat of government, drug-related shootings and street violence dictated that the only glass left at street level was bulletproof. At the front doors two heavily armed private security guards watched warily as people filtered in and out.

Del and Leah walked up to the front desk where an officious manager with tufts of gray hair surrounding his head like a halo instructed a bank of clerks working the computers. One well-groomed young woman smiled like a robot and asked, "How may I help you?"

"We need a room," Del said, handing over a plastic-card.

"Two rooms," Leah corrected, shoving hers over the counter beside his.

"Adjoining rooms," he countered.

She shrugged as the clerk swiped both credits, then went to work. The manager fingered his tufts and smirked. After a lengthy series of keystrokes, the clerk handed over two key cards. They carried their single bags themselves, heading toward the elevators.

"You think your grandfather's going to check up on our sleeping accommodations?" he asked as they slipped into a deserted elevator.

Leah chewed on the inside of her cheek. "You know better. No time for playing house. You have to contact Gracie and I need to see if any former BISC agents will talk to me."

"You need privacy for that, I guess," he said somberly. He knew it couldn't be easy for her to reenter the world of assassins and the bureaucrats who ran them, many of whom thought her a traitor for helping the FBI destroy their agency.

"And you don't want privacy when you talk whips and chains with Gracie?" she joked.

The humor was forced but he let it go. She'd been strung tight as a new wire fence since they met back in San Diego. Best not to push too hard. As they rode up, he thought about Gracie Kell. His computer guru was a bizarre combination of dominatrix, conspiracy theorist, and hacker who'd gotten inside the newly formed Euro Union's most secret programs less than a decade ago. Gracie had been thirteen at the time. Last summer she'd hacked into BISC for him—something no one in or outside the government was supposed to be able to do. There wasn't any system that she couldn't penetrate if given enough time. With a guy like Bernal peddling nuclear hardware inside the U.S., he only hoped there would be time.

Gracie had become an invaluable resource for him in spite of her kookiness. She persistently tried to get him to run stories about alien abductions and CIA involvement with extraterrestrials. Personally he felt contact with extraterrestrials might boost Company agents' intelligence quotients. As to the sex thing, well, he pushed the thought out of his mind. Mazola oil and whips weren't his thing.

Then the elevator door pinged and opened on their floor. When Leah unlocked her door, Del said, "Knock three times when you want to come over and play."

"Two times if I don't."

"I could run away with Gracie."

The image of that made her smile. As he slipped into the adjoining room, he realized how seldom she smiled and how much he enjoyed it when she did.

Leah sat at the functional hotel-room desk in front of the personal digital assistant and debated about turning on the vid. *Cut the games, Berglund. You don't want to turn on the PDA, period.* She took a breath and pressed aud/vid activate. If she was going to go begging for favors, she had to look Rhys Willis in his lecherous eyes to do it. Once he knew it was her he'd for sure turn on his screen . . . if only to tell her to drop dead.

But Willis surprised her. "Well, hello, Sweetums. Lookin' fine as always," he drawled, leaning his sizable girth against the back of an expensive leather chair. The skyline of Atlanta glittered through the vast expanse of glass beyond his corner office windows.

"Civilian life is treating you pretty fine, too, it would seem," she said.

He waved a pudgy hand fitted with a diamond pinkie ring that probably cost more than her last couple of months' salary at the rehab center. "Can't complain. Since starting my security consulting firm, bidness's been percolating right along."

"You trying to tell me I can't afford you?"

He grinned like a lecherous elf and leaned toward the screen. "For you, Sweetums, I'll arrange special terms."

"I'll bet." She scrubbed her hands through her hair. "Then you don't blame me—"

"No way. If I'd known how much money there was in the private sector, I'd never have signed on with BISC myself. Course, that's where I made some jim-dandy contacts. Much as I'd like to think it was my boyish charm, you looked me up because you need info," he said with a lazy leer.

Rhys Willis had been one of the best field operatives in BISC, even though at five feet six he'd barely passed the physical. Once transferred to desk work, his belt length had swelled to match his height. She smiled at his usual come-on. They were back on familiar ground.

"I adore your boyish charm, but what I need is information on a possible black-market weapons deal. Seller's from south of the border. ChiChi Bernal. He has a couple of small nukes. Entered the country illegally in late October, in Pinal County, Arizona." She gave him coordinates and a description of the plane and pilot.

He stroked his chins. "Haven't heard anything, but then, I wasn't asking either. Doubt he's in Arizona now. Any idea where he's heading?"

"Don't I wish," she replied. "Delgado's working on his Mexican connections. Maybe that'll give us some help."

"You and the newsman still together?" he asked, looking past her to the bed behind her, searching for him.

"That's personal, Willie. Just find me this Bernal and his nukes."

"Let me see what I can do. Oh, if we're talking nuclear problems, I assume Uncle Sam's offering a finder's fee, hmmm?"

"Let me see what I can do," she parroted.

"Oh, we'll work out terms, Sweetums."

"Your persistence is admirable, Willie," she said, shaking her head.

"I'm an admirable guy. That's part of my charm."

"You can reach me—"

He chuckled. "Oh, I won't have any trouble finding you when I need to. I'm in the security bidness, remember?"

She stared at the blank screen.

Willie was good. He knew everything that went down on the street and in the alleys. Thinking of darkened alleys, she realized she'd never checked in with the San Pedro cops since filing that hasty report in the middle of the night. They would want to do a follow-up and she'd left no forwarding address.

"Just what I need is to turn up on wants-and-warrants in LA," she muttered. In a couple of minutes she was put through to Captain Pablo Munez, who headed a special task force on drugs for the mayor.

A tough-looking Hispanic man's unsmiling face greeted her. "I'm happy you found time to report back, Ms. Berglund." The sarcasm in his voice was unmistakable.

"I apologize for leaving town before the investigation was closed but I explained—"

He waved his hand. "You had urgent business in Washington, yes," he said, glancing at her report on his desk. "Well, we have urgent business, too. Two men hospitalized by one unarmed female."

"I was a BISC agent," she said flatly. A knowing look hardened his eyes. "I was supposed to meet a client when those two jumped me."

"So you said. According to your statement, you thought they were members of Harbor Squad, same as the client who was a no-show."

Her gut twisted. "They weren't?"

Munez shook his head. "Those men have no connection to the gang. In fact, no connection in LA at all. Imported talent. Mickey Simon and Doug Schmitt are hit men from Vegas."

"Then they weren't after my client."

"Yeah, that client whose name is privileged according to your agency."

"You know the law regarding juveniles as well as I do, Captain. Besides, if those thugs weren't gang members after the *boy*," she stressed the word, "then why would they attack me?"

"You were BISC. Anyone out there with a grudge?" The question was rhetorical and they both knew it.

She clamped her jaw and stared stonily at him.

5.

Gracie made a new fashion statement every time Delgado saw her. He blinked at the vid screen and suppressed a shudder. Her hair was now snow-white with purple and red tips spiking across her head, shimmering like a fiber-optic lamp, or a psychedelic porcupine in heat. A sleeveless leather vest revealed matchstick-thin arms and a studded dog collar encircled her long neck. She used her tongue to flip a large gold nose ring back and forth as she listened to him give her the background on the missing nukes.

Although he wasn't supposed to share classified information, he'd stake his life on her discretion. In spite of her weirdness, she'd taken on BISC and won. If anybody could track down Bernal and those nukes, she was the one.

"I need everything you can dig up on ChiChi Bernal." He gave her all the info Oppermann had compiled on Ramirez's "minnow." "Can you start monitoring Cartel chatter, too?"

She grinned and stuck out her studded tongue. "Cat got an ass?"

"Good. Next, see what you can find on a Colonel Warren Tompkinson, deceased. He's the guy who picked up the nukes in Mexico, a buddy of Howard McKinney, chairman of the Joint Chiefs. If the general's linked to the missing nukes, I want you to find the connection. Nothing he'd like better than to undercut Samson's Secretary of Defense Karl Banecek. Ditto on Secretary of State Stuart Kensington."

Gracie Kell nodded, stirring her straw in a huge Coke. "Yeah,

I heard about Banecek's program for reducing the size of the military. Kinda like the guy for that, even if he is a gov stooge. You know the Army's been covering up UFO abductions for nearly a century now. With fewer boots on the ground—"

"Look, Gracie, can we talk about alien abductions some other time? Right now I need you to start digging."

"Sheesch! Okay, Lover. All those guys and the Cartel chatter, too. Anything else in my spare time? I do have a life, you know."

Just then an electronic buzz sounded inside her dingy apartment. Gracie lived in a terrible section of D.C. slums but the place was rigged with enough security to keep out a full-scale Special Forces assault. She had a fortune in computer equipment, all blinking and blipping contentedly around her, the queen in her hive. She pressed a key and the steel front door opened. A man roughly the size of Mount Whitney ducked as he entered the cluttered room.

Gracie's pale face actually took on a faint trace of color as she batted kohl-ringed eyes at her latest conquest. "Be with you in a sec, Baby Cheeks. Grab the Mazola oil and wait for me, 'kay?"

He shambled off and Delgado whispered, "Baby Cheeks?"

She gave him a crooked grin and picked up a whip, waving it slowly in front of the screen. "He's a real pussycat. Told you you don't know what you're missing. Now if you want—"

Delgado didn't want. "You actually have a kitchen?" he asked abruptly.

"Not to cook," she replied as patiently as a kindergarten teacher explaining to a five-year-old how to tie a shoelace. "I'll start monitoring the chatter this afternoon and see what filters out. The other stuff I'll get to work on tonight."

"After Baby Cheeks leaves."

She winked and nodded, uncoiling the whip. Just then Baby Cheeks sauntered back into view wearing nothing but jackboots and a lot of tattoos. Grinning, he held an open jug of cooking oil in one huge paw.

"I'll check with you in the morning." Delgado broke the link. This time he didn't suppress the shudder.

8:08 P.M. EST, SATURDAY, NOVEMBER 8
WASHINGTON, D.C.

"So those guys weren't part of the El-Op gang," Del said thought-fully, wiping his mouth with a napkin. They sat at the small table by the window in his room, comparing notes on their evening's work over a room-service dinner. "That means you were the target."

"That's what the LA cops think. The boys are from Vegas. Weird."

He shrugged. "Lots of weird in Vegas. Easy place to score a hit man."

"You ever think that El-Op with the M16 was after you, not your car?"

"Not until now, but it makes sense."

"That means someone here knew in advance that we were being brought into this along with my grandfather. I called him to warn him, but you know Gramps."

Del chuckled. "He'll make Abbie Rutledge crazy when he's president. He have any ideas about who the mole might be?"

"He's busy working his contacts on the Hill. He thinks Opper-mann's way off about McKinney. Kensington, too, but he'll keep an open mind."

"I'll have Paul put a call into San Diego and see if they've ID'd my carjacker yet."

She shook her head. "I'm going back. Let me handle that end."

"You don't trust Paul Oppermann?"

"Damn, Del, I don't trust the president."

He grunted an agreement. Wade Samson wasn't exactly at the top of his favorites list at the moment. "I could have Gracie check out both incidents."

"She's got enough to do. I'll drop in on San Diego's finest and see what they can tell me about the dead man on I-5 after I have a bed-side chat with one of the guys who tried to take me out."

He grinned. "You mean the one whose jaw isn't broken?"

"Captain Munez wondered how I did that." She carefully folded her napkin beside a plate of mostly uneaten food.

Del reached over and took her hand, covering it with both of his, massaging her tense fingers. "Sorry. Look, Leah, you did what you had to do. Let it go . . . let the whole damn thing go . . . the past—"

"Is past. Easy for you to say." She tried to pull away but he didn't release her hand. Instead he raised it to his mouth and kissed the knuckles.

"My shrink keeps telling me the same thing. At least you don't charge three hundred an hour." Her voice was flat with resignation as she withdrew her hand.

"I have a prescription guaranteed to make you sleep like a baby . . . and it won't cost you a thing," he suggested, waiting to see how she'd respond.

She looked into his eyes. "You may end up costing me most of all, Del . . . or I may cost you." She desperately wanted to release her pain in the oblivion of sex, but knew it would only be a temporary fix.

"I'm a big boy, remember?" He held out his hand. "I'll risk it."

She shook her head. "I won't, Del."

She crashed through the window where Mike and his mother were being held prisoner. But instead of finding them bound and gagged, they lay in pools of blood, their throats cut. The BISC agent grinned at her. "Too late," he said, holding up a gory knife.

She shot him, dead center, didn't miss. But he kept moving toward her in spite of the small red hole in the middle of his bulging forehead. She screamed, fired again . . . and again. And still he came. She lowered her weapon as understanding dawned. How much better to feel the slash of cold steel than face Delgado and tell him his son was dead? She had failed.

Del heard her cries and jumped out of his bed. He yanked open the door adjoining their rooms and stumbled over a chair in the dark before remembering to give a voice command for lights. She was damp with perspiration, tangled in the sheets, moaning in her sleep. He knelt beside the bed and gently touched her shoulder, murmuring, "Leah-Pia," Adam's pet name for her.

Leah blinked, her eyes coming into focus, drawing away from some black hell only she and maybe her shrink knew about. She huddled in the middle of the bed. "Guess I had a bad dream. Sorry."

"You told me the nightmares had finally stopped," he said, scooting onto the bed, wrapping his arms around her. She allowed it, but remained stiff and shivering.

"I lied. But they come less often."

He sighed. "Maybe if you'd tell me about them—"

She shook her head. "No, this is something I have to work out with Dr. Emmils." He held her, stroking her back, but she didn't return his embrace. Finally she pushed him away. "I need to sleep, Del."

"Alone. I get the message," he said gently. Giving a voice command to dim the lights, he walked back to his room and lay on the bed, staring at the ceiling in the darkness.

7:42 A.M. EST, SUNDAY, NOVEMBER 9
WASHINGTON, D.C.

"We have the place under surveillance." He watched the smarmy man on the other side of the vid, red-faced and demanding. In his most placating tone he added, "I'm using two of my best men."

"Well, your 'best men' let him get the fuck away in Arizona in the first place. Son of a bitch's been AWOL for a week!"

"One of my sources found him in a Texas jail—"

"Jail! You mean to tell me some sheriff wearing spurs has my nukes!"

"No, sirree. He was arrested by accident, a sort of fluke, but he hid the cases first." Dammit! He didn't want to admit how they had fucked up during Bernal's escape. "We handled everything."

There was a snorted obscenity on the other side of the screen. "Then why's Bernal still running around with those cases?"

Shit. For a stupid man, he asked damn good questions. "He slipped away, but we knew where he was headed by then. Now it'll only be a few hours till we have him. One of my men's due to report in a couple of minutes. When Bernal shows up, we'll nail the sucker. Believe me, if he doesn't have the cases, he'll talk when they get through with him. My money says he'll be carrying them."

"It's *my* money we're talking about—not yours! And don't expect a red cent until you recover my nukes."

Before he could try for more damage control, the screen went blank. That really pissed him off.

6:50 A.M. CST, SUNDAY, NOVEMBER 9
CORPUS CHRISTI, TEXAS

The wind coming off the bay lent an early-morning chill to the air even this far inland. ChiChi Bernal drove slowly down the narrow street, filled with salt-scoured jalopies in various stages of malfunction. The Chevy EV he'd stolen in Banquete blended in perfectly. Such rusted old electric vehicles matched the neighborhood of small clapboard houses with sandy dirt yards and fallen down Cyclone fences. In a few hours kids and dogs would fill the streets with noise. Now it was quiet.

Nina would be asleep, of course. She worked late on Saturday nights at the bar a dozen blocks away, a run-down joint but the best a floozy like her could get. Six blocks from her house he ditched the car and walked, keeping an eye out for anyone who didn't belong. Cops and feds were easy to spot, enforcers working for El-Ops harder, but his gut hadn't failed him yet. If it ever did, it'd be spilled over some sidewalk.

He slipped into an alley that ran behind her shack, passing a stray cat in search of breakfast. Nothing else moved. As he scanned rooftops and narrow passageways between houses, his right hand never left the butt of the Smith & Wesson concealed in his jacket pocket. He'd rigged it with a more effective silencer than a pillow. His weapon of choice remained his small deadly switchblade. Trash Dumpsters and tall weeds provided cover as he moved silently nearer his destination.

Then he heard the crackle on a link a few dozen meters away. The sound came from a dilapidated toolshed door directly ahead. ChiChi cursed and pulled out his knife. He circled and saw the man muttering into the link as he leaned against the shed. The guy had just finished reporting in. Perfect. His prey sensed him too late. Just as he turned, Bernal's blade slashed across his throat. Blood pulsed out like Old Spindletop striking oil, but he stepped back to avoid the essential carnage. Only his hand had a reddish smear on it.

ChiChi wiped it on the dead man's jacket, then pocketed his link.

He dragged the body toward a Dumpster and opened the lid. Heaving it over the side took all of his considerable strength, but he managed the job. He closed the lid, then checked the area for blood that might draw attention. Tall weeds soaked it up greedily. One concrete cinder block was splashed bright red. He kicked it over, satisfied that no one would find the dead man until collection day. Around this neighborhood that wouldn't be for at least a week. If the machine lift was working, his victim would end up in a landfill, vanished without a trace.

He moved closer to his destination, still watchful. The guy on the roof next door to Nina's place was facing the street with his head stuck up like a candy apple on a stick. How dumb was that? ChiChi could slip in her house without the clown seeing him. Of course, he was gambling on there being only two men staked out here. He played the odds and made his way across her yard, all the time watching his would-be watcher. Once by the back of the house, he fished an antique key from beneath a warped board on the deck and unlocked the rickety door.

Stupid broad still kept the thing where any nutcase could find it. Nobody ever accused his third wife of being smart. Lots of people thought she was a nutcase herself. He opened the door slowly, being careful to tug upward on the knob so as to keep it from sticking. The interior was as dingy and cluttered as he remembered. Pale light filtered from a narrow crack where the garish floral drapes didn't meet. Articles of women's clothing were strewn across mismatched kitchen chairs. She must have had a hard night, leaving a trail of discarded work clothes as she moved toward the bedroom.

He stepped into the dark hallway. Only the faint shadow at the corner of his eye alerted him to the arm raised to strike at his head. He swung his fist and backhanded her in the stomach. The blackjack in her hand clattered to the floor as she doubled over, grunting in pain.

"What the fuck you try that for?" he asked the moaning woman.

She straightened up, still rubbing her belly, and began to curse at him in Spanish. Nina was fortyish and rushing to fat, her once impressive breasts now resting comfortably on her expanding waistline. Tangled hair a shade of black seen only on Aztec priests framed her weathered face. With a big Roman nose and an overbite, she had never been a beauty, but her deep-set black eyes attracted him. That and her once-voluptuous body.

"You are a pig, a dirty, vicious brute." She embellished her diatribe with more very inventive Spanish oaths, clawing at him with chipped red nails. "I thought you were a thief—or worse!"

He caught her wrist and twisted it, stilling her. "Shuddup. You wanna wake the neighbors—or that man on the roof next door?" he said in English.

Her dark eyes narrowed, burning into him. "Man on the roof! What you do now, eh?" she replied, switching to English.

He released her wrist, which she began to rub. "I've stolen something your cousin Miguel wants . . . wants enough to pay a fortune for—that is, if he's got all them millions like you said."

She gave him a calculating once-over. "I don't see nothin'. What you got my cousin would want?"

"You think I'm dumb enough to carry a couple of nukes with me?"

That got her attention. "Mexican Navy don't have no nukes," she said, watching his face to gauge whether he was telling the truth.

"No, but the Americans do. Make me some coffee and I'll tell you about it. . . ."

They sat at the battered kitchen table as he wolfed a big plate of eggs scrambled with hot salsa and fatty bacon. Nina poured more coffee while he explained how he escaped from Mexico with two nuclear devices.

"So, the plane's about to land when I seen the glint off a rifle barrel. Then I spot two guys squatting in the brush and figure they ain't out there takin' a dump. Big shot who hired me's pulling a double cross. I ain't exactly surprised. So, I shove my gun in the pilot's neck and tell him to keep movin'. He puts up a squawk but does it. This time I pick the place to land near a highway so's I can get me a ride. I finish him and flag down a dude in a pickup. Piece of electric junk quit on me fifty meters down the road. I keep boosting wheels and ditching 'em before I get any cops on my trail—"

"If you're such a smart hombre," she said impatiently, inhaling an unfiltered cigarette, "how come it took you so long to get here, eh?"

He resisted the urge to give her another punch. Damned if he'd tell her he spent a week in a west Texas jail. Or that he needed her family contacts to market his wares. "I had to hide my tracks. That takes time. My old boss is looking for me. FBI and CIA, too."

ChiChi always liked to brag about what a big shot he was. All she cared about was his connection to Pacific drug traffic. Her cousin Miguel raised money for the cause dealing Elevator. And he was definitely in the market for nuclear weapons.

Her mouth went dry as she asked, "Where are the bombs?"

He smirked. "You think I'd tell you? I got 'em hid. You see if Miguel wants to deal. He deals with me direct or I find other buyers."

She huffed, pulling the lapel on her red satin robe. "Other buyers? You know one of them rag head sheiks? Or maybe North Koreans? I do'n think so. You need me to reach Miguel."

He gave her a measuring look, then shoved the last greasy strip of bacon in his mouth, talking while he chewed. "You want them nukes for your precious cause, you talk to Miguel. And not on your link. There's ways of listening in."

Remembering his mention of a man watching her place from next door, she took a deep drag on the Camel to calm her nerves. "I ain't stupid, Cheech. I call from my friend Tessie's place. You wait here. I go soon as I get dressed."

He shook his head. "Can't wait. It sometimes takes you days to reach that prick. I'm too hot to sit still. You set up a meeting, then call my uncle in Detroit. I'll lay low with the family up there till I hear from you."

"How much you want for the bombs?"

"The gringos I stole 'em for promised me ten mil."

8:15 A.M. PST, SUNDAY, NOVEMBER 9
SAN PEDRO PENINSULA HOSPITAL

Leah walked quickly down the crowded corridor as nurses, technicians, and doctors rushed past her, responding to the code in the room around the corner. She knew it was too late for Mickey Simon, the Vegas hit man whose jaw she hadn't broken. Damn rotten luck. She'd just have to do things the hard way.

When she reached Douglas Schmitt's room, the cop at the door was gone. She'd arranged for him to be sent downstairs to fill out more paperwork on her assailants' hospital admission. She figured she had about half an hour to get something out of the thug before his guard returned. It would've been a lot easier if she'd reached Simon before whoever killed him.

Entering the dimly lit room filled with beeping machines and IV bottles, she closed the heavy door. The man on the bed dozed fitfully. The lower half of his face was covered by a protective shield so the shattered bones in his jaw could mend. Her eyes glittered with determination as she took the call button from his lax fingers and carefully set it out of his reach. Then she began clicking keys and adjusting switches on the machinery around the bed. Nothing would alert staff to his elevated readings when she was done.

Schmitt awoke and blinked just as she was finishing up. He didn't recognize her until she leaned directly over him. "Hi, Dougie. How's it hanging?"

The look of horror on his face would have been comical if she had time to laugh. He tried to scoot away, clawing for the call switch. She immobilized him by grabbing his jaw shield. He emitted a high-pitched squeal of pain from his wired-shut mouth. She made a shushing sound and put one finger to her lips. He went very still.

"That's better. It would've been smarter if I'd busted your balls instead of your jaw. We could converse easier, but since your pal Simon is coding out down the hall, I'll just have to make do with you." He gave a startled grunt and his eyes widened with comprehension as he realized someone had gotten into Mickey Simon's room and finished him.

"Yeah, that's all the excitement you've been hearing. Someone slipped Mickey a mickey in his IV. All he had was a mild concussion and a couple of busted ribs when he was admitted last night. You saw how diligent the cop guarding you is. They'll get you next . . . unless you help me out."

He made a helpless gesture, pointing to his mouth.

"I know your jaw's broken but your hand isn't . . . yet. You can write, can't you, Dougie? Or isn't that a required course in hit man school?"

She picked up the clipboard she'd carried into the room and shoved a pen toward his left hand. "Seems I recall you're a lefty from the way you moved on the wharf. A name, Dougie. The Vegas connection. Then I get you serious police protection."

He was sweating now, the thin hospital gown clinging damply to his chest. She knew he was weighing the options. His boss would have him wasted for talking but if she was telling the truth, Simon was already toast. She smiled nastily. "Yeah, I mighta been the one who killed Mickey. But I'll for sure be the one who kills you if you don't talk. And I'll hurt you first . . . real bad."

His eyes traveled to the monitors around his bed. In spite of his heart and pulse pounding like a nag at Santa Anita, not an irregular blip registered on them.

"I used to be BISC. They taught us how to rig just about any kind of computer equipment. Now, who's your boss?" She punctuated her question by yanking the IV from his hand, leaving a trail of blood across the pristine sheet. When she reached for his jaw again, he seized the pen and started to scribble.

10:10 A.M. PST, SUNDAY, NOVEMBER 9
LOS ANGELES, CALIFORNIA

"Danny DeClue." Leah spelled the last name of Doug Schmitt's boss for Latifah Richmond. On the vid the large black woman typed it into her database. She was middle-aged with iron-gray hair framing a narrow, shrewd face, and she was one of Leah's best sources on crime in Vegas.

Being a money mecca filled with high rollers, Las Vegas had quickly become one of the Elevator distribution centers of the country after the Slaughter crippled drug enforcement operations nearly a decade earlier. One of the first casualties in the epidemic of deadly cocaine-Viagra use had been Latifah's son Ronald who had been shot to death during a deal gone bad.

In public, Mrs. Richmond railed against the authorities, saying her only son was an innocent bystander and the government cared nothing when African-Americans were killed by El-Ops. In private, she knew Ronald had been hooked on Elevator rides since he was a teenager and she'd been powerless to stop his downward spiral to violent death. She wanted to destroy every El-Op in the country.

Because Leah had lost her kid brother to an OD, a bond formed between the two women back when Leah had been a BISC agent. Latifah Richmond, antigovernment activist, had become one of her best sources. And as near a friend as anyone Leah could name.

Latifah tapped another key, then waited as her PDA worked. "Thought I remembered the name. Danny DeClue, strictly small-timer, works for Thomas Billinger."

"Are they El-Ops?" Leah asked.

"Gambling's their game. Numbers, casinos, ponies, you name it, Billy's your man. DeClue runs a cheap operation off the Strip for Billy. Always in trouble with the cops. Rigged tables, even runs numbers on the side. Lordy, how much can you make on that with the National Jackpot for competition?" Her PDA pinged again and she scanned the screen. "Now we're cookin' with gas. Those turkeys you put in the hospital work collections for DeClue. Strictly leg-breakers."

Leah chewed on her lip. "That doesn't track. Why would a small-time gambler send his enforcers after me? I've never set foot inside a track or casino in my life."

"There's rumors he's connected back East. Some big money man in Jersey. You want me to check it out?"

"Yeah. Jersey isn't that far from D.C."

Latifah nodded. "Could be a connection. This might take a while."

"I'll get back to you. Now I have a date."

"Delgado? Seen his picture in the papers. Looks yummy."

Sometimes Leah cursed the unlikely friendship she and Latifah had formed. "Not Delgado. Date's with a corpse, who definitely won't look yummy—except to a cannibal. I'm headed for the morgue in San Diego."

6.

Karl Banecek came from sturdy Polish stock and had a wide Slavic face framed by straight blond hair liberally sprinkled with gray. He walked briskly down the wide corridor, accustomed to working a seven-day week ever since he'd become Samson's secretary of defense. Banecek possessed the aura of a man accustomed to power, which he was. But inside this five-sided concrete monolith he always felt uncomfortable in spite of being its titular head. Still his piercing gaze was enough to give even Howard McKinney, chairman of the Joint Chiefs and his mortal enemy, pause when they locked horns over Department of Defense priorities.

He entered his office and closed the door, then took a seat and shuffled through various papers on his desk requiring attention. The week in Korea had really put him behind schedule. When the special link on the left side of his desk beeped, he picked it up immediately, flicking on the vid. Wade Samson's face filled the screen.

"Good afternoon, Wade. Anything new on this mess?" As soon as his plane had landed at National early that morning, Samson had summoned him to the White House and briefed him on the missing nuclear devices.

"Nothing yet. If that son-of-a-bitch Manchester's heard anything from his granddaughter or Delgado, he isn't sharing the information with me."

"I knew it was a calculated risk to bring him into the loop."

"No choice, Karl. If this debacle goes public, he takes the fall with us. Besides, Berglund and Delgado have contacts outside the government we can use."

"It's more Manchester's contacts inside the Beltway I'd worry about," Banecek replied. "I'll have my report on the Korean trip ready for you by morning."

"Good. Our esteemed secretary of state insisted on a meeting immediately after you left. I trust Kensington didn't give any of the representatives from the North the finger during the negotiations," Samson added dryly.

"He's too old school stick-up-the-ass for that but he sure wasn't happy. What did he want to talk to you about—Holy Arabia?"

"What else? He wants military intervention, Karl. Unilateral if the Euros won't back us."

"You know they won't. They've phased out fossil fuels more efficiently than we have. And we can't afford to go it alone. You know where the budget stands now." He hesitated for a fraction of a second, then asked, "You discuss negotiating for the royal family's release any further?"

"He's still furious, accusing me of signing their death warrants and destroying our credibility as a world power. The man thinks like a damned general."

"That's because he was one." Banecek laughed grimly. "He's fought our plans to downscale the armed forces from the get-go, but he can't stop us. Last time I checked, you still outrank him—even if he thinks only God does."

Samson gave a snort of grim amusement. "Sometimes I think he believes he outranks God."

"It's that old money mind-set. I went to Harvard with a hundred like him."

"But none of them happens to be the most popular secretary of state since George Catlett Marshall. If I want that Nobel, Karl, I have to negotiate with Holy Arabian leaders and convince them to release what's left of the Saud family. My reelection hangs on this . . . not to mention my place in history. I can't let Kensington destroy everything."

"You'll get the Nobel Peace Prize, Wade," Banecek said. "All we have to do is recover those missing nukes. I'm on it."

1:23 P.M. EST, SUNDAY, NOVEMBER 9
WASHINGTON, D.C.

"First of all, let me apologize for not responding to your message sooner, Adam. But matters in Korea kept me hopping for the past week," Stuart Kensington said as he shook hands with the senator.

The secretary of state and Adam Manchester stood in the balcony above the north transept of the National Cathedral, well to the back where they were not visible to worshipers remaining after the last Eucharist of the morning. Since both men were Episcopalian and frequently attended services at the Cathedral anyway, it was an inconspicuous and neutral place for them to meet without attracting media attention.

Considering the present situation with illicit nuclear weapons somewhere in America, the light shining through the rose window depicting the Last Judgment lent a somber tone to their meeting. Adam had sent a personal note requesting a face-to-face meeting but it was Kensington's staff who had made the arrangements as soon as he returned from Korea.

"No need at all to apologize, Stuart. I'm aware of how volatile the situation on the DMZ is. You've plenty on your plate. Frankly, I hate to add yet another item to it, but my staff—not to mention the party honchos—insisted on this meeting."

Kensington smiled at the taller man as they seated themselves while Secret Service agents stood watch at discreet distances, making certain that no one discovered the two of them talking. Both men spoke barely above whispers. Sound carried across the vast spaces of the nearly deserted Gothic cathedral.

"I believe I know what you intend to ask—or perhaps I should say what the formidable Ms. Steuben insists you ask."

"I'm not only acting on the GOP chair's wishes. Before I contacted you, I gave the matter considerable thought. You'd make an excellent running mate. That's never been an issue in my mind. The question is, would *you* be willing to do it?"

Kensington met Manchester's steady gaze, pausing as if to phrase what he had to say very precisely. Adam knew before he uttered a word what the "good soldier" was going to answer, and felt guilty as hell for putting him in this position. *Damned if I don't detest politics at times like this.*

"Nothing would give me greater pleasure than to place my resignation on Wade Samson's desk tomorrow morning, Adam. I'd consider it a high honor to make the run with you—especially considering that you're going to win," he added with a smile. "But when I took the portfolio for this president, I made a commitment that I can't in conscience abandon, in spite of the fact that Samson and Banecek have left me out of the loop. Hell, Bob Labat has as much influence with them as I do," he said with a trace of irony. "I don't mean to sound self-important, but if I were to leave now, there would be a public outcry."

"There'd be public outrage. It would leave the administration floundering and with the security issues we have on our hands right now, that would be very dangerous," Adam said. "When party leaders first approached me, I was unsure of your answer, but once the president brought me in for that briefing, I no longer expected you'd be able to give any answer other than the one you have."

"I hoped you'd understand. Nothing I would love better than to be on the inaugural grandstand with you, but I swore an oath to finish out this term, God willing, one I can't break under present circumstances. Your assessment of the danger is correct. We have to find those weapons before the media finds out and turns a volatile situation into a political circus."

"You're a statesman in an age of politicians, Mr. Secretary. I respect your decision. Please give my best to Jillian." Now Adam paused. "But I will leave you with this thought. God willing, if I do win the election, I'll need a secretary of state who shares my views on foreign policy."

As they stood and shook hands again, Kensington replied, "At that point, I'm your man, 'Mr. President.' I am your man!"

11:25 A.M. MST, SUNDAY, NOVEMBER 9
MAZATLÁN, MEXICO

Francisco and Serifina Mulcahey's home nestled in a charming section of the old city on a hill high above Playa Olas Altas on the bay. The yellow stucco house with wrought-iron window grilles, interior courtyard fountains, and lush bougainvillea looked like something out of a tourist brochure. Because they had raised a brood of children—their own as well as several orphaned nephews and nieces—the Mulcaheys had enough bedrooms to open a small hotel.

Usually it was as busy as one. But this morning the traditional gathering for Seri's after Mass Sunday brunch had been canceled in favor of a council of war. Elliott Delgado sat in his great-uncle's private study, a room as large and imposing as the old man himself. Bookcases lined the walls, filled with classics in Spanish, English, even Latin. Cervantes, Shakespeare, and Tacitus vied with modern political and literary works. Delgado's cousins Raoul and Ernesto flanked him, all three men sitting on heavy walnut chairs around Mac's massive desk. The old man reclined behind it and listened as the younger men spoke, taking everything in like the shrewd statesman he was.

Since Del's father had died when he was a small boy, he had spent summers with the tall gray-haired old man and these two grandsons. Raoul and Ernesto were as close to him as brothers. Raoul was darkly handsome as an early twentieth-century matinee idol with a narrow mustache and a devilish glint in his ebony eyes. His brother Ernesto, stocky and square as a cinder block, was round-faced and mild with a low-key sense of humor, the opposite of Raoul's wickedly barbed wit.

"I disarmed a dozen ten-kiloton devices aboard the *Cárdenas* that day," Ernesto said. "Removed their detonator couplers and replaced them in a separate case." He was an explosives expert with Mexican Special Forces.

"So there *were* twelve bombs," Delgado confirmed. "But only ten turned up at the Army storage base in Missouri. At least, that's what the FBI and Pentagon brass figured out last week."

"And they think we stole two of them?" Raoul asked, his eyes gone flat.

"They suspect it's more likely some of the goons Inocensio sent with you."

"Well, that's a relief," Ernesto said as his brother muttered a string of remarkable oaths.

"When you left your sergeant in the cooler with the weapons, was anyone else with him? Did any of Inocensio's men have access to them?"

Raoul shook his head. "Fernandez had his orders. He was locked inside with enough nitro-cordite to send the *Cárdenas* to the bottom of the ocean if anyone tried to break in. Once the ship was secured, I posted two of my men in rotating shifts until we reached Guaymas and rendezvoused with the Americans."

"When did you turn the material over to Thompkinson?" Del asked.

"July seventh. The colonel was waiting for us at the pier with a detachment of soldiers and a ton of official paperwork. I verified everything with Mexico City. Then we went to the reefer and opened the cases. I signed off and he signed on. Ernesto gave him the case with the arming devices. The Americans were responsible for twelve nukes after that."

"How long were Thompkinson and his men aboard ship?"

Raoul scratched his jaw, considering. "At least half a day while they waited for their plane to be refueled for their flight back to the U.S. Ernesto and I left before they did."

"We have to assume ChiChi could get into the reefer after you and Tompkinson did the sign-off check," Del said, trying to reconstruct the sequence of events.

Francisco Geraldo Esteban Mulcahey, the mayor of Mazatlán, was a tall raw-boned man of Irish-Mexican ancestry who remained vigorous in spite of being seventy-five. He'd let them talk. Now he leaned forward. "Bernal could have stolen two of those cases after Raoul and Ernesto left. But that would not explain why the American colonel signed off for only ten at the arsenal."

Del said, "Tompkinson had to be involved or else he'd have blown the whistle as soon as he found two missing."

"Give that man a cigar," Raoul replied with a cynical smirk.

"Convenient he died in a car crash a month after," Del said, combing his hands through his hair, frustrated. "Were any of his men with him when the two of you counted twelve weapons?"

"No, it was just Ernesto, me, and him. His detachment waited outside. As far as I know he didn't share the paperwork with them. They were just there for transpo."

"They never knew how many nukes were turned over," Del said. "But I bet Oppermann will find out the colonel's unfortunate demise was no accident."

"Could the FBI salvage his car?" Ernesto asked.

"Hell, Oppermann will exhume the body."

"I put the arming devices in a safe in the captain's quarters," Ernesto said. "When I took out the case they were housed in, its lock was intact. I didn't open it."

"Bernal could've gotten the combination to the captain's safe, a key for the detonator box, too, " Del said. "We need to find his pals—if they're still alive. Seems likely everyone mixed up in this ends up dead accidentally, or on purpose. So far as I know, ChiChi's the only one still breathing."

"As soon as I received your call, I made inquiries about Bernal," Francisco said. "Born in Culiacán but his parents emigrated to America when he was a boy. Rumor has it he returned here as a young man after getting in trouble with the American Navy."

When it came to rumors, Del knew his uncle could find out more with a few well-placed calls than he could with a week of legwork. Mac and his brother-in-law, the drug lord, had an understanding. Inocensio Ramirez left Mazatlán and his dead wife's family alone. There were no Elevator Operators on the streets. It was a clean and prosperous community surrounded by a literal sea of corruption.

"Bernal joined the Mexican Navy, but his real employer was Ramirez," Mac continued. "He was a cook aboard a series of coastal patrol ships trying without success to interdict drug traffic."

"Ramirez has an incredibly sophisticated organization," Raoul admitted.

"Men like Bernal use palm-sized digital units to give ship or troop movements to jets outfitted with communications equipment." Ernesto, the techie, loved gadgets. "The signals are disguised as overload satellite communications clutter. Never picked up by the government. We don't have the equipment or manpower to do the job. These flying communications centers are disguised as private corporate planes. They relay the information to Culiacán where Inocensio and his *segundo* Cabril have a central computer bank set up."

"And no one's tried to raid the joint?" Del asked.

"I have suggested it to my superiors. Perhaps now that we have a new president, the priorities in Mexico City will change," Raoul replied.

His grandfather looked dubious. "Inocensio Ramirez runs a drug empire that stretches across the ocean. He and the Cartel compete for Pacific Rim business. I do not believe President Higgins wishes to be squeezed between them. Times are very uncertain."

"Maybe that competition would be a reason for Inocensio to want a nuclear arsenal of his own," Del suggested.

The old man nodded. The implication troubled him. "He has never overreached before. But he has some reason to feel threatened. . . ."

"There are rumors circulating about the Cartel being in the middle of a shake-up. Some kind of power struggle," Raoul clarified for his grandfather, who remained deep in thought.

"You mean Benito Zuloaga's boys might start shooting each other? Wouldn't that be sweet," Del said. "But if they do have their own nukes, a shoot-out at the BZ Corral might not be such a hot idea."

His uncle said, "Precisely. Zuloaga is an educated man who understands the world situation. He's been a stabilizing force. If someone less . . . sophisticated gained control of the Cartel, the repercussions might be disastrous for Mexico and the United States."

"At some point maybe I'll go fishing to see what Benito knows . . . if he deigns to share. Since he already has his own stockpile, I doubt he'd be interested in two Russian dirty bombs. But first, I need to have a little talk with Inocensio."

"I imagined you would wish that. I have already put in a call to him, but he has not responded yet. I will inquire about the other sailors who were with Bernal on that raid. It might be interesting if any have failed to report for duty."

11:30 A.M. PST, SUNDAY, NOVEMBER 9
SAN DIEGO COUNTY MEDICAL EXAMINER'S OFFICE

Leah sat in the sterile room, like a thousand other government office cubicles she had visited over the years. The overhead fluorescent lighting cast everything including her in a sickly greenish shade. Fitting, she supposed for a building housing a morgue. God, she'd seen enough of corpses collapsed bonelessly in death, wide vacant eyes staring at nothing, slack mouths gaping without sound. Vital as it was to law enforcement, how could anyone do this work?

The ME was a busy woman, hardly surprising considering how many El-Op shootings they'd had in the past few days. Leah had caught a lucky break that the doc was working on a Sunday and willing to give her a few minutes. Determining cause of death was not the problem when dealers blasted each other with automatic weapons. She knew how the carjacker had died. That cannon of Delgado's packed enough force to stop a tank. The dead man's earlier life was of far greater interest to her.

Captain Munez had not been available to take her call. Her earlier admission that she'd been BISC had alienated him. Cops didn't like the way the defunct agency's personnel had operated, especially since not every BISC agent had turned in his personalized needle gun. They were rogues now, lethal threats to law enforcement. A few continued unauthorized cancellations of drug traffickers. Some even hired out to the El-Ops they'd been tasked with terminating. The money was a hell of a lot better than any federal agent's or police officer's salary.

Her ruminations were interrupted when the door opened and a petite woman in a pristine white smock entered. Her hair was cut functionally short and generously sprinkled with gray, but there was a surprising spring in her step as she smiled and extended her hand. "I'm Dr. Steller. The receptionist said you wanted to see me. An FBI matter?"

Leah's hand enveloped the ME's much smaller one. She had a difficult time imagining the woman sawing open human skulls for a living. "Yes, I'm Special Agent Leah Berglund." She felt like a fraud but technically it was true. She showed her badge to the doctor, who had doubtlessly seen enough of them to recognize the real deal.

"Please, won't you have a seat? My office is on the other side of this maze, but we can talk in complete privacy here."

They sat on two body-contour chairs that were surprisingly comfortable, facing each other. Leah went straight to the point, saying, "You worked on a man killed by a civilian last night on I-5 during an attempted carjacking."

"Oh, yes, a .50-caliber bullet wound is fairly unusual in this day of automatic weapons. It does the job, though. I can send you the report as soon as—"

Leah shook her head. "I've seen what a Smith & Wesson can do. We're trying to ID the El-Op. To see which gang he belonged to. Could I have a look at his personal effects?"

"Captain Munez, from the mayor's drug task force, was here a couple of hours ago and took them."

Leah cursed silently. A turf war was not what she needed now. The doctor's next comment startled her.

"Like many of the victims of violent death, he had no identification on him, but I can tell you he was not an El-Op. That will be in my report to the police. My technicians just completed the preliminary work on all the bodies from that incident."

"How can you be sure?"

"As I'm certain you know, we have pretty sophisticated means of testing for drug use. Even if a dealer never abused Elevator—or any other drug—our scans would pick up traces of it from simple physical contact, on the hands, for example. Breathing in particulate matter will also leave a signature. The residue's impossible to erase. It lasts for weeks. The men killed during the gun battle on the freeway were saturated. One vehicle in the crash was carrying a trunkload of bean bags and the gunfire smashed into them. I'd venture to say half the innocent civilians in cars nearby would test positive."

"But you're saying the man you just autopsied had no trace of drugs on him?"

"If he was ever near an Elevator capsule, it wasn't recent. He certainly had no part in the shoot-out on the freeway."

"No ID of any kind on him?"

"Well, there was one thing. . . ." The ME hesitated, giving Leah an uncomfortable look before continuing. "He had no fingerprints. They'd been surgically removed."

"Smooth as glass." Just like her own.

The doctor nodded. "I've heard rumors about BISC agents, although I've never met one."

Until now. Leah placed her hands palms down on her lap, wondering if the ME had noticed when they shook hands.

2:47 P.M., EST, SUNDAY, NOVEMBER 9
WASHINGTON, D.C.

Adam Manchester flicked off the link and pondered his next move. The call from Leah had been very disturbing. Someone had deliberately targeted her and Del in California. That meant someone in Washington knew they would be brought in to the investigation before they did and moved to eliminate them. She had a source in Vegas trying to connect the small-time gambler who'd ordered the hit on her with a bigger fish on the East Coast.

The one who went after Del had been BISC. That reeked of a connection inside the Beltway. His granddaughter had a contact trying to identify the man Delgado had killed. He looked down at the digipix she'd sent of the shooter. Hard to tell much when a man lay stone dead on a morgue slab.

Manchester leaned back in the big leather chair and looked around the well-appointed library. The walls were lined with built-in bookcases and the furniture was Chippendale. Since his old Senate colleague Brett Lowell had become the American ambassador to the Euro Union, he'd offered Adam use of his beautiful Georgetown home any time he visited D.C. Having given up his own residence in the capital when he retired, Adam was grateful.

He had not slept since receiving Wade Samson's call in the wee hours of Saturday morning. "I'd better get used to going without sleep if I accept the nomination," he muttered, rubbing his eyes. Down to work. The attorney general had legal access to BISC records. With some luck they might be able to identify the man who'd tried to kill Del, then link him to someone in Washington.

Leah had her own leads on the thugs who'd come after her. Just thinking of his granddaughter with hired killers stalking her made his blood run cold, but he knew nothing he said or did would keep her out of this. Manchester muttered an oath. Did he really want back in the snake pit? Then he sighed, admitting Leah came by her stubbornness honestly. Damn right he did!

He poured himself another cup of coffee from the silver pot on the side table, took a swallow of the strong black stuff, and picked up the link, bracing himself to speak with John Scarletti.

3 P.M. EST, SUNDAY, NOVEMBER 9
WASHINGTON, D.C.

"What the hell do you mean, you can't find Bernal? You guaranteed you knew everything about this turkey! How the hell did you lose him a second time? Bad enough he slipped our of our hands in Arizona after all my trouble getting him here. Now he's running around with *my* nukes, trying to make a deal for himself!"

On the other side of the vid link, the man leaned back and let his employer rant. *If only his colleagues could see him now*, he thought with amusement.

"What if that reporter and his assassin find him before you do? I won't pay you one thin dime, dammit! I told you to kill them and you botched that, too!"

"Mistakes happen." He shrugged. "But I still say they might lead us to Bernal—if I don't find him first. You'll get your nukes back."

"As soon as you find Bernal, kill them both—and him."

"Not to worry. I have a score to settle with all three of them. You just make the deal with the rag heads."

"I'm on top of that. Aziz al Ambas is a ballsy bastard. Locked up in a concrete cell at Gitmo and still acting like he was in a Riyadh palace. He's dying to use bombs on us that our CIA swiped from the Ruskies. Convenient that the nukes are already inside the country.

His cells have their targets picked out. All we need is to kill Bernal and deliver the goods."

"I can do that. Just so we get out of Dodge before they go boom."

"We will. And traveling first class, too. We're gonna be rich, boy. Rich!"

7.

As Adam Manchester drove up to the sprawling white frame house surrounded by tall sugar pines, he felt distinctly uneasy. Was this the kind of home he and Anne Beresford would have had if they'd married? He knew she and her husband Frank Scarletti had bought the place when John was a young boy. After Frank died, Anne had moved to a condo in Silver Springs and left the large house to their son, who had a growing family. For such a large and diverse metro area, Washington was an amazingly clubby town. Learning about her situation had been accidental, before his own wife had passed on.

For a moment, the idea of Annie being there teased the back of his mind. He dismissed it. All John Scarletti had said was that he was grilling burgers for the family and they'd be delighted to have Adam join them. The casual invitation had surprised the senator. It did not fit the "Scar's" icy public image. Manchester was not certain why he had accepted. Curiosity? He picked up the small folder from the seat beside him and got out of his car. This was business, after all.

As he walked up the driveway, he could hear the sounds of children's laughter through the heavy storm door. He pressed the bell and a soft chime brought footsteps down the dimly lit hallway's parquet floor. A small, slender woman with the regal bearing honed by New England's finest finishing schools approached and opened the door.

"Adam, it's been so long, but I'd recognize you anywhere—and I'm not just saying that because your pictures are all over the newspapers these days either." Anne Beresford Scarletti smiled as she ushered him inside.

"The same for you, Annie," he replied. "You'll never change." Except for a few highlighted silvery streaks in her sable hair and tiny smile lines around her eyes and mouth, it was the truth. She seemed as slender and athletic-looking as she'd been when they were college sweethearts.

They stood, taking each other's measure for a moment, uncertain of what to say or do next when two boys approaching teen years came barreling down the hallway. "Grandma, you gotta come stop Dad from adding that sucky steak sauce to the burgers," the younger one said. "He always ruins them that way," the taller of the pair added.

They skidded to a stop beside her, looking inquisitive as she introduced the senator to her grandsons, John and Frank. In moments Adam had met the whole clan, the AG's wife Sally, a striking blonde with a generous smile, and their daughter Violetta who was a freshman at Georgetown. They settled in the large family room adjacent to the kitchen where John was mixing ground beef with a plethora of ingredients as the younger boys protested.

While Sally set the table, Violetta diverted her brothers to a fierce battle at gaming stations across the room, leaving Adam and Anne on the sofa. She smiled comfortably at him, settling back and kicking off her flat-heeled shoes. "Never could abide the things," she said.

"I remember. I used to think you had shoe leather on the soles of your feet, running over the rocks on the beach when we were at Yale."

"I never was very good at holding up the Beresford traditions," she said with a laugh. "Jillian was the lady and I was the tomboy. I understand you've kept up with her and Stuart over the years?"

"You know how social obligations are when you're in politics. We've run across each other, mostly back when I was in the Senate and Stuart was at the Pentagon." Stuart Kensington's wife was Anne's sister, the one who had made the proper marriage while Anne had fallen head over heels in love with an Italian immigrant's son attending Yale on a scholarship. The Beresford family had never gotten over it.

For totally different reasons, neither had Adam Manchester, until he met Dorcas. As they talked of inconsequential things, mostly funny memories from college days, he wondered if she ever thought about how their lives might have been if they'd married. But any idle curiosity about that was quickly interrupted by the aroma of spicy burgers. John Scarletti carried a heaping platter in from the backyard grill. His demeanor with his family was utterly at odds with the way he acted inside the Beltway.

When the meal was finished, Adam and John adjourned to the AG's private office. "Pull up a chair, Adam. I know that packet of documents is burning a hole in your hand," Scarletti said in his deceptively soft voice. A hint of his usual guardedness returned now.

"I just found out today that the attempts made on my granddaughter's and Elliott Delgado's lives last night were coordinated to keep them from reaching Washington." He gave the file and digipix of the dead "carjacker" to Scarletti as he explained what Leah had told him.

"So, he was BISC. Doesn't surprise me. Since we shut them down, lots of the former agents have gone rogue," Scarletti said.

"I've heard some of them still have activated needle guns."

"We did a recall of all agents we could access, having the chips removed from their hands so the guns wouldn't fire." Scarletti scanned the lab report attached to the morgue pix of the man Delgado had killed. "This one obviously had his chips removed. The scars are noted."

Adam remembered the small neat incisions in both palms of Leah's hands. BISC agents had been trained to shoot with deadly accuracy, left- or right-handed. "The trick now is to identify him and connect him to whoever hired him," he said grimly.

Scarletti sighed. "When I said we had chips removed from those we could access, I meant there were records destroyed at BISC Central in Reston before Justice moved in to shut them down."

"You mean we may never get a line on this guy?"

The AG shrugged. "He had the chips removed. That improves the chances we can ID him . . . after wading through the mess Central left. Their bureaucrats were thorough and vindictive. And I might add, are now awaiting trials charged with the obstruction of justice." The grim hint of a smile played around his mouth.

3:32 P.M. MST, SUNDAY, NOVEMBER 9
PAPAGO INDIAN RESERVATION, SOUTHERN ARIZONA

Paul Oppermann scanned the desert landscape filled with little more than sand and cacti. Leah Berglund sat in the seat beside him while he drove their Ford TE rental car. He had reached her link a couple of hours ago, saying he was en route to interview a Border Patrol agent who knew how Bernal got into the country. Was she interested in meeting him to question the guy?

Leah had intended to be in Mexico with Del to put Inocensio Ramirez's feet to the fire. She knew Uncle Mac would track the bastard down for them. But she was curious enough about what Oppermann expected to learn from the Border Patrol here to schedule a detour through Tucson en route to Mazatlán. While waiting for the changed connection at San Diego International, she had checked in with Rhys Willis and Adam Manchester. Willis had nothing to report on Bernal or his merchandise yet.

But her grandfather had amazed her. He'd eaten dinner with the AG and his family. Scarletti grilled burgers on an antiquated charcoal brazier nearly as primitive as Manchester's own. Apparently the senator wasn't the only living anachronism in Washington. She only hoped they had more luck than Willis seemed to be having with his search.

She and Oppermann met at the Tucson airport. During the hundred-kilometer drive to the small outpost on the reservation they exchanged information.

"I assigned agents to search for the soldiers Tompkinson took with him when he picked up the nukes," Oppermann told her. "In Missouri my men are checking junkyards to locate his car. A forensic team at Quantico's waiting for delivery of his body from Arlington. Getting the court order to disinter him was easy. When Scarletti yanks chains, he gets results."

"You admire him." It wasn't a rebuke, just puzzlement. Obviously

Paul and her grandfather both found the AG far more human than she did. During that interview in the White House, he had creeped her out big time.

"He's tough but he knows his job now that he's been turned loose to do it."

Leah did not reply, just stared straight ahead.

"Sorry. I'm a klutz. I didn't mean—"

"Yes you did and you're right. BISC undercut the whole Department of Justice. It was dangerous and I'm glad it's gone."

"You helped put the agency out of business. That took guts. We need more people like you in Washington."

"You'll be getting Adam Manchester. From what he's told me, I don't think you or your boss will have to worry about your jobs."

Oppermann laughed. "Maybe we only look good by comparison. Samson's picked some beauts. His CIA director just let the whole Middle East blow up in his face, his secretary of defense wants to dismantle the military while his secretary of state's itching to put it to use. And don't even mention poor Bob Labat."

"The secretary of Homeland Security is out of his element in Washington," Leah agreed. At best he had the most thankless cabinet post in the government.

Oppermann snorted. "It'd be a *mitzvah* if Samson just let the Rabbit sort paper clips."

"It's a far cry from lying down in front of hazmat trucks to whipping Homeland Security in line," she replied.

"But you gotta admit, if he'd do his protest shtick on the Fourteenth Street Bridge it'd be a great opportunity to finish off an inept politician. Not a car would touch their brakes."

Leah couldn't suppress a laugh, but protested, "That's awful, Paul! He's a decent guy."

"With dirty bombs inside the country, we need a *mentsh*, not a 'decent guy,'" he replied, gazing out on the bleak desert landscape.

The border area's only claim to fame this time of year was an occasional saguaro cactus. The magnificent giants bloomed in spring. Otherwise, the unremitting tan and dusty pale green of greasewood and other scrub vegetation covered the red, rocky earth, flowing uninterrupted into the hazy distance. Overhead the sun blazed through thin dry air like a predator eager to suck the life from any living thing.

A sign ahead indicated they were nearing the Border Patrol outpost. Oppermann turned the rental car onto the broken asphalt of a small parking lot. The building was made of unpainted cinder blocks, squatting like an ugly spider caught without the protection of its web. "Some fancy digs," he muttered, killing the engine.

"Tax dollars at work," Leah said as they walked to the door and entered. Both of them blinked, trying to refocus their eyes from the blinding sun outside and adjust to the much dimmer artificial lighting of the windowless interior.

A short, muscular young man wearing the green uniform of a Customs & Border Protection officer sat behind a battered desk surrounded by an array of outdated computers and surveillance equipment. He wore a buzz cut and a worried expression.

"You're Oppermann, the FBI director," he said. His name tag identified him as Ken Robinson.

"Glad I'm so famous," Oppermann said, deadpan, flashing his badge anyway. "This is Special Agent Leah Berglund. She's working on this investigation with me."

Leah nodded, checking out the cluttered area. A small office and a restroom appeared to be the only other rooms in the facility. The doors to both were ajar. She could see no one but Robinson was in the place.

Noting the same thing, Paul got right down to business. "You indicated that you know how that Cessna crossed the border and you weren't talking to anyone but me. Okay, I've come a long way. So talk already." He grabbed a chair and wheeled it around, then straddled it.

Leah pulled up another chair and sat on the opposite side of the young officer.

Beneath his sun-darkened skin Robinson looked pale. "I didn't know Harry was doing anything wrong, I swear. God, I wish I hadn't come in that afternoon. . . ."

"Maybe you'd better start at the beginning," she said quietly. The young man was scared to death.

Robinson gulped. "I wasn't supposed to be on duty, but I came in anyway. Wanted to score points, you know. Harry Busch—my supervisor—was running air surveillance ops that day. We monitor the ninety-mile stretch of Mexican border on the reservation. Most of the land on either side's pretty desolate."

"You ain't kiddin', " Oppermann muttered with a big-city shiver. "So what was good old Harry up to?"

Robinson swallowed. "You know Globe Net monitors all air and land traffic for the NRO." They nodded. "If any unauthorized activity occurs in our jurisdiction, Globe Net sends us the coordinates and we check it out." He swung his chair around to show them the console. "I read the report on the screen while he was . . ." he hesitated, red-faced. "Uh, he was using the bathroom."

Whether Robinson was embarrassed about his unauthorized peek at the equipment or Harry Busch's indisposition was unclear. "Agent Busch has a stomach problem, especially the day after he's tied one on."

"Harry the Hurler," Oppermann said. "So you saw the report on this plane, huh?"

Robinson nodded. "I didn't think much about it then. He said it was a glitch in the Globe Net system because Papago Security forgot to tell them they'd sent up their Cessna to go after a couple of local kids who'd stolen a car. They fly over the border now and then when they're not paying attention."

"That would explain why the NRO had no unauthorized entry on record," Oppermann said. "Busch misled Globe Net so they never filed a report."

"What led you to question what Agent Busch had told you?" Leah asked.

"I didn't . . . at first. There's lots of unemployment on the rez. Drinking, Elevator tripping, theft to support their habits, you know. But a couple of days later I read an article in the *Tucson Citizen* about a plane crash and an unidentified man found murdered inside it. The authorities said it was a drug deal gone bad . . . but that plane was a Cessna, too, and it was found about seventy klicks from the coordinates I'd seen."

"Had to be the same plane your pal Busch let fly in from Mexico illegally," Oppermann said.

"I didn't know that then. But Harry called in sick Tuesday and then word came from Tucson that he'd resigned, no forwarding address. I checked out his digs in town but the landlady said he stiffed her out of a month's rent."

Oppermann asked, "Address?" He jotted down what Robinson gave him.

"When I cleaned out his desk I found these." He handed Leah several brochures from a GMC dealership in Tucson. "Harry always wanted one of those fancy TE all-terrain vehicles, but on his salary he couldn't afford it."

"Looks like our boy was anticipating a big payday—and not from Uncle Sam," she said, handing the brochures to Oppermann, who tucked them in his shirt pocket. The boys in his Tucson office would be busy for quite a while.

Leah watched the young agent. There was more he hadn't told them. "What did you do after Harry was gone?"

He hesitated a moment, then swallowed and said, "I decided to check his story with the rez police. They never sent their plane up that day. It was down for repairs. They didn't have a report about a stolen vehicle either, so everything he told me was bogus."

"Why did you wait until now to report this? And why not go to the FBI in Tucson?" Leah asked.

"Two days ago a guy claiming to be FBI came here, asking about Harry. I told him I didn't know where he'd gone."

"The Bureau didn't know *bobkes* about Busch. None of my agents talked to you."

"I know. Something about him wasn't . . . right. I called the Tucson office after he left. Just sort of checking, you know? They said there was no agent named Jim Barnes working there."

"So, you didn't trust the local FBI. Why'd you wait until today to call Washington?" Leah asked.

Robinson shifted uneasily in his seat. "That Barnes or whatever his name was . . . he knew about Maria." When they both sat forward, he cleared his throat, more nervous than ever. "She's Harry's girl. I told him I didn't know anything about her. She's got enough trouble. I wasn't going to get her in any more."

"She didn't have a green card," Leah surmised.

"An illegal and a Border Patrol agent. Match made in heaven," Oppermann said with a sigh.

"Nobody knew about them. They were real careful. After that phony agent pumped me, I went to warn her but the owner of the coffee shop where she works said she'd quit a couple of days ago and gone home to Mexico. I knew that wasn't true. Her folks there need the money she sends real bad. She'd never quit unless she was scared . . . or maybe she'd run off with Harry and lied to her boss to throw that Barnes off the trail."

"Okay, so Harry's gone. His girlfriend's gone. You got any idea where they might be?" Oppermann asked.

"Harry said she was from someplace in Sonora, but never mentioned a town."

"That really narrows it down," Leah said dryly. "Full name?"

"Maria Montoya."

"Just a guess but there are probably about five thousand Maria Montoyas in Mexico," Oppermann said.

"Nah, there are at least that many in Sonora alone," she replied. "I'll see if Del's uncle can trace her family. Maybe she'll lead us to Busch. Where'd she work?"

"In Sells. A place called the Coffee Cart."

Oppermann jotted down notes as the young officer gave him details. Leah had a gut intuition the kid was probably infatuated with Maria himself. "What did this Barnes look like?"

"Tall, thin, stooped shoulders, gray hair. He smoked one cigarette after another. Some funny foreign kind. Smelled like a fire in an outhouse. And he acted weird. Everyone else who smokes out there"—Robinson gestured to the parking lot outside the door—"they flick their butts. He took his with him."

She and Oppermann exchanged looks. "He's gotta be Company," he muttered.

"CIA?" Robinson said in a hushed whisper, paler than ever.

"You were real good at keeping secrets up till now. Not a word about this to anyone." Leah's tone was enough to make Ken Robinson shrink back in his chair.

"Yes, ma'am."

"Special Agent Al Trask will pick you up in a couple of hours," Oppermann said. "He'll show you some digifiles. See if you can finger the *mamzer* who's impersonating an FBI agent. If you can't, we'll have a compu-sketch tech work with you to create a likeness."

"He isn't BISC," Leah said with absolute certainty as they left the building. "BISC agents weren't allowed to smoke. Bad for wind and stamina. Worse, it leaves trace evidence. This guy made sure he didn't." *CIA. I'd bet my ass on it.*

"The odd 'foreign' brand might be a lead," Paul suggested, opening his link. He held a brief conversation with Special Agent Trask, then signed off as they climbed into the Ford TE. "I got Tucson searching for Harry Busch. Techs will be here to go over his vacated premises ASAP."

"My money says he's dead," she replied.

"Only a *meshugener* would take that bet."

"Our smoker's Company. Finding him won't be easy. How good's your sketch tech?"

He shrugged. "How good's Robinson's memory? You know witnesses. He might ID me if I was in the vid file."

"Nah, he recognized you the minute you walked in the door. Besides, you don't have hair." She grinned at him.

"You, I like," he said with a laugh.

"I'll have my contacts snoop in CIA records once we have a visual to work with. Look for the Montoya girl, too."

Oppermann nodded. "You feel an uncontrollable craving for caffeine?" he asked as he turned the ignition. The turbo-electric engine started with a whine of protest. "Wouldn't one of those big GMCs with flash drive be sweet?"

"Too bad Busch didn't get one either," she replied. "Let's go have a cup of joe on Uncle Sam."

The owner of the Coffee Cart turned the color of guacamole when they flashed their badges and asked about Maria. He swore he didn't know she was an illegal and had no idea where she'd gone. The only thing helpful he could give them was an address. En route they stopped by Busch's apartment in Sells, but found nothing useful. FBI techs from Tucson arrived to sift the dump while he and Leah questioned neighbors. No one had seen anything unusual or knew when he left town. The guy was a natural loner. After wasting nearly an hour, they headed for Maria Montoya's run-down shack on the outskirts of town.

Busch's second-story unit was a palace compared to where she had lived. When they questioned the women and children on the street, Leah applied her newly-acquired language skills. A couple of old women said they'd seen an Anglo man pick Maria up after dark on rare occasions. He was in civilian clothes and no one ever got a good look at him.

"It's progress," Leah said. "No one at Busch's place ever saw him with a Mexicana."

"Hardly saw him at all."

"I think Robinson was right. Busch probably kept his little romance pretty quiet. Playing hanky-panky with an illegal is a definite no-no for Border Patrol agents."

Then they found Matt Lone Deer hunkered in front of a dirty shed, whittling on a piece of greasewood with a pocketknife. He was dirty and thin, about ten or eleven, with wary eyes and hair that had never seen a barber. But the blade of his knife was clean and sharp.

"You know Maria Montoya?" Leah asked him after she and Paul had identified themselves.

"Yeah, I knew her. She's gone."

"How about this guy?" Oppermann flashed a pix of Busch they'd taken from the Border Patrol computer.

"I seen him around. He don't live here."

"But you know he's Maria's boyfriend," Leah said.

He nodded. "I followed them a couple of times . . . late at night." A smirk that was part little boy and part street smart crossed his face.

"Where'd they go?" she asked.

"They had, like, a sort of place . . . you know, where nobody would mess with them," he said, shoving a long hank of straight black hair out of his eyes.

"Will you take us there?"

"I might," the boy said. He turned then and stared defiantly at Oppermann.

Leah studied him appraisingly. His black eyes were hard beyond his years. *Like Joey Buccoli's.* She pulled a fifty out of her handbag and watched his face betray him. It was probably more money than he'd ever seen. Only the El-Ops on the rez had this kind of cash and he was too young to deal . . . yet. "We'd pay for a good guide and tracker," she said with a smile.

"You just hired one." He grabbed the fifty.

They drove several miles on what passed for roads, then had to abandon the car and go on foot, down an embankment to where a dry streambed cut an erratic gouge in the red rocky soil. Leah was glad she wore sport joggers and slacks that protected her legs from spiky cacti and brush. Paul's soft loafers weren't as practical and his best blue suit was ruined by the time they reached the small cluster of cottonwoods where Matt Lone Deer stopped.

Oppermann was sweating and short of breath in the cool, dry air. He noted with aggravation that the woman and the boy weren't even winded. "You wait here while we have a look around," he said to Matt.

Sullenly the boy kicked a stone in the dust, ignoring him. As soon as they walked out of earshot, Oppermann asked Leah, "If I'd left the keys in that junker, you give me odds he wouldn't boost it?"

"Nah. Me he likes," she said with a grin.

They walked a little farther. She scanned the trees growing at the edge of a dry streambed. Bare roots from the hardy cottonwoods were exposed where water had eroded the soil away. She approached the twisted mass. Then she saw it. "Paul, I think I just found Maria Montoya . . . or at least part of her."

A woman's foot was wedged firmly in the roots, detached above the ankle by what looked to be a predator's gnawing. Oppermann noticed the boy was moving closer. He motioned for him to stay where he was, then walked over to where Leah knelt, carefully examining the ground.

"Clumped dirt. Looks like someone dug too shallow a grave," she said, pointing to the mound of dry reddish soil that had been disturbed, probably the preceding night.

The bodies had been partially disinterred. As they used broken off tree branches to shovel the dirt away, it was apparent the exposed parts of the bodies had been savagely chewed by the local carnivores. "What do you think?" Paul asked, pausing to wipe the sweat from his forehead. "Wild dogs? Coyotes? What the hell lives out here?" He gestured around the rugged landscape.

"Don't look at me. I grew up in Minneapolis. Wouldn't know a panther from a pack rat," she replied. "Delgado would. He's the great white hunter type, but I can give you cause of death and it wasn't by wild animals."

Oppermann squatted beside her as she gently brushed the dry dirt from the victims. "Yeah, I don't feature a coyote packing heat," he said grimly.

"Professional job," she said. Busch and Maria had been shot in the head at close range, execution style.

"My mother wanted I should be a rabbi. Days like this, I wish I'd listened to her." Paul looked down at what had once been a pretty young woman, shaking his head.

7:00 P.M. MST, SUNDAY, NOVEMBER 9
MAZATLÁN, MEXICO

"Anything to report?" Delgado asked Gracie Kell. He could tell she was in her favorite D.C. haunt, a bar near her apartment where he'd met her several times. It was decidedly low-tech but otherwise as grungy as the place she lived.

A small hand with well-bitten nails clutched a huge Diet Coke as she stared into the vid screen. "You pick the crummiest times to call a gal, Delgado. I'm meeting a guy in ten minutes."

"Baby Cheeks?"

"No way. Strictly business. People besides you pay computer interrogators, you know." She was in her usual rear booth, back to the wall, but her eyes still scanned every rickety bar stool before she replied. "Zip on Kensington and McKinney, other than what the media—you are they, right?—already knows. The Pentagon brass are in a battle to the death with the administration over cuts in military size. You know, I could really have a thing for Karl Banecek if he weren't ex-CIA morphed into defense secretary.

"Cartel chatter's interesting. Seems to be some trouble in paradise. Between Zuloaga and a dude named Fuljensio Noriega. A mean mother. Grew up in the mountains around Cali, working in the fields and cocaine processing plants."

"You don't grow in that environment, you metastasize," Del said. "He's number two dog now? You think there's a coup in the wind?"

"From what I gather, could be. I'll keep on it. Oh, yeah, that Bernal guy is a real charmer."

Del leaned toward the screen. "What've you got on him?"

"You know the old cliché, *cherchez la femme.* ChiChi really believes in the institution of marriage. Got six wives that I've found so far. One in every port where the Mexican Navy's ever put in." She snickered at her own pun.

"How many in the U.S.?" Del asked.

She made a few swift keystrokes and said, "Seattle, Frisco, San Diego, Corpus, New Orleans, and, get this, the Big Apple. Your boy gets around."

"Give me their names and addresses."

She transferred the information to Uncle Mac's PDA. Del glanced at it and said, "Gracie, you're a genius."

"You gotta get more original with your flattery, Delgado. I *know* that. Uh, here comes my client. Gotta run. I'll let you know soon as I find out anything more."

"Especially about Bernal," he said.

She nodded and her spiky hair shimmied like the tentacles of a hungry sea anemone. Then the screen went blank.

"Damn, I'd love to see who her 'client' was," he muttered, then gave a voice command to connect him to Oppermann.

Without preamble the director said, "Leah should be in Mazatlán in an hour or so. We know where Bernal entered the country and how. The Rabbit's Border Patrol is in deep drek."

Del listened as he outlined what they'd learned on the reservation. "I'll see if my uncle can dig up any leads on Maria Montoya. The CIA connection makes me nervous."

"Can't say I'm thrilled either. Especially considering it was one of their spooks who brought those dirty bombs here in the first place. *Meshugeners*, all of 'em. If our sketch tech can work with Robinson and get a decent likeness, Scarletti may be able to track him down." Oppermann didn't sound optimistic.

"Maybe Gracie Kell'll have better luck. She just hit the jackpot. Like all good sailors, ChiChi had a girl in every port." Delgado gave him the info on Bernal's wives.

"My gut says Corpus, considering it's closest to where he entered the country, but since you and Leah were hit in southern California, I'll have that checked out, too."

"Keep me posted on Tompkinson. Wanna bet his accident wasn't?"

"What's with you *goyim*, always offering sucker bets?"

11:50 P.M. MST, SUNDAY, NOVEMBER 9
NAYARIT, MEXICO

The jungle closed in on them like a living thing, darkening the huge gold moon that had danced over the ocean when they left Mazatlán. The farther south they traveled, the denser the canopy of vegetation. And rougher the roads. Leah felt her jaw snap with enough force to loosen a molar when the ancient Jeep bounced across another muddy rut. Raoul didn't even hit the brakes, just continued at breakneck speed down the barely discernible trail that narrowed with every kilometer.

"You sure you know where you're going?" Del asked his cousin.

"I know Grandfather's information is seldom wrong. Bartolome Cruces's family lives about five miles down this road—distant cousins, admittedly, but he has no other living relatives."

"A long shot that Ramirez hasn't figured this one out yet," Leah said bleakly.

According to Francisco Mulcahey's sources, Inocensio had moved heaven and earth to find ChiChi and the other three men on the *Cárdenas* mission. So far he'd had no success with Bernal or Cruces but the other two had turned up dead in the past week. So had several of Inocensio's "security forces," leaving a trail of bodies down Highway 15, scattered like rat droppings from Hermosillo to Guaymas.

The harbor police report of a shoot-out between drug dealers at the San Carlos Marina had slipped under the radar until Uncle Mac started asking questions. The only solid lead they had was the slim connection of ChiChi's coworker to this remote backwater.

Del swatted a mosquito lucky enough to make a skin landing while the Jeep bounced through the encroaching thicket. "It'd be easy to lose a body in this jungle."

"It'd be easy to *become* a body in this jungle. Maybe you'd better slow down and kill the lights when we get close," Leah suggested.

Raoul's teeth gleamed whitely in the dim glare from the headlights as he grinned. "She always this bossy?"

"From the first time I met her," Del answered from the backseat.

Leah rolled her eyes. Mulcahey slowed after the next turn. He came to a stop in the middle of the road and doused the lights. "From here on, we move on foot, *con su permiso, señorita*?" he added with a chuckle.

She knew he was teasing. The past summer they'd fought their way through the Sonoran desert and the wilderness of northern California together. "*Desde luego, mi Coronel*," she replied.

"She's been studying Spanish," he said to Del. "That's a good sign." The whole Mulcahey family wanted Del to marry her. Raoul wondered why they hadn't done it yet but knew better than to press the issue. Yanquis were strange sometimes.

They started out using one electric torch on the lowest setting, moving quietly with Raoul in the lead. He was used to jungle maneuvers. Del had spent summers with his Mexican family while growing up, but he'd become more accustomed to urban warfare since his FBI days. After about twenty minutes they saw a small cluster of shacks in a clearing. The primitive glow of lantern light cast them in shadowy relief. Several people moved around inside the largest building, a clapboard and corrugated tin monstrosity with only cheesecloth to hold the mosquitoes at bay outside a couple of windows. The door was closed but looked little more substantial than the "screens."

"I doubt they have guards posted. Mosquitoes would carry off anyone crossing the clearing," Del whispered. "They may live without electricity but I bet they buy Buggone pills by the case."

"No guards," Leah agreed. "They're easy targets through those windows. Not the way someone who expects trouble would act," Leah replied.

Raoul grunted an assent as they knelt in the dense undergrowth, watching the activity inside the shack. "I make three adults. If they have kids, they're asleep by now."

"Let's not spook them, just the same. I'll cover from that giant tree over there since my Spanish still sucks," Leah said.

"Good plan. An Anglo arriving in the middle of the night would frighten them, even if she is a beautiful woman." Raoul turned to Del. "Give me five minutes to skirt the perimeter and find a position in back of the shed, then go calling, Tigre."

"Use that good old homeboy charm, Delgado," Leah said.

"Right." Del watched the illuminated dial on his wrist unit as they moved into place. After enough time had passed, he began to walk slowly toward the front of the shack. He was dressed in cheap cotton pants, an open shirt, and sneakers, the kind of clothes least likely to advertise any official status, this side of the border or the other. Only his watch and his haircut gave him away, but he figured if he got close enough to talk to Bart Cruces, that wouldn't matter.

He patted the Smith & Wesson tucked into the small of his back for reassurance, then called out in Spanish, "Hello inside. My name is Delgado."

The soft murmuring increased, growing harsher as two men and a woman argued. Then a child cried and he could hear the sounds of the mother's voice murmuring soothingly.

"I mean no harm." He raised his hands and stepped into the light spilling from the door as it opened enough for him to see inside. The room was eerily reminiscent of a similar shack in the wilds of Alabama where a former BISC agent named Gary McCallum had met his fate. Delgado's gut gave a sick twist as he remembered that night when all the sounds of the woodland had suddenly gone quiet. Here in the tropics nothing silenced the cacophony of insects and nocturnal animals.

His eyes quickly accustomed to the light as a thin figure opened the door wider, peering out at him. Del saw a table situated in the middle of the room. Remnants of beans and tortillas encrusted five tin plates.

A second man stood up, his chair hastily scooted back as he studied Delgado with frightened black eyes. A bottle of cheap mescal and a couple of half-empty glasses indicated they'd been drinking. On the hard-packed earthen floor two small figures huddled together while the woman knelt protectively with her arms around them.

"What do you want, man?" the one by the table asked, edging nervously toward a shelf on the side wall. Delgado couldn't see a weapon but he'd have bet his pension one lay hidden in the tangle of implements piled on it. He recognized the man by the door from his naval ID pix. It was Cruces.

"I need to talk to Bartolome Cruces. Maybe I can save his life," Del said, moving to block the thickset man's path. At once his eyes darted to his companion. Accusation filled them. The woman gasped aloud, clutching her children tighter.

"You were with ChiChi Bernal the night Special Forces raided the *Cárdenas* last July," Del said to Cruces. "He took something that belongs to the Americans. You helped him." He watched the cousins closely as he added, "Look, I don't work for Ramirez."

"How can I believe you?" Bartolome Cruces asked, crumbling back onto the wicker chair and seizing his glass to polish off its contents for courage.

Delgado pulled his FBI badge from his front pocket and tossed it on the table. "You read any English?" He knew Cruces did, although it was doubtful his cousin even spoke it.

"You're FBI?" His voice cracked.

"If this dumb gringo could find you, so will Cabril," his cousin snarled, lunging past Delgado.

Before he could reach the shelf, Delgado's left fist plowed into his solar plexus. Del pulled the Smith & Wesson from his belt and leveled it at Cruces's cousin. "Sit down. I'm not here to hurt you or your family."

Doubled over, he staggered back to his chair. Del replaced the gun in his belt, still within easy reach, but he could see both men were glassy-eyed from the cheap booze. "I know Ramirez had his *segundo* looking for you ever since Bernal pulled a fast one. You give me what you know about the theft of those two suitcases and I'll see you're protected."

"Pah! No one can escape Inocensio's reach. Not even here," Cruces's cousin said. "I told you they'd find you."

"The more we argue, the more likely that gets," Del said, concentrating on the man called Bart. "How did Bernal get to those cases after Colonel Mulcahey placed them under guard?"

Cruces hesitated, then said, "He waited until the Mexicans left, when the Americans took over. They had some kind of deal. We weren't told why Ramirez was able to get this done, just that the gringo colonel would turn over two cases to Bernal."

"Then what?" Del asked, still keeping an eye on Bart's cousin.

"Bernal came topside carrying two metal suitcases and a little package, something he said he'd taken from the captain's safe earlier. He always had the combinations to the locks on any ship where we were posted. Courtesy of Ramirez."

"Detonator couplers," Del muttered. "You delivered them and the cases to Ramirez?"

Cruces nodded.

"Any idea why Inocensio wanted two dirty bombs?"

Bartolome blanched and crossed himself. "No, sir. I did not even know what was in the suitcases, I swear by the Virgin."

"But ChiChi did?"

"I guess. He was the one who reported directly to Ramirez's *segundo* Cabril. They told him things that we did not need to know . . . or want to know. My brother Tomas and I only wanted the extra money. Times are tough, you know?"

"They'll get a lot tougher if those nukes go off, believe me," Del said. "Bernal must've double-crossed your boss. What do you know about that?"

"Nothing, but a couple of weeks ago . . ." He scrubbed his hand across his beard-stubbled cheeks, sunken and gray in the dim light. "We were on leave, in Guaymas, me and Tomas and our cousin Gilberto. ChiChi didn't go with us. Two days later Cabril brought us in for questioning about Bernal. Did we know where he was? Did we have those suitcases? When we couldn't answer, they beat us."

Del noted the faint bruises on the man's thin face. Several of his fingers had been smashed and he moved like a man who was nursing broken ribs. "I take it they didn't believe you?"

He swallowed, hard. "I knew they were going to kill us. I convinced Tomas and Gilberto that we had to escape. We were locked in a warehouse in Culiacán. We piled boxes up to a high window and climbed until we reached it. I broke the glass with a board but that must have set off some alarm. Ramirez's men came running with submachine guns. I jumped through the window and fell to the ground just as they opened fire. The boxes crashed down. I could hear my brother and cousin scream over the sound of bullets. But I ran. . . ." He broke down sobbing.

"Until you found shelter here."

"And now you have brought him here and my family is in danger," his companion said. "How did you find us?" he asked Del.

"My uncle is Francisco Mulcahey."

The man cursed beneath his breath. "He will tell Ramirez."

"Never. Ramirez can't touch any of you if my uncle gives you protection—and he will if you come with me."

"Go," his cousin said, with a sharp gesture. "I will protect what is mine."

Bartolome looked pleadingly at his distant cousin, accepting the truth. He had nowhere else to turn. "I will go."

Del heard the muffled report of a silenced weapon coming from the jungle. Immediately he doused the lamp on the table and shoved Cruces to the floor. "Is there a back way out of here?" he asked.

8.

"I have friends waiting outside to help us," Delgado said to Cruces.

"You have already helped enough, gringo," Bartolome's cousin growled as he crawled to his wife and children. "That is the only door."

As Leah waited in the jungle outside, the pop of the silencer caught her off guard. Whoever he was, he had gotten near enough to Raoul to fire, no easy feat. She peered into the darkness, wishing for night-vision goggles they'd had no time to obtain. The house was dark now. Good. Another shot, unsilenced, rang out. The colonel was still in business and that was even better.

Hold the fort, Delgado.

Leah climbed the tree with the economical movements of a born athlete, using an outstretched branch as an observation post. If there was one shooter, there would be others. Then she heard the soft rustle of movement nearby. A burst of automatic weapons fire sounded across the clearing. Raoul would be in a cross fire if he hadn't hit his first target. If only she could see, dammit! A man screamed and she knew Mulcahey had scored.

She listened for the rustling again. Nearer. *Come to mama.* Then she could make out two men, walking about six meters apart, weapons raised as they approached the clearing. One would pass directly beneath the tree limb. She waited, barely breathing, in the zone where pure instinct and years of training took over. The head shot to the farthest one was easy. Jumping the guy below her before he could raise his assault weapon was a little trickier but she landed on him. Hard.

His MP5 went flying as she flattened him. Before he could recover, she smashed the butt of her Ruger against his skull, feeling the crunch of metal penetrating bone. Leah rolled off him, seizing his weapon. She made a quick lunge for the other dead man's stubby submachine gun while she was at it. Slinging the second MP5 across her shoulder, she shoved her Ruger into her belt. If she could reach Mulcahey this would even the odds.

After taking out the first opponent with his Beretta, he slipped up on another before the man fired his Uzi. Raoul was very good with a knife. A sudden shotgun blast whizzed by him, buckshot clattering through the dense vegetation. Cursing, he flattened himself against the thick trunk of a podocarpus tree. Hearing the single shot across the clearing, he knew Leah was at work.

He tugged at a love vine snaking its way up the tree. When he yanked hard on it, the branches above him started to rustle and his stalker fired another load of buckshot at the sound. Ramirez's thugs didn't know jungle warfare. He pinpointed his target and started to move silently.

Leah beat him to the kill, opening up with her commandeered submachine gun when she caught sight of her target. He went down and she dived for cover, yelling to Raoul. "*Como estas*, Mulcahey?"

"*Muy bien, gracias*," he replied, zigzagging toward her. They converged, all the while listening for any more shooters.

"Cover me. I'm going in," she said, offering him one of the MP5s she'd taken.

He knew her. This was no time for machismo. "Take the second MP5 to Del," he whispered with a grin. "The guy you just finished has a shotgun. I prefer that for brush fights—a Benelli Super 90, from what I could see."

Inside the shack, Del crouched at the door, listening to the sounds of the firefight. Cruces's cousin and family huddled together in the small room at the back of the shack. It had no windows and the man had one gun—the old single-barrel utility shotgun he'd taken from the shelf to protect his wife and children. They couldn't chance leaving the shelter of the house with an unknown number of hostiles in the surrounding jungle.

Delgado had explained that he had two "men" with him and both were professionals. Their best bet was to wait it out. He moved from the door after shoving it closed, crawling to the second window in search of a better view of the jungle fight. Bartolome held his position at the other window. All they could see was an occasional faint flash of gunfire through the undergrowth. Then a figure darted into the clearing.

"Someone is running this way," Bart hissed to Del.

As soon as he caught sight of her he felt the tightness in his chest loosen. She sprinted like an Olympic runner, the two assault weapons not slowing her stride a bit. A burst of fire aimed at her was returned from across the jungle. Raoul.

Del jerked the door open a second before Leah tumbled through it. "What the hell did Inocensio do, send in his whole friggin' army?" she asked.

"I don't think he wanted us to find out he was briefly a nuclear power," Delgado said, peering into the darkness. "How many did you and Raoul take out?"

"Five so far. How the hell did they follow us? We were so careful leaving Mazatlán."

"Worry about that later," he said as another exchange of fire erupted. "Right now, we'd better find a way out of here before the reinforcements move up."

Suddenly a loud whooshing explosion rocked the small shanty, shaking it like a terrier worrying a rat. The crackle of fire and stench of burning creosote filled the room. "A napalm grenade!" she said incredulously, looking up at the roof where it had landed.

Sparks already bounced down from the corrugated tin, glinting like fireflies at the windows. The makeshift house composed of ancient chemically treated railroad ties would be a death trap in moments. Choking black smoke rolled in the door and the children in back began coughing.

"Two kids, a woman, and another man." Delgado answered her unasked question.

"You know how to use one of these?" she asked Bartolome, holding out the MP5.

"Yes, señorita," he replied, seizing the weapon with injured hands.

"Somehow I figured you would."

The children cried from the unventilated hellhole in back while their mother's voice made soothing sounds and their father cursed. Cruces called to his cousin in Spanish, "Come out! You'll suffocate in there! We must make a break for it. I have a weapon. I will protect you." Swearing and soot-stained, the heavyset man led his desperate family into the front room.

Delgado said, "We have to find cover they can't burn. We'll go behind the shed, then make a break for the jungle there." He pointed to the closest point between them and the dense vegetation. "You follow Leah," he instructed Bart. "I'll cover our rear and our friend out there will keep those bozos busy." His voice was already raw from the smoke.

Leah knew what he was going to do. "Let me stay here and draw fire until Raoul can spot the bullpen," she said, coughing.

"No." He played his ace. "You run faster and we have kids to protect."

The acrid stench of burning creosote filled the room. He was right. She turned to the woman, who now appeared resigned but ready to follow orders. "Don't let go of your son." She placed the little boy's wrist in his mother's hand. Strong brown fingers gripped tightly in understanding. Leah repeated the exercise with the older boy's father. All the defiance had drained out of him. He did as she commanded. "I'm going out first to give them something to think about," she said to Cruces. "Soon as I make the shed, you cover them as you follow."

He nodded. "*Sí, señorita.*"

Smoke burned her eyes, blurring her vision when she looked at Delgado. This might be the last time she saw him but she couldn't afford time to think about it. Instead, she handed him the MP5 as she drew her Ruger. "Don't wait until you're a Mexican marshmallow."

With that she rolled out the door and hit the ground, firing as she leaped up, sprinting toward the shed. A man rose out of the undergrowth to toss another grenade. Raoul took him down with a blast from the Benelli. The grenade rolled from his lifeless hand to explode in a spectacular bonfire.

At the corner of the shed, Leah motioned for Cruces to bring his family. He covered them as parents ran with children in death grips, shielding them with their own bodies. An automatic weapon chattered from across the clearing. Delgado laid down an answering stream of fire from the burning house while Leah and Cruces did the same.

They made it almost intact. Cruces's cousin was bleeding profusely from a bullet that had slashed across his thigh and Leah had a shallow scratch on her left arm. They crouched in the undergrowth. She gestured for them to stay silent, virtually impossible as the children and their mother fought not to cough out the poison they'd inhaled.

Both boys' dark eyes were wide with terror as they saw the blood on their father. When the youngest tried to speak, his mother immediately covered his mouth with her hand and held him close. Biting down on his lip, her husband stretched his leg out in front of him and used his knife on his pant leg. He cut a strip big enough to serve as a tourniquet and fastened it quickly.

Leah watched for Delgado. The roof was starting to buckle from the heat. Soon it would collapse. Smoke billowed from every window and the door like the roiling boil from the forges of hell. *Come on, Del, dammit! Perfect cover.*

Then she saw his shadowy shape climb from the side window closest to the shed. He wasn't carrying the submachine gun. Probably out of ammo and better off without the excess baggage. He wasn't much of a runner with his bum knee. The bullets spattering the mud in erratic patterns around him served as incentive. He moved pretty fast.

By the time he reached the shed, the house was completely swallowed by the fire. The scene was out of Dante—a blazing shack and in direct counterpoint across from it, the diminishing fire caused by the dead killer's grenade. Burning wood snapped and twisted metal groaned over the jungle sounds.

Were there any gunmen left? They heard the retreating sound of someone crashing through the brush. "And then there were none," Leah whispered, still on guard.

Del spoke quietly. "I'm going to check the perimeter and look for Raoul."

"You . . . may need . . . this," Cruces murmured haltingly, handing the automatic to Delgado. Then without a sound the fugitive crumpled and fell on his back, revealing a spreading blackish red stain on his chest.

Del seized the weapon as Leah knelt over Bart. "He's gone," she said after a swift check. The mother shielded her sons from the ghastly sight, burying their heads against her breast while their father adjusted his injured leg.

Del reminded her of their all-clear signal. "I'll fire two shots five seconds apart."

Before he made it a dozen meters Raoul appeared at the edge of the clearing, then vanished back into the undergrowth. Delgado joined him in one more sweep.

In a couple of moments Raoul fired the all clear before strolling out of the bush holding a napalm grenade. "This is a dandy toy. Only read about them in *Guns & Ammo*, never saw one in action before. Wish our army had a few thousand of these babies."

"Well, you have one now. Great for barbecues," Del said as he fell in beside his cousin.

They found Leah calmly adjusting the tourniquet on Cruces's cousin's leg. When Del saw the blood running down her arm, he cursed. "Let me—"

"No time, Del."

"She's right, Tigre," Raoul said. "We have to get these people out of here before more troops come in."

"How the hell did Inocensio find us?" Del asked as he and Leah helped the injured man to stand.

"No idea. I know for sure our Jeep is clean." Raoul had scanned it with utmost care before they set out.

"What if these men weren't sent by Ramirez?" Leah asked.

Both cousins looked at her grimly. Neither had an answer.

6:05 A.M. EST, MONDAY, NOVEMBER 10
WASHINGTON, D.C.

"What do you know about a casino owner named Richie Viviano?" Adam Manchester asked John Scarletti, who blinked owlishly into the vid screen.

Looking decidedly rumpled as he groped for his glasses, the AG sat up on the side of his bed. "We have a couple of gigabytes on him at Justice. Started out as a small-time hood in Jersey back twenty years ago. He's strayed from his ethnic roots. Formed an alliance with some Russian mobsters from Brighton Beach and pretty soon he's behind a bunch of the biggest casinos in Atlantic City. He's connected and dirty but we haven't been able to pin anything on him—yet. What's your interest?"

"I just received a call from my granddaughter. She's still in Mexico but her source in Las Vegas just gave her some news she wanted us to work on immediately. Those two men who attacked her were hired by a small-time thug named Danny DeClue. DeClue works for a local casino operator, Thomas Billinger, who's involved in numbers running, all sorts of illegal scams. Leah's source just traced Billinger to a big-time East Coast gangster—"

"Richie Viviano," Scarletti said, coming awake quickly now. "How the hell did Leah get anyone connected to Viviano to give him up?"

"That's not important now." Having a pretty good idea about how Leah had gotten the man she'd put in the hospital to give up DeClue, Manchester went on. "Whoever wanted my granddaughter eliminated in San Pedro contracted the job through Viviano. You said he was tied to the Russians?" Adam felt his gut clench.

"Yes. Richie plays no favorites. He's got his finger in every pie from the Fidelista Liberation Front to Holy Arabia, but we've been concentrating on his Cartel connections. And, yes, he dabbles in the arms trade. Who doesn't, these days?"

"You think Bernal may contact him?"

"If Bernal does, we might finally catch a break. I'll put Viviano under surveillance immediately."

5:10 A.M. CST, MONDAY, NOVEMBER 10
CORPUS CHRISTI, TEXAS

Paul Oppermann was glad he was Conservative, not Orthodox, and that he had an understanding rabbi. He hadn't seen the inside of a shul since this crisis had erupted, much less had time for regular prayers. As soon as his field agents in Texas notified him that they'd located Bernal's wife, he hopped a flight from Arizona, wanting to talk with her firsthand. He arrived too late.

The local police had ceded jurisdiction to the Bureau immediately since Special Agent Gabe Tolson had found Nina Dolores Rosario Maria Alvarez. Technically she wasn't Mrs. Bernal. The one in San Diego apparently had legal custody of the name—at least until another one in his harem with an earlier date on her marriage license claimed the honor. Paul knelt beside Nina's body.

"Somebody really worked her over good," the tech said with a grimace, staring down at the ruins of the middle-aged woman crumpled on the filthy, blood-soaked carpet.

He was young and hadn't seen this sort of thing enough to harden him . . . yet. That would come with the job, Oppermann knew. "Whoever did this knew his stuff," he said with the shield of dispassion that was his thin link to sanity when he dealt with dead kids . . . or tortured women.

Her face and body were swollen and discolored from repeated blows. Someone had held her down while a second *mamzer* punched. According to prelims, both of them wore gloves. When that punishment hadn't worked, they had started on her nails. Oppermann looked at the bloody, torn remains of her right index finger. Acrylic fingernails gave excellent leverage to someone wielding a pair of pliers. He stood up and dusted himself off, scanning the cluttered bedroom.

Cheap brightly colored clothes and undergarments were strewn carelessly around the unmade bed, but the room had not been tossed for information. Nina was a messy housekeeper. Tchotchkes of every imaginable variety covered the particleboard dresser and nightstands, all shrouded with dust. Cobwebs grayed the unevenly hung drapes. Nothing had been disturbed.

"She must've told them what she knew about Bernal," Special Agent Tolsen said.

"Wouldn't you?" Oppermann replied with a sigh. Suddenly he felt the same queasy way the young tech did.

Her throat had been quietly cut when they finished their "interrogation." Traces of the wad of cloth used as a gag to muffle her screams were visible in her broken mouth. The bloody cotton sock had already been bagged for evidence when he arrived. He watched as the guys from the Medical Examiner's Office loaded the corpse onto a stretcher for transpo.

"I want this place combed closer than a grand champion Persian cat. After finding that stiff in the Dumpster, I'm betting Bernal was here. If only we could figure where our boy's gone now."

"And who's on his tail," Tolsen said.

"Yeah, that, too."

8:00 A.M. EST, MONDAY, NOVEMBER 10
WASHINGTON, D.C.

"You got any idea where those n-nukes are?" Bob Labat asked. He hated it when he stuttered, but John Scarletti made him nervous. Hell, the AG made everyone in D.C. nervous, he thought, gaining assurance.

"Wish we did, Bob," Scarletti replied calmly. "What have you learned?"

"Finally got the report from my Border Protection division chief in Arizona. One of my agents let Bernal in. Falsified evidence with Globe Net so nothing was reported to the NRO, if you can believe that."

The Scar was already ahead of the Rabbit. "According to Paul Oppermann, your Border Patrol officer, Harry Busch, has been murdered along with his girlfriend."

Labat looked frustrated. "Great. Our only solid lead and he's dead."

"We do have a composite of the character who set up the deal with Busch, courtesy of Officer Robinson," Scarletti said. "A Company man."

Labat sighed. "Great. Not a snowball's chance on the Salt Flats that anything'll come of that."

Scarletti watched Labat fold himself into a chair across from his desk, awkward as Ichabod Crane. The Homeland Security director moved like a man who wasn't convinced his limbs would remain attached to his body. The low Danish chair was not a good fit. Labat's knees could've touched his chin if he'd leaned forward. Instead, he gripped the wooden chair arms with big, raw-boned hands and braced himself against the low back.

"It's not an ejection seat, Bob," the AG said quietly.

Labat snorted. "Wouldn't surprise me. No one's kept me in the loop on this. Oppermann isn't even in town and damned if anyone at the Bureau'll tell me where he is. Still out in Arizona, I suppose. Hell, John, I'm responsible for the Secret Service protecting the president. I need to know if this Bernal fellow's anywhere near Washington."

Scarletti thought Abbie Rutledge could handle Samson's safety without any help from "the Rabbit," but did not say so. Labat's far-flung department was in even more chaos than the CIA and that was saying a lot these days. To thwart his enemies on the Hill, Samson had chosen an outsider to head Homeland Security. Robert Labat's appointment guaranteed that the career bureaucrats now combined under the HS umbrella would not be forced to share information with each other, much less with the administration's opposition in Congress.

Of course, holding on to presidential power was Samson's reason for making Scarletti AG as well. But John was far from an outsider. Now with the FBI's powers expanded and Justice in charge of prosecuting drug traffickers, he had become one of the most feared men inside the Beltway. He liked it that way.

Labat's nose twitched and he massaged it with blunt knobby fingers, then fixed Scarletti with as near to an accusatory stare as he could muster. "What's going on with the Bureau, John? Oppermann doesn't make like a field agent just to check on how my Border Patrol screwed up. I'm gonna take a lot of heat over that, I know—"

"Paul's following a lead on Bernal. His wife—or one of them, he has several—was found dead in Corpus Christi this morning. She'd been tortured, we assume, to give up Bernal's location."

"Did she?" He leaned forward, hands on his knees like a tall skinny frog ready to leap.

"From the way Paul described it, I imagine she talked, Bob. But whether or not she knew where Bernal was going . . ." He shrugged.

"But you think this CIA guy killed her?"

"Or someone working for him did."

Labat snapped his fingers and his eyes lit up. "You say this Bernal fellow has more than one wife? What about the others? That could be where he's lying low."

"We're checking on all of them." Scarletti hesitated, then asked, "Have you ever heard of a casino owner and mob type from Jersey, Richie Viviano? He's linked to a couple of local boys from your neck of the woods, Danny DeClue and Thomas Billinger."

"Dunno about DeClue. Billinger's a nobody from Vegas. There was a Gaming Commission investigation of him a couple of years ago. No indication he was connected on the East Coast. You saying he is?"

Scarletti decided sharing what Adam had given him might keep the Rabbit from leaking anything by fumbling around on his own trying to find out what Justice knew.

After the AG finished his report, Labat leaned back in the low chair. "You trust Manchester? If he takes credit for finding those nukes, he'll beat Samson. Then we'll both be out of a job."

The faintest trace of a smile played around Scarletti's thin lips, then vanished. *We might be if he is reelected, too.*

8:30 A.M. EST, MONDAY, NOVEMBER 10
WASHINGTON, D.C.

"I told the son of a bitch nine and you know how punctual he is, so we only have half an hour," Wade Samson said as the secretary of defense walked into the Oval Office.

"Sorry I wasn't here sooner, but I couldn't get away from McKinney. The chairman's going to fight us every fucking inch of the way,

Wade. He was pounding on my desk like Khrushchev at the U.N. So much for that laid-back Carolina charm," Karl Banecek said as he poured himself a cup of strong black coffee and took a gulp.

"How the hell can you do that?" the president asked.

"Cast-iron mouth. Or so my wife says."

"Helen sends her best to Alice. We need to all have dinner when this mess is over—if it ever *is* over." Samson picked up his cup of coffee, pale blond with cream, and sipped, then said, "Recap on our Joint Chiefs' positions. Any in our camp?"

"Don't I wish. Air Force *could* go our way. They'd benefit most from the new technology and don't have the manpower issues of Army and Naval Operations. Still, McKinney swings a lot of weight. General Kirk is sitting on the fence, waiting."

"In other words, he's waiting to see who'll win the pissing contest, me or my secretary of state. Stuart Kensington's just waiting this out, licking his chops." Samson swore quietly.

"McKinney's convinced the only way to deal with Holy Arabia, Korea, or the mess in the Balkans requires boots on the ground. I think all the Chiefs but possibly—and I stress possibly—Kirk will support his recommendations."

"Playing right into Kensington's hands," Samson said. "Damn me for listening to the party honchos. You told me to offer Kensington the vice presidency, but never State. I should've listened."

"Just lousy timing, Wade, not your fault, " the secretary of defense insisted. "If Malton hadn't dropped dead and left State open the week after Vice President Waterman was killed, the whole thing wouldn't have been an issue. You had enough on your plate last summer."

Stuart Kensington, a much revered and hugely popular military hero, refused the vice presidency, which, as one former holder of the office said, "was not worth a bucket of warm spit." Samson's whole administration had been in shambles after the dismantling of BISC. When Kensington would only accept the First Portfolio, Samson had appointed Aiden Grover, an elderly senator from Rhode Island, to the lesser office. Grover could barely remain awake through a ribbon-cutting ceremony.

"We have to stop Kensington from taking his agenda to the media.

Without support from the Pentagon, our plans for modernizing the military are sunk. Who can we count on individually?"

Banecek ran down a list of two- and three-star generals who supported their position. "I'll keep working on General Kirk. The Air Force might be cajoled with a few carrots like those innovations for Globe Net and the three additional cutters might sweeten the bargain for the Coast Guard, too. NRO's in our camp—"

The sound of Samson's inner office link interrupted them. Irritated, the president flicked voice only. "Yes, Marti," he said.

"Secretary of State Kensington's here for your nine-o'clock, Mr. President," she replied blandly, knowing full well how heartily the two men detested each other.

"Tell him I'll be with him momentarily," Samson said, eyeing his wrist unit. He had one minute and thirty seconds until nine and he was damned if Kensington would get it. He and Karl Banecek wrapped up their discussion on strategy. Then the secretary of defense left by another door.

Samson couldn't resist letting Kensington cool his heels until five after nine. When the secretary of state walked into the Oval Office, his expression was placid as pond water. *Ivy League and old money, Karl would say.*

Kensington was an aristocrat to his well-manicured fingertips. Compactly built at five-ten, his presence gave the impression of greater height. He was elegantly turned out in a dark gray Caraceni suit and pale blue shirt that accented his heavy silver hair and deep blue eyes.

Those laserlike eyes met the president's head-on as they shook hands stiffly. "Please have a seat, Stuart." Samson always felt like he was interviewing for a job as a Senate page when he met with Kensington. The only other man alive who made him that damn uncomfortable was Adam Manchester. He shut down the unpleasant thought and concentrated on the issues at hand. "I want to go over the message from al Ibrim and formulate a proper response. We can't afford to wait until matters escalate beyond redemption."

"They already have . . . in my opinion." Kensington spoke quietly, placing no emphasis on the last three words.

"I disagree. Al Ibrimi's Holy Arabian government wants recognition from the international community. In return, he is willing to entertain a discussion regarding the release of the remainder of the royal family."

"Mr. President, those savages have slaughtered most—if not all—of the House of Saud already. Negotiation is not an option. Al Ibrim and his mullahs are nothing more than blackmailing terrorists. If we cave in to them, why not negotiate with the Cartel? Give them an embassy on the Row just as you'd give one to this so-called Holy Arabia."

"World opinion isn't with you on this one, Stuart. The Euros and the Pacific Rim both want a peaceful resolution, not another destabilized area they or we will have to occupy and administer. In any case, the situations in the Middle East and in South America aren't at all analogous and you know it." He couldn't quite keep the snap out of his voice.

"Since when has the United States made its foreign policy based on what the Euros or the Pacific Rim wanted? The Rim is too far away to be affected and the Euros are too fat and comfortable to disturb themselves. We're the only power with hope of restoring order on the Arabian Peninsula and we can only do that by quickly and effectively moving to topple the rebels' hold on Riyadh. They're only a few thousand fanatics with no military experience. They don't have more than a couple dozen pilots to put in the air against us."

"True," Samson conceded. *Damn McKinney and the CIA for feeding Kensington intel.* "But the fight wouldn't be aerial. It'd take place on the ground. Crossing thousands of miles of sand. Taking and occupying each town and city. We're talking guerrilla warfare, General, and you know it—"

"Yet you and your secretary of defense want to downsize our armed forces. The logic of your position escapes me."

"We only need a large army if we let ourselves be dragged into that kind of a war. There is another option right now," Samson said impatiently. "You have to admit the overthrow of the Saud family was a popular uprising. A foreign invasion would only result in al Ibrim and his government raising an army of millions—every man between the ages of eight and eighty would fight us."

"If we move decisively, don't vacillate, we can sweep them out of Riyadh before it comes to that. Just as we did in Iraq."

"Yes, and that ended so well after we pulled out. A tripartite con-federation of Sunnis, Shiites, and Kurds in a perpetual hatchet fight. Turkey and Egypt have already been destabilized in that mess and the civil war in the Balkans is endless."

"The Balkans are the Euros' mess. The Middle East is ours. I needn't remind you that we still require their oil while the Euros and the Rim do not."

"Yes, the Middle East, the recently reunited and very unstable Ko-rea, the shaky democracy in Cuba, and the Cartel—they're all our 'mess.'"

"If we handle Holy Arabia expediently, it will be an object lesson for the North Korean extremists, the Fidelista Liberation Front, and Benito Zuloaga. We've been a paper tiger too long, Mr. President."

Samson sighed and shoved back his chair, fixing Kensington with a level stare. *Time to play hardball.* "I've drafted a personal message to al Ibrim's government. I will go to Riyadh and personally negotiate the release of the Saud family, and I will discuss diplomatic recogni-tion for Holy Arabia. You may deliver the message for me . . . or, re-gretfully, I will have to ask for your resignation." Samson put his best game face on. If Kensington resigned, it would virtually guarantee the election of Adam Manchester.

"You're capitulating to terrorism if you do that," Kensington said, ignoring the threat of resignation.

"Your opinion is crystal clear on that point, Mr. Secretary. Will you deliver the message or not?" He felt the acid pooling in his gut and took another sip of pale coffee, suppressing the urge to upend the cream pitcher directly and give his ulcer some relief.

Kensington stood and made a slight bow. "Very well, Mr. Presi-dent. I shall deliver your message." With that, he turned smartly on his heel and left the office.

Samson poured the cream into a fresh cup and drained it.

9.

The lush rolling hills were brown with winter's chill but the tall spikes of sugar pines soared green against a brilliant blue sky. Jillian Beresford Kensington looked out the picture window, admiring the view from her sitting room. The twenty-one-room manse had been the family's ancestral home since the Revolutionary War. Modernizing it without disturbing its historical integrity had cost a fortune, but Jillian had possessed money enough for the task.

A well-preserved sixty-eight, with silver hair fashioned in a sleek chignon, Jillian required little makeup. Her patrician face was slim and angular with ageless cheekbones, more handsome than beautiful. The Beresfords were a long and illustrious line, the nearest equivalent to aristocracy America could claim. Jillian and her sister Anne had grown up in a society where fox hunts and steeplechases were still enjoyed by the privileged few and outsiders were not welcome. She always wore conservative clothes by American designers. A string of rare gray pearls, a silver anniversary gift from Stuart, was the most ostentatious jewelry she owned.

After years following his rising star in the military, enduring postings in Middle-Eastern and Asian pestholes, she had been overjoyed when her husband retired and they returned to northern Virginia, the home of her heart. His tenure with the think tank and teaching at George Mason University had been idyllic, but Stuart was born for public service, once again in the spotlight. And in conflict with his president.

"Mrs. Kensington, your husband is on the link," her personal secretary said after a discreet tap on the open door.

"Thank you, Clarice. I'll take the call from here." Clarice quietly closed the door as Jillian gave a voice command opening her PDA. At once Stuart's haggard face filled the vid. He was in his office, which meant he'd be unable to make Dolly's luncheon. Her heart clenched, but she smiled. "You look tired. The meeting with the president was unsatisfactory."

He sighed and leaned back in his leather chair. "Ironically, you always were more the diplomat than I, my dear. Samson should've tapped you for State. The man's an imbecile."

"He wants you to approach those Arab terrorists." In spite of her pressing social obligations, Jillian made it a point to keep up with international events because of her husband's work.

"He threatened me. Either deliver his kowtowing plea for negotiations or resign."

"Oh, Stuart, I'm so sorry."

"I'll have to do as he demands, but let's not worry about that now. I haven't forgotten the reception. My driver may have to risk a speeding ticket or two, but we'll be in Middleburg by eleven. It's not every day a man's only daughter is feted by the DAR," he said with a smile. "Dolly's worked very hard and I want her to know how proud we both are of her."

"Stuart . . ." she hesitated, moistening her lips. "Anne will be there. That won't be a problem, will it?" She knew her husband had never approved of her sister's marriage. Neither had she since it had broken their parents' hearts, but she and Anne tried to keep up appearances for the sake of the family.

Kensington smiled. "Of course not. We haven't seen her since Dolly's last birthday."

"She keeps rather busy with her grandchildren," Jillian said with a pang of envy. The Kensington's only son, Stuart Junior, had been killed in the late war, leaving no children. Dolly was devoted to her career and had never married.

"Now that he's back in Washington, do you think there's any

chance of her and Manchester getting back together?" he surprised her by asking.

Jillian appeared thoughtful. "When she called yesterday evening, she mentioned that the senator had been at John's house with her for dinner. But you know how Anne is, so guarded about her feelings."

Kensington snorted. "She should've married Manchester in the first place."

She smiled. "You're only saying that because you think he'll be the next president."

"Be a considerable improvement over Wade Samson, wouldn't you agree?"

**10:05 A.M. EST, MONDAY, NOVEMBER 10
WASHINGTON, D.C.**

"I have a complete surveil on Richie Viviano," John Scarletti said. "We won't know anything until we see who he plays footsie with. We're running a trace on any connections he might have with the players here in D.C."

"Any other good news to share with your tea?" Adam Manchester smiled. The "Scar" was a tea drinker. Earl Grey with lemon. He'd ordered a pot to be steeped as soon as the AG had called.

"Unfortunately, lots. Our Vegas Bureau chief sent agents to bring in Viviano's pals, Danny DeClue and his boss Billinger, early this morning. Sweat them about their connection to the two hit men who tried to take out your granddaughter." He paused for a sip of tea.

"And?" Adam prompted, knowing he wasn't going to like it.

"DeClue and Billinger walked out of their club not ten minutes earlier. Then a carload of thugs opened up on them. Both DOAs. No trace of the shooters."

"Viviano's men?"

"He—or whoever's behind him—figured they were a liability." Scarletti shrugged.

Adam digested the implications. "We have to tie our friend in Jersey to their deaths. Can we do it?"

"Viviano's a lot smarter than Billinger and Danny. But between physical and electronic surveils, we'll turn something."

Adam studied Scarletti as he took a deep swallow of tea. "What else?" he asked with dread. He knew there was more.

"Holy Arabia's terrorist cells inside the U.S. are studying at least half a dozen sites around the country—Wall Street, the Golden Gate Bridge, the Statue of Liberty, the Arch, Mall of America, Arlington Cemetery. God help us if they get their hands on those nukes. Bad enough with conventional explosives." The AG paced back and forth in Brett Lowell's spacious library, cradling the Sevres cup in both hands.

"Did this intel come from Aziz al Ambas?" Adam asked, dubious that the old fanatic could be broken by Torquemada himself.

"No, but I might've figured you'd know about our friend Aziz."

Manchester grimaced. "I wouldn't be a candidate for my party's nomination if I hadn't kept contacts on the Hill, John. Aziz is Holy Arabia's highest-ranking terrorist. Currently a guest of our government at Guantanamo Bay. If he didn't give you this information, where did you get it?"

"Paul Oppermann's had a man inside a Muslim extremist sleeper cell in St. Louis for several months. They just received a wake-up call. Our agent's met the head honcho, a sweetheart named Ahamet bin Bergi, who graced the local peons with a visit a few days ago. Apparently, he's been contacted by someone pretty high up in the government who wants to sell two dirty bombs."

Manchester froze. "No idea who it is?"

"No. All we have is the target list. We don't even know if Bernal's turned over the nukes to the American middleman yet. But somehow this ties into Viviano and his mob connections. We just have to put the pieces together."

"Someone in Samson's administration is dealing with Holy Arabia and Bernal's still on the loose. We haven't got time for jigsaw puzzles. Any chance the Bureau could arrest this bin Bergi?"

"He's a phantom. Almost an urban legend until Paul's man met him. He was long gone by the time our agent could report it. Even if we got lucky and nabbed the guy, these groups are like a hydra, Adam."

"Cut off one head and another just takes his place in the plan." Manchester understood all too well. "Tracing his activities would be more useful—if you can trace him."

"Right now all we have for sure is al Ambas—who won't ever talk—and Viviano, who might lead us to the inside man who set up this whole nightmare."

"So we wait and watch Richie Viviano," Adam said, resigned.

"There are a few other leads. The DNA run on that BISC agent Delgado killed should be completed tomorrow unless Central deleted his records before we shut them down. Maybe we'll get a break there."

"Or connect the dots from Viviano to that someone high in the government who's selling nuclear weapons." Adam ran his hand through his hair, frustrated. "I can work on Viviano's operation with Del's computer interrogator."

One of Scarletti's eyebrows rose. "Read hacker?"

"That, my friend, is the very least of it."

Scarletti could've sworn the old man blushed. Must be a trick of the light. He couldn't imagine the venerable senator flustered by anything, least of all some computer geek.

2:20 P.M. MST, MONDAY, NOVEMBER 10
CULIACÁN, MEXICO

The place hadn't improved much since last summer. In fact, in the harsh afternoon sunlight it looked even more filthy and run-down than it had under cover of darkness on their first visit. The huge old warehouse was constructed of utilitarian corrugated tin but Del and Leah knew the insides of this dilapidated building were reinforced with dura-blocs thick enough to survive a tank assault. Judging by the looks of some scorched places where the ancient metal curled away, perhaps it had.

The smell of fecund tropical vegetation and the rot of garbage filled the air. "One thing you can say for Ramirez, he doesn't waste money on the high rent district," Del said dryly as they climbed out of his uncle's Lincoln.

"Yeah, a real man of the people," she replied, eyeing their welcoming committee. "If those thugs try to frisk me like they did last time, they'll have to gargle to wash their balls."

"Temper, temper, Special Agent Berglund. Aggressive behavior's frowned on by the Bureau."

"I'll take my chances with Oppermann. Me, he likes," she said with a sharkish grin.

Two burly men armed with Uzi submachine guns watched them through narrow dark eyes that shifted to check the quiet street. One signaled to a lookout on top of the building across the way, then approached the visitors. They were expected. It had taken Del's uncle nearly three days to reach Inocensio Ramirez. The drug lord finally agreed to meet with them only after Francisco Mulcahey described the firefight in the jungle and told him that Bartolome Cruces had implicated Ramirez in the theft of the nukes.

"Come with me," the taller of the two guards said in Spanish, gesturing with the Uzi to make his point.

"That car belongs to my uncle Francisco. Be certain it's here—intact—when we come back," Del said in Spanish to the guards. The second man nodded, then spat a wad of brown well-chewed tobacco on the cracked pavement as they walked by.

"A dental hygienist's nightmare," Leah muttered as they stepped into the dim interior of the cavernous warehouse.

The door slamming behind them had the sound of a vault closing. Or a coffin lid. Unidentified crates and barrels filled just enough of the space to give the illusion of an import business, but they both knew the only goods Ramirez imported were cocaine and sildenafil citrate, the powdered pharmaceutical that gave the "lift" to "Elevator."

"How much you suppose this stuff's worth?" Del speculated as they wended their way through the labyrinth toward the metal door at the back of the building.

"Too high to tally if it's all coke and sil-cit."

When they were in range of the vid sweepers, the guard stopped. Two more men came forward. She recognized the little one wearing the leer as the jackoff who'd frisked her with such enthusiasm on their last visit. "Bite me," she said through clenched teeth, holding out her arms to show she carried no weapons. She'd deliberately worn a sleeveless blouse and fitted slacks to give them no excuses. The furrow on her arm throbbed just enough to make her want to hurt somebody—especially if that somebody was a drug-pushing perv.

The smirking guard shoved a hank of greasy black hair from his eyes and made a lewd suggestion to his companions in Spanish. She caught just enough of it to want to punch the grin off his face but restrained herself, turning in a circle for their inspection.

"If I were you, gentlemen," Delgado said dryly, "I wouldn't mess with her this time of month."

This elicited an outburst of laughter as he raised his arms and they made a cursory pass at frisking him. Although he had spoken rapidly, she caught it and glared. In English he said, "Just trying to oil the waters."

"Why does grease come to mind, not oil?" she snapped, striding toward the door, which now opened.

They entered the inner sanctum of Inocensio Jesus Emanuelo Ramon Ramirez, arguably the most powerful man in Mexico. The office remained every bit as garish as Leah remembered, with blood-red carpeting so thick it took a couple of inches off their height. Dark walnut panelled the walls. Two enormous cut-crystal chandeliers hung suspended on gilded chains, lighting an immense mahogany desk inlaid with rosewood depicting fanciful mythological scenes.

Instead of the tropical print shirt he'd worn before, Ramirez was conservatively dressed in a plain black turtleneck sweater. He'd lost a considerable amount of belly but not his taste for jewelry. Several anchor-weight gold chains hung from his thick neck while rubies and diamonds glittered on his hairy fingers. As he leaned back in a butter-soft leather chair, he gestured grandly for them to sit on the two Paoli chairs that looked like kneelers in front of the high altar at Mass.

Beneath the grizzled gray-black of his beard, his face was pale. He clenched an expensive Cuban cigar in the narrow slash of his mouth. "Good afternoon, my friends. It is good to see you once more." The unctuous, oily smile from their first encounter was decidedly missing.

"Could've fooled me. Uncle Mac practically had to raise the dead to get you to meet us."

Finally, seeming to force it, Inocensio's big teeth gleamed brown and gold. He grinned without removing the cigar, then released a puff of smoke. "My enterprises are vast, my schedule demanding. I regret I was unavailable until now."

"Until Bart Cruces told us how you had Bernal steal those nukes," Leah said.

"Ah, señorita, always the outspoken one."

"She speaks the truth, my friend," Delgado said. "Suppose you tell us why you did it."

"And why you tried to kill us last night," she added.

His face lost all traces of false joviality as he looked at the fresh bandage on her bare arm. His brother-in-law had told him she'd been injured. He leaned forward and placed his elbows on the gleaming desktop. "Upon my wife's grave, I swear to you, I did not try to kill you. If I had . . . you would be dead," he said simply. "Tell me more about this attack."

"My uncle was able to trace Cruces to a distant cousin who lives several hundred klicks south of here. He told us how Bernal stole the two nukes for you."

"And you believed him?"

"In a heartbeat," Leah said. "His brother and cousin were with him and Bernal aboard the *Cárdenas* when the deal went down with Tompkinson. Your *segundo* Cabril tortured and killed them. Cruces escaped—until last night." She watched his body language, intuiting that he was weighing his options. His arms were crossed on the desk, big hands rubbing his biceps, his eyes far away. He inhaled the cigar as if it were his last smoke before a firing squad.

"Yes, my *segundo* ordered those men to be shot—but only when they tried to escape. Once I was certain they had not helped that traitor Bernal, I would've turned them free to hide in the jungle as Cruces did. What did I have to fear from them?"

"That they could finger you, for openers," Delgado said quietly. "You stole two tactical nuclear devices, property of the American government. Uncle Sam gets mighty testy about things like that."

"What were you going to do with dirty bombs?" Leah asked, not wanting to give Ramirez time to regroup. He was sweating now in spite of the cool air in the big room.

"Nothing, señorita. Absolutely nothing. Do not scoff," he admonished her. "I would not use any weapon—most especially this kind of 'dirty bomb' as you call it—anywhere near my own people."

"How about the people halfway around the world, say Pacific Rim drug dealers?" Del suggested.

"They are my business associates. They supply me with, er, certain pharmaceuticals and even cocaine when my suppliers here in Mexico run short. And do not be so foolish as to suggest I would use such puny weapons in a preemptive strike against the Cartel. Do I look like a fool?" he asked, his black eyes piercing them. "I assure you, I am not."

"I dunno, it was pretty stupid to steal them in the first place," she said.

"Why did you do it?" Del asked, going along with her good cop/bad cop routine.

"Just because I would not start a war against the Cartel does not mean I do not require protection from them. Especially now that the organization is, *como se dice?*"—he groped for the expression—"in flux."

"We've been picking up rumors about Zuloaga being in a tug-of-war with a nasty character named Noriega," Del said.

Ramirez's eyes narrowed. "You are as smart as your uncle. *Sí*, this Noriega is one bad hombre. If he takes control of the Cartel, he will invade my territory—unless I have *la amenaza*."

"A deterrent," Del translated. "Makes sense in a risky sort of way. If Noriega's half as bad as everyone thinks, why wouldn't he call your bluff?"

"*Es malo, no es loco*," Inocensio replied, grinning at Leah. "It would be what you gringos call a Mexican standoff, no?"

"So you only wanted to use the bombs to protect your turf. How'd you get your hands on them? This had to be planned days in advance while the ship was returning to port," Del said. "People high in our government were involved."

"An Americano came to me that first week in July, when my men—led by that dog Bernal—were helping your cousins aboard the *Cárdenas*. He gave me information about Noriega and Zuloaga. The

increasing danger their struggle meant for my business. And he offered . . . helpful suggestions. Might not a few nuclear weapons be
aces I could hold?"

"How did he get inside information on the Cartel beyond what
your own spies feed you?" Del asked.

"*Lo siento*, my only man inside the Cartel was found out. He is no
longer . . . working. This Americano comes and goes from Bogotá to
Mexico to the U.S. and back."

"A good source?" she asked, a hunch itching at the back of her
neck. "Does he smoke a lot?"

Ramirez blinked. "Señorita Berglund, you continue to amaze me.
One nasty filtered cigarette lit from another. Nothing like a fine cigar," he said, puffing luxuriously as he appeared to relax. These two
and his brother-in-law now knew much of what happened, so he
might as well talk.

In for a dime, in for a dollar, huh, Inocensio? "And he pockets the
butts when he finishes each one." Delgado leaned forward now, catching Leah's excitement. "Show him the drawing."

She pulled the folded compu-sketch from her shirt pocket and
handed it to Ramirez.

"*Sí*, that is the man, only his nose is more hooked, his face a little
thinner. He said he could guarantee your government would not
know the weapons were missing. He'd stolen the devices from the
Russians several years earlier. They were forgotten until General Sommerville took them to use against the Cartel. The Yanqui colonel returning them was in charge of the fort where they would be stored. If
twelve were removed and ten returned, *quien sepa*?"

Leah and Del exchanged quick glances at the mention of the man
she'd dubbed the "Ashtray" after her brief time with Paul in Arizona.
Now they knew he was the one who'd stolen the dirty bombs from
that Russian lab. "Twistier and twistier," he murmured.

"Unfortunately the colonel had a fatal accident and his replacement
found out about the two missing nukes," she said to Inocensio. "What
did the spook want in return for giving you this tip?"

Ramirez frowned. "He said it was in his government's interest—I
would say instead it was his agency's interest—to maintain the bal-

ance of power between my organization and the Cartel. It seemed like a good plan at the time."

"You were set up. He intended to use Bernal to steal from you," Del said.

"*Sí.*" Ramirez's face was creased with an odd mixture of fury and chagrin. "I have spent the past weeks searching every rat hole from Hermosillo to Acapulco to find that *bastardo*. I would never be so foolish as to anger your president by sending such weapons to your country."

Leah looked dubious, but Del nodded.

As Inocensio leaned across the desk and pounded his chest with one meaty fist, a diamond half the size of a golf ball winked counterpoint to the chandeliers. "Never would I do anything to place my family in danger." He stared hard at Delgado. "Cisco Mulcahey and his are mine, even you, El Tigre of the FBI . . . I would never have used those bombs."

"I believe you . . . *Tio*," Delgado said.

The vertebrae popped as Leah corkscrewed her neck to stare at Del.

As they drove away from the warehouse, Leah chewed on her lip, deep in thought. "Why use Inocensio and ChiChi? Why not just have Thompkinson steal the two nukes in July and bring them into the U.S.? It doesn't add up."

"Unless our smoking spook wanted someone else's prints all over this mess. Someone to take the fall if the deal went south," he speculated.

"Whitherspoon?" she asked, thinking of the recently disgraced CIA director.

Delgado shrugged. "Maybe, but I doubt he's the head man. It has to be someone higher up the food chain—someone who's still on the inside. Couldn't be easy getting a full bird colonel to commit treason."

"What game is the CIA playing?" Leah asked, more to herself than to Del. She remembered the treachery inside BISC and shivered. She'd been their unwitting tool. Had the mysterious man she dubbed the "Ashtray" also been used by his agency?

"What if the Company isn't in on this?" Del suggested. "What if your Ashtray set this up for someone else? If Paul finds a link between Thompkinson and a player in D.C., we're in business."

"Whoever's behind this wanted Bernal to bring the nukes into the U.S. so he could set up the guy who's buying them," she said.

"Yeah, but I think our boy ChiChi's taken a page from his former employer and become an entrepreneur. He's eliminated the middleman, although I doubt he knew about the guy behind his buyer."

"Yeah, he used the buyer to get into the U.S., then gave him the slip." She could see it now. "With a dozen terrorist groups, not to mention the odd El-Op wanting to expand his turf, ChiChi could have one dilly of an auction."

Delgado nodded grimly as he drove south on Highway 20.

After a moment's silence, Leah couldn't help herself. "*Tio?*"

Del shrugged. "Technically true in the ways of extended families. At least Mexican style. By marriage Inocensio Ramirez is my great-uncle."

"I never thought you'd acknowledge him."

"Neither did I."

Serifina Maria Estrella de Mulcahey y Guzman was plump, regal, and always smiling, free with hugs and treats for every child she met. As soon as Del and Leah pulled up at the Mulcahey house, she took one look at Leah's injured arm and said, "I will call Dr. Cisneros at once."

Leah got out of the car, arm still throbbing. It was nothing she wasn't used to. "No, really, it's fine. I've had a lot worse." The minute the words left her mouth, she could see Aunt Seri's startled expression quickly masked by acceptance. His family knew she was a killer and yet they welcomed her. It just didn't add up, no matter how hard she tried to make sense of it. Of course, they were grateful she'd helped save Del's son Mike last summer, but . . .

"You will come with me and I will decide what to do," the older woman said authoritatively, taking hold of Leah's uninjured arm to lead her inside.

"She'll hogtie and drag you if you don't go along," Del said with a smirk.

Leah gave in and followed Seri while Del and his great-uncle remained outside, discussing the meeting with Inocensio Ramirez.

"You are just in time for supper. Tonight it will be only the four of us, can you believe it?" Seri asked with a big smile. Hordes of children, grandchildren, nieces, and nephews often filled their large home. It was no matter to her if there were four or forty at the table.

As she clucked over the bullet slash across Leah's arm, expertly applying disinfectant and bandages, she said, "I know you wish to discuss business with the men, but perhaps after we have eaten, you and I can talk, no?"

No! Leah wanted to shout the word, but all she could do was nod. These people were so kind, so open and generous. They knew nothing of the black emptiness deep inside her. Or the nightmares . . . oh, God, the nightmares. What if she woke Uncle Mac and his wife with her screams as she had Del the other night?

She vowed to stay awake until they left in the morning.

While Del and his family wolfed down Seri's marinated beef, spicy rice, and fresh green beans, she knew the older woman was watching her. The men discussed their meeting with Ramirez and Leah put in her opinion several times between making obligatory small talk with her hostess. Then a servant came in to clear the table after they'd finished dessert, a luscious fresh pineapple concoction.

"Come, *mi hija,* let me tell you stories about *El Tigre* that you have never heard," Seri said to Leah. Tiger was the family nickname he'd earned during a boyhood hunting incident.

"Hey, no fair, *Tia!*" Del protested. "She's already heard about how I got tagged with '*Tigre.*' That's embarrassing enough."

Leah sat glued to the chair. Trapped.

Seri made a dismissive gesture in her nephew's direction, a wide grin on her small round face. "No, we will have our coffee and talk," she said, picking up a small tray the houseboy had set on the dining table. It contained a pot and two mugs along with a good-sized pitcher of hot milk for the traditional *café con leche.*

Leah followed like a convicted felon en route to the execution chamber as Del's aunt led her down the hallway.

———

The moon was waning by the time Leah wandered from her room, still deeply disturbed by her conversation with Seri. She stepped onto the second-floor gallery overlooking the courtyard fountain and stared up at the star-filled sky. A cool breeze made her wish she'd worn a jacket. She wrapped her arms around herself, then sensed him behind her.

"Couldn't sleep either?" Del asked. His voice was low, mellow as the heavy Rioja wine they'd drunk with dinner. "That must've been some discussion you and my aunt had . . . or was there another nightmare?"

She could hear the concern in his voice. "No, only girl talk, Delgado. I can't betray a confidence," she said lightly.

Too lightly. "So, she got to you, did she?"

"What's that supposed to mean?"

"She told you about Diana and me, how my work with the Bureau tanked our marriage—only the Gospel according to St. Seri puts the blame as much on Diana as on me. Not entirely fair but, hey, she's family. Who am I to argue?" he said with a wry grin.

"As a matter of fact, she mentioned that in passing," Leah replied pensively. *But mostly she wanted to talk about how I suited you much better.*

"She wants you to marry me. Funny thing. So do I. For a while last summer, I thought you agreed. What happened, Leah?"

She didn't answer at first. Finally, knowing he wasn't going to let it rest, she said, "I . . . I can't do it, Del. You know about the nightmares. You've seen how I am—how I get when the action starts—when I do what I do best. Kill people."

"Wrong. You aren't ChiChi Bernal. You're not a stone killer, just a trained agent who happens to be very good at saving my ass. I've kinda gotten used to that. We'll work this out."

She hugged herself harder, shaking her head. "You need a real life for you and Mike. I can't give you that, Del."

"That's not what my aunt told you. She must've struck a nerve. Always had a way of doing that, ever since I was a kid."

"We're not kids anymore. She's never lived in our world—my world," she amended. "When it's dangerous . . . I get . . . I don't know. . . ."

"A rush?" he supplied.

She turned and looked at him, startled.

"Hits you like a dose of Express Elevator, doesn't it, with every new chance to go after the bad guys." He felt her stiffen, wished he could read her expression more clearly in the moonlight.

"I suppose when you worked for the Bureau, you felt it, too."

"And as a reporter. The adrenaline rush kicks in whether you're facing an El-Op with an automatic or meeting an anonymous source who has hard evidence that the head of a major corporation cooked his books. I still got it when I was hot on a story."

"You said you 'got it.' Past tense, Delgado. You're a bureau chief now. I still get that . . . that high." She shuddered at the word, hating that it sounded like a narcotic, which she knew it was. "When Gramps called I felt it tingling up my spine."

"That's why you didn't want to bring me in on this. After all we've been through, why are you still afraid I'll see something I don't like in you?" He cupped her face in his hands and forced her to look at him. "I already know Leah Berglund, remember? Ab Fenster had us pegged the minute he met us." He stroked a wisp of pale hair from her eyes. "We never have called him about that wedding. After he saved our asses last summer, we owe it to the old codger. Who knows how much longer he'll be around?"

She shook her head, breaking the spell. "I don't think getting married just because an eccentric old man wants us to is the world's smartest idea." She paused and gathered her thoughts. "I'll never change, Del. Even working at Clean Ride, I get a boost when I'm out in the field. When it's dangerous."

"That's why you've stayed away from me and Mike. To protect us. Poor Leah-Pia, always so damn noble, even when she's so damn wrong," he murmured.

"How did you beat it?" she couldn't resist asking.

"I have a son who's growing up fast, who hasn't had much time with his father. You can bet Tia talked to me about that! Family has a way of anchoring you, making you realize there's more to life than the juice you get saving the bloody ungrateful world."

"That's part of it, too," she said in a small voice. "Your family. I don't understand them. They're too accepting, too generous—nothing like mine."

"Oh, I don't know. Seems as if Adam and you have a great relationship."

"Well, my parents didn't. And after all I've been through, I'm not sure I'd do much better. Your family—you, Mike—you all deserve more than I can give. You need a stable home for Mike. With a woman like Diana."

"Already tried that. You saw how well it worked out. Diana gave it her best shot. The basic problem is she never understood what I was. Still am."

"But you don't get that rush anymore, you admitted it."

He grinned and kissed the tip of her nose. "Why do you think I open up the flash drive and go 120 kph on unrestricted highways whenever I get the chance? Why did I jump at the chance to go to D.C. with you?"

"I don't think it will work, Del."

"I won't push you," he said quietly.

She read something else in his eyes, the weariness in his voice. "But you can't wait forever, can you, Del?"

10.

ChiChi Bernal climbed out of the beat-up little EV after parking it in the darkest corner of the yard under a makeshift carport. He had arrived in Detroit day before yesterday riding Greyhounds in a zigzag route until he was sure no one followed him. His back ached from the misery of sleeping on bus seats and his cousin Edmundo's lumpy sofa. He'd left Ed's place in the dead of night, not telling him where he was headed, only instructing him to wait for calls from Nina and from him.

Earlier he'd used cash to buy the beater Chevy he'd driven to this burg just over the Ohio line from Toledo. Adrian was good cover because of its large Mexican-American population. He'd blend in, living with a distant cousin by one of his marriages. Then he would wait until Nina got the deal set up with Miguel.

Following the muddy driveway to the front yard, he surveyed the ugly frame house. The dim glare of Dorothy Street's lone functioning light revealed an old washing machine and microwave oven littering the bare ground. A few straggling weeds had withstood the onslaught of southern Michigan winter, brown and beaten-looking as the house itself.

Two rusted-out pickup trucks sat in the drive. He'd had to pull around them to reach the cover of the carport and cursed Salvador's lazy stupidity for not moving them. The place looked deserted, but he knew Sal, his wife, and three kids were sleeping inside. Sal was related to Teresa, his wife in New York. He grinned. There was no possibility anyone could beat that information out of Nina or Ed. They had no clue.

He picked up the two suitcases and waded across the small yard, glad the dark house had no porch light as he set down one case and fished behind a big clay pot filled with dead coleus until he found the key just where Sal said it would be. The door creaked open, made of flimsy half-rotted wood that he could've kicked in quicker than groping for the key. Some dump. Reminded him of Nina's place in Corpus.

As he let his eyes adjust to the dim light from the street, he suddenly got a bad feeling. She should've called him at Ed's place by this evening. After a few decent hours of sleep he'd check on her. Very carefully. No way did he want to leave a trail like some hick leaving boot prints in the mud. He'd gone to too much trouble to hide it. He saw the rollaway bed in the corner and muttered an oath. It looked worse than Ed's sofa—if that was possible.

He stashed the cases under the ratty bed, then collapsed onto the groaning springs. That nagging feeling about Nina made his gut churn. *Nah, it was just those lousy burritos I ate at that joint on Highway 52.* Damn, he forgot how bad American "Mexican" food could be in Michigan.

Sal's little rug rats would be up at daybreak getting ready for school. Better catch some sleep while he could. He pulled up the cheap poly blanket and concealed the deputy's automatic underneath it. ChiChi never took chances. After all, one of Sal's kids might hurt himself if he got his grubby little fingers on it. He chuckled and fell asleep.

4:50 A.M. EST, TUESDAY, NOVEMBER 11
WASHINGTON, D.C.

Gracie Kell positively loved it! Pulling an all-nighter in front of the screen was worth every minute. She couldn't wait to roust the old buzzard out of bed. After all, how often did a professed anarchist get the chance to piss off a president? The first time he'd called and gotten an eyeful, she thought he'd choke. Looked sort of like Santa Claus, complete with white hair and a very red face. Guess Delgado hadn't warned him. Then again, maybe he had. People from Maine weren't exactly on the cutting edge of hip. Adam Manchester probably kept a moose as a house pet.

She touched up her black lipstick and gave her fuchsia and lilac Mohawk a pat. The new "do" gave her slight frame an extra couple of inches in height. Her dog collar with the cubic zirconium spikes added a nice touch, too. Did the snake tattoo show? She looked down, then tugged at her red leather bustier. Damn thing was way cool but made for a woman considerably more endowed than she was. Wriggling to pull it down so he'd catch the full effect of the design, she checked her appearance in the reflect-vid on her screen, then switched it to trans-vid and touched the send key.

Presto. "Wake-up call, Senator," she murmured, chewing on one lilac nail. He probably slept in striped pajamas. Hot damn, she wished he'd turn on his vid so she could see. Expecting him to be sound asleep, she prepared to wait until he stumbled out of bed and remembered how to open his PDA for the call.

"Manchester here," came the resonant voice almost immediately. Other than sounding a bit hoarse, he was wide awake.

"Doncha ever sleep? I guess if you wanna be president you have to give that up, huh?"

"Ms. Kell?" His tone went from hoarse to tense. "I trust this isn't a social call at such an ungodly hour. What have you found out?"

"First, check your encryption status. This is pretty hot stuff I got for you." She waited a beat, watching the elaborate readouts on her equipment to make certain he did it correctly. She could've done it from here but what the hell . . . if the old geezer was going to be president, he needed to get with modern technology.

"Everything's secure," he said after a moment. "Now, what have you uncovered?"

"Put your vid on, why doncha? I like to deal face-to-face."

"Considering you make your living communicating from machine to machine, I find that a peculiar sentiment, Ms. Kell."

She was surprised when she saw him fully dressed, shirtsleeves rolled up, hair rumpled, looking very tired. "You pulled an all-nighter, too," she said with a touch of sympathy. Jeez, he had to be sixty or so, practically one foot in the grave already. She felt a sudden pang of guilt.

"It comes with living in Washington. Now . . ." His voice faded away as he looked at the apparition in front of him and wished devoutly that his PDA didn't have such a large screen. In fact, he wished it didn't have vid on it at all. He cleared his throat and tried again. "What have you got for me?"

Del had insisted he use this creature to track down information that he and Scarletti were unable to find. The first time he'd contacted her, she had been dressed in dark purple spandex that made her emaciated body look like a grape Popsicle, with matching hair and eye shadow. That wouldn't have bothered him much, if not for the whips and chains—not to mention the motorcycle—clearly visible in the background of her living quarters. After a brief rant about alien abductions, she had made a few smart-mouthed comments in response to his requests, then signed off.

He never expected to hear from her again. Or maybe he just hoped.

"Karl Banecek's still got some juice with the spooks. Too bad because he's righteous about cutting the military."

"Yes, regrettable," he replied, rubbing his eyes to blot out the clash of colors on the screen. "But hardly surprising considering that he used to be CIA director."

"Yeah, that sucks, too. But last Thursday he talked to Ralph Whitherspoon."

"The man Samson fired as CIA director?" he said, suddenly energized. "Any idea what they talked about?"

"No way to know unless they made discs of the conversation and stored them where I could access. But I can tell you this much—ever since the Holy Arabia thing blew up and Samson cleaned house at the CIA, Banecek's been talking to the ex-director pretty regular. I set a tracer. Next time the secretary of defense has a confab with Whitherspoon, I'll try to pick up what they're talking about."

"Let's hope it's soon. I need to know what he's up to and if Samson is aware of it."

"That's not all. That gambler from Jersey you asked me about—

Viviano? I ran a few scans into his computer network. Really dumb for a 'wise guy,' " she said with a smirk.

Now she really had his attention. "I told you he's connected to an attempt on my granddaughter's life."

"Yeah, he had those guys from Vegas on the string, all right. Richie Viviano said jump, they asked how high. Heard they got canceled."

"Yes, DeClue and Billinger are dead. I told you they were connected to Viviano, but we can't legally nail him. If you're able to get inside his computers that might give us something to work with." He pointedly didn't mention whether that was legal.

"Piece of cake getting inside. And it's pretty interesting. Viviano keeps detailed books on the customers at his casinos. Like I said, a dumb wise guy. All I had to do was watch the algorithms on—"

"Please, spare me the technical details of hacking and tell me what you found out," Adam said, throwing up his hands. "I'll be the first to confess I'm a troglodyte who still prefers pen and paper to keyboards."

"Paper?" Gracie blinked. The image of anyone actually *writing*— *on paper*—was as alien as one of her UFOs. Del had warned her Manchester was weird, but jeez. . . .

"The casino records?" Adam reminded her.

"Yeah, well, they were in code when the customers were, ah, 'sensitive.' Strictly amateur night," she said with a snort. "Figgered only gov hacks might try and they wouldn't break it. Guess Richie and his boys thought they were protecting their high rollers so nobody'd get wind."

Adam could feel his pulse skip a beat. "High rollers like whom?"

"Lots of Pentagon hotshots, including one full bird colonel name of Thompkinson. You mentioned he was dead, too, didn't you?" When he nodded, she continued. "He owed Viviano serious bucks. Waaaay past what a frickin' general could afford and he wasn't anywhere near a promotion."

"So someone blackmailed him into stealing those weapons," Adam said thoughtfully, more to himself than to her. "Any idea who Viviano's working for?"

"Not yet, but you wouldn't believe the piles of crap I have yet to wade through. Viviano's operation reaches all the way from the Big

Apple down to Miami. Been reading screens filled with numbers and code names until my eyeballs bleed. I'll get back to it, but thought you'd want a heads-up on our boy Banecek and the connection from Jersey to Thompkinson."

"I'd be interested in the names of any other Pentagon officials or Washington insiders who're in hock to this mobster."

"Can do. Now I gotta get back to work."

"Fine job, Ms. Kell, thank you," Adam said with genuine admiration.

When he smiled that way she liked him. Looked like somebody's grandfather, which, of course, he was—none other than Delgado's babe's. If only he weren't a pol.

7:05 A.M. MST, TUESDAY, NOVEMBER 11
MAZATLÁN, MEXICO

"Just got off the link with Paul. Thompkinson's tragic accident wasn't so accidental," Del said as Leah entered the big dining room where Seri had already laid out a buffet breakfast of huevos rancheros, fresh grilled salmon, and pan dulce dripping with honey.

"*Quel* surprise," she said, yawning, as she poured a cup of steaming black coffee without benefit of the hot milk. She needed a straight jolt to start her heart beating after a sleepless night. She told herself she'd stayed awake because she didn't want to wake the house screaming like a nutcase. She knew that wasn't the truth. The scene with Del had left her feeling empty and scared. She'd pushed him away too often. Maybe this time he'd walk. *That's what you want, isn't it?*

"So what about Thompkinson?" she asked, taking a seat. All business.

He shoveled another mouthful of eggs and chunky salsa into his mouth, then explained as if nothing had happened last night. "The agents from St. Louis found the car. Brake lines were tampered with, among other items assured to make him lose control on those lousy curving hilly roads around the Army base. Just to guarantee he played tackle with a tree, his body was pumped full of enough ketamine to make that backcountry highway seem like the Yellow Brick Road."

"And Highway Patrol didn't pick up on any of this at the time of death?"

"It was late, driving conditions were horrible because of a beaut of a Midwestern thunderstorm, and they'd had a busy night carting the living ones to local ERs. Whoever set it up did a good job."

"As good as a BISC sanitation squad could do," she said flatly.

He sighed. "Yes, if they were still in business. Whoever killed Thompkinson, they were pros."

She nodded. "Raoul find any trace of Maria Montoya's family?"

"Not yet, but I'm afraid even if he does manage to locate them, they won't know anything. Busch isn't a much better bet. He was a real loner. Even if he had family, I doubt he talked to them." Del polished off the eggs and went for seconds. "You need to eat."

"No thanks, I never eat before my heart and lungs restart. A working stomach's too much competition for them."

"You skip the most important meal of the day and then scold me about my lousy eating habits."

The old familiar grouse was oddly comforting, even though she hated to admit it. "I only said pizza and McDonald's were junk food." Then she returned to business. "Oppermann have anything on that plane or the pilot ChiChi iced?"

"Finally traced the plane with Raoul's help. Stolen from a small private strip in Sonora. Whoever did it had the paint job redone, registration number and all. The pilot may have been a former spook. Looks like he was freelancing as a mercenary in the Balkans recently."

"Apparently someone stateside made him a better offer. Too much to hope the Bureau knows who."

"Not yet," Del said, sopping a soft piece of bread in the puddle of honey and holding it out to her. "We're walking on eggs, Leah. Can't get the job done that way. Peace offering?"

It smelled so heavenly she couldn't resist. "Yeah, you're right." When she took a bite the honey dripped on her chin and she licked it off. He looked at her mouth like it was the Hope Diamond and he was a jewel thief, which made her want to kick herself. *Why am I doing this to both of us?*

He broke the tension by shoving another piece of bread in his mouth. "Adam called a little while ago."

"What did he say?" she asked, miffed that Gramps hadn't asked to speak to her directly.

"Karl Banecek's been meeting with Ralph Whitherspoon." He filled her in on the information from Gracie about the secretary of defense and the incriminating ties between Thompkinson and Viviano.

"So now we know Thompkinson's motive," she said, sipping her coffee thoughtfully, grateful to be back on track. Away from the personal. "If Gracie can only come up with more people in Richie's debt—higher up—we might hit the jackpot. Who knows how twisty this rat maze is? Could Banecek be involved?"

Before Del could reply, Seri bustled into the dining room. "Good morning, Leah. Francisco said to tell you an encrypted signal has come over his PDA for you."

"Willis," she said to Del and his aunt, quickly excusing herself to speak privately with her source.

"Well, aren't you all bright and chipper, Sweetums." Willis's big grin filled the screen. "Gotta be, what, crack of dawn down in siesta land?"

He knew she hated mornings. "Get on with it, Willie. Where are the damn nukes?"

"Bogotá's a good bet."

"The Cartel?" That didn't add up with the other information they had about people high in the American government being involved in the theft. Of course, if they just wanted to sell to the highest bidder, maybe Benito had made them a better offer than Holy Arabia. "What makes you think it's Benny?"

"Don't know that it is Zuloaga. He's sittin' on a nest full of rattlers. Word is any of them would love a way to bite him where the sun don't shine."

She cursed beneath her breath. "Great. Noriega and his crowd could set off a couple of dirty bombs and then preside over a nuclear wasteland from the Andes to the Amazon basin. He that crazy?"

Willis shrugged his meaty shoulders. "Could be. He's a hard case. Might be a head case, too. One of ours took a job with him."

She knew "ours" meant a former BISC agent. "Let me guess. A hit on Benito."

"Give that lady the prize Kewpie doll," he said, pointing one chubby finger at the screen. "Didn't get the job done. Got done himself instead. Noriega likes results, guaranteed."

"He'd use dirty bombs." It wasn't a question.

Willis only nodded.

She signed off, then joined Del and his uncle in Mac's study. Both men looked expectantly at her. She quickly outlined what she'd learned.

"This Willis, is he reliable?" Francisco asked.

"Willie gave me the information that proved BISC had set me up to kill Del last summer. If he heard rumors about someone in the Cartel buying nukes, there's a damn good chance Bernal sold to him."

"But why would ChiChi have to come here to do that? It doesn't fit. We know there's a Washington connection," Del said.

"I agree. Someone in D.C. pulled many strings to get Bernal inside the U.S.," Francisco said thoughtfully.

"But who? And why?" Del asked.

"One way we might find out," she said.

"I hear Bogotá's lovely this time of year," Del replied.

His uncle looked from Del to Leah and back, a worried expression on his face.

10:15 A.M. EST, TUESDAY, NOVEMBER 11
WASHINGTON, D.C.

"They've made the connection between Viviano and Thompkinson. I don't want this to get any closer, dammit. You sure that fucking pilot can't be traced? He was Company, after all."

On the other side of the vid, the man took the burned down stub of his Macedonian cigarette and lit its glowing tip to another fresh one. "He's dead." He inhaled deeply, held the smoke, then let it out. "Dead men don't say much."

"Neither do live ones when you can't find them. Where in hell's Bernal and my nukes?"

"I have a lead in Detroit. We'll have him soon. You just do your part and focus on the deal with the 'Rabs."

"Scarletti knows about their targets in the U.S. FBI's got a mole in one of their cells. I tell you, I don't like it."

"No one at cell level knows anything." The man exhaled a cloud of smoke. "Do you care if they blow up Wall Street?"

"Let those damn rag heads blow up Congress." He snorted. "Do every taxpayer in the fucking country a favor. Now, you listen to me. I want those nukes and I want them now. Not next month, not next week—now! My pal al Ambas is ready to deal and I want him to pay me before the FB-fucking-I busts in and stops the party."

"My sources in Detroit are interrogating Bernal's cousins. We'll find him, Mr. Secretary. Just be ready to take delivery of the suitcases." The former CIA man blew a wreath around his face, then the screen went black.

Arrogant prick. Damned fool knew more than was healthy. He might have to deal with his chain-smoking spook.

He smiled coldly. Dead men didn't say much. . . .

8:20 A.M. MST, TUESDAY, NOVEMBER 11
MAZATLÁN, MEXICO

"It wasn't easy, believe me. Like getting an audience with the frickin' pope or something." Gracie shivered, remembering the cold black eyes of the thug in Cali she'd just spoken to. He almost made her believe evil could ooze through a vid screen. "You're being granted an interview with his royal highness, Benito Zuloaga. Tomorrow. Soon as you can arrange flights."

"Pick up any more chatter about his difficulties with Noriega?" Del asked.

"If you mean is his rival on the lookout for a bomb or two, yeah, sounds like it to me."

"That's what Leah's source says. Maybe that's why Benny agreed to see us."

"Before you go flying to Cartel land, there's one thing you oughta know. I just told Leah's granddad. Ya know, he's not so bad for an old pol—if only he'd loosen up a little." She grinned, thinking of the senator, then returned to business. "Fibbies in Detroit followed a lead I gave them on a guy named Edmundo Sanchez. Found him and his family killed, execution style. Looked like a professional hit." She waited a beat. "He was ChiChi Bernal's cousin."

As soon as he signed off with Gracie Kell, Del put in a call to Paul Oppermann, who was by that time back in the capital. The director of the FBI was not a happy camper. His shirt looked as if he'd worn it for a week—which was nearer the truth than he'd ever dare admit to his wife—and his face was lax and gray from lack of sleep.

"It's as if those *mamzarim* are one step ahead of us every time we catch a break," he said, scrubbing one meaty hand over his shiny scalp. "Same deal as Bernal's wife in Corpus. But this time I don't think they got anything. Way it looks, they tried to get information out of Sanchez by using his wife and kids."

No wonder he looks like shit. Paul Oppermann never got over the deaths of women or children. Del knew he'd lost his younger sister and her teenage son during the Slaughter, when the Cartel had struck at drug enforcement personnel with heavy collateral damage. A thirty-seven-year-old woman and a fourteen-year-old boy. Paul still mourned them after all these years. "You mean whoever this was, they shot them one at a time, thinking Sanchez would talk."

Oppermann nodded, muttering a Yiddish curse. "But I don't think he knew where Bernal was. Poor schlemiel just had to sit there and watch them execute his whole damn family."

"That means they don't have any more idea where Bernal is than we do."

"Some bright side," Oppermann said, massaging his temples. "But we were able to find a witness who ID'd Bernal. He was there overnight, then flew the coop. Right now I've got every available man in southern Michigan looking for him. Might take a while though. That area's full of Mexican-American communities."

"Exactly why ChiChi'd go there to lie low. He's waiting—either to take the money and escape to Canada . . . or he hasn't made the deal yet."

"Give my best to Benny. I hope like hell he's got the nukes." Oppermann didn't sound like he believed it.

Neither did Delgado. But if there was an auction, no way would a player as rich as Zuloaga not know about it. It was the only lead that was hot at the moment. They might as well go for it. And who knew, it might be to Benito's advantage to partner up with the FBI.

11 A.M. EST, TUESDAY, NOVEMBER 11
WASHINGTON, D.C.

Adam Manchester flicked off his PDA and leaned back in his chair. Scarletti had given him the DNA report on the former BISC agent who'd tried to kill Delgado. His name was Roland Bolmer, recently hired as a security supervisor for the Bureau of Customs & Border Protection. It would not be difficult for a man trained by BISC to hack into Border Patrol files and select Harry Busch to let ChiChi's little plane fly into the country undetected.

"But who did Bolmer work for?" The senator poured himself another cup of coffee and took a sheet of paper from a desk drawer. He began to write names and connect them in a free-associating schematic, a technique that he'd always found to be a good analytical tool. There was the line from Viviano to Thompkinson, who'd covered up the stolen nukes in the first place, which created another line to the Pentagon and the colonel's boss, General McKinney.

Manchester couldn't believe a man of McKinney's integrity would unleash a dirty bomb anywhere, least of all within the United States. He was not in any way connected to General Sommerville's failed coup last summer. Yet he had defended Thompkinson who owed a fortune in gambling debts to Viviano . . . who used Vegas connections to make an attempt on Leah's life.

Bernal came into the country through bribery of a Border Patrol agent. Customs and Border Patrol were under Homeland Security . . . Las Vegas . . . there was a common denominator: Bob Labat, the former governor of the Silver State.

Wildly unlikely in spite of all the converging lines, but then many of the conspirators last summer had appeared unlikely, too. He gave a voice command to the PDA. "Get me Brett Lowell. Secured channel."

Ambassador Lowell encrypted every communication going out of his home. It was nearing the cocktail hour in London and he had a dinner at the Russian Embassy that evening. The senator caught him in full black tie regalia, a martini in hand. The slim and elegant Brett had been able to drink truck drivers twice his weight under the table since college days, then walk away stone sober. An asset for a diplomat.

"How's my house treating you, Adam?" he asked, grinning. "Or should I anticipate and say, Mr. President?"

Manchester waved away that lurking possibility. "I'm not even a senator at the moment, Brett. I have a favor to ask," he said, going directly to the point. "You have connections inside Riyadh. I need to know more about Aziz al Ambas. . . ."

It took several hours and by the time he returned Adam's call, Lowell was decidedly out of sorts. He'd missed out on Beluga caviar and 1990 Moët & Chandon champagne to do a favor for his old roommate. "Well, you were right about al Ambas. He may be confined in Guantanamo but he's had some very important visitors in recent months. And, yes, one of them was a shadowy CIA sort with enough phony names to fill a London teledirect. Haven't the foggiest who he really is and don't think you'll be able to trace him."

"I hear the 'but' in your voice, Brett," Adam said impatiently.

"According to my sources—and I double-checked using some highly illegal methods, for which you owe me at least a half kilo of Beluga—the secretary of Homeland Security went to Havana on October 15, supposedly to hold talks with President Ruiz on coastal security. Keep out those nasty Cartel boats filled with Elevator, you know."

"Then he made a side trip to Gitmo."

"Yes, the next day he apparently met with our friend Aziz. Sounds perfectly innocent if you disallow the secrecy hovering over it. A personal interrogation since the secretary's concerned about terrorist cells inside the U.S." Lowell scoffed. "As if that cutthroat would tell Labat anything. Better men than the Rabbit have struck out, believe me. I know a few Euros who've dealt with al Ambas over the years.

Never thought I'd say this, but considering everything, I'd rather be posted to the Balkans than back in the U.S. right now."

"I could give you a list of places to avoid," Adam said in a dead tone of voice.

After signing off, he sat alone in the office for several moments, mulling over what he'd just learned. Suddenly he felt an inexplicable need to reassure himself that Leah was all right. He opened a link to Mazatlán. When Francisco Mulcahey's face appeared on the screen, his usually genial expression was grave. The mayor was obviously worried about something.

· Adam's gut clenched as he asked, "Is my granddaughter there?"

"No, I am afraid she and Del are en route to Bogotá."

11.

"Bogotá!" Adam echoed. If Mulcahey had said she'd gone straight to hell he couldn't have been more horrified. "I need to reach her." His gut was churning now.

"Security inside Colombia is very tight. Even I cannot speak with them until they are out of South America." Francisco explained why his nephew and Leah had requested an audience with the Cartel head.

"You don't like the smell of this, do you?"

Mulcahey nodded. "No, I do not. The situation is very unstable with Noriega and Zuloaga engaged in a power struggle. If Bernal sold the weapons in South America—"

"Why go to all the trouble of coming to the U.S. first?" Adam finished for him.

"Precisely. But they felt it was the only lead they had to pursue and time is running out."

"How well I know," Adam said, scrubbing his hands through his hair, thinking about Labat's possible complicity. "Here's hoping Zuloaga knows something he's willing to share."

"He must be frightened enough if he is willing to speak with agents of your government," Francisco said.

Adam couldn't help but feel that Del's uncle was trying to reassure himself as much as his American friend. After they said good-bye, he couldn't shake a premonition that something awful was about to happen to Leah. Knowing he could do nothing to help her, he remembered all she'd survived in her troubled life.

Leah will be all right. He forced his concentration back to the matter of Lowell's intel. He had to find proof that Bob Labat was behind the nuke theft. "Gracie," he muttered reluctantly. Of course, she was unavailable. He left her a message, outlining what Brett Lowell had told him. Delgado's hacker could track down any cyber evidence. The issue was time—time they did not have.

Just as he opened his link to call John Scarletti, he suddenly closed it. What if Brett's security had been compromised? He remembered all the encryption precautions Leah had taken when she was working against BISC. Could he be under e-surveil?

He looked around the gracious walls of the Lowell family library. Every dark shadow against the high ceiling suddenly appeared ominous. Being a ranking member of the Diplomatic Corps, Brett had his home swept regularly. The ambassador employed every imaginable device to prevent anyone from hostile governments to the news media from listening in on classified conversations. It was fail-safe. Or maybe it was not.

Someone had been one jump ahead of them from the time this nightmare began. Every time they got near Bernal and his deadly cargo, ChiChi and his mysterious pursuers escaped. The cabinet member in charge of America's first line of defense from terrorism might know their every move. Whatever plan was devised to trap Labat must remain secret.

Swallowing his gorge, he knew he had to start at the top. Samson had egregiously poor judgment in selecting people to serve under him, but he was still the president. *If only no one from the CIA or Homeland Security has the Oval Office bugged!* He gave the command to the PDA. "Connect me to the White House. Adam Manchester to speak with President Samson. Immediately."

Wade Samson's haggard face appeared on the vid screen a moment later. "I understand you've learned something important, Senator," he said in his most stentorian tone. He waited like a chess player, expecting Adam to make the next move.

"We need an immediate face-to-face, Mr. President," Manchester replied. "I have information too sensitive to discuss any other way."

Samson digested the demand, allowing his expression to register some of the irritation he felt dealing with the old warhorse. But he'd brought Manchester in because his opponent had invaluable resources. "I'll have Vera clear my calendar and assemble our team. Say half an hour?"

"Half an hour's fine, but I'd prefer only the attorney general be present," Adam replied. "In fact, in light of what I've found, I must insist."

Samson stiffened, taken aback by the bald nerve of the old man. His eyes narrowed. He considered his options, jaw clenched. Manchester waited him out until he finally nodded. "Very well. I'll send a car for Scarletti. Half an hour."

The screen went immediately blank. *Pissed him off. Good.* Adam allowed himself a tight smile.

Stuffing his notes in a battered old leather briefcase, an anniversary gift from his wife forty years ago, he headed toward the library door, then stopped. He walked behind the desk and pushed the panel that revealed Brett's wall safe. Then he pressed his right eye to the retinal scanner and waited impatiently. The heavy door swung open soundlessly.

He removed a short-barreled Colt Python that he used to take backpacking and placed it inside his jacket. Although he had two Secret Service agents assigned to him, Manchester went with his gut instinct for an extra measure of protection. Growing up in the Maine woods, every man and woman learned how to handle firearms. He admitted he was an anachronism in the twenty-first century. But, by damn, he might still be the next president . . . if he lived long enough.

1:19 P.M. EST, TUESDAY, NOVEMBER 11
WASHINGTON, D.C.

The two agents in the front seat of Adam Manchester's Chevy TE remained watchful as they chauffeured him to his meeting. After all, they were taking a potential president to confer with a sitting president. Not exactly a low-profile assignment. Heading from Georgetown to the center of the capital, they knew the danger from El-Op–related violence increased.

After they approached Washington Circle, Adam considered the beautiful warm day and thought of how walking the last blocks would allow him time to gather his thoughts for the confrontation with Samson. He said to the Secret Service agents, "I can remember when it was safe to walk all the way from my house in Georgetown to the Capitol."

Special Agent Larry Jacobi looked at the shabby streets as they headed southeast and replied, "No disrespect intended, Senator, but it isn't even safe to walk down the aisle of a church around here nowadays."

Adam nodded. "I understand." El-Ops ruled the northeast section of the district, but tens of thousands of public employees worked in buildings around the National Mall and the White House. They kept the area relatively danger free. "Relatively" being the telling word. Even in the shadow of the Washington Monument, drug deals were common and only slightly more covert. No place in any American city was safe.

Just after they passed Washington Circle, traffic quickly snarled on Pennsylvania Avenue. "Must've been a shooting somewhere nearby," Jacobi said, opening his link to check on the reason for the congestion.

While he talked sotto voce into the link, the other agent, who was driving, slowed to a complete stop. "Dammed gridlock," he muttered uneasily, his eyes scanning right and left in a practiced pattern.

Both men were on high alert. Jacobi pulled out his SIG-Sauer as he spoke quietly into his link again. "I don't like this, Manny," he said to his partner.

Even when BISC agents had been legally terminating El-Ops, the streets were never safe from random gunfire if a deal went south. When the cops got lucky the dealers and their hardcase clientele offed each other without civilian casualties. But D.C.'s finest weren't noted for their luck or their arrest records. Since BISC had folded, the rate of violent crimes in the nation's capital had grown higher than ever.

"What's HQ say?" Manny asked Jacobi. His eyes looked like a German shepherd's.

"A shoot-out between rival gangs going down."

"How far away?" Manny asked.

Before Jacobi could answer, a deafening explosion shook the small electric vehicle. Adam's ears rang from the impact. The car's windshield shattered as if a giant fist had punched through it. Pebbles of glass flew like beebees, spraying the two agents in the front seat. But more than safety glass penetrated the car. Manny slumped against the driver's door. His head hung at an angle that told Manchester he was dead.

Jacobi yelled, "Stay down, Senator!"

Adam was already crouched behind the seat in the narrow space on the floor, his weapon pulled from inside his jacket. Agent Jacobi's eyes searched the area, looking to see who had fired the shot, his SIG-Sauer ready.

"Down East is under fire. Penn at Eighteenth," he yelled into the link. "Repeat, Down East—" A second blast rocked the car, sending more glass flying. Jacobi's body slammed back against his seat.

Adam knew this was not El-Op automatic weapons fire, but some pinpoint accurate high-powered rifle. Both agents had been taken out with surgical precision. He tried to grab Jacobi's gun but when he heard the sharp metallic whine of a cutting tool on the door lock beside him, he peered out the window.

The operator crouched beside the door, not looking up, busy at his task. Manchester aimed directly at his head and fired through the glass. The cutter tumbled backward against the curb. Wasting no time as a second cutter unlocked the opposite door, Adam jumped out onto the street, stepping over the dead man.

The senator knew the attack wasn't random drug violence. Someone had provided the killer with too much fancy hardware. He was the target. *Damned if they'll get me.*

He took a step but before he could turn, a rough voice said, "Drop the gun, Senator, like the smart guy everybody says you are." The second cutter aimed an M16A1 at his chest, moving around the front of the car.

Manchester ducked behind the door and squeezed off a shot, grazing the man's shoulder, but by that time a third thug materialized behind him. "If you ain't so smart, you'll end up like them guys inside," he said, his automatic aimed directly at the senator's head.

Adam was caught in a cross fire. Slowly, he dropped his Colt Python and waited as the two men seized his arms and started hustling him toward the intersection. *Why do they want me alive?*

1:22 P.M. EST, TUESDAY, NOVEMBER 11
ADRIAN, MICHIGAN

ChiChi Bernal closed the link with an oath. Nina's cousin Rosario said she was dead. The fucking FBI had swarmed all over the place, looking for him. Rumors in the barrio said Nina'd been tortured before she died. Rosario told him never to call her again. She was leaving town, going back to Mexico. Bitch.

He knew the burn in his gut wasn't from lousy food now. Eddie wasn't answering his phone. He called a pal of his cousin's in Detroit, already knowing what he'd hear. The feds were keeping the deaths out of the media. The brief conversation held no surprises. The whole Sanchez family had suddenly disappeared. Bernal knew they were dead.

"No way could they give me up," he muttered, taking a swig from a can of cheap Yankee beer. It tasted like piss. Sal couldn't afford a decent import. He'd give Dolores a few bucks and send her over to Meiers for some good stuff when she got off work. Tossing the empty into a cheap plastic wastebasket, he paced across the creaking floorboards. Time to think before his cousin's rug rats got home from school.

He'd have to handle the deal himself. It might be safe enough here for another day or two but someone was closing in fast enough to make him sweat. Not the feds. Bad as they wanted the suitcases, they wouldn't have done that to Nina or Ed. It was either Inocensio Ramirez or someone working for the big shot who'd hired him to steal the nukes from Ramirez. He wished he knew who the skinny, chain-smoking Yankee worked for. It might be a good life insurance policy.

Then again, it might also get him dead. The spook's boss had plenty of juice in Washington. He decided the best thing was to get the hell out of Adrian as soon as he had Sal buy him a car. ChiChi had enough cash to pay for something that would run for fifteen hundred miles. That would get him close enough to his destination. Reaching

Miguel once he arrived . . . that was another matter. Hell of a hard man to find, even if he desperately wanted what Bernal had to offer. Had Nina contacted her cousin before she died? No matter. He'd do it himself.

"I'll find you, you nutcase El-Op," he muttered with a grin.

ChiChi Bernal always beat the odds. He pulled open the ancient fridge in the hallway and grabbed another lousy beer. Barely cold but what difference did that make? Pretty soon he'd be drinking Modelo Negro in the Big Apple, watching the world go by from some high-rise condo. He downed the swill in one long chug, then squeezed the can in his meaty fist until it crumpled.

When he heard Sal's beater pickup pulling in, he knew luck hadn't deserted him. Must have knocked off work early. Sweet. They could go shopping for that used car now. Too bad Sal would know the make and model.

That made him a loose end.

1:25 P.M. EST, TUESDAY, NOVEMBER 11
WASHINGTON, D.C.

From down the wide street, Paul Oppermann saw the armed men forcing the senator away from the destroyed EV. Two of his agents ran toward the kidnappers, weapons raised but unable to fire for fear of hitting the old man.

Come on, come on already! Where the hell was the sniper who was supposed to be on top of that delivery truck in front of the World Bank Complex? He raised his link and said, "Seal off Eighteenth. It's a one-way heading north. If those goons get the senator in a vehicle at the intersection and make it past Mount Vernon Square, we'll never see Adam Manchester alive again."

He observed three vehicles with engines running, all too close for comfort, and cursed in Yiddish. Pandemonium had already broken out all around him. Motorists ducked low or crawled out the opposite sides of their cars as soon as they saw the distinctive FBI jackets.

Down the street, one of his agents yelled at the armed gunmen. "Stop! FBI. Drop your weapons and raise your hands."

Just then Oppermann received the signal that his sniper was in place. "Do it," he ordered. His men were well ahead of him, but he started running flat out past the cars lining Pennsylvania Avenue.

He heard the sharp whine of a .308-caliber bullet end with the soft whump of connection. The kidnapper exposed on the left was slammed to the ground. His companion tried to hold the old man as a shield, but Manchester was tall, in better physical condition than most men half his age. The instant the FBI sniper dropped one kidnapper, the senator jabbed his elbow into the other man's gut, then seized his gun arm.

They tumbled to the ground, wrestling for the weapon. Manchester's big hand wrapped around the thug's wrist, pinning it to the pavement as he smashed his other fist into his kidnapper's face. In a moment the agents ahead of Oppermann reached them. The old man didn't require their help.

Paul grinned. "Pretty amazing."

The driver of the Pontiac TE on Eighteenth decided waiting for his passengers was a bad call and peeled rubber from the curb. A couple of blocks north the shriek of metal twisting at high impact told Oppermann that the getaway vehicle hadn't fared any better than the kidnappers on foot. Two of them lay dead, the other bloodied and unconscious. Agents swarmed around them.

"How the hell did you know I was going to be kidnapped?" Manchester asked Oppermann when he came running up.

"Dumb luck . . . as a matter of fact." He paused for a minute and got his wind. "I walked out of Hoover when I heard the report of an El-Op firefight by Murrow Park tying up traffic like crazy. Lots of shooting but nobody's hitting anybody says the cop on the link. Then all of a sudden, the 'rival gangs' disappear like Aladdin's Genie. Fight's over before the cops get off a shot but cars up and down Penn are in gridlock."

"So you smelled a trap?"

Oppermann shrugged. "AG told me you were on the way to the White House from Georgetown. He was gonna meet you there. What kind of nebbish tries to kidnap a presidential candidate, I ask you? And I'll ask him," he added as two agents placed the surviving kidnapper in a cruiser.

"Why kidnap me? Why not just kill me?" Manchester speculated.

"Don't know. But whatever you have to tell Samson and Scarletti must be the reason someone wanted you out of commission—or maybe they just wanted to know what you know before they killed you."

Adam grunted. "Makes as much sense as any of the rest of this mess."

1:52 P.M. EST, TUESDAY, NOVEMBER 11
WASHINGTON, D.C.

"One of the El-Ops is in custody, the other three dead. Manchester walked." The terse staccato delivery held no inflection. If the man exhaling a stream of tobacco was upset by what he had just reported, his tone indicated nothing. He took another drag, waiting for his employer's response.

"That is very unfortunate. At least those thugs assigned to kidnap the senator didn't know anything. Holding Manchester would've bought us more time." He leaned back and took a sip of whiskey, breaking his five-o'-clock rule. Things had not been going according to plan lately. "Any news on Bernal?"

His normally drooping mouth downshifted. "Our technical support followed the lead from Bernal's wife in Corpus, but Detroit was a dead end. Maybe our boy's on his way to make a deal with his in-laws down south."

"You know we can't have that. The weapons must go to Holy Arabia. Both targets have been agreed upon." He took another sip, resisting the urge to polish it off.

"We'll retrieve the nukes from Bernal. You want me to set up a hit on Manchester? A lot easier than snatching him."

"Too late for that now. He's already speaking with Samson." He paused and considered, then said, "Let's distract them another way, with a little more evidence. Bin Bergi is in St. Louis finalizing his plans, isn't he?"

"Right now. Tomorrow night he'll head to New York."

"Put a flea in bin Bergi's ear about the suitcases being 'misplaced.' Then he'll be screaming for a meeting with our man . . . in St. Louis.

164 I ALEXA HUNT

As soon as the FBI follows them, bin Bergi can disappear. He's good at that. Just be sure our man gets away, too. You'll probably have to keep him under wraps until the deal's ready to go down."

The chain-smoker's normally dour face betrayed a hint of wry amusement. "Another nail in his coffin. Can do." He pressed the tip of his cigarette butt to a fresh one as the vid went blank.

2:00 P.M. EST, TUESDAY, NOVEMBER 11
WASHINGTON, D.C.

The AG observed the two antagonists in the Oval Office. Manchester leaned forward in an uncomfortable wing chair, his clothes rumpled and dirty. He hadn't even bothered to comb his hair after fighting off his would-be kidnappers. The thick white shock stuck out in unruly clumps. Samson sat with his fingertips steepled, looking from behind the leather inlaid desk with the seal on the front.

He wraps the grandeur of the presidency around himself like a flag. Scarletti knew the senator was thinking the same thing as he briefed them.

"The very secrecy of Labat's contact with al Ambas indicates a deal in the making," Adam concluded.

Samson cleared his throat as soon as Manchester gave him an opening. "I still think it's possible Bob was interrogating al Ambas. He is in charge of stopping terrorist activity inside the U.S., after all."

"You've already admitted he went to Guantanamo without your knowledge. That would raise flags for me, Mr. President."

If you were president, which you are not. "A president can't keep track of the complete itinerary of every cabinet member on a daily basis. Jimmy Carter tried it and look where it got him," Samson said with an ingratiating smile. "I did know Bob had talks with President Ruiz in Havana. This other bears watching, I agree." He turned to Scarletti. "I'll have him come by for a little chat this afternoon."

When Adam didn't jump in, the AG said what he knew Manchester wanted to say. "Mr. President, perhaps that's not the best approach. If he is involved in selling these weapons, we're only warning him to lay low and cover his tracks better. I can order the Bureau to record all his communications. Assign my best agents to watch him."

Samson appeared to consider, then reluctantly nodded. "I can't imagine Bob Labat capable of treason, but given the circumstances, I'll allow it."

"This brings us to the next item," Manchester said. "I have evidence that Warren Thompkinson was being blackmailed by a New Jersey hoodlum named Richie Viviano. The colonel owed him over half a million dollars."

"I have Director Oppermann's report on Thompkinson's death. It would appear he was complicit in stealing those bombs." Samson looked as if he'd swallowed a prune.

"General McKinney vouched for him. That indicates—"

"Nothing," Samson said sharply. "McKinney and the Joint Chiefs were one hundred percent behind me during last summer's attempted coup. I'd trust Howard with my life."

"More than your life—or mine—rides on this, sir. We know someone at the top level inside the Beltway is involved. No one, no matter who, can be ruled out," Manchester replied. "For what it's worth, I agree the general is a long shot. I worked with him for years when I was in the Senate."

The implication to Samson was clear. *Long before I was even a hick congressman from Michigan.* "John, what do you think?" the president said with a friendly warning in his voice. Dammit, the AG worked for him, not this old warhorse!

"Given his long association with Colonel Thompkinson, I'd say a discreet investigation is in order. As soon as the senator's source completes the survey of Viviano's records, we'll be in a better position to proceed. It's possible McKinney might be involved with the gambler, too. Meanwhile, I'll have him surveilled." He paused a beat. "With your permission, of course."

Adam knew the AG was sticking his neck out and Samson could likely chop it off, ending a distinguished career for a dedicated public servant. *Too few people like John Scarletti in government these days.* He remained silent while the president ruminated.

"Permission granted. If the report about terrorist targets is true, the use of dirty bombs would make the possibility even more horrific."

Now Manchester braced himself to raise the most touchy issue of all. "My source has also learned that Karl Banecek's been in contact with Ralph Whitherspoon. Did you know that, Mr. President?"

Samson dodged the question, saying, "The secretary of defense was formerly head of the CIA. Whitherspoon was his closest subordinate. That's hardly incriminating. I can see no relevance to Bernal and the missing nuclear devices."

"We're sure the man who set up the original theft for Inocensio Ramirez and then got Bernal to steal the weapons from him was a Company man. That makes this damned relevant," Adam replied. "What's Banecek talking to Whitherspoon about?"

"I'm not at liberty to say, Senator."

"You're not at liberty!" Manchester roared. "You dragged me into this debacle—one that your own administration has created, *again*, and now you have the unmitigated gall to say you can't tell me why the secretary of defense is holding secret meetings with the discredited former director of the CIA! Did you or did you not know Banecek and Whitherspoon were in contact?"

"Calm down, Senator," Samson said, assuming his most presidential air. His opponent had lost as much sleep in the past days as he had last summer when he knew someone was planning to assassinate him. *Learn how it feels, old man.* "I have complete faith in Karl. If he's using Whitherspoon for some purpose, it's perfectly valid, I assure you."

"Plausible deniability," Scarletti said quietly.

"It won't wash, Mr. President," Manchester said flatly, cutting in to deflect Samson's anger back to him. "This has something to do with the rogue CIA agent. We have a right to know."

Samson deflated a bit. He had not expected Labat of all people to be hip deep in this shithole. Now Manchester was after McKinney, even Banecek. Where would it all end? Visions of a mushroom cloud and years of fallout rose like a nightmare from hell. He closed his eyes and tried to think of an answer.

"I have no idea who the CIA rogue is," he said wearily. "I'll deal with Karl. I do *not* want him surveilled." He turned to Scarletti. "Do I make myself clear?"

The AG nodded. "So noted, Mr. President."

Manchester leaned forward and placed both hands on the edge of Samson's big walnut desk. "Let's lay our cards on the table, Mr. President. The only reason you brought me in on this debacle was so that I could share the blame if the worst happens. Well and good. I accepted the risk, but now you have no right to withhold information from me."

"That is my call, Mr. Manchester."

Samson stressed the "Mr." intentionally. Manchester ignored it. "You've taken a beating in the press and with the American public since last summer, but this isn't the time to back off investigating high-ranking members of your administration. Being reelected isn't worth it. Neither is a Nobel Prize."

Samson froze. "You think I'd risk those bombs going off to obtain a Peace Prize?" His voice was icy.

"I think you're making a mistake if you don't share everything you know with us the same as we've done with you." Adam could see by the set look on the president's face that he would get no further information. "We've told you where we are with the investigation. We'll continue to share information. Good day, Mr. President."

Manchester turned to leave, but as Scarletti rose, Samson motioned for him to sit. "Please, a private word, Mr. Scarletti."

Manchester threw up his hands in disgust. "If Bob Labat is innocent, I'll win the Boston Marathon next spring!" He and Oppermann sat in Brett Lowell's library. While the AG was being grilled by Samson, Adam asked the FBI director to have his techs scan the house for listening devices. Two were found in that room. So much for Lowell's vaunted security system. Small wonder whoever was behind this almost succeeded in kidnapping him.

"I've already got my best agent setting up surveillance. That *mamzer* won't so much as belch without we know about it.

"Samson's letting his obsession with being a Mideast peacemaker blind him to catastrophe right here at home. My God, we know Holy Arabian terrorists have targeted every place from San Francisco to Arlington!"

Oppermann paused, shaking his head. "Who'd have thought the Rabbit would turn out to be the wolf?"

"I only wish that thug who tried to kidnap me knew something," Manchester said.

"*Bobkes.* Just one of four goons hired by another El-Op named Louie 'the Jar' Jarvis. Driver killed in the Pontiac was his, too. The Jar's gone underground. We might get lucky and pull him out of some sewer." Oppermann didn't sound optimistic. "I wonder what kind of grief our commander-in-chief's giving my boss."

Manchester smiled grimly. "You can bet John's getting a damn good dressing down for consorting with the enemy."

After leaving Paul, Adam asked his newly assigned driver, accompanied by a second bodyguard, to take him to the Rayburn House Office Building. If the two men knew that their predecessors had just been murdered, their square-cut, watchful faces gave nothing away. *Hell of a job. Damn, I admire them.* He wanted to talk with an old colleague who was a senior member of the House when Adam had first been elected to national office.

Albert Braveheart was full-blooded Lakota Sioux and chaired the House Intelligence Oversight Committee. The outspoken representative from South Dakota had turned down his party's repeated offers to run him for the Senate, saying, "If the voters don't like what I do, they ought to have the chance to kick me out every couple of years." Even though Al was a Democrat, Adam had recognized a kindred spirit when they lifted their first glasses of bourbon together three decades ago.

During the conspiracy last summer, Braveheart had been one of his best sources in piecing together the ties between BISC and ranking Pentagon officers. He needed to bounce his suspicions off someone who knew Washington inside out. Al had agreed to meet him at his office in Rayburn.

After the driver pulled to the curb, he and the second Secret Service man flanked their charge as soon as he stepped out of the car. Adam approached the building named after one of the most powerful and ruthless Speakers of the House. His link beeped as they climbed the first tier of steps. Annoyed, Manchester's first impulse with all modern technology was to turn if off, but he couldn't afford personal eccentricities when fast communications were this essential.

He checked the machine hoping it was Leah. Gracie Kell's ID came up. He turned it on at once, fumbling clumsily with the controls. Leah had insisted he learn to use the damned new gadget but he would never have the knack. "Ms. Kell, what do you have for me?" he asked.

"Where are you? This might be big," she muttered.

He told her and she instructed him to go inside the building and find an isolated place in the large open reception area where listening devices wouldn't work. Melodrama. But after his experience with Brett's home, he did as she said, then asked, "All right. What have you learned?"

"I've been scanning those lists of Viviano's, running them against anyone with juice in the gov, you know, like we talked about. Got several pings, but one's really a biggie."

Although he had no vid on his simplified link, Adam could sense the excitement radiating across town from whatever her squalid location. "Who?"

"Does the name Frank Scarletti ring any bells with you?"

Only the man who took Annie Beresford away from me. Aloud he replied, "You mean the AG's deceased father? He was tied to Viviano?" He couldn't believe it.

"He was a high roller. Liked to play but he could afford to pay, too. Over the last five years before he died—I didn't take the time to go back further—he gambled away a mil five. Must've had some kind of law practice to be able to afford that."

Adam's gut clenched as he thought of Annie . . . and John. Frank Scarletti had been one of the most brilliant trial lawyers of his generation. Often he was compared to Clarence Darrow and F. Lee Bailey. He was known for his pro bono work, but to cover his expenses, he'd also taken some pretty messy criminal cases for millionaire defendants. He'd been born to poverty but died a rich man. Adam was uncertain what this meant. Had Frank Scarletti been involved with East Coast crime syndicates? El-Ops? Dear God, what if John . . .

Mustering his thoughts, he asked, "Do you have any other connections between Frank and Viviano besides his weakness for the cards?"

"Not just cards. Ponies, dogs. Damned if the man wouldn't bet on which sparrow'd fly off a fence first. Sometimes he won big, too. Never was in hock to Viviano. Just played his casinos and tracks. If you're gonna gamble, it's pretty hard to play big time and not use Richie boy's facilities. He's got the lock, all the way down the coast."

"What about Scarletti's son?" Adam knew on a government salary John couldn't afford his father's vices.

"Nada. But I did come up with a few other brass asses."

"McKinney?" he asked, horrified as visions of everyone he knew or thought he knew swirled around in his head.

"Not the general but two others, another colonel and a captain, both assigned to the Pentagon."

The names she gave rang no bells but he asked her to check on their relationship to the chairman of the Joint Chiefs. Would Howard vouch for them, too? he wondered. "Oh, Ms. Kell, please continue very discreetly—"

"Everything I do is discreet, Senator," she replied.

He could hear the affronted tone in her voice, but coming from a woman with lime and fuchsia spiked hair who wore leather bustiers and tattoos, the term discreet seemed inappropriate. "Yes, of course. You've been most helpful and reliable. It's just that I want you to check further on the AG and any possible connections between him and Viviano . . . or Bob Labat."

"When you asked about that poor Homeland Security sucker this morning, I couldn't believe it. If he's mixed up in this, wow, wouldn't that be a pisser," she said with renewed enthusiasm in her voice.

When he signed off, Adam Manchester felt as if he'd been gut-kicked. As soon as he spoke with Al Braveheart, he was going to have a serious talk with Annie. *I'll know if she's lying . . . I think.*

But he really was no longer sure of anything.

12.

Braveheart's office was large but did not appear that way since stacks of books, loose papers, and bound documents were strewn across every available flat surface, from the desk and tables to the floor where some grew knee high. He'd been known to threaten more than one House clerk with a Lakota curse for disturbing his "filing system."

A thickset man of medium height, Al wore his salt-and-pepper hair in a pair of braids that reached just past his shoulders. "A damned pain in the ass but the voters back home like it," he'd once confided to Manchester. In recent years the Native American voting bloc had grown dramatically, due in no small part to the registration drives on reservations sponsored by Braveheart.

He was hunched over a report, drinking a vile herbal concoction his mother brewed in South Dakota and shipped to him in pouches. Adam had tasted it once, a mistake he'd never repeat. When he tapped on the open door, the old man muttered, "Put the files on that stack left of the door, Hal, then back quietly out."

"How the hell do you keep clerks, the way you treat them?" Manchester asked.

"Adam, you young bull, how the hell are you!" Braveheart's face split into a wide grin as he shoved back his chair, an old-fashioned six-wheel monstrosity he refused to have replaced, and walked around the desk to shake hands.

"Not so young. Tough as old leather just like you," the senator replied. "But right now I'm feeling like a freshmen rep sitting in on his first presidential briefing."

Braveheart studied Manchester with shrewd black eyes as they sat down. He'd been careful to close the door before returning to his desk. "I figured this must be serious when I found out you and Wade had a little White House tea party over the weekend."

"I should've known you'd get wind of that. We have a nuclear threat inside the country." He knew Braveheart had his offices and home swept for bugs so often that no one inside or outside the government bothered planting any. Adam spelled out what they had learned about the two nukes and all those who might be involved, then sat back, rubbing his eyes, still dazed by the horrific potential.

"I know where those bombs came from." He smiled thinly when Manchester's head jerked up. "See, Karl Banecek arranged a black-op back when he was CIA director. Worried about stray Russian nukes being sold on the black market. He had intel on a base a little over two hundred kilometers outside Moscow, Arzamov-16, where some ex-KGB types were supposed to be brokering a deal with Iran. Sent in a team to bust up the party. His hand-picked leader was a spook who'd survived half a dozen administrations. Guy dropped off the screen shortly after the mission when the joint House and Senate Intel Committee called Karl on the carpet. Last I heard, the nukes were stored at Little Lennie in southeast Missouri. Now I know different."

"We need anything you can find out about where this rogue CIA agent is now and who he's working for since he left the Company."

"I'll get on it. Still have one source inside who's always been reliable—or as reliable as those ghouls can be. Can't say I'm surprised about the Rabbit."

Manchester's jaw dropped. "You're the only one in Washington who's not. What do you know about him?"

"Nothing I could prove. Rumors from way back when Lem Fredericks was governor of South Dakota. He always said Labat was in bed with the Vegas crowd."

"You never blew the whistle? Demanded an investigation?"

Braveheart shrugged. "He may have been a son of a bitch but he was *our* son of a bitch, Adam. Besides, state politics were out of my bailiwick. I did warn Samson when he nominated the jerk to be director of Homeland Security." He snorted. "Hell of a lot of good that did. Samson wouldn't budge. Neither would our colleagues in the Senate. Sometimes I think you had the right idea when you chucked this whole thing. Maybe you should've stayed in Maine. Gone fishing."

"Instead of 'kicking at cow chips on hot days'?" Manchester asked, using one of Al's favorite expressions. "Yes, my friend, right now a boat off Machias Bay sounds damn good," Manchester said wearily.

1:35 P.M. CST, TUESDAY, NOVEMBER 11
ST. LOUIS, MO

Ahamet bin Bergi stood at the base of the long flight of steps sweeping upward to the towering stainless-steel arch that gleamed in the cold autumn sunlight. The wind off the Mississippi whipped his neck scarf around his face. He stuffed it back inside his jacket, then raised the camera, clicking off a few casual pix just as any tourist would. The Gateway Arch had become the most recognized monument in the world, surpassing even the Eiffel Tower. Nearly two hundred meters high . . . and right in the heart of the Great Satan. The United States.

The St. Louis cell had been chosen to use one of the bombs. Bombs American infidels had stolen from Russian infidels. How brilliant the plan. He smiled coldly. The other device he would personally place and detonate, dealing the final, crippling blow to America. The damage—financial psychological, and physical—would be incalculable.

His link vibrated. Sliding the camera inside his jacket, he took it out and answered, listening for a moment. "I must speak with him. Sooner." His voice was curt and imperious. He had found it to be most effective in dealing with Americans. "Good." He gave the address on South Grand Avenue where members of the local cell rented a modest apartment in a neighborhood filled with immigrants from around the globe. "I will expect him. Be certain he is not followed."

After hanging up, bin Bergi climbed the stairs briskly, then walked across the park to the reflecting pool near the north leg of the Arch. He strolled casually around, taking pix of the grounds, then descended the slope to the facilities beneath. All the while his mind worked furiously. After he met with the American traitor he would instruct the cell members to move to another location. When dealing with vipers it was wise to take no chances. He had arranged his ride to St. Louis via private jet. No one would know he had been here or where he would be tomorrow.

When the infidel handed over the weapons, he would expect the agreed upon price. A hundred million dollars was a great deal of money, but bin Bergi had paid sums of such magnitude before. To bring the United States to its knees would be worth every cent . . . but he did not intend to pay it. He smiled coldly. Betrayers should beware of betrayal.

3:25 P.M. EST, TUESDAY, NOVEMBER 11
SILVER SPRINGS, MARYLAND

The neighborhood was typical of suburban America's retreat from the violence and drugs inside its cities. Anne Scarletti lived in a gated community of condos and single-unit dwellings, blended carefully into manicured landscaping on a hilly patch of ground that had been heavily forested only a decade ago. Adam positively hated bringing Secret Service personnel but there was no way to avoid it. Somehow it seemed an intrusion into her privacy after she'd graciously invited him into her home when he called.

He felt traitorous enough considering what he intended to ask her. Had to ask her. Her place was part of a cluster of adjoining condos intended for one-person occupancy, each compact but elegant. It fit her. Walking up the curving pavement past winter-brown grass and glossy evergreens, he touched the chime. Almost instantly the door opened and a beaming Anne ushered him inside.

"Special bodyguards," she said, glancing at the two men sitting in the TE parked out front. "My, but the powers that be must be very certain you'll be elected." That same old smile he remembered from their youth lit her face. She was a lifelong liberal and he was a staunch conservative. Anne had always teased him about politics.

If only this were a teasing matter. "I have no idea if I can beat Wade Samson, but the GOP seems to think so." He followed her inside past a comfortable sitting room decorated in soft blues and greens, down the short hallway to a sunny kitchen where a sturdy oak table and two chairs sat in a bay window. Yellow place mats were set with cups and small plates. A fresh pastry wafted its welcome aroma around the room. Annie had always been a sensational cook and baking was her specialty.

But the rich smell of freshly brewed coffee and strudel only made his gut clench the more. This was not going to be easy. They took their seats and she poured coffee into his cup. "Black with one sugar, right?" she asked.

He held his hand over the cup when she offered the sugar bowl. "Now just plain black. I quit sugar."

"White sugar kills," she said with a chuckle. "Wasn't there some health guru movie star back in the last century who used to say that?" Observing him take a hearty gulp of coffee and show no interest in the strudel, she asked, "This isn't a social call, is it, Adam? Something's bothering you."

He studied her beautiful gold eyes. "You always could read my moods. But, no, this isn't social, much as I'd like for it to be. Seeing you at John's on Sunday brought back wonderful memories." He felt guilty as sin when she beamed at him.

"When I overheard John inviting you to join us for dinner, I'll confess I was hoping you'd say yes." Her expression changed as she sipped from her coffee, studying him over the rim of the cup. "What's this all about, Adam?"

He set his cup down with a clatter and ran his fingers through his hair. "There's no easy way to say this, Annie. . . ."

"Then just say it, Adam," she replied softly.

"I'm involved in a national security matter—Samson brought me in. I won't go into his motives for that, but while I've been investigating some issues, your husband's name came up."

Her breath caught softly. "Frank? But why? How? He never held any government office."

"Were you aware of his gambling habit?" he asked bluntly.

She flinched, then let out a long sigh. "Of course. Did you know he supplemented his scholarships—which were never enough for him to live on—by playing cards with the wealthier students at Yale? They could afford to lose." Her tone was hard now.

"But he couldn't. I take it he mostly won?"

"He stayed to graduate at the top of his class," she said with pride. Then she stirred the cream in her coffee for a moment, gathering her thoughts. "When we were first married, he was very careful about finances, seeing that the children and I had what we needed. But after he started to make a great deal of money, it was as though something inside him was . . . free.

"He truly loved cards, horse races . . . I suppose I always knew it was a form of addiction, but he never lost more than we could afford. He left me very comfortable and saw to it that all his children had the best educations. Adam, what has Frank's gambling to do with national security?" she asked, biting her lip, studying him closely.

"Probably nothing. Have you ever heard or did he ever mention a man named Richie Viviano?"

She thought a moment. "Not that I can recall. He had so many clients over the years and I'll admit some of them weren't the best in terms of morality, but what's so important about this Viviano?"

"He's part of the East Coast's gambling syndicate. Frank's name came up as a significant loser at his casinos."

If he'd struck her, she could not have looked more hurt as she started to digest the full implications.

"I see. And since Frank's dead, you're wondering if his son shares his father's addiction, isn't that right, Adam? Are you and the president investigating John?"

"No. The crisis has nothing directly to do with the AG. But his father's name came up along with several Pentagon officers who're involved—all of them spent huge sums of money with Viviano. We know one was being blackmailed—"

"John detests gambling," she said abruptly, cutting him off. "In fact, when he found out how much his father spent that way, he tried to intervene. It didn't work, but my son has never bet a penny on anything in his life. And there is absolutely nothing in John's life anyone could use to blackmail him."

The senator could see how badly she was hurt, not just for her son, but for what Adam had come into her home and dared to ask. He stood up, swallowing hard at the sudden lump in his throat. She looked so small and vulnerable sitting there. "I believe you, Annie. Please accept my deepest apologies. John and I are working closely on this matter. I would appreciate it if you didn't say anything to him about this conversation . . . but then that's up to you."

Her lips thinned bitterly. "He genuinely admires you. I should hate to disillusion John, so no, I will not mention your implications."

After he let himself out of the condo, Anne remained seated at the table, staring at the untouched strudel. Finally she got up, took it over to the sink, and shoved it down the garbage disposal.

3:29 P.M. EST, TUESDAY, NOVEMBER 11
BOGOTÁ, COLOMBIA

Eldorado International Airport was packed with people speaking a babble of languages. Although Spanish predominated, the wide accents of Australian English blended with the guttural growl of German and the musical purr of French. Asian dialects too numerous to count outnumbered the rest. The newly constructed facility was made of gleaming steel and smoky glass, a paean to the most expensive modern architectural design. A sprawling, high-tech, and showy airport was good for the Cartel's business image.

Over the past decade Bogotá had eclipsed Buenos Aires and Rio as the premier city in South America. The wealth of the Cartel poured into Colombia and Benito Zuloaga saw to it that a generous portion was devoted to civic improvements, in his home city of Cali as well as Medellín, Cartagena, and the seat of the puppet government through which he operated, the nation's capital.

Del and Leah walked down the wide concourse headed toward the public transit station. They both traveled light with one small carry-on apiece. There'd been no time for packing more even if either had the inclination. As far as Leah was concerned an overnight in the Cartel's nerve center did not merit dress clothes. Her hard-soled boots clicked on the creamy marble floors. With the practiced eye of a trained agent, she eyed the mass of humanity pouring by her. No one seemed particularly interested in them.

"Damn long flights," Del groused, also on guard, feeling vulnerable without his Smith & Wesson.

"We lucked out on that early connection from Havana. We're here an hour ahead of schedule. Don't bitch."

Since neither Mexico nor the U.S. had diplomatic relations with Colombia, they'd been forced to travel via Cuba, adding hours onto the flight from Mazatlán. As American citizens, they'd been given intense scrutiny and had their persons as well as their bags thoroughly scanned before boarding the Aereo Colombia plane. Once deplaned, they'd had to go through another inspection. The officers were amazingly efficient, using newer and more complex screening devices than any airport in North America possessed.

"We could use the extra time for sightseeing. I hear the city's had quite a facelift in the last few years. Low crime rate, too."

"And they just love Yankees. Right, Del. Benny's granting us an audience at seven sharp. We don't dare be late for dinner."

"Pity I didn't have time to pack my tux. He's supposed to be a stickler for protocol."

"What you see is what he gets," she said, striding along in a pair of crisp polymere slacks and a soft sea-green sweater.

He gave her a quick appraisal. "Lucky fellow."

She ignored his compliment. They rounded a curve on the concourse and she spotted the signs ringing the huge geodesic dome of the main terminal. "There's ground transpo."

They headed toward the pix of a big red accordion bus, a Transmilenio made by Volvo. The city owned a huge fleet of them, shuttling people the fifteen kilometers from El Dorado IA southwest into the heart of the city. The goliaths held up to 160 passengers but could thread their way through the narrow streets of the historic central district where the seat of government was located.

They'd booked reservations at a modest hotel near the edge of La Candelaria. Zuloaga's palatial mansion was to the north of there. The plan was to check in and wait until he contacted them. No one entered or left the capital without his knowledge.

About halfway across the terminal they spotted two men, dressed in khaki, carrying the "Micro" version of Israel's TAR-22. The compact weapon was the Cadillac of small submachine guns, standard issue for every Colombian paramilitary. One of the men spoke into a link, nodded, and closed it up, then approached them with a welcoming smile.

Del could sense Leah go on alert. His old knee injury started to throb, too. Not a good sign. "Beware of Colombian military police baring teeth," he muttered beneath his breath.

"Good day, Mr. Delgado, Ms. Berglund. I am Colonel Liam Santander. Welcome to Colombia. Mr. Zuloaga sends his compliments," he said in fluent English with only the faintest hint of an accent.

"We weren't expecting a ride," Leah said guardedly.

"But once he found out your flight plans, Mr. Zuloaga made arrangements. We would not want important guests riding on public transit, no matter if it is the finest in the world." His face was Indio, swarthy and flat with slightly crooked white teeth that gleamed when he smiled.

Del nodded and said, "We're staying at—"

"A thousand pardons, but the reservations in La Candelaria have been canceled. You are to be Mr. Zuloaga's guests for the duration of your visit. I can assure you his accommodations will far surpass those of a five-star hotel."

"I don't think the rooms we reserved even rated three," Del said. He and Leah exchanged glances. Benny wanted to keep his eye on them. That could work both ways.

"We look forward to Mr. Zuloaga's hospitality," she replied as the colonel extended his hand with Latino chivalry to take her bag.

They followed him from the terminal through a wide set of crystalplex doors. A vintage 1965 Rolls-Royce Silver Cloud III in pristine condition waited. The flashy car sat in a zone that was strictly designated no parking. A tall, slender man in an Anderson & Sheppard suit climbed out of the front passenger seat and bowed smartly. His face was narrow and finely chiseled with striking blue eyes. He sported a three-hundred-dollar haircut and the officious smile of a bureaucrat.

"I am Mr. Zuloaga's personal secretary, Doroteo Suma. If you please?" he asked, indicating they should climb inside as he opened the right rear passenger door for Leah while a second man, the driver, stood with the other rear door open for Del.

In spite of their expensive tailors, both the suit and the uniform revealed concealed firearms to their trained eyes. "So much for Bogotá being safe for *turistas*," Del murmured to Leah. She was eyeing the two stubby Micro TAR-22s in a custom-designed rack attached to the front passenger door.

"Benny's prepared for trouble. Noriega?"

They sank into butter-soft gray leather while the driver placed their bags in the trunk. "Probably," he agreed, then fell silent as the black-clad driver slid behind the wheel. Colonel Santander saluted Zuloaga's secretary smartly before returning to the terminal. Mr. Suma took his seat and the driver pulled away from the curb, weaving expertly into the mix of buses, cabs, and private cars.

"Once Bogotá was a city of mules and Maseratis, mud bricks and mansions, but no more," Suma said proudly. "Now we are a model metropolis of beautifully restored historic buildings and modern architectural wonders."

Thanks to billions in drug money. Leah sat rigidly, observing the deep green vegetation along the wide ribbons of new superhighway, saying nothing as Del made small talk with Zuloaga's honcho in a polyglot of Spanish and English. Doroteo had been delighted to learn Delgado had grown up bilingual.

She tuned them out and concentrated on what she knew about Bogotá. It was situated on a mountain plateau at more than twenty-six hundred meters elevation, with steep cliffs rising to the east. She had observed a stunningly beautiful country from the air. On the ground Colombia's natural beauty was even more impressive.

If only all the newly improved living conditions had not been bought with blood. She refused to think of Kevin, dead at nineteen of an Elevator OD. And now they were going to partake of his killer's hospitality. Who was it that had said, "Use a long spoon when dining with the devil"?

Her reverie ended abruptly when the driver said something in rapid Spanish. She recognized agitation even if she didn't catch all the words. Something about being followed. Like Del and Suma, she looked behind them. A black Jaguar was closing fast. Trouble. She wished desperately for her Ruger as Suma unfastened a TAR from the door and opened the window.

"I would advise you to crouch on the floor," he said to his passengers. Just then a second car, a blue Bentley Amage T, came flying down from an overpass and pulled directly in front of them in an attempt to cut them off. Their driver swerved into the next lane and accelerated ahead of the Bentley. Suma fired at it, transforming the windshield into an opaque mosaic of webbed glass.

The Bentley careened wildly out of control, its driver either dead, injured, or simply unable to see. It flew over the berm and vanished into a ditch as they sped away. But the black Jag remained on their tail, gaining ground. Both cars wove in and out of traffic, cutting off other vehicles. Blaring horns and bellowed curses blended with the high-speed hum of traffic. Suma leaned outside just enough to line up his weapon for a shot at their pursuer.

Del and Leah crouched down but kept tabs on the action as Zuloaga's "secretary" fired off several rounds, hitting the Jag's hood, which was apparently reinforced steel that took the shots with no damage besides a ruined paint job. "Bulletproofed," Del heard him mutter, aiming for the tires. If the grille and hood were bulletproof, he must have reasoned that the windshield would be also.

Just as he pulled the trigger the Rolls lurched sharply to avoid another car attempting to cut them off. Then all hell broke loose. Suma's shot went wild, hitting a Maserati not in the contest. It crashed into one of the Transmilenios, creating a horrifying tangle of twisted metal and screaming people as other cars and buses were unable to avoid the wreck.

Another of the Bentleys came streaking down an entry ramp and pulled alongside them. Suma swung his submachine gun and fired at the driver's window. It cracked just as the first Bentley's windshield had but the driver must not have been hit as he pulled ahead of them, attempting to cut them off.

The sound of helicopter blades overhead drowned out the frantically hissed exchange between the driver and Suma. The driver changed lanes twice, executing the dangerous maneuver one-handed while he fired his Beretta at the first Jag which had now pulled abreast of him on the left. The passenger window held. Suma leaned out and fired up at the copter, yelling for his companion to do the same.

Leah leaned over to Del and whispered, "Have you noticed nobody's returning fire?"

"Yeah, like they don't want to risk hitting us. But it sure isn't keeping these clowns from blazing away. Kinda makes you wonder who the 'good guys' are, doesn't it?"

"I think we got suckered by Noriega's men."

"I think you're right," he whispered just as she slammed against his chest when the car swerved sharply. "What are we going to do about it?"

3:04 P.M. CST, TUESDAY, NOVEMBER 11
ST. LOUIS, MISSOURI

"I have him on visual now," the agent said. "He's entering the building." He repeated the address, then sent the vid on his specially equipped porta-link. This was the latest in FBI technology, but from across the wide boulevard at over fifty meters, he knew the pix could not give them much. "Do you want inside surveil?"

On the other end of the transmission, Paul Oppermann said, "You have Padorski in position?"

"Yes, sir. Back entry."

"Do it. Very careful."

Special Agent in Charge Donnell Washington's face glowed with perspiration in spite of the cold autumn day. This was the biggest case in which he'd ever been involved—following the secretary of Homeland Security since his landing at a small private airstrip in Jefferson County. Apparently Bureau honchos in D.C. had been surveilling Robert Labat for an unknown length of time. For an unknown reason.

This was a career-making assignment. Washington and a hand-picked cadre of agents from his St. Louis office had located the wrecked automobile of some army colonel who'd been roadkill on a rural high-way last summer. Big hush-hush deal when the totaled car was taken away for inspection a few days ago. He'd heard no more until an hour ago when he rushed to assemble his team at the airstrip.

"We can't see *bobkes* on this pix," the director's aggravated voice said.

"I can have my man move in with the vid shot after Padorski's in place. Too far away from here for any better resolution," Washington said.

There was a pause on the other end of the link. "As soon as you have the building surrounded, haul your *tokhes* up there and get what you can. Just be sure Labat doesn't make you."

As the black SAC in the rusted-out Ford TE spoke with the director, someone else monitored their conversation from far away with equipment that made the government-issued junk obsolete. He smiled to himself. A damned good thing his erstwhile employer carried the homing dot. Time would come soon when that dot would bring him down. But not until he'd done what he was supposed to do.

He made a voice-only transmission to his own field agents. Former BISC, they were good as gold. Beat the piss out of any FBI hot-shots. He leaned back and smiled, then lit up a smoke.

Inside the old brick flat, a furnace somewhere belched out excess heat, making sweat bead his forehead, but he didn't intend to be here long enough to shed his cashmere topcoat. "This place stinks like 'Rabs," he whispered to his bodyguard, who only grunted his agree-ment, watching every door along the hallway as they neared the second-story room at the rear of the dump. Down the corridor a baby cried. A man's and a woman's voice rose, arguing in some for-eign language.

The guard slipped an extended clip into his fully automatic Glock 18C, then knocked on the appointed door. After a cursory inspection through a peephole, it creaked open, letting out more heat and the smell of garlic. A pot of chickpeas boiled unattended on the stove in the small kitchen. The lone woman in the room, covered head to toe in black, diapered a baby on a ratty old divan. She did not look up, but when one of the four men gave her a sharp command in Arabic, she quickly finished her task and headed into the kitchen, child on her hip.

Ahamet bin Bergi looked at the tall American infidel with utter contempt, reserving his haughtiest warrior's sneer for the bodyguard and his machine pistol. "I have heard some very distressing rumors, Mr. Secretary, rumors I hope you can dispel immediately. . . ."

Before the secretary could reply, his guard received a transmission from his partner standing watch at the rear of the building. "This looks like a setup, sir! We gotta get out of here—now!"

"Do you have the bombs or not?" bin Bergi asked stubbornly, ignoring the outburst from the guard. He always had his escape route planned before he ever entered a building.

"I'll deliver them as promised," the secretary replied, already backpedaling out of the apartment.

His guard led the way down the hall to a rickety door marked STORAGE in faded letters. "Good thing I cased this joint earlier," he muttered, opening the door and shoving the secretary inside. The musty room was filled with beat-up furniture, piled haphazardly in every available space. The aide climbed over it, reaching a filthy window with fresh marks from when he had jimmied it open earlier. It protested but raised. He threw a rope secured to a massive monstrosity of a sofa out the window. "Nobody'll be watching this side of the building." *I hope.*

"You expect me to climb down a goddamned rope! I'll break my neck."

"You wanna stick around and explain to the FBI what you're doing with a group of Holy Arabian terrorists?" the guard dared to ask. Damned if *he* wanted to.

The secretary put one leg over the sill and took hold of the slender nylon cording, looking uneasily at the ground below.

"Just let your gloved hands slide along it," the aide coaxed. "I got a second car waiting behind the shed."

"What the hell do you mean, he got away!" Paul Oppermann yelled on the vid screen.

SAC Washington winced. "We've torn the place apart, sir. Padowski and his men came up the back stairs, we came in the front. Had the fire escape covered, too, even though it was too rusty to blast loose with a cannon. He just isn't there. We know there were at least four terrorists besides bin Bergi in the unit. We got two of them and a woman with a baby trying to slip out an ancient coal chute. The building's been sealed off and we're continuing the door to door, but after finding that cord out of the second-story window, I doubt we'll find Labat."

"What about that tracer dot on him?"

"He ditched it. One of my men found it a few meters away from that cord."

Oppermann swore in Yiddish and rubbed his head. "We should've had the *mamzer* dead to rights. Who the fuck is he, Harry Houdini?"

"No, sir, Bob Labat's not Jewish," the SAC replied, deadpan. He was fucked anyway. What the hell.

13.

The deafening whir of copter blades and crack of gunfire almost drowned out Leah's words. Leaning close to Del, she said, "I'll take the gunman." She quickly slid the slim belt from her slacks and slipped it to him.

Crouching with his bad knee thrumming in pain, he prepared to swing the belt over the driver's head. Luckily for them, the two men in the front seat paid no attention to their passengers. If a hostage negotiation began, Delgado knew that would instantly change. Right now their kidnappers were occupied firing at the Black Hawk copter flying low in front of the Rolls-Royce.

Then the Jag slammed into their front fender and the Rolls shuddered and veered into the right lane, nearly smashing a small Volkswagen as it was merging from an entry ramp. Its driver swerved and hit the berm. Leah made her move. Legs like steel springs lifted her up and over the seat. Her arms came down, seizing Doroteo Suma's throat in a viselike grip with one hand. Her other hand pressed against his temple. She broke his neck with one powerful twist, putting the full weight of her body into it.

The sound of vertebrae snapping was drowned out by the chopper but the driver caught the sudden motion in peripheral. Still holding on to the wheel he tried to aim at her but Delgado had the belt around his throat before he could raise the weapon. Leaning around the headrest, he growled, "Be a good boy and pull over before you black out and kill us all. Life is sweet." To emphasize the point, he tightened the belt. The driver had one hand on the wheel while the other still clutched his Beretta.

Leah had moved out of his limited range of vision. He gave in to the inevitable and eased off the gas. The copter overhead had pretty well cleared away the traffic on the busy highway by this time. Cars were exiting or pulling onto the berm, some even driving into ditches to escape the mayhem. The aircraft set down in front of them as the Rolls stopped in the far right lane.

Delgado kept his stranglehold on the man's throat while Leah ripped the gun from his hand. By this time his face was approaching the shade of the roof tiles on the houses scattered along the hillside. In spite of the attempted kidnapping, they were definitely in a high rent district. He watched as she concealed the Beretta inside her bulky green sweater.

"Think they'll search us like Inocensio's boys did?" she asked.

"At this point, I doubt one handgun will do much good," he said, watching as a squad of heavily armed men in khaki swarmed out of the copter and several of the cars that had been pursuing them. They were dressed exactly like Liam Santander. "We may be out of the frying pan into the fire."

"I don't think so," she replied. "If Benny wanted us dead, why go to so much trouble to rescue us? All he had to do was let the Hellfire missiles on that Black Hawk open up and we'd be toast."

She had a point. Still, it never hurt to be prepared if they had to defend themselves again. They were in Cartel headquarters, after all. "Slip me Doroteo's piece, will you?" he asked. She slid her left hand between the seats to where Suma's sidearm was holstered inside his impeccably tailored jacket, pulled the gun out, and dropped it into Delgado's jacket pocket.

The man who appeared to be in charge drew near with a worried look on his face. Del greeted him in Spanish, still not relinquishing his chokehold on the driver's neck. "We appreciate your help, Major."

The officer leaned inside the front door that one of his men had opened. He looked at the dead man slumped in the passenger seat and the red-faced driver. "It would appear, Señor Delgado, Señorita

Berglund, that you did not require much assistance," he replied dryly in slightly accented English. "Please allow me to apologize for this mistake. Señor Zuloaga sends his sincerest regrets. We did not expect your flight to arrive for another hour."

"We caught an earlier hop from Havana," Del explained as he released the driver, who doubled over coughing and spit up a basket of "oysters."

The major nodded, unable to keep his eyes from flitting swiftly back and forth from Leah to Suma's grotesquely twisted neck. "My men will take care of these vermin."

He motioned for one of the officers standing behind him to take charge of the driver and the dead man. Two soldiers pried open the badly dented back passenger doors so Del and Leah could get out. If anyone noted that the kidnappers' handguns were missing, no one made a comment. The soldiers dragged the driver away and carted off Suma's body.

Zuloaga's Yankee guests were escorted to the Black Hawk. After taking their seats inside, the major smiled and asked, "Would you please be so kind as to turn over the handguns you so cleverly liberated in the car? Señor Zuloaga has strict security procedures at his home. He would be most embarrassed, as would I, if you were to set off his weapons detection system."

"We aren't here to assassinate Señor Zuloaga, but after what just happened, you can see why we took precautions," Leah said calmly as she handed over the Beretta. Glumly, Delgado did the same.

The major smiled genially, then gave a signal and the copter lifted off the highway.

Bogotá was a city of contrasts, Leah thought as the copter approached the helipad carved into the steep side of the mountain. Benito Zuloaga had a splendid view from the heights. Cartel money had refurbished the nation's capital until it lived up to its name as the Paris of Latin America. Magnificent mansions whose architecture reflected every style from Moorish to Bauhaus sat on broad tree-lined boulevards. The central district's public buildings were almost medieval in austere grandeur, given the new polish afforded by unlimited restoration funding. But the northernmost section was all glass and steel, glittery as the skyline of Tokyo.

And even more soulless. Leah studied Benito Zuloaga's compound. It sprawled over the verdant evergreen covering like a ten-carat diamond set on a field of emeralds. Floor-to-ceiling windows arched skyward, jutting out from the hillside. She speculated about the steel reinforcing the frame and the thickness of the glass. "I bet that sucker could survive a direct nuclear hit," she muttered to Del over the noise of the copter.

"Even if it couldn't, I doubt Benny'd be aboveground if he had any warning. I bet that palace is cut at least a kilometer deep in the side of the mountain," he replied.

"With an express elevator—this one going down, not up," she said as the copter landed smoothly. Two guards ducked under the draft of the blades to pull open the door. She had to arch her neck to see the top peak of what looked like a cedar shake roof above the glass, although she was certain it was a very excellent steel facsimile. "One-way glass."

"Probably half a meter thick, nondistort-plex. Security with a view," Delgado replied dryly as they were escorted toward a low spiral of artfully hewn granite stairs leading past elaborate Japanese gardens to where the house sat regally above them.

A pair of wide glass doors glided soundlessly open as they approached the lower level and a slightly built man with light brown hair and eyes the color of a winter sky emerged flanked by two burly men in paramilitary uniforms that bore an eerie similarity to those worn by Hitler's SS. Their very non-Aryan Indio faces were neutral yet watchful. With an almost imperceptible nod of dismissal, Zuloaga strode ahead of them, extending his hand to his guests.

He wore custom tailoring well, Leah thought bitterly. Even though she did not recognize Gieves & Hawkes of London, she knew high-end clothes when she saw them. His three-hundred-bucks-a-pop stylist made the most of his fine thinning hair. He shook her hand gravely. His accent almost startled her until she remembered that he'd been educated in England. It was pure upper-class Brit.

"Please accept my sincerest apologies for that most regrettable incident at the airport, Ms. Berglund. My security people were told to verify your flight arrival but someone was derelict in his duty."

She could well imagine what that "poor sod's" fate had been.

"I assure you, no further disturbances will mar your visit to Colombia," he said as he and Del exchanged handshakes.

"Our flight schedule changed suddenly in Havana. Threw off the arrival time," Del explained. "Was our welcoming committee from Fuljensio Noriega?"

"Possibly," Zuloaga replied, dismissing the topic as he led them toward the glass palace.

The doors opened as they approached, revealing the soaring ceiling a dozen meters above them and open space sufficient to house several small aircraft. Floors gleamed with the gold patina of polished hard maple, strewn with brilliant blue and amber area rugs. Two impossibly long Dansk sofas made of buttery soft natural leather stood like parentheses around an immense low glass table, its geometric design at various odd angles. The surface was set with an array of finger foods—water crackers, fresh fruit, imported cheeses, Beluga caviar, and other rare morsels.

Both rear walls in the diamond-shaped room were constructed of thin stacked stones, from palest gray deepening to blue where a waterfall splashed down, forming a boomerang-shaped pool that curved around the back of the room. Electric-bright tropical fish flitted in its depths. Potted ferns and marble urns filled with exotic flowers softened the ultra-modern harshness of the décor.

Zuloaga approached the onyx bar at one side of the room to play host. "May I offer you a drink?" It was clear from the selections of top shelf liquor, malt beverages, and wines on the shelves behind the counter that the bartender in the tux could fill any request.

Delgado shrugged and said, "Cervesa. Pacifico."

"Ah, yes, manufactured in your uncle's city, I believe." He turned to Leah. "And for the lady? I have an exceptional bottle of champagne. Krug, 1988."

"Just mineral water, please," she replied.

"Still abstemious. A holdover from your days with BISC, I assume,"

Zuloaga said with a slight smile. He turned to the bartender. "Open the Krug for me after you've seen to my guests, Mateo."

"Now that you've made it clear you did your homework on us, can we talk, Mr. Zuloaga?" she asked as he handed her the glass of bubbling water.

"In due course, Ms. Berglund," he replied, gesturing for them to be seated on the sofas after Del took a frosted mug of foamy beer from Mateo. Benito joined them with a Waterford flute of champagne in one well-manicured hand, lounging casually as he took a sip. "A fine vintage. Pity you haven't the taste for it." He raised the glass. *"Salud."*

Delgado returned the gesture. Leah hesitated for an instant before joining him. This urbane pseudo-Englishman was responsible for the death of her brother and uncounted others dead by drug OD or assassination.

Sensing her feelings—or because he knew her family background—he remarked, "Let me begin by saying that I regret the policies of my predecessors. The Slaughter was not my idea, nor did I have any part in implementing it. A senseless waste of life that only brought further reprisals from your government."

"You seized control of the competing cartels a year earlier," she said.

"Not entirely. I had several competitors to deal with, both here and abroad. At the time the unfortunate decision was made to attack your federal judiciary and drug enforcement agencies, I was in Geneva. The attack was . . . ill advised. If I had the reins of power fully in my hands at that time, I assure you, I would never have permitted it. Quite frankly, it was—"

"Bad for business?" Delgado suggested blandly.

"Quite so. Do try the Stilton," he urged, slicing off a chunk of veined white cheese and placing it on a cracker. "More hearty than the Roquefort. In many ways, the English are a superior race. Terribly civilized. That's why my father sent me there for my education. My son is at Eton. In fact, my wife is visiting him now, else she'd be joining us for dinner this evening. She's English, as I am certain you already know."

"An illustrious lady from a distinguished family," Leah said with a smile.

Butter wouldn't melt in her mouth. Delgado took a long swallow of beer and tried a chunk of the Stilton, playing the genial guest while he made a subtle inventory of the facilities. Two doors at opposite corners, an elevator at the intersection of the stone walls at the back of the room. *Benny's escape hatch.* The Stilton was damn good cheese but he still preferred Roquefort.

"With all due respect for your hospitality, we didn't come for a social call, Mr. Zuloaga," Leah said.

"You came to inquire what I know about two missing nuclear devices, which your government originally stole from a Russian lab several years ago." He smiled revealing teeth that had provided some orthodontist a lavish retirement.

Leah put down the water glass. "A reliable source of mine indicated you may have purchased them."

"Ah, I wish that were true, but I did not. I only know who stole them." He paused a beat. "Inocensio Ramirez. As you know, I'm certain, he was the original thief."

"He wanted insurance against the little 'unrest' going on down here," Del said, studying Benito over the rim of his beer mug as he sipped. "Noriega's getting pretty bold," he fished.

"Noriega has nothing to do with the situation in your country," Zuloaga said, dismissing the subject. His internal problems were obviously not on the table. "I did hear rumors several weeks ago about an auction of the weapons. Dirty bombs, I believe you call them." He grimaced in distaste and took another sip of champagne as if to cleanse his palate.

"Who was selling?" Leah asked.

"In matters of such international delicacy, one does not inquire. One only asks the cost and to inspect the merchandise, of course."

"Of course," she echoed, waiting like a chess player for him to continue.

He daubed at his mouth with one of the small linen cocktail napkins from the table. The delicate gesture was at sharp odds with the wintry gray of his eyes. "I would have bought them—but not because I require such crude devices."

"You have your own nuclear arsenal, one of infinitely higher quality," Del said. "But one you'd never use in a first strike capacity, *es verdad?*"

"*Es verdad*," Zuloaga agreed.

"If that's true, then why would you consider buying the dirty bombs?" she asked.

His smile was warm but his eyes remained winter ice as he replied, "Why, for the goodwill of your president, what other reason? I would have returned them as a gift."

"A very expensive gift," Delgado said.

Leah leaned forward. "Why weren't you able to buy them?" Money sure as hell couldn't be a problem.

"A preemptive offer ended the auction before I could act. Holy Arabia made it, according to my sources."

Leah set her glass down with a slight clink against the crystal surface of the table. Delgado could hear her mentally cursing. He wasn't too happy having their worst fears confirmed himself. "We know Bernal double-crossed Ramirez and whoever he smuggled the nukes into the U.S. for. Our people will track down Bernal." *We hope.* "But if you really want to win our president's goodwill, find the identity of the American buyers."

"I see I am not the only one with . . . internal difficulties." He nodded with a grim smile as he signaled Mateo by holding up the empty flute. Mateo instantly materialized to refill it. "Whoever this person is, he must be highly placed in your government."

"We know that much." The bartender poured more sparkling water into Leah's glass and silently offered Del another beer. "*No, gracias,*" he said, draining the mug.

"You must be tired after such a long and . . . eventful journey. I'll have my servants show you to your quarters so you may rest and refresh yourselves. Dinner is at eight. I trust that will be a suitable hour? Latinos prefer eating barbarically late, but Edyth has convinced me it's better for digestion to dine early."

He barely nodded to Mateo and almost instantly the elevator doors opened. Two uniformed maids smiled shyly. As she and Del walked to the elevator, Leah wondered how often the help here got to fete FBI agents . . . or CIA operatives.

They were whisked up several floors and the door at the opposite side of the elevator opened onto a wide corridor lined with doors. The top level of the house was set back behind the great room's soaring peak. They were ushered into a suite with two bedrooms off a spacious sitting room. Del walked over to the huge window after one maid drew open the drapes, revealing a stunning view of the city below. Bogotá winked to life with a million brilliant lights as darkness fell.

An enormous spray of flowers so rare Leah couldn't identify half the colorful blooms sat in a cut-glass vase on a teak table in the center of the room. Brocade sofas done in soft mauve lined the walls and her shoes sank into pure white Karastan carpeting. A fully stocked bar was placed on the wall by the outside door.

"Some hospitality, and on such short notice," she said, walking to the window to inspect the view.

He glanced back at the suite. "Yeah. Kinda makes you wonder what he'd do if we were business associates or heads of state and he had time to plan the welcome."

"Yeah, I'd love to know where the smoking rooms are," she said.

"I doubt Benny's guards will let us explore much." He moved up behind her, felt her tense when he stood so close. "You're like a coiled spring," he murmured, massaging the tight muscles in her neck and shoulders.

It felt so damn good. She let herself relax, tipping her head back as his thumbs skillfully loosened her cervical vertebrae. Every bone in her body suddenly turned to mush. *My brain, too.* With a smothered oath she turned swiftly and pulled his body against hers, raising her parted lips to his.

Delgado felt the hunger burn in his gut. He knew she was acting out of pure instinct. They could've died in a car wreck shoot-out. Sex was life. But he knew she would regret it afterward. He should stop her but she was fragile as glass. Rejection would shatter her. Instead, he kissed her hard and deep.

They started tearing their clothes off in silence. This was not the time to talk of love or permanence, just to feel. She yanked her sweater over her head. His fingers, suddenly clumsy with the buttons, made him impatiently rip his shirt open and shed it. In less than a moment skin pressed to skin. Without a word, they moved toward the open door of the nearest bedroom, unable to keep their hands off each other.

The sheets still tangled around them, a silk comforter lay piled on the floor at the foot of the bed. Del cradled her head against his chest. Leah could feel the harsh pounding of his heart and knew her own hammered in her chest. She fought the urge to press her palm on his chest and snuggle close as they had done so often in the past after making love. Love.

I lived in a dream world and thought I could become someone I'm not.

When she'd first moved to California and taken the job with Clean Ride, it had been a huge leap of faith. Or perhaps more of desperation. She wanted to believe that she could live like any other normal person. Get married, maybe even have children with Delgado. Fit into his big, happy family.

She'd only been on the job a couple of weeks when the dream ended. She was caught in a cross fire between the LAPD and an El-Op gang while trying to get a thirteen-year-old girl away from her pimp. The child was prostituting herself to support her Elevator habit. Cassie was hit by a stray bullet. Leah watched her die on a stretcher while paramedics fought to save her. When they pulled the sheet over Cassie's face, Leah slipped into the alley behind the warehouses. The police and El-Ops continued their shoot-out but Tuttie Bazan, the pimp, had a hidey-hole that the girl had told Leah about.

She found him jamming cash and drugs into a bag. And she killed him with his own knife. The only witness was another of his "stable," a fifteen-year-old who sat impassively in a corner of the dump during their fight, so high on an Elevator ride that when her pimp's blood spattered over her, she didn't even notice. Leah took her to Clean Ride after getting them both a change of clothing.

The nightmares started that night. She would never be "normal," didn't even know what that was—or if she ever had, the time was too long past. Leah swallowed hard and rolled off him, swinging her legs off the bed, sitting with her back to him when she spoke.

"If you don't say you're sorry, I won't either, just as long as we agree this was a mistake."

"I'm not sorry and it wasn't a mistake, Leah. Just human. Natural." His voice was soft. He let her walk out of the room and collect her clothes. In moments, he heard the shower go on in the bath of the adjoining bedroom. He cursed and pounded the pillow, then forced himself to concentrate on the job they'd come here to do. After all, he knew that was what Leah was doing.

7:15 P.M. EST, TUESDAY, NOVEMBER 11
WASHINGTON, D.C.

Ralph Whitherspoon was a tall man with a faint white fringe of hair surrounding his bald head and a scholar's frown of concentration creasing his high forehead. He'd been a professor at the University of Washington, held the Gates Distinguished Studies in Political Science Chair before he entered government service. Academe had never looked so good as it did at the moment, facing Karl Banecek across the dimly lit table in a small Georgetown café.

"I want Sievers, Ralph." The secretary of defense's pale eyes bored into his former colleague's face.

"I can't reach him. I've tried every trick in the book, Karl." Whitherspoon ran his hand over his smooth scalp and massaged his aching neck. He shoved a glass of St. Emilion in tight circles on the checkered tablecloth as he spoke.

"He led the team that snatched the bombs from Arzamov-16. He's our boy."

Whitherspoon nodded glumly. "Yes, he's ours, all right. And I will contact him. Just give me time."

"The mullahs are getting restive. So's Samson. This whole mess could blow up in our faces if we don't get it together—immediately."

"I already told you, Karl. Holy Arabia's in the deal."

"Great. Just get me Sievers. That's all I ask."

Whitherspoon upended his glass and called for a refill as Banecek shoved back his chair and stalked out the back door.

As his driver took off, Banecek leaned back to consider how he was going to handle his meeting with Howard McKinney. Within half an hour they pulled into his reserved space in the Pentagon parking lot. The secretary of defense rubbed his burning eyes, unable to remember the last time he'd spent more than four hours horizontal. Weeks.

Cursing, he got out of the car and made his way upstairs to the conference room where his nemesis waited. Neutral ground, neither his office nor that of the chairman of the Joint Chiefs. The useless conversation with Whitherspoon had made him late. He cursed some more as he strode down the busy hallways, ignoring the deference of his subordinates. If any curious two or three stars wondered what the hell he was doing here after hours, fuck 'em. McKinney had better not have breathed a word to a soul—not even Eisenhower's ghost!

"We're in trouble, General. Your duty—"

"Don't lecture me about duty. I was fighting a real war while you were riding herd on a pack of spooks who couldn't slap their asses using both hands!"

"Under my watch the CIA was solid," Banecek said.

"So solid you green-lighted the theft of a dozen highly experimental dirty bombs from a Russian lab! And no one in the Pentagon was informed. What the hell—"

"You weren't informed because it was a rogue operation, start to finish. I personally cashiered the men who handled it as soon as I found out."

Not believing Banecek's story for a moment, McKinney snapped back, "And hid the weapons at Little Lennie."

"What the hell was I supposed to do with them—detonate them over mainland China? No, don't bother to answer. You probably think that would've been a capital idea."

McKinney forced himself not to reach across the table and place his big hands around the bull neck of the secretary of defense. Instead, he leaned back stiffly in his chair and drummed his fingers on the tabletop. "While I am against negotiating with terrorists in the Mideast, Mr. Secretary, I am not 'nuke 'em Nate' Sommerville. My point is that the CIA and the past several administrations have kept the Joint Chiefs out of the loop on critical national security matters. When those two weapons went missing, I sat in that briefing room filled with *civilians*"—he paused for emphasis as if it were a dirty word—"and heard about that CIA black op for the first time."

"Was it really the first time?" Banecek asked, studying the general carefully.

McKinney leaned forward and locked gazes with the secretary of defense. "What exactly are you implying? That I'm involved in the sale of nuclear devices to Arab terrorists?" The look on his narrow, harshly chiseled face was incredulous.

"You have to admit, General, it would serve your cause if extremist elements within the Holy Arabia movement were caught with those weapons. There would be no chance whatever for the president to negotiate after that."

"Extremist elements! The whole damned lot of them from Mohammed al Ibrim to Aziz al Ambas are certifiable madmen! You can't negotiate with them."

"You sound like Stuart Kensington."

McKinney stiffened. "If you believe I'd stoop to endangering American lives—innocent civilian lives at that—just to knock Wade Samson out of the box, you prove it, you damned bean counter! You were never cut out to head the CIA. OMB was the perfect place for you. Pity you didn't stay there."

"Two presidents did not happen to agree with your assessment, General."

"The 'Peter Principle' at work." McKinney once again leaned back and gave the big arrogant blond a look of pure disgust. "I've convinced General Kirk that it's in the Air Force's best interest to stand with the rest of the Chiefs against your reorganization plans. The military defense of the country will remain in our hands."

Banecek played his last ace. "Kensington's delivered the president's message to al Ibrim's government. They're considering it."

"Then Kensington sold out. All you're doing is giving those cut-throats more time to consolidate their power . . . and just maybe set off a dirty bomb or two right here in America. It will be on your head if they do."

Banecek stared silently at the wall as the general unfolded his six-foot-six frame and strode out of the room.

8:00 P.M. EST, TUESDAY, NOVEMBER 11
BOGOTÁ, COLOMBIA

The dining-room table could have seated half the United Nations General Assembly, but its gleaming burled mahogany surface was de-void of place settings. Instead, in an intimate alcove at one end, a small round table was laid out with the finest Belgian linen and Irish crystal. Windows stretched from floor to ceiling on three sides, af-fording them a splendid view of the brightly winking lights of the city below. Their host, dressed casually in Bill Blass shirt and slacks, stood silhouetted against the glass, politely smiling.

"Good evening. I hope you have an appetite. My cook has prepared a standing rib with Yorkshire pudding, a favorite of mine since uni-versity days." He walked a few paces to another sleek bar, this one built into the wall, and asked, "Would you like a before dinner libation?"

Too terribly civilized. Leah opted for more mineral water, wonder-ing if his crack about having an appetite was a subtle joke because he had the bedroom on vid. His veneer of propriety was thin as a cheap paint job as far as she was concerned. That type made the best pervs. Just thinking of his watching them made her skin crawl, but then she got hold of her animosity and realized an entrepreneur as busy as Benito Zuloaga had better things to do . . . she hoped.

Del declined another beer. She knew he was a recovering alcoholic who strictly watched his consumption. There would be wine with dinner and that would be his limit for the day. Their host smiled ge-nially as he joined her in drinking mineral water. *Got to keep a clear head to deal, Benny?*

"While you were resting, I made a few inquiries regarding the weapons transaction, which appears to have your government in quite an uproar."

Letting us know he has spies in high places. "Wouldn't you be a tad upset if Noriega had two dirty bombs in Colombia?" Del countered.

"Point taken, Mr. Delgado. Or I should say Special Agent Delgado." His pale eyes moved from Del to Leah. "I am surprised that you have joined the competition, so to speak, Special Agent Berglund."

"It's only temporary," she said flatly.

"You mentioned inquiries about the nukes?" Del prodded.

At that moment, a servant dressed in a faultless black tux glided across the carpet and pulled out a chair for Leah. She took a seat and the men joined her. Zuloaga didn't respond to Del's question until they'd been served the sumptuous meal. Then, raising his glass of '82 Château Margaux, he proposed a toast. "To a repast as splendid as the view," he said, gesturing to the glittering city so far below them.

Del and Leah raised their wine bowls and sipped. She forced a smile as she cut into the tender beef, waiting for their host to reopen the conversation.

"As I said," he began after the servants had completed their tasks and left the room, "I learned some things which should be of interest to you. There is a man who has spent many years in Latin America under various names and nationalities. Quite a clever chap. We found each other . . . useful from time to time."

Del stopped chewing, not even needing to glance at Leah to know where this was going. "CIA," he said flatly.

"Formerly, yes, but his allegiance was always flexible."

"More than his smoking habit," she said. "We know he was the man who persuaded Ramirez to swipe the nukes."

Zuloaga smiled. "Inocensio was a fool to fall into that mouse trap, betrayed by his own man."

The son of a bitch knows a hell of a lot about this deal. She felt a sudden surge of adrenaline that killed what little appetite she had. "Does this spook still work for you?" she asked.

Zuloaga shook his head. "Not for the past six months or so."

"When the coup against Samson hatched, he bailed," Del speculated.

"Didn't want to glow in the dark if Sommerville made his strike . . . or end up with a bullet in his head if the general failed."

Zuloaga nodded. "It would have been awkward for him either way, yes. But shortly after the debacle in your capital, someone in your own government offered him better—or at least more secure— remuneration than my organization."

They both stared at him, willing him to quit playing games. "Who?" Leah asked.

He shrugged. "My sources have been unable to establish that, alas. But I am certain this individual must be someone in your president's inner circle."

"What makes you think so?" Del asked.

"The elaborate orchestration of this scheme. The CIA rogue sets up a deal for Inocensio to steal the weapons but he had to be able to guarantee two cases will not be missed. Then he bribes a cat's-paw to double-cross Ramirez and bring those nuclear weapons into your country where terrorist cells of various denominations would most love to detonate them."

He paused and took another sip of wine. "There is also the speed and efficiency of the operation. By the time I heard of it, Holy Arabia had already agreed to the purchase."

"But no one counted on ChiChi Bernal taking off on his own," Del said.

"A major misjudgment . . . perhaps," Zuloaga replied. "But realize that to date all your attempts to reclaim those weapons from a lone petty thief have met with failure. Each time your FBI gets close, they are thwarted."

"Inside info. Someone in that briefing room must want those nukes. He's the seller to Holy Arabia," Leah said to Del.

Zuloaga nodded. "In spite of Bernal's clever thwarting of the original plan, consider that it could not have worked at all without coordination between various agencies. The rogue CIA man has contacts, yes, but this involved your Border Patrol, NRO, the Pentagon, perhaps even someone high in your Justice Department."

"You're telling us we can't trust anyone in Washington," Del said. " 'Fraid I already knew that."

"Any ideas on how to find our nameless spook?" Leah asked Zu-loaga.

"Perhaps these might be of some help." He took a small plasti-sealit from his shirt pocket and handed it to her. Inside were several cigarette butts. "He is not always as careful as he would like to believe he is."

She peered at the crumbling artifacts through the clear container. "They're some expensive foreign brand. Hard to find?"

"But maybe easy to trace," Del said hopefully, wondering how long this "evidence" had been gathering dust in one of Benito's vaults. *When you play with the jaguar prepare to be mauled.*

Zuloaga smiled quietly and sipped his wine. Excellent vintage. "Oh," he added conversationally, "your 'spook' has a name. Sievers. Leonard Sievers."

14.

They took a redeye out of Bogotá immediately after dinner. Del and Leah were both anxious to trace the "gift" Zuloaga had bestowed on them. Could Sievers's bizarre foreign cigarettes actually lead them to him? During a plane change in Havana, waiting for their flight to D.C. to board, they found a deserted corner in a martini bar off the main concourse and used the links Gracie had given them. She'd scoffed at Oppermann's "primitive" devices and assured them what she built would be untraceable—unless she did the tracing, of course.

The news from home was not reassuring. Adam Manchester had nearly been kidnapped. Bernal still eluded capture with the weapons, and the body count was rising. The secretary of Homeland Security was most likely involved in the sale of the nukes. Labat had miraculously escaped from an FBI attempt to catch him meeting with known Holy Arabia terrorist cell members in St. Louis. But the nearest thing they had to proof of his treason was more information from Leah's friend Latifah Richmond.

The antidrug crusader had dug up some real dirt about "the Rabbit's" political career in Nevada. While in the state legislature and as governor, he had taken substantial bribes from Vegas gambling interests. Two of the key players, weasels named Thomas Billinger and Danny DeClue, had been canceled Monday morning minutes before Bureau agents could arrest them. But once their connection to Labat was known, other small-time local hoods had been pulled from under their rocks. Now the DA in Carson City had enough evidence to indict the former governor on corruption charges.

"Labat's a wanted man in Nevada, but we still don't have any evidence tying him to the nukes," Leah said, combing her fingers through her hair until it stood up in silvery spikes.

Delgado nursed a cup of coffee to wear off the effects from the dinner wine. It seemed an eternity ago. Leah looked as exhausted as he did, but somehow they had to keep going until those bombs were recovered. "If only the son of a bitch hadn't dropped out of sight. Paul'd wring the truth out of the bastard."

"*Mamzer*," she corrected, using Oppermann's word unconsciously.

"Where the hell did a Lutheran-Episcopal girl from Minnesota learn Yiddish?" he asked, too jet-lagged to keep on track.

"My best friend in high school, Lev Barnov, an Israeli. We were seventeen the first time we 'did it.' Pretty good sex but we decided we were better off just being friends by the time we were sophomores in college."

"What happened to him?" he couldn't help asking.

"He went back to Israel when his mother got sick. Served his time in the Army, decided to make it a career. Last I heard, he was working for Mossad. Kinda spooky considering that I ended up in BISC. We used to correspond. . . ."

"Except for your grandfather, you don't much keep in touch with people, do you?"

"We have more important things to talk about than my social life—or lack thereof, Delgado," she said, massaging her temples as she pulled up her notepad on the vid screen and reviewed the distillation of their combined conversations with her grandfather, Latifah Richmond, and Paul Oppermann. "We know Labat made a deal with Holy Arabia, but I don't buy him being the only hairball in the soup."

Del nodded. "Yeah, but who's pulling the strings?"

"I say we can't trust Samson and Banecek after what Gramps told us about Whitherspoon. We know we can't trust anyone in the Pentagon or any of the other Cabinet members. Even Scarletti, since his old man was linked to Viviano."

He shrugged. "I vote for Oppermann only. If not for him, Adam might be dead now."

"Can't argue with that," she said, remembering the devastation she'd felt when she believed her grandfather had been killed last summer. "Can Gracie run sources on Ashtray's cigarettes?"

"She could if she knew the brand name. For that, we'll need Quantico."

The announcement for their flight to Washington quavered down the concourse in four languages. Leah stood up, closing her link. "Then let's get the hell to Quantico."

1:35 A.M. EST, WEDNESDAY, NOVEMBER 12
SOMEWHERE ON I-75, SOUTHERN GEORGIA

It was time to change plans. Again. ChiChi Bernal had spent an exhausting thirty-six hours driving nonstop, except for a brief pull-over in Atlanta when he'd almost driven off the road because he'd fallen asleep at the wheel. Operating on four hours' sleep over nearly three days wasn't conducive to clear thinking, but he had lots of practice living on the run. The car he'd had Sal buy him in Adrian was making ugly noises and he was on a particularly deserted stretch of highway. If it quit on him, he couldn't take the chance of running into any Motorist's Assistance trucks.

Would it be better to stop in the next berg and boost a new set of wheels or take a bus? He wanted instant transpo when he reached his destination, but there was anonymity among the poor and displaced on a Greyhound. He was running low on cash after buying this piece-of-shit old Pontiac TE. That used car dealer in Michigan would get his payback. Someday. But right now, he had to decide whether to risk driving a stolen vehicle.

Unless he stole it from someone who couldn't report it missing. Grinning, he slowed for the exit sign and headed into the next town, cruising down the side streets, checking out residential neighborhoods. This was definitely white-picket-fence country, a southern version of Adrian, Michigan, with a mix of poor neighborhoods and elegant century houses. He bypassed the fancy homes, figuring they'd have security too sophisticated for him to penetrate.

On the far side of the town, he found what he was looking for—an isolated trailer park, run-down and rusty. The smell of neglect hung limp in the air like the cheap awnings covering the windows of the double-wides. The owners' vehicles were out in the open for his inspection. On one stretch of the winding gravel road a dog barked. He drove on until the noise faded. Then he saw it. A cheap single unit with the siding peeling off it, half hidden by high weeds and scrub pines. He slowed, then pulled into the drive and concealed his beater behind some bushes.

After creeping carefully to the trailer, he found what he was looking for. A Chevy EV, only a few years old, gleamed in the faint moonlight. The owner's car was far better cared for than his lodging. He examined the tires and used his penlight to check the odometer. Low mileage. A codger's car if ever he'd seen one.

Bernal walked to the door and extracted a small tool from his pocket. The lock was easy enough for any street kid from Detroit to open. He entered soundlessly, pulling the knife from his belt. The placed reeked of stale cigar smoke and carry-out food. He let his eyes adjust to the dimness, then made his way to the trailer's only bedroom. Its door was ajar. An old man's soft snores came from the rumpled bed where he slept alone. . . .

7:45 A.M. EST, WEDNESDAY, NOVEMBER 12
WASHINGTON, D.C.

"Sweetums. Good to see your not-so-smiling face," Willis said genially as soon as Leah had him on screen.

"Yeah, Willie, I've run out of smiles," she replied. "That trip to Bogotá nearly got us kidnapped and your tip on Benito was way off the mark. Neither he nor Noriega have the nukes. Any other bright ideas?"

His grin faded. "No shit! It's a dangerous place, but you and your former fibbie know how to take care of yourselves. As a matter of fact, I have scrounged up some new info. Seems Bob Labat took a trip to Mexico City a couple of months ago. Supposedly for some high-level talks with their new presidente. Clemente Diaz Higgins used it as a photo op, then scratched old Peter Cottontail between his ears and went back to bidiness as usual."

"So?" she prompted.

He grinned again. "Our boy didn't report straight back to Washington. Seems he made a little side trip to Puerto Vallarta."

Sorta like the one to Gitmo when he talked with al Ambas. "Let me guess. He met ChiChi Bernal."

"Can't prove it, but Bernal was on leave and in town that night. My sources place Labat on a mysterious boat ride 'round midnight. Then he flies home on a red-eye, slick as cow slobber."

"He made a deal with Bernal to steal the nukes from Inocensio," she said.

"'Pears to me that way. Kinda careless, I'd say, but then the bunny never was the sharpest knife stuck in the block." He chuckled.

Leah told him about Labat's escape from Oppermann's carefully laid trap. "The homing dot planted on him must've been spotted by Labat's security people when they got him out of there. Now he's vanished just like Bernal. But we know he's still after the bombs. His Holy Arabian buyers are all set to deal."

"And Samson doesn't dare go public with a manhunt. 'Fraid of causing a panic," Willis surmised.

"Any idea where the Rabbit's warren might be?" she asked.

"I'm working on it. Bet your boss is, too."

"Paul Oppermann isn't my boss." It was reflex to deny that she carried a badge, but the minute Leah uttered the words, she felt stupid.

"I understand, Sweetums. A gal's gotta do what a gal's gotta do. I may get lucky with Bernal. I got contacts in the Hispanic underground from Michigan to Miami."

"Clock's ticking, Willie. We have to get to those nukes before this deal goes down, whoever the hell's trying to make it."

They discussed the theory that Labat was not the only player involved. Willis agreed, saying, "Makes sense that someone smarter than Bobby Boy's behind this."

"The point man is that CIA ashtray. Leonard Sievers is his Cartel handle."

"See, told you ole Benny'd give us something for our trouble."

"*Our* trouble? You weren't the one being shot at. Besides, this fucker must have a dozen names—or more."

"Told you I was sorry." He shrugged impenitently. "Guy's a chameleon. No Company connections I can find yet, and that's saying some." He looked aggravated. "But I will."

When the screen went black, Leah stood up, rubbing her aching neck. Sleeping on airplanes made chiropractors some serious money. They'd driven straight from National to Quantico with the "sample" they'd received from Zuloaga. Oppermann had alerted the lab people to make identifying it a priority. Just how long that would take was anyone's guess.

She walked from the small private office and rejoined Del and her grandfather in the big study of Brett Lowell's spacious Georgetown house. She could hear them arguing from down the hall.

"I won't leave John Scarletti out of the loop," Adam said flatly. "I know his family . . . his mother—"

"And Gracie found out his father was one of Viviano's best customers," Del replied.

"I went to see Annie. We went to school together," he added, glancing quickly at Leah. "I asked her about Frank's gambling addiction. She was very forthcoming about it. According to the records, he was never in debt, always paid what he owed."

"A mil five that Gracie's found to date." Delgado sounded skeptical.

Leah looked at her grandfather, startled. She dimly recalled one of those old-fashioned albums Adam loved to collect. There were several pix of him with a smiling little brunette named Annie in it. When she'd asked him who the woman was, he'd brushed it off, saying she was just an old girlfriend. "Anne Scarletti was the Annie in those old pix?" she asked.

Agitated by his argument with Del, Adam only nodded. "She told me John hated his father's habit and tried to get him help. John's never had anything to do with scum like Viviano except to prosecute them."

"That we know about so far. Look, Adam, I'm inclined to agree— Scarletti's probably squeaky clean. Paul thinks so, but Paul's new to Washington and we just can't be sure at this point. Look at the possibilities—Banecek, Kensington, McKinney—" he ticked off using his fingers. "We're sure Labat's somebody's goat—most likely somebody in Samson's inner circle. Even your source on the Hill knew the Rabbit was dirty from the get go and Samson didn't do squat about it."

"And your friend Oppermann's the one who let Labat slip through his fingers," Adam snapped, then immediately apologized. "I didn't intend to accuse you, Del, but I'm just tired . . . and sick of this whole mess. Men I've known my whole life could be involved in treason."

"I know exactly how you feel," Del said quietly, remembering last summer.

"So do I." BISC had been Leah's ultimate betrayer, using her to silence Delgado.

"Are we agreed we have to narrow the loop on this?" Del asked as he took an unenthusiastic bite from some cold pasta he'd scrounged out of the fridge.

Leah said nothing, just looked at her grandfather, waiting for his answer.

Adam asked, "You want to keep only Oppermann in?"

"We have to. Without the Bureau, we're operating in the dark. Besides, we're only three people—we don't have the manpower to do this without him."

"Damned if I trust Samson himself," Leah said. "Now he has incontrovertible proof that Labat's in the hip pocket of the Vegas mob and he won't let Paul put him on the Most Wanted list."

"Bad election politics. Remember, this hasn't been an exactly sterling year for our peerless leader in terms of his Cabinet choices," Adam said. "I doubt Samson's involved in this nuclear catastrophe, though. No way to maneuver it to his credit that would make it worth that kind of risk."

Del felt a belly laugh in spite of the grim situation. "You have as high an opinion of him as I do. Say, what are you telling your party pals about taking a hiatus from campaign planning? I'd imagine they're champing at the bit to capitalize on the ax fight among Banecek, McKinney, and Kensington. Not to mention Holy Arabia's less-than-positive response to the prez's olive branch. That made headlines," Del said.

Manchester grunted. "I spoke with Stuart Kensington last night to reassure him I understood about his delivering Samson's idiot initiative to them. He feels it's unworkable, but Samson's intent on pursuing recognition for that terrorist government. As secretary of state, Stuart's hands are tied." Manchester still regretted that Kensington could not make the run with him.

"Isn't his wife Scarletti's aunt?" Del asked. "Seems I remember—"

"Jillian is Annie's sister," Adam replied. Wanting to head off any discussion about Anne, he immediately redirected the conversation back to his campaign. "Laurie Steuben's been in a Texas-sized snit, but I delighted her with that press conference yesterday and made a little hay after the botched kidnapping. Streets not safe, El-Ops running loose in America while Samson placates Holy Arabia, that sort of thing."

"Too bad you can't leak how Wade Samson's Cabinet choices have put the country in danger from a couple of nukes," Leah said.

The old man resisted the urge to grind his teeth. "High-level treason undermines public confidence in our whole system of government. The American people have already been through enough over the past decade to shake their confidence to the core. And by bringing me—and you—into the loop on this, Samson's effectively tied my hands. If I try to tar him, he can use the same brush on me."

"Well, we have another nail in Labat's coffin now. Willis just told me he met with Bernal in Mexico back in September." Leah relayed the details to them. "Still not absolute proof but enough to indict him."

"I'd say," Del agreed. "The crusading 'Mr. Jones Goes to Washington' guy to everybody. Earnest and dumb. A brilliant piece of acting."

"Cunning men can hide their warts up to a point, but greed will out," Adam said. "I imagine our CIA friend approached him with the deal of the century and he was so blinded by the chance to make millions that he was willing to take chances he'd never taken before."

"Bottom line is we still don't have him or Bernal or the nukes," Leah reminded them. "Not to mention the setup man behind it all. What about bringing in Viviano?"

Adam considered her question. "The Bureau's had him under surveillance, but now that he's assassinated his Vegas connections, that might be an option."

"He'd just lawyer up," Delgado said, shoving the plate of mostly uneaten pasta away.

"Might be worth a try. He knows we've made him or else he wouldn't have hit DeClue and Billinger," Leah said.

"I'll discuss it with Paul," Adam replied.

"Paul's got two of the terrorists from St. Louis he's sweating, although I doubt they're any more likely to talk. We could probably use the talents of your friend Lev. I bet he'd make the *mamzarim* sing."

Adam glanced at Del, surprised that Leah would discuss Lev Barnov with him, but said nothing. "Since Labat doesn't have the weapons, let's focus on the man who does. Bernal."

"And 'Ashtray,'" Leah added. "He's our ticket to whoever's pulling the Rabbit's strings. Willis is working that end."

"I hope it pans out better than his lead in Bogotá," Adam said grimly. He knew what they'd told him about their brush with Noriega had been a considerably sanitized version.

"You think your sources on the Hill can come up with anything on Leonard Sievers?" she asked her grandfather.

"I have people on it. Nothing so far," he replied.

"Old Benito's 'Ashtray gift' may just be our ticket to break this thing," Del said speculatively. "Zuloaga has enough trouble at home without getting in a pissing contest with Samson."

Gracie really wanted to gig the old senator, but as luck would have it, when she beeped his link, Delgado and Berglund were sitting at the table behind him. Adam quickly turned her over to Del. "How was Zuloaga's hospitality? I hear his place in Bogotá really rocks."

"Not half as much as the ride we got from the airport." He glossed over the story about their welcoming committee, then asked, "What have you got for us?"

She grinned, revealing tiny, nicotine-stained teeth. "After ChiChi's wife numero three turned up dead in Corpus—pardon the pun—I did a little snooping on her family. Bernal isn't the only one in the drug biz. Seems poor Nina Dolores Rosario, what all, had a cousin who's real involved, too. Name's Miguel Lopez."

"*The* Miguel Lopez?" Del asked, feeling his heartbeat accelerate.

"None other. The drug kingpin of Miami—"

"And leader of the Fidelista Liberation Front," Del finished for her. He'd done a story on him a couple of years earlier.

"The guy who wants to oust President Ruiz and take Cuba back to the golden days of communism?" Leah asked, her interest rising. She had followed the news about former "revolutionaries" who had been forced to flee Cuba after Castro's death when the Marxist regime came tumbling down and the Miami Cubanos reclaimed their homeland. Ironically, now their positions were reversed.

Cuba presently had a capitalist democracy and the followers of Fidel Castro had become exiles in Florida and Puerto Rico. But most of the exiles this time entered American territory illegally and quickly moved underground, seizing control of the lucrative drug traffic pouring into the U.S. from the Cartel stronghold in the Yucatán. During her three-year tenure with BISC, she'd made a number of terminations in Miami, but had never been able to get close to the elusive Lopez.

"Lopez is practically an urban legend," Adam said.

"All too real," Del replied. "No one outside his organization even knows what he looks like. Word is, most of those inside it don't either. He keeps his identity a closely guarded secret and he's one of the richest El-Ops on the Eastern Seaboard."

"And on the lookout for a couple of nukes to use against the Cuban government?" Leah speculated.

"Your lady friend's got smarts, Delgado. She'll get a slow learner like you up to speed in nothin' flat," Gracie said, giving Leah a wink with an eyelid that looked too weighed down by black liner and mascara to raise and lower without a crane.

"So now we know where Bernal's heading," Del said. "Any idea about how we can track him in a city with over a million Spanish-speaking inhabitants?"

"When I was hiding from BISC in Havana last summer, I made some contacts. I'm working them even as we speak," Gracie replied.

"I wonder if Bernal has a direct conduit to Lopez?" Del asked.

"I doubt it. That was what he needed his wife for," Leah speculated.

"But those goons who tortured her asked the wrong questions— she gave up ChiChi in Detroit, not her connection to Lopez," Del said.

"They must not have known about it." Adam rubbed his chin, considering the possibilities. "Maybe we're finally going to steal a march on whoever's orchestrating this nightmare. Any further information on what's going on between Banecek and Whitherspoon?" he asked Gracie.

"I'll get to that," she replied. "But first, the best news of all. You'll never guess who sent me a message for you. Hot off the press—ain't that what newspaper guys used to say?" she crowed.

"No time for games, Gracie," Delgado said tightly.

"Benito Zuloaga! He knows no one will ever break my encryption. Didn't trust yours," she sniggered. "He wants to do you a favor—to make up for the 'unfortunate incident in Bogotá,' so he says. He's giving up Miguel Lopez, all gift-wrapped—even a pix!"

"He knows about Bernal's connection to Lopez and wants to stop the Fidelista Front from blowing up the Gulf of Mexico," Leah said. "Bad for business."

Delgado nodded, humming with excitement. "If we get to Lopez, we get to Bernal and his nukes. We'll need a plane—"

"Willis has a contract for private jet privileges. Let me call him and see if he can get us down there," Leah said.

"Quicker than regular airlines," Gracie agreed as Leah picked up her link. "You better stick with this gal, Delgado. Say, Miami should be mag this time of year." As she spoke, the pix of a swarthy, handsome face slid out of the PDA's repro, followed by a map and contact names.

Del studied the info as Adam asked, "What about Banecek and Whitherspoon?"

"They met in a Georgetown café last night. I couldn't pick every word up, but they were talking about some spook. Whitherspoon's trying to find him—and get this, Banecek said this Sievers guy was the one who stole those nukes from someplace called Arza-something-16, wherever the hell that is."

Adam couldn't help a grim smile of satisfaction. Thanks to Al Braveheart, he'd finally stolen a march on the infallible hacker. "It's in Russia, not far from Moscow."

Gracie blinked. "No shit?"

"Any more details on Banecek's and Whitherspoon's conversation?" Leah asked Gracie after finishing a brief conversation with Willis.

"They agreed this Sievers guy was theirs—I kinda got the impression they've lost control of him—"

"I just bet," Adam said. "Can you forward that tape to me?"

Gracie sighed. "Senator, tapes went out even before DVDs did. We use a whole new tech now, see—"

"Can you send me a copy of their conversation?" Manchester asked in weary resignation.

"Will do." She touched several keys and their PDA began to download the aud-surveil.

"That arrogant bastard," Manchester said under his breath, thinking of his feckless interview with Samson. "I wonder if he has any idea what his friend Karl Banecek has unleashed on us?"

Del said to Gracie, "We're waiting for a report from Quantico, a new lead on this Sievers." He explained about their "gift" from Zuloaga. "If those smokes are as rare as we hope they are, you might be able to pinpoint where he buys them."

"Probably in hundred-kilo bales," Leah said. "We gotta beat feet to Miami."

Gracie stared directly at Adam. "It's you and me working from D.C., right, Senator?"

When she winked, Manchester's face turned brick-red. Del suppressed a grin as the vid went blank. "We should bring Paul into the loop on this right now."

Leah shook her head. "Let's play this one by ear. We can be in Miami in a couple of hours, check out the Lopez deal. You know Paul will want to have his most trusted locals dogging us and I think they'd draw more attention in Little Havana than we can afford right now."

"We cut out John Scarletti for a hell of a lot less reason," Adam said. "What she says makes sense—but only until you verify Zuloaga's information. Then you let the Bureau help you take Lopez down."

Reluctantly, Del and Leah both nodded.

15.

ChiChi ditched the stolen EV several blocks from a run-down section on Calle Ocho where he could rent a cheap motel room. The last thing he needed was someone finding that old man's body and the cops putting out a BOLO on the junker. Abandoned cars were as common as mosquitoes in the drug-infested slums of the Caribbean section of Miami called Little Havana.

He picked out a sleazy stucco courtel with peeling green paint and walked inside. The desk clerk was a Nicaraguan with the smell of an illegal about him. If the skinny little fart thought it was peculiar that he was carrying two suitcases but had no vehicle, the clerk asked no questions. Bernal needed a few hours of sleep before he dealt with Miguel Lopez. He knew negotiating with Nina's cousin would require a clear head. Maybe she'd managed to reach Lopez before she got wasted, but ChiChi had no way to know for sure.

Once in the dreary room, he called several Cartel men he knew in town. Keeping tabs on his old boss's competition had been one of his jobs while he worked for Inocensio Ramirez. Felix refused to touch the offer but Sancho, who was always in hock to gamblers, agreed to set up a meet with one of Lopez's men. Just after nine he called back. For once in her miserable life, his bitch of a wife had done something right. Lopez knew about the "merchandise" and was ready to deal.

A Haitian dude with some serious scars met him at the entrance to Domino Park. Ravel was a scary-looking character—if ChiChi had been inclined to scare. Still, the Colt concealed under a loose print shirt reassured him.

"You are the man's cousin?" he asked in a singsong Caribbean accent, pronouncing "man" like "mon."

Bernal nodded. "Let's walk. Too many old people around here." The tiny park's tables were already filled with elderly players, setting up their dominos for the day's games.

Ravel's laugh boomed out. "Okay, man. We walk."

ChiChi knew he wasn't fooling Ravel. He needed to watch for a tail and that would be easier if they weren't sitting still. The streets were busy, filled with men and women chattering away in a polyglot of "Spanglish," drinking strong Cubano coffee and eating pastries. Here and there a drug deal went down. No one noticed or cared as long as shots weren't fired.

"You tell my cousin that I want ten mil in cash and I deal with him in person."

"Ten million is a lot of money," Ravel replied.

"Shit, a big-time El-Op like Miguel's got that much laying around. It's loose change to the guy. You and I both know it. His organization's been saving their bucks for a big bang. Well, I can give it to 'em."

"Let me see what he says," Ravel replied, pausing to pull out a link and press in a code.

As Ravel relayed the information quietly, Bernal watched the street, keeping his back to a brick wall at the edge of an alley. The conversation didn't take long.

"Okay, man. You come to Ponce de Leon Street at one-thirty this afternoon. Bring the suitcases."

Now it was Bernal who laughed. "You tell my primo to go fuck himself if he thinks I'm crazy enough to walk into the wolf's lair with the merchandise." He started walking again.

Ravel followed, reconnecting with his boss. The hushed conversation was again brief. "All right, man. I give you a vid code and you call your primo at one-thirty. You and Miguel will talk about how to set up the exchange."

"Now, that's more like it," ChiChi said with a sly grin, accepting the slip of paper with the number scrawled on it. "I think it's time we part company. Until this afternoon?" he asked cordially.

Ravel nodded as Bernal slipped around the corner. ChiChi knew he would be followed. If Lopez tailed him to the nukes he was a dead man. That was why he arranged transpo with Sancho, offering the small-time El-Op enough money to retire on if he provided a getaway car. ChiChi vanished inside the back door of a leather shop owned by Sancho's brother, then cut across the street, emerging on SW Seventh where a rusted-out Ford TE was waiting.

He leaped into the backseat and dropped on the floor as Sancho pulled into traffic. The car looked like hundreds of others around the neighborhood and had stolen plates. "Drive around for a while. Be damn sure you aren't followed," he hissed at the fat little El-Op.

"Whatever you say, ChiChi."

After a couple of turns, Bernal raised his head and checked for a tail. Once he was satisfied Ravel hadn't been able to make them, he said, "Now drive me to the airport."

9:32 A.M. EST, WEDNESDAY, NOVEMBER 12
THE PENTAGON

"Adam, good to see you," Howard McKinney said as he ushered the senator into his office and closed the door. "I really appreciate your making time in your schedule for this visit."

"You said you had an urgent matter to discuss with me." The senator scanned the spacious office, the paneled walls filled with pictures of McKinney beside presidents and prime ministers as well as ranking members of Congress, even Supreme Court justices. On the drive, he'd mulled over how to handle the general's questions. Given the decision he had reluctantly reached with Leah and Del, he knew he would have to withhold information. But denying access to the chairman of the Joint Chiefs was going to be very tricky, especially considering that if he was elected, he wanted to keep McKinney in his post.

The general offered him a seat in an oversized, comfortable leather chair. "Would you like some coffee? As I recall, you used to drink it by the quart, black as ink, in your Senate days," McKinney said, pouring from the antiquated percolator on the table beside the window.

"You still keep that artifact working? Makes the best damn coffee in Washington," Adam replied, nodding as McKinney handed him the steaming mug. "Thank you."

"We always did share an affinity for doing things the old-fashioned way," the general said, refilling his own mug and taking a sip. He folded his large frame gracefully into the chair across from Manchester. "That's why I wanted your read on how Samson's handling this situation. Frankly, I can't get a straight answer out of him or any of his boys on the Hill."

"I take it your own intel shops haven't come up with anything," Adam hedged.

"My sources say not only has CIA been kept out of the loop, but even DIA and NSA. Hell, we control eighty percent of the intel budget and look where it's got us! The whole thing's the FBI's show from where I'm sitting." He ran his hand over his sleek silver hair.

Adam knew it was a nervous gesture that signaled he was pissed. "And since my granddaughter and her friend are part of that FBI investigation, who better to ask, eh?"

"I know Samson's political motives for dragging you into this. What's he think this reporter and Leah can accomplish that our own security agencies can't? I know about the cover-up inside the Bureau last summer, Adam. Why trust them now?"

Manchester wasn't surprised. The Pentagon had at least half a dozen intel resources besides the Defense Intelligence Agency and National Security Agency. "Howard," Adam began carefully, "Oppermann is our best hope to recover those weapons without starting a national panic. He's been very selective of which agents to run."

"This Delgado, you trust him and he trusts Oppermann, that it?"

Adam nodded. "We're looking at a conspiracy that goes pretty high. Homeland Security is completely compromised."

McKinney shook his head. "I knew when Labat's people let Bernal in the country no one over there could be trusted. Only thing, I thought it was because of his incompetence." McKinney leaned forward and fixed his slightly protruding gaze on Manchester. "He's the one who wants those weapons from Bernal, isn't he?"

"The FBI has a pretty good case that he planned to sell them to Holy Arabia," Adam admitted, but knew he dared not say anything about Bernal and Lopez or where Leah and Del were headed at that very moment.

"That damned roosting dove in the White House wants to give those savages diplomatic recognition! Adam, what in hell's the world coming to when we stand by while terrorists topple the governments of our allies and come after us inside our own borders!"

"Wade Samson wants a Nobel Peace Prize," Manchester said, glad the discussion was on a track they could discuss openly.

"He's a self-serving egomaniac. I hope to God you beat his ass next November, Adam. We can't afford to dally around while the whole Middle East goes up like tinder."

"Would you advocate a preemptive attack against Holy Arabia?" Adam asked, fishing. If McKinney was that hawkish . . .

"In a heartbeat." The general paused, his creased face losing some of its tension. "Question is, would you?"

"A Rubicon I'll only have to consider crossing if I'm elected, Howard," Adam replied.

"That's a politician's answer, Adam."

"Much as I dislike the breed, we can't get around the fact that anyone running for president has to be one," Manchester replied with a grimace.

On the drive back to Georgetown, Adam considered how many relationships he might lose before this nightmare ended. He'd equivocated and put off Howard McKinney until the chairman knew he was not going to reveal what the FBI, including his granddaughter and Delgado, were doing. He'd already evaded Stuart Kensington's questions. But it was John Scarletti who bothered him most.

No, much as he admired the younger man's dedication and intelligence, it wasn't just John he was forced to mistrust. It was Annie. And that hurt most of all.

He'd tried to call her yesterday evening after their unhappy meeting, uncertain of exactly what he could say to alleviate her pain. But she had not answered. He'd let the PDA messenger blink for several moments, then broke the connection without saying a word.

When he reached Brett Lowell's home, his PDA signaled waiting messages. Like the house, the computer had been swept and newly encrypted. Only he could access it. He skimmed several reports and dismissed them, then came to one from Paul Oppermann, delivered only moments earlier. It was marked top priority. He'd discussed bringing in Richie Viviano with the director after he, Del, and Leah had agreed it was a good idea early that morning. So did Oppermann.

Maybe the Jersey gambler had given them something! Excitedly he gave a voice command to reach the director. In moments Paul Oppermann's haggard face appeared on the vid screed and Adam knew the news wasn't good. "What's happened, Paul?"

"It's been a rough few days for the gambling establishment. Richie Viviano got in his Caddie this morning and turned the ignition. The explosion took out all of his garage and half the house. All of Richie, too."

9:50 A.M. EST, WEDNESDAY, NOVEMBER 12
AIRSPACE OVER CENTRAL FLORIDA

"Diana Shrewsbury's got to be there. She told me she and my son were staying at the Four Seasons. I damn well know there aren't two of them in Manhattan," Del growled into his link.

Leah watched his frustration build. He felt guilty as hell for having to miss Mike's Science Fair in New York tomorrow. *I'd suck as a parent.* He had called Diana from his uncle's home in Mazatlán as soon as he learned about the terrorist targets, pleading with her not to take their son to New York. But Diana had refused to deny Mike his big day.

Del had even broken his oath and explained that New York was on a Holy Arabia list of possible targets for a bombing. After living for so long with Cartel thugs roaming the streets of D.C. and San Diego, Diana insisted that terrorists didn't control their lives. Some heated wrangling followed before they compromised. She promised to leave as soon as the fair was over and Del promised to be there for his son Thursday morning.

Now that the Lopez connection in Miami made it impossible for him to keep his word, Del had spent the past hours trying in vain to reach his ex-wife and explain. But her link did not respond and the hotel where they were supposed to be staying insisted Mrs. Shrewsbury had not checked in.

He clutched the link in a whitened fist. "You overbooked." He sighed and combed his fingers through his hair, struggling to keep his temper. "Any ideas about which hotel she was referred to? I know after a mistake like this a five-star hotel wouldn't just turn her away!" After an obviously unsatisfactory response, he slammed his fist on the plane's armrest and broke the connection, then punched in his ex-wife's number again. "Come on, answer, Diana!"

"Her link's down. Happens all the time, Del. She and Mike are okay. As soon as she realizes it's broken, she'll buy another link and call you," Leah said, trying to calm his frazzled nerves.

"Dammit, I won't be able to be at the fair tomorrow and Mike's going to be heartbroken. How can I expect a kid to understand the sorry world we live in? And the sorry excuse for a father he has," he added under his breath.

"Quit beating yourself up. He thinks you're a pretty terrific dad and you know it," she said.

He looked at her. "He tell you that?"

Leah knew he was testing her. She and Mike had forged a special bond since they met last summer and her withdrawal from his life had been hurtful. But this was not the time to lose focus. They had a job to do. "Yeah, he told me that," she said. "Nothing's going to happen in New York. The bombs are in Miami, remember?" Was she trying to ease his mind or her own?

"Let's nail Lopez and take out Bernal."

She nodded at him. "Paul will find Labat. Once he talks, it'll all be over. We're coming in for a landing. You okay?"

How could he feel okay when he didn't know where his son was? But Del knew there was nothing he could do until Diana called. He nodded and stared out the window, forcing his gut to unclench.

They had a job to do.

As the plane taxied across the ill-maintained runway, he looked out at the flat southern Florida landscape. Brilliant sunshine flooded the small jet's cabin, a Lear 45/60 owned by Willis Security, used for flying key personnel quickly and quietly wherever they needed to be. Low buildings, mostly ramshackle-looking in the distance, had the harsh edge of poverty blunted by a scattering of palm trees.

"Not exactly the high-rent district," Leah said, trying to gauge their distance from Little Havana.

The pilot stepped out of the cockpit wearing a genial grin. "Welcome to beautiful downtown Miami—or as near thereto as I can get you folks." He was a compactly built man with a bullet head and dark eyes that missed nothing. "Car's waiting outside, courtesy of Mr. Willis." If he was interested in the high secrecy surrounding the pair, he was too well trained to ask about their assignment. "I was told to wait for you here."

"We'll be in touch. Hopefully it won't be long," Leah responded as they headed for their transpo. Knowing driving was Del's thing, she crossed to the passenger door. The car was a Chevy TE, faded paint and lots of dents, the sort of vehicle unlikely to attract the attention of El-Ops cruising to carjack vehicles they could use for their illicit trade. Miami was one of the largest hubs for moving Elevator into the country and the Metro-Dade Police were understaffed and badly outgunned. Most of the area's six million more affluent inhabitants avoided the central city like it was radioactive. Soon it might be.

"I'm calling Willie. See if he's come up with a nuclear signature yet." Del nodded as she opened her link. Almost immediately, Willis's round face appeared on the tiny vid. "Anything?"

"Just like I warned you, Sweetums. Your pal ChiChi must've figured out that once some boogeyman like me got close enough, he could pick up a glow from those cases. He's sealed them—or else he isn't in Miami yet."

She drummed her fingers on the roof of the car. "Possible. But we know for sure he's coming. I doubt our buddy Benny lied to us." Leah signed off with Willis and looked over at Del. "Still no sign of Bernal."

"If he keeps those cases under wraps, Lopez is our only way to nab him. I vote for taking out Lopez first. He's ChiChi's only customer. If he gets his mitts on those nukes he'll turn Havana into one giant radioactive crater to retake his homeland."

"And toast south Florida in the process. I can see your point." She kept tapping the dull paint as her mind raced. "Once he's neutralized, we might be able to run a sting on Bernal. Lure him in. We'd need some help from Willie. . . ."

Del climbed inside the car while they talked, noting the shabby interior hid some special features. "A GPA and flash drive," he said as he turned the key and read the panel.

"Don't get us pulled over for speeding, Delgado."

"Hey, in this baby, I might be able to outrun the fuzz," he said, noting the special high-performance turbo engine. "This junker packs a lot more juice than it looks like. Hot damn, Willis!"

"Boys and their toys." She shook her head. "Here's hoping Paul grabs Labat while we're rounding up Bernal and his nukes."

"Your good pal Paul won't feel so grateful if we go after Miguel Lopez without his agents."

"I worked Miami when I was BISC. The El-Ops know every agent and own half their snitches. That's why no one's ever been able to nail Lopez."

"Until Zuloaga turned him in. Ironic. Leah, we need Bureau backup."

"Can't do it, Del. Even if we had time to get a search warrant, when we knocked on the gate and announced we're FBI what do you think he'd do? We'd have a full-blown shoot-out with media coverage swarming all over us and Bernal would skip town with the nukes, then start looking for another buyer."

"So we violate the basic constitutional rights we took down BISC to restore." He knew that was hitting below the belt when she paled.

Her mouth was a slash of silence for a beat. Then she asked coldly, "You want to risk a nuclear catastrophe that could melt Florida and Cuba?"

"You win. Strike that last remark," he said, picking up his link to try Diana again.

She gave him points for being under personal stress. Families and this kind of work just didn't mix. In a conciliatory voice, she said, "Mike's all right, Del. We'd have heard if there was anything wrong." *He should be with his kid.* She stared out the window, scanning their surroundings as they shot up I-874 for the I-836 interchange, then turned due east headed for the southwestern quadrant of the sprawling city, to the place still called Little Havana.

Before the death of Castro, affluent Cubanos had gradually moved out of the central city, buying lavish homes in the Gables, the Grove, and more outlying areas. Their workingclass countrymen gravitated toward the modest neighborhoods in and around West Miami. When the Communist regime toppled, many of both classes had returned to rebuild their historic homeland.

Now Little Havana had been infiltrated by a polyglot of Nicaraguan, Haitian, and other Central American and Caribbean immigrants. Some had fled the Cartel; others worked for it. But over the years, a new breed of Cuban exile replaced the original refugees. These were the true believers led by the Fidelista Liberation Front. Once again Cubanos became the power brokers in the "Spanglish" world of Miami.

But this time many were also the Cartel's south Florida conduit for Elevator. And they shared one dream with the previous exiles—to return to Cuba. Their vast wealth garnered through the drug trade, combined with their utter ruthlessness, made that dream the nightmare of the Ruiz Administration in Havana.

"Exit on Seventeenth and head south," Leah said, reading the GPS console. "If Benito wasn't shitting us, we should meet his man in a couple of miles." Zuloaga had given them a contact who could get them inside the crumbling mansion in Coral Gables that Lopez used as his fortress. The Cartel agent was a Haitian named Ravel, identified by a large white scar running across his chin. He would approach them at a *botanica*, or Santeria shop, on Calle Ocho.

Delgado studied the fruit stands, cigar factories, street-side cafeterias, and shoe shops lining Little Havana's main thoroughfare. Vivid colors and the beat of Latin rhythms pulsed from every street corner. One eat-at window offered fried plantains and *chicharrones* on special.

He loved the spicy fried pork dish but felt no appetite. The *botanica* was just past Twelfth Avenue. They were close. "We could have a problem taking Lopez down if his place is big as Benito indicated. Damn, I wanted him holed up in some storefront apartment here on Eighth."

"Crowded buildings could provide cover for Miguel to slip away, too. It worked for bin Bergi and Labat in St. Louis," Leah said. "Let's see what Benny's man Ravel has to say."

"If the Bureau can't help, we'll need more backup than this Ravel," Del replied.

"He promised a guided tour of Fortress Lopez. Willie will cover us if we need help—and his people won't stand out like fibbies."

"Hey, the Bureau has Hispanic agents. You're looking at one."

"We can't take the chance on more like me showing up. Face it, Del, I stand out like a Christmas tree in a shul." She checked her disguise in the mirror again, not reassured. She'd darkened her skin by drinking a chemical cocktail, used brown contacts and a black cosmipen on the roots of her white-blond hair. Her last experience with wigs in the Sonoran desert had taught her they couldn't fool anyone close up. Besides, they made her sweat like a pig. She spotted a scar-faced black man loitering in the door of a Santeria shop and started to sweat anyway.

10:12 A.M. EST, WEDNESDAY, NOVEMBER 12
WASHINGTON, D.C.

"Brett, damned glad I caught you," Adam Manchester said as his old friend's face appeared on the vid screen. Lowell didn't look as if he shared the senator's sentiments.

"So help me, if you make me miss another reception—"

"This is vital, Brett," Adam said. His tone and facial expression were enough to sober the ambassador.

"What do you need?"

"Between Quantico and a rather unorthodox source I've been working with here in Washington." He paused and cleared his throat, trying to block the mental picture of Gracie Kell's latest incarnation in neon snakeskin. "Well, anyway, we've linked the rogue CIA agent to a tobacconist in London. Leonard Sievers favors a particularly nasty blend of Turkish and Egyptian cork-filtered cigarettes called Macedonians. The shop's in Piccadilly—"

This time it was Lowell who interrupted. "The Eur-east Connection. I've heard of the place." He grimaced with distaste. "Macedonians are bloody awful but they don't come cheap. Still, safer than Elevator. Just barely. Do you have a pix of this spook of yours? I assume you want me to play detective at the tobacconist's."

"I'm transmitting it now. He's obviously using another name when he orders the cigarettes, and from what we've learned, he's a very good customer. Must support at least a four-pack-a-day habit. Use whatever leverage you have to find out."

"Good enough. Give me an hour or two."

"I appreciate it, Brett. The whole country would, but please God, don't let them ever have cause to find out why."

An hour later, Adam stared at the blank screen on Lowell's PDA, mulling over what his congressional colleague Al Braveheart had just told him. Leonard Sievers had a "safe house" in New York City. The senator stared at the address, which he'd scribbled on a slip of paper. Might the CIA agent possibly be hiding Labat there? He gave a voice command to reach Paul Oppermann but the ping of an incoming transmission interrupted. "Brett, I hope good news?"

Lowell's face on the vid looked smug. "I'm getting rather good at this cloak-and-dagger stuff. Used a bit of blackmail, playing a Euro customs official after the manager sold me a really potent hash blend. Of course, my source in Interpol will choke me when he finds out I compromised his undercover agent. But the manager recognized the drawing you sent and knew the pricey rot our spook smokes. Called the guy Mr. Neighbors, if you can believe that one."

"An address in the U.S.?" Adam prompted.

"A little shop in New York, where else?" He studied his friend's expression. "Say, you already knew it was New York, didn't you?" the diplomat accused. Sighing, he gave Manchester a street number in a cut and shoot area of the Bronx.

The congressman had given him an address in Riverdale, a quiet residential neighborhood north of Manhattan. "I really appreciate this, Brett."

"Just don't forget the caviar, champagne, and"—he glanced down at a bill on his desk—"two thousand pounds for that hash laced with God only knows what."

"God has nothing to do with this, Brett."

"He had nothing to do with the hash, either, believe me," Lowell said, signing off.

In less than a moment Adam was on the link with Paul Oppermann.

11:20 A.M. EST, WEDNESDAY, NOVEMBER 12
MIAMI, FLORIDA

"That is the tour, man," Ravel said in a musical Caribbean accent. His voice was surprisingly soft for such a hulking brute, his manner deceptively gentle. But Delgado and Berglund had met Cartel killers before and knew he'd use his Glock or knife on them in a heartbeat if he felt the necessity.

He had taken them on a reconnaissance of the perimeter of Lopez's hideout in an area long ago populated by millionaire orange growers and cattlemen. The mansions in the vicinity were mostly Italianate or Spanish Rococo, crumbling and fading under the merciless on-slaught of tropical sun and hurricane wind. Live oaks, poincianas, and huge tropical ferns fought with kudzu and creeper vines inside the large compounds whose walls had been breached by vegetation and vandals. Swimming pools were either slimy green breeding grounds for mosquitoes or empty peeling holes gaping at the lost grandeur that surrounded them.

The homes had mostly been deserted by owners unable or unwill-ing to pay the taxes on large hunks of real estate. Squatters, recent im-migrants from Central America and the Caribbean, subdivided them. Shoot-outs over occupancy were everyday events that the local cops ignored. El-Ops strutted along cracked pavement and stood laughing and talking in the shade of ancient trees, their M16s and AK47s slung carelessly over their shoulders. Deals went down in plain sight on any street corner in the bright south Florida sunlight. It was a no-man's-land offering perfect concealment for the Fidelista Liberation Front.

Lopez's house had once been a vibrant rose stucco, now faded to dirty pink. The elaborate cornices overhanging the roof were filled with jagged holes. Chunks of plaster littered the lichen-covered patios and smashed fountains like a warning to intruders. But the overgrown yard would furnish excellent cover for a raid . . . if it had not been mined and electronically surveilled.

Ravel pointed out, "Someone must get inside first and cut the power. Miguel has his own generator."

"See if Willis is picking up any trace of Bernal yet," Del said to Leah. "And when the hell are his people going to get here?"

"Let us not worry about ChiChi Bernal for another two hours," Ravel interjected. "I gave him a Cartel vid code instead of Lopez's. If he calls early, they will tell him a fish story until I call him back. Once we have control of Lopez's compound, the Cartel link will feed Bernal's call directly to us. Then we can trace the call with Miguel's equipment and we will have him. Simple, no?"

"Lots could go wrong," Leah said, chewing her lip as Del nodded a second.

If Ravel was bothered by the Yankees' lack of faith, his round ebony face revealed nothing. "I take your man in, lady. He plays Bernal. Miguel has never met Nina's husband but considers him family and that is important."

"Bernal got Miguel's cousin Nina tortured to death. Somehow I don't think kinship will count for much if he knows about that," Leah argued.

"Too late for debate. We only have a couple of hours," Delgado said. "I can pass for a Mexican national."

"I hope Nina never described her husband to Miguel," she said. Del had used her makeup kit to pencil more gray into his hair. There was not much he could do about weight or height differences, although they were considerable.

"I'll tell Lopez I joined a fitness center."

"And grew six inches?" she shot back.

"That's about how much Oppermann will cut off my *schlong* when he finds out we went after Lopez without telling him."

"If he cuts six inches off your hose, you'll have to put a straw in the hole to pee," she shot back. "Enough about Paul. Let's get this done."

They worked out their plans as they cased the crumbling estate. Willis was assembling a team of Miami operatives to help them. If he couldn't pinpoint the radioactive signature on the nukes, their only option would be to wait for ChiChi's call to Ravel at one-thirty. Because Ravel had infiltrated Lopez's organization for Zuloaga, he knew every detail about the Front's security. He brought architectural drawings of the building and grounds that included Lopez's escape tunnel and the layout for the minefield in the yard.

While they waited for Willis's call, they devised a way for six highly trained and well-armed people to overcome the fifteen unsuspecting Front members currently on the premises.

Leah's link beeped and she opened it to Willis's leering grin. She listened, nodded, and signed off. "He's got a three-person team set up. We meet them in Little Havana. Let's roll."

Ravel drove them to a cinder-block grocery with peeling white paint liberally decorated with spray-can graffiti. The ugly building squatted next to a mud-rutted parking lot overgrown with weeds and littered with junker cars. El Siglo XXI sold fresh produce and Cuban specialties. While the Haitian and Del waited in the car, Leah went inside. The musty interior smelled of smoked meat and overripe tropical fruit. A couple of ancient window box AC units wheezed in the humidity. At once she spotted the three operatives.

Both men were Hispanic and the woman Italian-American. They were discussing the quality of the smoked hams hanging on ropes from the ceiling. Mustering her best Spanish, Leah greeted them, pretending to be the wife of the second man. Both males were dark complected and compactly built. Ortega was slightly taller than Bermudez, who sported a heavy handlebar mustache curled at the ends like a bad parody of a Frito Bandito.

Ortega leered at her and pulled her to his side with one brawny arm, giving her a quick peck on the cheek. The woman who Willis had identified as Ida Martenelli was taller than her "husband," with a braid of luxuriant black hair that reached halfway down her back. Leah recognized the defined musculature of a serious gymnast. She was one herself.

Ortega pointed to the ham, but softly said, "The weapons and explosives are in our truck. We got everything on your shopping list."

"We don't have much time. I'll let our pal from the Cartel explain the layout to you," Leah said as they strolled to the checkout with a six-pack of beer and a couple of bags of fried pork snacks. They made the purchases, then walked out.

Bermudez looked at Del and Ravel lounging under the shade of a couple of scrubby palms. "I don't know about a Cartel guy covering our backs."

"Then why the hell did you come?" Leah snapped as they approached the TE.

Martinelli laughed in a husky voice. "He wants the money just like we do. Bernie'll do his job."

Leah made quick introductions as Ortega opened beer cans, passing them to the others. They meandered toward a withered live oak for what looked like a casual social gathering. In fifteen minutes they were back at Lopez's compound, armed with Glock machine pistols, MP5s, and enough explosives to blow the escape tunnel and half the crumbling mansion.

Leah climbed a thick bougainvillea vine on a side wall. Ravel had assured her it was no longer connected to the sensors since he'd rerouted it hours earlier. Using her monocular, she watched as the gates swung open. Ravel drove Delgado up the driveway in his shiny new Cadillac. After they stepped out of the TE, three of Lopez's men led them toward the house.

"They're in," she said to Ortega.

He checked his wrist unit, then nodded. Martinelli and Bermudez covered the rear and opposite side of the compound. Ortega moved to his position. Leah headed for the front gate, casually strolling like a hooker waiting for a pickup. Her black spandex mini and halter top were covered by an open knee-length red coat that concealed not only her Ruger but a Glock 18C machine pistol, three thirty-round clips, and enough nitro-cordite putty to blow the heavy iron gate.

16.

Delgado heard the soft scurry of rats across the filthy marble floors as his eyes adjusted to the dim interior light in the huge entry hall. A curving staircase with threadbare carpet so stained and varmint-chewed its color was indiscernible led to the second story where he knew four guards slept. He didn't see Lopez.

"You're early. Why didn't you bring the cases?" a wizened older man with cold gray eyes asked in rapid-fire Cubano Spanish, studying with overt suspicion the man he thought was ChiChi Bernal.

"You think I'm stupid, man? I don't work on no timetable and I told Ravel I don't walk into the wolf's den carrying my picnic basket," Del replied. "I deal only with my cousin. Where is he?"

"How do you know I'm not him?" a younger man with a flat round face asked softly.

"Nina, she told me what her cousin looks like. I want to see Lopez."

"You want to see my money, eh, *primo*?" Miguel Lopez said in un-accented English. He was standing at the top of the stairs, looking down at them with faint amusement in his dark eyes.

"Damn straight," Del replied, switching to English. Lopez would know Bernal's history, expect him to be able to do that.

"For a man who's just lost his wife, you don't look so grief-stricken," Lopez said, moving down the steps like a jaguar stalking a deer.

Shit! Del shrugged. He was afraid Lopez would've found out about Nina. "Men in our line of work make enemies. She was in the wrong place at the wrong time. I'm sorry, but I still got two nukes. You wanna buy?"

"She always said you were a cold fucker," Lopez replied. Then he laughed. "But Ninita, she always was a bitch, even when we were kids. She was older than me. Used to sneak drinks from my mother's wine, then blame me. I got lots of beatings because of her."

"No time for family stories," Del said as Ravel wandered down the hall, taking one of the three men who'd brought them inside with him. "Let's talk somewhere private. Finish the deal."

"Okay, big fella, that's enough," Leah whispered to the guard at the front gate who was massaging her breasts. "First you pay, then we play." She leaned back against the gate, pushing him away with one hand while the other shoved a piece of nitro-cordite putty with a timed detonator on the iron lock behind her.

He leered at her slender body. "How much you want?" the fat youth asked, wiping his sweaty paws on the sides of his jeans.

"Two hundred for a BJ. Three fifty for a roll." She had to make it so outrageous that he'd immediately back off.

The kid blinked in amazement. "You'd have to be a natural blonde first," he said with a snigger.

Leah laughed. "Don't know what you're missing, pussycat." She pushed off the gate, holding his attention by wriggling her hips while she sauntered a dozen meters down the sidewalk.

Inside the house, Lopez said to Delgado, "Come with me." He strolled to a big wooden door that one of his underlings opened.

The third man remained in the entry, watching the front of the house from a monitor mounted on the crumbling plaster wall. Off to the left, the door stood ajar to a big room filled with electronic equipment, the nerve center of compound security manned by two geekish types who Del assumed were as proficient at killing as they were at surveillance.

He followed the head of the Fidelista Liberation Front inside his office. Obligingly, the guard closed the door from the outside. That might buy him a nanosecond or two. The musty library's walls held dusty volumes of what once had been an expensive collection. Garcia Lorca and Cervantes probably didn't interest Miguel Lopez. Machiavelli might have some practical applications, if the rats hadn't chewed half the pages. Del noted the Benelli shotgun stashed in a corner of the room. It was in better shape than the books but too far away to do him any good.

Lopez moved toward the big desk where Ravel said his boss kept a Mach 10. Del had walked through a metal detector when he entered the house. He needed the firepower ASAP. To distract Lopez, he asked, "You have the cash in here?" He moved toward a two-meter-square steel door built into the wall, obviously a recent addition to the shabby old room.

"Ten mil? No, I don't keep that kind of money lying around."

Del's eyes narrowed as he touched the safe. Lopez did as he hoped and followed him. "Looks like it could hold that much. Why else you got it?" he asked, positioning himself between Lopez and his desk.

Leah hit the detonator and the iron gate flew off its hinges with a twisted groan. The armed man who watched her backside was knocked forward with a hole in his chest the size of a basketball.

She shoved the twisted wrought iron open and ran past him. *Close as you'll get to any pearly gates.* She zigzagged across the yard, carefully watching for the mines Ravel had diagrammed. One shot and the first blew sky high, taking with it an armed guard who'd rushed out the door just in time to die. She could hear the sounds of gunfire as Ortega, Martinelli, and Bermudez came over the walls. She prayed Ravel had taken out the power or they'd all be sitting ducks.

Lopez glared at Delgado. "Quit stalling. You know I'm good for the money. Where's my merchandise?" All pretext of geniality was gone.

Suddenly the light from the cobwebbed chandelier overhead flickered, then went off. Ravel had cut the power. When the first explosion rocked the house, Lopez lunged past Del. Plaster fell in hunks from the ceiling and the walls cracked as Delgado tackled him. Leah and her team were in action. So was the guard stationed just outside the doorway. Gun raised, he crashed through the door and tried to shoot Del without hitting his boss.

12:20 P.M. EST, WEDNESDAY, NOVEMBER 12
MANHATTAN, NEW YORK

Diana Shrewsbury stood at the front desk of their hotel in Lower Manhattan, her temper fraying as she waited for that lazy clerk to fetch her room key. The place was closer to Mike's Science Fair than the Four Seasons, but woefully understaffed. It seemed every convention imaginable, not to mention a special session at the United Nations, had brought record crowds to the Big Apple.

She had tried to reach Elliott yesterday when the Four Seasons could not accommodate them, but his link was not open. They needed to discuss where they would meet at the fair, but it was just like him to put details off to the last minute. And now her link was down. It served him right.

"Here is your key, Mrs. Threwsbury." The young man's accent was Eastern European and quite thick. He kept mispronouncing her name but she was too distracted to care.

"When are we gonna buy a new link, Mom? What if Dad's trying to call?"

"I'll track him down eventually. Remember, he had to go with Leah on some special secret mission, so maybe he can't call even if I had a working link." *Damn you, El.*

Mike's face fell. "I still wish we could go to Central Park."

She didn't want to explain the reason they had been avoiding tourist spots, but this was an easy one. "I'm afraid Central Park is too dangerous, kiddo. Just like Balboa at home."

"You mean it's filled with El-Ops, too?"

She nodded. What kind of a world were they bequeathing to their children? The limo they'd taken from the airport yesterday had bulletproof windows and special locks inside the passenger doors. Even the regular taxis had similar precautions against carjackings. She had hired one for a sightseeing trip along a scenic stretch of beach in southern New Jersey. "Let's just go up and rest now. I'll try your father again on the PDA in the room."

Diana was willing to bet once Mike flopped on his bed, he'd be out for several hours. But she'd have to come up with some diversion to occupy him until she could reach Elliott. If he didn't show up for Mike's big day tomorrow, she'd ream him a new asshole!

12:20 P.M. EST, WEDNESDAY, NOVEMBER 12
MIAMI, FLORIDA

The guard's shot grazed Delgado's ribs as he punched Lopez, then dived behind the desk. He clawed at the upper left drawer. It was spring-loaded to open instantly. A good thing since he'd no sooner seized the Mach 10 than bullets sprayed the heavy wood top, biting deep into the oak. He returned fire with one short burst that sent the guard diving behind a chair.

Lopez lay behind him on the floor, yelling obscenities in Spanglish. "*Puto* motherfucker! Don't shoot me—him! *Matas* Bernal!"

Delgado grabbed Miguel's arm, then smashed the gun into the side of his head. As he pulled Lopez behind the desk, the guard risked another burst of fire. Del rolled around the side of the desk and blew the heavy brocade chair to kindling.

The force of the barrage knocked the guard against the bookcase behind him. He slid down the shelves like a bloodstained rag doll. Rare volumes tumbled over, their pages fluttering red as they landed around him. Outside, the sounds of explosions and gunfire drowned out their fight, but Del knew Lopez's men would quickly come to aid their leader.

Miguel Lopez had taken enough hard knocks to recover quickly. He shook his head to clear it, then lunged at the man he still thought was ChiChi Bernal, shrieking to anyone outside who might hear, "*Ayudame!*"

One of the techies from across the way poked his head inside, shoving the door ajar with the barrel of a .40-caliber Smith & Wesson until he could see his boss and Del struggling. He raised the automatic for a shot.

Leah knew she and Willis's agents had to equal the odds before the four men upstairs joined the fight. She fired at another mine. Bingo. Similar sounds were coming from around the yard. Just so no one made a misstep reaching the house. A shot pinged a meter away from her and she knew someone inside was trying to set off a mine close enough to take her out. She jumped forward as the second attempt hit its mark. Dirt and weeds rained down on her as she fired from behind an overgrown palmetto.

Halfway to the house, she'd triggered three of the mines and the guy inside had obliged her with the fourth. She knew the minute she hit the front door a welcoming committee would be waiting. But without juice for the cams to reveal her position, the odds had just improved. In the front courtyard, she slammed against the side of the fountain, hitting the uneven bricks hard with her knees as another burst of fire tore directly over where she had just stood.

The sleepers had awakened. She scanned the upstairs windows, looking for movement, but the glass was dirty enough to obscure anyone standing behind them. When a hand pulled a drapery back slowly at the side of one window, she fired just behind it. The whole swathe of velvet tore from its valance, clutched in the hand of the man who went down. She knew there were more men upstairs.

Show me, dammit! She waited, counting off the seconds, not allowing herself to think of Del inside with Miguel Lopez. Then the ground rumbled and shook beneath her feet. Ravel had blown the escape tunnel! Lopez couldn't slip away now. Two more mines exploded, set off by the force of the underground blast. One sent a scrub palm flying as if it were caught in the path of a class-five hurricane. It was close enough to the house to smash into a second-floor window.

When she heard the scream of someone inside, she used the distraction to round the fountain and hit the wall of the house. She eased her way toward the front door, the schematic for the first floor flashing through her mind. Big entry hall. Security room to the right.

Lopez's office to the left. With no power, the geeks might run but she doubted it. Everyone in the Fidelista Liberation Front was a soldier.

The gunfire and explosions sounded like the D-day landing but she knew Miami-Dade PD wouldn't venture into the fight if Adolf Hitler rose from the dead and invaded the city. Flattened to the wall, she sidestepped carefully to the arched entryway. Some sixth sense— and years of BISC training—alerted her to the tiny snick of an automatic over the din. She looked up at the shallow second-floor balcony on the other side of the front doorway.

A mean-looking mother zeroed in on her, his finger whitening on the trigger. Leah raised her Glock and fired. He pitched backward and tumbled over the rusted wrought-iron railing, landing with a thud. She was too exposed to stay outside. Now or never, she slipped into the outer entry and flattened herself against the big door that was closed. Probably locked manually when the juice quit.

She took another small glob of putty from her coat, pressed in the detonator, and stuck the charge onto the lock, then jumped back against the wall. Three seconds later the blast tore the rotted old wood from its frame. The door crashed to the floor. She leaped on it, sweeping the cavernous space for targets. When the door shifted under her feet, she realized one lay pinned beneath it. He wouldn't be moving anytime soon. She made a quick dash into the security room. Clean. One of the geeks was still out and about.

Then she saw him whirl around in the doorway of Lopez's office, disoriented by the blast. Where the hell was Delgado? She fired, a clean head shot, and he crumpled to the filthy carpet. The place was dark and musty as a tomb. Leah almost shot her foot off when a rat the size of an overfed house cat scurried across her left boot.

"Talk to me, Del!"

"I'm busy right now," his voice grunted from inside the office.

She could make out the sounds of a struggle. Lopez! She started across the hall when the winding stairs above her creaked in warning. A fat man wearing a red do-rag fired a burst that grazed her arm. She took his head off with a swift burst from her Glock machine pistol, then ran for the door. The sound of footsteps racing down the hall made her crouch and aim. She held her fire when Ravel appeared.

"Dumb-ass thing to do. I could've shot you," she snarled.

"Your friends, they are good. So are you," he said, unperturbed.

The sounds of fists pounding flesh came through the door. "Cover me. Delgado's inside," she said, then stepped over the dead geek's body and slipped into Lopez's office.

A dead man sat propped against the bookcase. The revolutionary leader fought like a crazed animal, willing to take any punishment to kill Delgado. She saw a Benelli shotgun propped in the corner by the window but it was the Mach 10 they struggled over. Leah could see Delgado's knee give out on him when he tried to lever himself above Lopez and use the receiver of the machine pistol to crush Miguel's throat.

"Give it up, Lopez," she said, walking toward the two sweating men. He ignored her. She took aim, then saw the movement outside the window.

Someone was sighting in on Delgado through the glass. She adjusted her aim but before she could fire glass shards flew outward in a glittering rainbow. The man outside went down. Ravel grinned from the doorway. "I am good, too."

Delgado's full concentration was on Lopez. Their little tug-of-war wasn't going his way. He felt his bad knee start to go, then shifted his weight to the good one, toppling them onto their sides. Neither man lost purchase on the Mach 10 until Lopez suddenly let go, shoving it at Del when he saw his chance to grab his shotgun in the corner. He seized it and turned with a snarl.

Leah aimed for Lopez but Del was in her line of fire. Miguel's finger whitened on the trigger of the Benelli but his blast went into the ceiling. Ravel downed him with a hail of bullets that virtually cut him in half at close range.

Blood-spattered and aching, Del struggled to stand up. He could see blood running down Leah's arm. "Dammit, you're hit."

"Son of a bitch outside tore open the scratch I got in Sinaloa. Nothing serious but it'll leave a hell of an ugly scar."

The sounds of gunfire fell silent. Outside Martinelli and Bermudez called to each other. From upstairs, Ortega yelled, "Three dead men. Floor clear."

Del limped around the desk. "You can always have plastic surgery—unless you want to keep your battle scars."

"You look like the one who'll need surgery," she said, seeing the red stain on his shirt, noting how he favored his bad knee. "Can you walk?"

He checked his watch. "We have less than an hour before Bernal calls. You bet I'll walk. Hell, I'll dance to catch that fucker."

12:40 P.M., EST, WEDNESDAY, NOVEMBER 12
MIAMI, FLORIDA

The place wasn't any more of a dump than the joints in Michigan or Nina's place in Corpus, for that matter. But the humidity made it worse. Shit, he could smell the stink of ripe green mold blowing through the wheezing window box. Noisy outdated piece of crap, it didn't do squat to take the south Florida moisture from the air.

ChiChi Bernal sat up in bed and felt the lump from a broken spring press into his right cheek. The bed wasn't any better than those in Michigan either. At least he'd had time for a catnap to sharpen his wits before he called Lopez.

He scooted off the mattress, rubbing his ass, swearing as he reached for a pack of cigarettes lying on the burn-scarred Formica table near the window. The slip of paper Ravel had given him lay beside the smokes. He checked his watch, then peered through a slat as he lit up. The street below him teemed with life. A fruit vendor yelled out he had the freshest mangoes, three women from the cigar factory down the street took their lunch break, sipping inky Cuban coffee while standing at the window of a cafeteria, and a shoemaker stood outside his shop, listlessly smoking in the unseasonable heat.

ChiChi took another drag on his own cigarette and scratched his hairy belly. He was built like a fur-covered football, but the thickness around his waist and moon face often made people underestimate him. When his motel door lock snicked and opened, he moved with amazing speed, diving for the Colt lying beside his pillow. A single shot, a silenced ping barely audible over the babble coming from the street, skittered the weapon off the bed.

The shooter stepped calmly into the room. He closed the door as he spoke. "I wouldn't try that again."

Bernal stared into the barrel of what looked like an old-fashioned Ruger .22-caliber target pistol, ominously equipped with a silencer. He went still. "I got nothin' worth stealing." He gestured around the shabby room, stalling.

The intruder glanced down at a small device in his left hand and smiled. "You're a lousy liar. I'll take the cases." He placed the electronic device in his pocket and nodded toward the bed.

Knowing this was his last chance, Bernal didn't play dumb. He walked around the bed and knelt, reaching for the first case with one hand while his other slid beneath the mattress for his backup piece. He touched the cool smooth butt and felt reassured.

The shot caught him by surprise, smashing into his chest with more force than he would've believed a little forty grain .22 slug could deliver. He tumbled backward against the wall, looking up with glazed eyes at his murderer.

"It was worth a shot," the man said with a chuckle. "Too bad for you it was mine, not yours." He fired again, this time directly into Bernal's forehead, then knelt beside the corpulent corpse and finished sliding the case out. He fished for the second one and extracted it, too, then stood up.

The acrid odor of burning cloth filled the room. Bernal had dropped his cigarette onto the bed when he'd tried for the Colt. His killer calmly smothered the fire with the garish purple bedspread until he was certain it was completely out, then picked up the two cases. After placing a DO NOT DISTURB sign on the door, he departed. He doubted any maid would bother the room for days in a dump like this.

Grimacing with distaste, he muttered, "Miserable cheap tobacco."

1:05 P.M. EST, WEDNESDAY, NOVEMBER 12
WASHINGTON, D.C.

Wade Samson did not bother to stand when Adam Manchester was ushered into his office. Karl Banecek stood at one side of the president's desk. The secretary of defense wore a glowering expression on his broad pale face. Pointedly, he did not extend his hand to the senator. Samson nodded curtly for both of them to be seated. "I believe we have some things to discuss, Mr. Manchester."

Adam had been expecting this call, but when he found John Scarletti was not present, he was considerably relieved. Samson and Banecek, his right-hand man, he would have no trouble dealing with, but the AG was entirely a different matter. By keeping Scarletti out of recent developments, he had jeopardized Paul Oppermann's career. But worse from a personal point of view was the lack of faith in John. He was certain it was a mistake.

"Precisely what do you want to discuss, Mr. President?" Adam asked neutrally.

"Against my specific request, you've been investigating Karl and the CIA, for openers," Samson snapped.

Adam reached into his pocket, deciding to lay his cards on the table. If Del and Leah recovered those nukes, he'd hear within a few hours at most. Paul had the tobacco shop and Sievers's New York apartment under surveillance, hoping to catch a break on that end. All he could do was to buy them time now.

"You might want to play this. A source of mine recorded it early on Tuesday evening." He handed the copy to Banecek, who accepted the offering as if it were a live snake.

The secretary of defense placed the disc in the elaborate PDA against the wall and gave a voice command for audio play. The conversation, broken up but mostly audible, came through. Banecek's voice was unmistakable as was that of the recent CIA director Ralph Whitherspoon. Other than a slight tightening of his prominent jaw, Karl Banecek betrayed no emotion.

Wade Samson, on the other hand, was clearly livid when the transmission ended. "I brought you in to help us find two nuclear devices smuggled into the country by relatives of your granddaughter's boyfriend and you spy on the secretary of defense! What the hell has this got to do with finding Bernal and those weapons?"

"You know Leonard Sievers, don't you, Mr. Secretary?" Adam asked, ignoring Samson's outburst. "In fact, you were the one who sent him to Arzamov-16 to steal a dozen experimental bombs when you were the head of the CIA. I wouldn't bother denying it since I have proof." Actually, he wasn't at all certain that Al Braveheart could prove it, but he had no doubt Banecek was involved up to his eyebrows in the mess.

Banecek leaned forward in his chair and pierced Manchester with an icy stare that made most men back off. The senator didn't blink. "Ralph and I knew Sievers led a black op to obtain those weapons. Since we now know a former CIA agent is involved with Bernal, I figured it was Sievers. We're trying to track him down. If you have any information about where he is, you'd fucking well better give it to us—now."

Adam leaned back calmly, indicating that he was unconcerned by Banecek's posturing. "If we knew where Sievers was he wouldn't be on the loose. It's perfectly clear from developing events that whoever set this potential nuclear catastrophe in motion is highly placed in the government—and I'm not referring to Bob Labat who was merely a means to an end."

"We need to be informed about every piece of intel you uncover— immediately," Samson said.

"You refused to tell me what your secretary of defense and Whitherspoon were working on when I asked. Frankly, right now, I'm not interested in trusting you any more than you trusted me. The contents of this recording are pretty damning."

"I closed down that black op and cashiered Sievers when I was director, dammit! You can't walk in here and accuse me of treason. I had nothing to do with Sievers turning rogue. That's why the president decided not to tell you we were using Ralph Whitherspoon to locate Sievers. You'd only turn it to your political advantage," Banecek said, his temper fraying as he stared at the old man.

Now Manchester let his own anger show. "Political advantage?" he asked incredulously. "Is that what you think this is about? Polls? Peace Prizes? Your record in the history books? Gentlemen, we are looking at the greatest homeland security threat in the history of this nation."

"And you think we're unaware of that?" Banecek asked. "You're an old warhorse on the opposite team. We haven't got a reason in hell to trust you."

"The feeling is mutual, I assure you."

"You arrogant troglodyte, you have the mind-set of Teddy Roosevelt!" Samson said. "You'd be a disaster as president."

"If hundreds of thousands of Americans are killed in bombings and even more maimed by radioactive waste, what the hell difference will it matter who wins the damned election!" Manchester said. "My only concern is to find those bombs and capture the people responsible for bringing them here."

He stood and started to leave the Oval Office, then paused at the door and added, "I devoutly hope it is yours as well. Impossible as it may be for you to comprehend, it really doesn't matter if either or neither of us wins the next election—just so America survives."

17.

"Bernal's not going to call," Delgado said. There was hard resignation in his voice.

From where she paced inside the front entry, Leah scanned the wreckage of Miguel Lopez's compound. She looked over at Ravel, who sat calmly smoking a Cuban cigar. "You still say he agreed to call at one-thirty to set up a deal?"

Ravel shrugged. "That is what the man told me."

"I can't believe ChiChi'd pass up ten mil unless something—or someone—stopped him," Delgado said.

"If only you hadn't lost him after your meeting this morning," Martinelli accused Ravel from her post in the security room. One of Willis's best techies, she was in charge of manning the restored surveillance equipment.

The Haitian shrugged again. "This Bernal is no fool. He has come all the way from Mexico without being caught. Zuloaga had five other men besides me on his tail. Bernal knew Lopez would order this. He must have hired a driver to help him vanish."

"So where does this leave us now?" Leah asked, abandoning her position by the door. "Bernal's not calling. He's either made us, which I doubt, or somebody's made him. We have to assume whoever set this in motion has the bombs."

"Time to let Paul be the *moyl* at my bris," Delgado said with resignation. "See if the Bureau can do what Benito and Willis haven't been able to."

Leah knew he wanted to say "I told you so," but was too tired to bother. She felt guilty. *You made a stupid call, Berglund.*

Delgado winced as he picked up his link, dreading the exchange with Oppermann. He left the house, not wanting Ravel or any of Willis's people to overhear. By the time he finished, he felt even worse. He turned to Leah, who had followed him outside. "Did I say six inches? He took that and one of my balls."

"What's the deal with Bernal?" She'd overheard the end of the conversation. "Paul get a lead on the prick?" Leah said.

"Yeah, he was even willing to share." He let the irony sink in. "Those fibbies you think can't slap their asses have been monitoring local police. An unidentified Latino male matching Bernal's description was just found shot to death in a motel on Eighth Street. They checked it out. It's ChiChi."

"No nukes." Leah knew the answer. She cursed and kicked a clump of weeds across the yard.

"Let the lady pass go and collect two hundred dollars," he replied bitterly. "It was a fluke they found the body so soon. Had a new maid from up north somewhere. Couldn't read Spanish and thought the DO NOT DISTURB sign meant clean the room. Went screaming to the manager who called the cops. When our techs checked the dump, they found a trace signature of radioactivity but no prints."

"I'm guessing whoever killed Bernal probably opened the cases to make sure the bombs were inside," she said, already on her link to Willis. Their conversation was brief and she signed off, nodding. "I was right. He picked it up in a scan when I gave him the address. So faint he might've missed it otherwise."

"The shooter had to be Sievers. This fits his M.O.," he said.

"Look, Delgado, I was wrong. We should've brought Paul in. Hell, nothing the Bureau could've done to make this a bigger cluster fuck than we managed playing Lone Ranger."

He gave her a crooked grin. "What do you mean *we*, white woman?"

She didn't feel like smiling. "Tonto means stupid in Spanish. I'm the one who should deliver that old punch line."

He looked at her bandaged arm. "That must hurt like a bitch. You take your pain meds like a good girl?"

"I'm not a good girl, remember, Del?" She turned away and took out her link. "Better check in with Gramps and give him the bad news—if Paul hasn't already."

"Paul had more news."

She canceled the link command. "What?" The tight brackets around his mouth indicated it was bad.

"Between Adam, Gracie, and Quantico, they have some possible leads on Sievers in New York. Paul has addresses for a shop that stocks his cancer sticks and an apartment that might be a safe house for him. They're keeping both under watch."

New York. Instantly she thought of Mike and his mother. "If Ashtray's base is New York, you can bet that isn't going to be one of their targets," she said, trying to reassure him.

He didn't buy it. "I'll try Diana again while you dismis Willis's troops."

"You think we should just let Ravel walk?" She couldn't help asking.

"He did his job, blew the tunnel, and backed us up. Zuloaga doesn't know any more than we do about this mess. Not much point in losing what may be a valuable asset in the future," he replied.

Leah knew he was right. "Make your call while I brief Gramps. Then let's head over to that motel. See what the Bureau's forensics people have." She tried Adam but he didn't answer. She left a brief report on his PDA, taking the blame for losing the nukes.

Thanking Willis's people was easy. They'd done their jobs superlatively. President Ruiz's government would be happy to know the Fidelista Liberation Front was out of business. Thanking Ravel was hard. Leah knew the Cartel drug operation in Miami would quickly regroup. Ravel would be part of it.

How did it feel having the enemy cover your back?

4:49 P.M. EST, WEDNESDAY, NOVEMBER 12,
INDIANAPOLIS, INDIANA

The Holiday Inn was modest, a mid-range hotel that was comfortable without being ostentatious. The kind of place average middle-class families used on vacations and traveling salesmen frequented. Exactly the place where an ordinary-looking white guy like Bob Labat, with a little hair dye and a mustache, could be stashed without being noticed. Leonard Sievers had a network of such places across the country to keep assets out of enemy hands. His definition of enemy had become flexible over the years but the government had never been privy to his safe houses even when he worked on their side.

He knocked on the door and waited until Labat opened it, glad to see the jerk had enough sense to check the viewer before unlocking the double dead bolt he'd installed himself. "Special delivery. Here's your merchandise, just like I promised," he said, placing the two cases on a well-rumpled bed. One of the rules had been no maid service.

"About goddamned time. I've been cooped up in this lousy room forever."

"You want to go out on the town?" Sievers asked sarcastically as he removed the bombs from the specially designed container in which he'd transported them.

Labat snorted. "Some town. Indianoplace. They roll up the sidewalks at nine. Least you could've done was put me in Chicago."

"This is closer to St. Louis and bin Bergi. He wasn't very happy about the delay. I'll call and tell him you're bringing the goods tonight."

"Just so he has a hundred mil cold ones waiting for me. Then I'm out of this shithouse of a country. I busted my ass all my life and all I ever got was laughed at behind my back by Ivy League pricks like Kensington and Scarletti—all Samson's jerk off cabinet."

Sievers had heard the rant a dozen times before and tuned it out as he pressed the contact on his encrypted link. Bin Bergi's voice answered in Arabic. Although Sievers was fluent in the language, he knew the fucker spoke it just to piss him off. He'd be more than glad to see the last of both the Rabbit and the rag head.

"You can take delivery of your goods tonight on the terms we agreed," he replied in English. Just to piss bin Bergi off.

As darkness fell, Robert Labat, the secretary of Homeland Security, drove west on Highway 70 to give a terrorist two nuclear devices. In exchange he would become a very rich expatriate.

7:15 P.M. EST, WEDNESDAY, NOVEMBER 11
WASHINGTON, D.C.

"I appreciate your seeing me after hours, Mr. President," General McKinney said as Wade Samson ushered him into his private office on the second floor of the White House.

Samson gave his most ingratiating smile. "When the chairman of the Joint Chiefs wants to discuss new options on military policy, I'm always willing to accommodate. So's Karl."

Banecek was waiting inside Samson's office where he and his friend had speculated about what McKinney was willing to give them. Far less the politician than Samson, the secretary of defense shook hands stiffly with the general and all three men took their seats.

McKinney began. "I spoke with the Joint Chiefs this afternoon. They might be persuaded to consider some policy shifts you advocate. General Kirk is interested in that new satellite array and the Navy would like a fleet of those Corvette pocket frigates built in Louisiana."

"And the Army?" Banecek prodded.

McKinney smoothed his big hand over his silver widow's peak carefully. "Troop reductions and—or—redistributions are not on the table until after this nuclear crisis is over. Then and only then, I'll entertain—"

"You want something, General, yet you're sitting here making demands. How about telling us just what that is before we waste any more time?" Banecek said, his irritation clear.

"Now, Karl, let's take this one step at a time," Samson soothed. "We can discuss implementation of the new Defense Department initiative with the Joint Chiefs at an appropriate date. What do you want tonight, General?"

"The Chiefs have been left completely out of the loop on this nuclear mess. I have it on damn good authority that that idiot Bob Labat is responsible. I want to know just what in hell's going on. And don't spare any of the details if you expect to get one iota of cooperation with your so-called defense initiative." He leaned back and crossed his arms over a chest full of medals.

Samson and Banecek exchanged glances. Less than they'd hoped for but about what they'd expected. The president let his old friend the secretary of defense play bad cop as they'd agreed.

"First you agree to get the Seventh Fleet the hell out of the Mediterranean and those carriers out of the Gulf of Aden so the president can negotiate with Holy Arabia." Banecek's laserlike eyes skewered the general.

McKinney met his gaze calmly. "I don't take well to threats, Mr. Secretary," he said quietly. "If we end up fighting a war with those bastards—"

"Do you want to know what the FBI has learned or don't you?" Banecek said flatly. "If a couple of dirty bombs go off inside the United States, your three-million-man Army won't mean jack."

"But if such an unthinkable catastrophe occurs, the Joint Chiefs will be forced to deal with Holy Arabia—and I don't mean by appeasement," the general shot back. "If those devices go off, you'd be a fool to believe Holy Arabia would negotiate unless America had the Seventh Fleet on their doorstep."

"The way I see it," Samson began carefully, "is that saber rattling would stiffen Holy Arabia's resolve to initiate terrorist attacks within the U.S.—to say nothing of the deaths of every remaining member of the Saudi royal family."

"The hell with the House of Saud," McKinney snapped. "The American public will be incensed when they find out your secretary of Homeland Security is selling nuclear devices to Holy Arabian terrorists. Voters will be screaming for war. You'll be run out of office quicker than the carpetbaggers left North Carolina in 1877."

Samson stiffened, red-faced. "I don't take well to threats either, General."

"I'm not threatening, Mr. President." He ignored Karl Banecek, who'd leaned forward menacingly. Instead he kept his eyes fixed on Samson. "Let the Chiefs know what's going on or I go public with the information I have."

"That would be a grave error resulting in panic across the nation," Samson said, trying to hide his gut-kicked reaction.

"I'll have your job, you son of a bitch," Banecek said through gritted teeth.

McKinney shrugged. "Dismiss me . . . if you have the balls." His eyes never left the president's.

Samson hesitated, swallowing his amazement. The good old Carolina boy played hardball with the best of them. When Banecek stood up, he shook his head. "No, Karl. We have enough to deal with already." He took Paul Oppermann's latest report from his desk and began to outline what the Bureau, Justice, and the wily Adam Manchester's various sources had unearthed to date. The thought of an alliance between McKinney and Manchester was enough to start his ulcer bleeding until he'd need a transfusion.

7:19 P.M. EST, WEDNESDAY, NOVEMBER 11
NEW YORK, NEW YORK

"Be careful, please, Stuart. I always worry when you're in New York. The drug situation there is even worse than in the District and the United Nations is a hotbed for terrorists to boot."

Stuart Kensington smiled reassuringly at his wife's face on the vid. Such a lovely woman. Why men with intelligent and handsome wives wanted to have sordid affairs on the side had always mystified him. Jillian had been the only woman in his life since the day they'd wed nearly forty years earlier.

"I'm delivering a very important policy speech in front of that august body, Jillie. I even get to outline a few ideas I agree with in it," he added with black humor. "Give those damned Euros hell."

"Just be careful, darling. According to the news, New York's filled with drug gangs fighting turf wars," Jillian said.

"The president's provided me with a whole phalanx of Secret Service agents."

She made a face. "Only because he wouldn't dare risk having his most popular Cabinet member gunned down. I wish I were there with you. This is so soon after that awful trip to Korea."

He knew she'd been worried sick the whole time he'd been in that highly volatile part of the world. "I'll be home day after tomorrow as soon as the private meeting with the Security Council is over. Say, why don't you ask your sister to come down to Middleburg for an overnight stay? It'd do her good to get out of that gated compound and spend some time in the country."

Her face lit up at the suggestion. "We scarcely had a moment together at Dolly's reception. I'll give her a call right now." Jillian blew him a kiss before signing off. She always did that.

He liked it.

7:30 P.M. EST, WEDNESDAY, NOVEMBER 12
NEW YORK, NEW YORK

Leah sat glumly in the seat of the FBI car. Willis's jet had flown them to La Guardia. Oppermann wanted them to work with the Bureau and locate Sievers. Damned if she knew why after the way she'd blown it in Miami.

"You don't have to act like a prisoner facing execution. Paul blew his gasket on me. You he likes, remember?"

"And that's supposed to make me feel better? Bad enough we cut the AG. That one pissed off Gramps. Now I've alienated Paul."

He shook his head. "You do love self-flagellation."

"Look who's talking. You're eaten up with guilt because you don't know where Mike and Diana are staying. They're okay, Del."

"Wish I knew where the hell they are tonight," he said, looking out the window as the FBI car sped over the Bruckner Expressway headed for the address of the tobacco shop in the Bronx. To the south the glittering lights of Manhattan rose like something out of a fantasy, filling the night sky.

Mike and Diana were in those canyons of steel. She had left him a message while he was busy being shot at in Miami, giving the number for her new link and their new hotel. Her link had gone out and she bought another one. She explained that she was taking Mike out for an early dinner and then to a cine. Since he needed rest before his big day tomorrow, they were going to bed early. She expected Del to be at the fair tomorrow at nine sharp. No excuses.

He had left a message on her new link, explaining the change in plans, asking her to call him as soon as she could. Then, just as backup, he called to leave the same message at the hotel desk. The clerk insisted there was no Diana Shrewsbury registered. He had no idea where in that huge, dangerous city his son and ex-wife were.

Leah watched him redial Diana's link again and drum his fingers nervously. She knew he worried about the mix-up in accommodations and felt rotten that he couldn't be there for Mike's big day. Obviously there was still no answer on the other end. "She's turned off the link while they're in the theater, Del. That's all."

He grunted and broke the connection as the Bucar slowed in a shabby neighborhood. Even for the Bronx, this was bad-ass territory. Leah's instincts started humming. Empty storefronts stared at them like dead men's eyes and steel bars shielded the windows of those still occupied. Graffiti smeared on litter-filled sidewalks put a Technicolor finish to a scene made even more sinister by the occasional streetlight that had not been shot out. This was the sort of place where she'd hunted when she was with BISC.

The car pulled to the curb and they got out. Del unconsciously reached inside his jacket to check his Smith & Wesson. Leah scanned the alleyways and second-story windows up and down the narrow, dirty street, trying to see in every black corner.

"Guess the borough's street department doesn't feel this is a safe neighborhood to work in." He kicked an empty can out of his way as they approached the Full Gospel Temple in a storefront down the block from the tobacco shop.

"Can't say I blame them." She saw a black man dressed in clerical garb standing in the door. He looked as much like a preacher as she did.

"I'm Special Agent Brock Little. Two of my men and I"—he gestured to a pair of more convincing-looking vagrants sitting on folding chairs near the makeshift altar—"have been monitoring the tobacco shop for Sievers. Zip so far." As they walked farther inside, he offered them coffee. When they declined, he said, "The director wanted to update you as soon as you arrived." He pressed in the code and handed Delgado the encrypted link.

Oppermann got straight down to business. "I had to go to Scarletti to get a bug on the tobacco shop."

"What did he say?" Del asked apprehensively. Damn, he'd hate it if Paul lost his job over this!

"Not much. John's the quiet type. But he and Berglund's grandfather just had what you goyim would call a 'come to Jesus talk' right after I got my tap."

Delgado winced. "I hope Adam blamed the whole thing on me."

Leah leaned forward and said, "About our not keeping you—"

"Forget it. This whole mess is enough to make anyone *meshuge*. It's pretty obvious that someone got to Bernal while you were taking down Lopez."

"You mean someone knew we were occupied baiting a trap for Bernal. Zuloaga?" she asked, once again thinking of Ravel.

"You did Benny's dirty work," Oppermann said. "Got rid of a loose cannon in his organization. He'll have the drug operation up and running in a heartbeat. Without the inconvenience of a nuclear war set off by Lopez and his revolutionaries."

Leah nodded, but something about it didn't ring true. "Why not give us the nukes, too, if that was his game? He made it pretty clear he doesn't need them."

"Good point. I don't think Zuloaga double-crossed us either. My undercover agent in St. Louis just got word to me that Labat's on his way there with the nukes. The charmer running the show's the same *mamzer* who got away during the raid yesterday, Ahamet bin Bergi. Deal's set to go down sometime tonight."

"Your man know where?" Del asked.

"That's the problem. He doesn't and he has to restrict his communications. Several others in the cell are already suspicious of him."

"And you can't just round them up and hope to sweat where bin Bergi's rendezvousing with the Rabbit," Del said, anticipating the answer.

"Not with a super sauna. These cells always have backup plans. If we bust bin Bergi now, some other Holy Arabian crazy'll take over and grab the nukes from Labat. We have to rely on Ben Shehabi to get us word. If we lose him, that's the ball game. I'm en route to St. Louis right now."

"Any idea about when the fireworks are supposed to go off?" Del asked.

"No, but I'd bet my *tokhes* both blasts will be at the same time. If we don't recover the nukes in St. Louis, I have teams in place to search all ten targets for radiation signature, but I'd bet the farm that one of the bombs is set for the Arch. My agent didn't know for sure, but that was his gut guess and he's been living under the skins of these *mamzarim* for months."

"I'd go with that. It's one of the most widely recognized monuments in the world," Del said.

Leah nodded. "Yeah, bin Bergi wouldn't waste time setting up a deal in St. Louis if the Arch wasn't one of the sites."

"I'm putting the two of you in charge of the New York leads. There's another team watching the Riverdale apartment. I figure you can flip a coin and see who gets to take over which site. Kosher with you?"

"Better than we deserve," Delgado replied.

"You got Lopez. And if not for Special Agent Berglund's grandfather and your hacker, we wouldn't have either lead on Sievers. Now get to work—oh, yeah, and keep in touch, will you?"

The vid went black.

11:31 P.M. CST, WEDNESDAY, NOVEMBER 12
ST. LOUIS, MISSOURI

Ben Shehabi crouched in the corner, trying to make himself invisible in the crowded room. They were in big old flat just off South Grand Avenue, in a neighborhood that had yet to see the gentrification taking over parts of the area. Dirty yellow paint peeled from the walls and plaster on the high ceiling crumbled where a bathtub on the floor above had overflowed recently. The only furniture in the room was a single rickety table that bin Bergi used for his diagrams of their target. The cell members sat at his feet like disciples.

Several new men had arrived with the leader of the terrorist network. After losing two men in the FBI raid yesterday, everyone eyed his fellows with distrust. Ahamet first harangued everyone about the debacle that could have ended his mission. If not for careful planning, Labat, too, would have been captured before he could bring them the bombs.

The FBI infiltrator was a Lebanese-American who had spent the past seven years working counterterrorism. Ben Shehabi excelled at his job, motivated by the loss of his aunt, uncle, and four cousins to Muslim extremists in Beirut when he was twelve years old. This was his most frightening experience in what had been a harrowing life. He could not mess up, even though he knew Selim and several of the others remained suspicious of his family's affluent American background. If his parents had been Lebanese Christians instead of Muslim, he'd never have been accepted into the cell.

He listened as bin Bergi spoke.

"Think of it, my brothers! What marvelous irony. We will use weapons the American infidels stole from the Russian infidels—given to us by the offal who was charged with the Great Satan's own Homeland Security!"

Ahamet was a charismatic speaker, a slender man with deceptively wiry strength. His face was narrow, his black hair falling around it in a cheap haircut that matched the ill-fitting off-the-rack brown suit he wore. Although Ben knew he owned a Rolex and a closet full of Armanis, he did nothing to attract attention to himself when he worked in a poor neighborhood of struggling immigrants such as this.

"I will make the announcement about the origin of the bombs when we claim credit for the waste laid to these people and their wealth."

Unfortunately, bin Bergi would not divulge to this cell when or where he would take delivery from Labat, or what the other target was. Shehabi had just learned both weapons were scheduled to explode sometime tomorrow afternoon. The second detonation could be on the East Coast or the West.

He watched intently as bin Bergi described the positions each man was to take at the Arch. Their key player would be a blond-haired, blue-eyed all-American boy from Wisconsin who had taken the Muslim name of Selim when he converted to their perverted brand of Islam. Selim could easily pass the security checkpoint inside the museum below the monument. He would wear a uniform and have the proper ID for a safety engineer scheduled to inspect the tram that took tourists to the observation deck on the top of the Arch. A team had already broken into the home of the real inspector earlier that evening, disposed of him, and taken the materials they needed for the switch.

Once Selim was inside the stairwell that zigzagged alongside the tram, he would climb over a thousand steps to the top and conceal the bomb. By the time he and his men were flying from a private airstrip just across the river in East St. Louis, the Jefferson National Expansion Memorial Park, filled with tourists and schoolchildren, would be ground zero. A dirty bomb would send radioactive waste sweeping across the American heartland.

Timing was tight in spite of their careful months of planning. Every cell member knew their window to reach the plane and escape was very narrow. They embraced the risk of martyrdom. None more than the convert, Selim.

Ben Shehabi paid rapt attention to Ahamet's words and studied the diagram. His exceptional memory had proven invaluable to the Bureau over the years. Unfortunately, he doubted the terrorist leader would reveal the second bomb's destination. This cell did not need to know it. But if he could find out where bin Bergi was meeting Robert Labat and get away long enough to relay the information to Special Agent in Charge Donnell Washington, the Bureau might have a chance to nab both bombs before the nightmare went any further.

He knew several of the old-timers from Syria and what had been Saudi Arabia mistrusted him, especially since the raid yesterday. Getting away from their watchful eyes without blowing his cover would be very tricky. He had an encrypted link that their highly portable technology couldn't break, but since newer cell members were subject to frequent searches, he'd been forced to conceal it inside the engine of his old Pontiac EV down the street.

Just say where you're meeting Labat!

"I will return within the hour with the weapons. Until then my personal guards will see that everyone remains here," bin Bergi said, his glittering black eyes moving across the assembly on the dirty floor, studying each face.

Ben Shehabi cursed silently. He had only one ace up his sleeve. Playing it was a real long shot, but it might be the only one he would have. His racing thoughts were cut short when the terrorist leader spoke directly to him.

"You, Shehabi, come with us. Jabbar and Faisal say they doubt you even though they do not doubt Selim, who is not of our blood."

"But he is of our faith," Ben replied calmly. "That is all that matters."

Bin Bergi grunted, turning toward the door. Apparently it was the right answer. "Jabbar, you too will come along." A sly expression touched his lips. "To watch Shehabi. You can each carry a suitcase. You are strong men, eh?"

18.

The wind off the Mississippi was icy cold and whipping briskly as they pulled the beat-up old TE van off the road and into an abandoned warehouse located in a rusty manufacturing district. Nearby the shadow of a crumbling bridge loomed over them, long closed because the states of Missouri and Illinois were still wrangling in court about who was responsible for its repair. Their footsteps echoed on the concrete floor as they stepped out of the van.

Ahamet motioned for the driver to pull farther into the shadows while he led Shehabi, Jabbar, and two of his men to a small enclosed office from where the light emanated. He flicked it off, then checked the electric torch he'd brought from the van. Once satisfied it worked, he switched it off.

"Now we wait."

Fifteen minutes crawled by. Ben could sense the presence of Jabbar beside him. *I bet the fucker can see in the dark like a rat.* If he moved, the squat powerful man would be all over him. So would bin Bergi's goons. He had no weapon. After the FBI raid yesterday, bin Bergi had responded to Jabbar's and Faisal's suspicions by stripping Ben of his gun and knife.

Just as his eyes adjusted to the darkness, the low hum of an electric engine sounded at the opposite end of the warehouse. Two doors opened. One of the passengers coughed as he inhaled a cigarette. Its tip glowed, visible through the office door. They approached using a pencil torch for guidance. Ben could hear the smoker's hoarse voice say, "This is as far as I go. Collect your money, Bob."

He shooed Labat into the little room where bin Bergi switched on his bright torch. The secretary of Homeland Security looked like a jack-lighted rabbit. Tense as he was, Shehabi almost laughed at the image. Until he saw the suitcases Labat clutched in each big hand. The secretary stood frozen, squinting as he turned his head to avoid the sudden light.

"Turn that damned thing off!" he yelled.

"I do not think so." Bin Bergi rounded the table quick as a cat, keeping the beam shining on his target. "I believe those are mine," he said to Labat.

"Where's my money," Labat said stubbornly, casting a quick look back at the smoker whose cigarette glowed from a dozen meters away. "Sievers, you promised me protection, you son of a bitch! Haul your ass in here." Labat backed up a step but one of Ahamet's men anticipated his move and slammed the door behind him.

"The cases and detonators, Mr. Secretary?" bin Bergi said. His voice was soft, cordial . . . delighted.

"When I see the hundred mil," Labat replied, his Adam's apple bobbing as he swallowed hard. He tried to look mean, as Richie Viviano had when he ordered a guy to pay up or have his kneecaps busted, but he knew it wasn't working. *Rag head fuckers are crazy!* He damned Sievers for bringing him here, himself for believing the deal would still go through after all the mess-ups. "Come on, fellows, I know a hundred mil is chicken feed to your bosses in Riyadh."

"And you are no more than a chicken . . . but I do not believe I shall feed you," bin Bergi said.

"Now just a fucking minute! You—"

Labat's outburst ended with a sudden gulp as one of bin Bergi's men yanked the cases from his hands while another shoved him against the door. He tried to regain his balance, sweat beading suddenly on his forehead. "I got those damned things for you. I'm helping your cause," he said, trying to placate the nasty-looking thugs.

"Silence!" bin Bergi hissed.

The first man set the cases carefully on the floor. Obviously knowing what he was doing, he opened them, then used his own pencil torch to examine them. He nodded to his leader.

Bin Bergi pulled a small .32-caliber Beretta Tomcat from inside his jacket and turned it on the secretary of Homeland Security. "N-no! Don't kill me! Forget the money. I'll—"

His plea ended as a series of harsh pops rent the silent warehouse. Bin Bergi fired point-blank into Labat's chest three times. He kicked the body aside after the secretary crumpled to the floor. "Bring the bombs," he instructed Shehabi and Jabbar.

The smoker had vanished. They could hear the sound of his EV fading into the darkness. All that remained when they neared their van was a faint aroma of pungent tobacco.

"A useful man, but one day I will have to kill him, too," Ahamet purred as they climbed inside and exited in the opposite direction.

2:25 A.M. CST, THURSDAY, NOVEMBER 13
SOMEWHERE OVER ILLINOIS

"The deal's done on this end," he said, lighting another cigarette as he reported to his boss on the encrypted link. As he spoke, he looked down at the darkness below. From the window of the Cessna Citation he could see pinpoints of light winking faintly. Late-night television viewers, cars on the highway. A pity they'd all be dead in less than a day, but everything had its downside. "Our man will arrive by noon. I'll be at my place."

On the other end, a crisp voice said, "No, the place in Riverdale is being watched by the FBI. So is the shop where you buy those vile cigarettes. Go directly to bin Bergi's rat hole and set up recon. You know whom to call and when. We can't afford a mistake at this stage of the game." He signed off without waiting for acknowledgment.

Using the end of one cigarette to light another, the former CIA agent inhaled deeply, laughing until it started up his cough. *It'd serve the prick right if I died of a heart attack before I made those calls.*

2:48 A.M., CST, THURSDAY, NOVEMBER 13
ST. LOUIS, MISSOURI

"This is not the way to our rooms," Jabbar said as the van took a left turn onto Shenandoah. He looked at the driver, one of bin Bergi's men, who did not answer.

Bin Bergi replied, "Selim has already moved the rest of the cell to new quarters. It is a precaution. We do not want a repeat of that FBI raid." In the reflected glow of streetlights, his eyes were like black coals of fire, piercing each man in turn.

He lingered longest on Ben Shehabi. *This is it. He's made me.* Despite his gut reaction, Ben returned bin Bergi's stare. He'd had lots of practice pretending to be a zealot. After a moment, bin Bergi broke contact with a sly grin. *The bastard's playing me.* Then the thought occurred to him. His car with the encrypted link hidden in it had been left behind. He had to reach that link.

Then the driver said, "All our vehicles have been brought here while we accomplished our mission. They're parked out on the street, ready to use in the morning."

Ben breathed a small sigh of relief and turned his attention to the deserted street. Still in the south city off Grand Avenue, a couple of miles from the other place. The two suitcases lay beneath an old tarp in the back of the van. If the police pulled them over, six Arabic men should raise flags, but considering the El-Op-infested neighborhood, cops were in decidedly short supply. When Ben recognized his beaten up old EV parked beside several of the other terrorists' vehicles, he breathed a little easier.

"This is it," bin Bergi announced as the van pulled up a driveway. The big old house was completely dark and the surface they drove over was bumpy. The van stopped beneath the ruins of what had once been an elegant porte cochere and a side door to the mansion opened.

"Did you get them?" Selim asked, his yellow hair faintly visible in the black void around him.

"Of course," bin Bergi replied as he climbed from the passenger seat and quietly closed the door. One of his men opened the back of the van as their leader commanded, "You, Shehabi and Jabbar, bring the cases."

Ben couldn't decide whether it was a taunt or just a simple order because he and his accuser sat closest to the prize. They carried the heavy cases inside and Selim lit the way with a small electric torch, guiding them to a large living room. The rest of the cell sat on their sleeping bags, thrown on the bare wooden floor. Heavy drapes were drawn on both big windows and the only light came from a small lamp in one corner. The room was filthy and devoid of any other furnishings.

"Prepare yourselves to submit to the will of Allah. I go to rest and pray." With that, bin Bergi snapped his fingers. His two key men relieved Ben and Jabbar of the cases and followed their leader.

Shehabi could hear them climbing the rickety staircase in the hallway as Faisel said to him, "Your sleeping bag is over in the corner, Shehabi."

"I'm starving. We've had nothing to eat for hours. There anything in the kitchen?" Judging by the condition of the deserted house, he doubted it.

"Pah, you act like a fat old woman," Jabbar sneered at Ben.

Ignoring his antagonist's taunt, he said, "We passed an all-night Bosnian place on Grand. I'm going to get something. Who's got the keys?" At least he knew Jabbar couldn't have them since he'd been with Ben during the move.

But his plan was thwarted when Faisel said, "I, too, could eat, even if it isn't Halal." He tossed Ben's keys to him. "You drive."

Two others agreed they were hungry also. Accompanied by three terrorists, Shehabi could do nothing but play along. During the drive to pick up lamb kabobs and bottled water, he considered every option for reaching his link without alerting the men. There were none. They returned with several sacks of food and he was forced to wolf down the spicy meat while his stomach protested.

The bombs were right here, one call away from being safely retrieved by the FBI and all he could do was toss on the hard floor with indigestion through the endless night. He could sense Jabbar's eyes on him and knew there was no way he'd ever get out of the house alive.

When he reached his link in the morning, one bomb would already be gone with bin Bergi, headed anywhere his private jet took him.

But Ben had one last, desperate ace to play. . . .

7:00 A.M. EST, THURSDAY, NOVEMBER 13
MIDDLEBURG, VIRGINIA

Jillian placed her Limoges cup in its saucer and stared at the delicate pattern around the edge. The set had been in the Beresford family for generations. After Anne had married Frank Scarletti, their parents had changed their will, giving all the heirlooms to her and Stuart. Jillian knew it wasn't fair, but she'd been so hurt by her sister's rash elopement that she'd made no protest. Odd, after all these years how she should think of that as the two of them sat across from each other sharing breakfast. Anne had never cared about the china, crystal, or linens, even the lovely old house filled with priceless furniture.

"I think you should call him," she said to Anne. "He's left three messages now."

Anne smiled sadly, using the sterling spoon to stir black coffee. "Mother and Father always wanted me to marry Adam. Are you still matchmaking for them?"

"Better late than never," Jillian said, reaching out to clasp her sister's delicate hand. She swallowed hard, then looked into Anne's soft golden eyes. "I know you loved Frank deeply. The family was wrong to do what they—what *we* did."

"Jillie, we don't—"

"Yes, we do. It's long past time to clear the air. I'll be honest. You hurt me because you hurt Mother and Father, but they were wrong and so was I. We had no right to judge him unworthy because he wasn't in the social registry."

"You know we did have problems," Anne said softly, shoving the coffee away. "Oh, he became financially successful, but . . ."

"Not other women?" Jillian couldn't believe her sister would have put up with that.

Anne shook her head. "No, nothing like that. He was the love of my life, and I of his. He gambled. Compulsively. John tried to get him to stop but he never did. That's what Adam and I quarreled about."

"How on earth would Adam Manchester know about something that happened so many years ago—unless he's been keeping watch over you to see that you were all right."

"I seriously doubt that. No, it has something to do with John. He all but accused my son of being some sort of national security risk because of Frank's gambling!" She tried for anger but her face betrayed deep hurt instead.

"It had to be a misunderstanding, Anne. If you can't forgive Adam . . . will you ever be able to forgive me?" Jillian asked in a small voice.

"Oh, God, Jillie, yes, yes, of course," Anne said as she stood up and rounded the small table to hug her sister.

After that, they talked about the past, their marriages and children, Jillian's terrible loss when young Stuart had been killed, everything that had touched their lives. Everything but Adam Manchester.

7:30 A.M. EST, THURSDAY, NOVEMBER 13
NEW YORK, NEW YORK

Delgado awakened and sat up in the narrow hotel bed. Across the small room, Leah worked on the small PDA she carried with her. After monitoring the stakeouts at both the Riverdale and Bronx sites since yesterday, they'd finally given in to exhaustion and left Paul's hand-picked agents to continue the surveil. They checked into a small hotel in Lower Manhattan around three that morning. Because of overbooking, they had to share a room. He knew Leah had been uncomfortable with that after what happened in Bogotá.

But he was too worried about Mike and Diana to give a damn. Still no response on his ex-wife's link and the hotel continued to insist she wasn't registered. *At least New York doesn't appear to be a target.* The consolation was small. He rolled out of bed, saying, "Time to hit the shower. Then I'm off to talk to that manager face-to-face."

Leah looked up, distracted. How often had she seen him rumpled from sleep like this? But in times past, she had slept in the same bed with him. The past night they had spent a few tense hours in separate beds, each intensely aware of the other. *At least I didn't have any nightmares.* She knew that was only because she hadn't been able to fall into a deep enough sleep.

Her mouth felt dry when she said, "Pull your badge, Delgado. They'll find Mike and Diana quick enough." She wanted to ask to go along, but it was wiser to stay here and monitor the stakeout sites. At least, that's what she told herself.

In moments he showered, dressed, and walked out the door. Within the hour, he was back. "The day manager double-checked the guest registry. No dice. All I can do is show up at the Science Fair and pray Diana and Mike are there."

He looked gut-kicked. Deep grooves bracketed his mouth and his eyes were red from lack of sleep. "They will be," was all she could say.

"Any news from the Bronx or Riverdale?" he asked.

"I just received negative reports from both surveils," she said.

They waited nearly an hour for the PDA to signal a break or his link to beep with a call from Diana. Neither happened. Finally, Del checked his watch, then said, "You want to come with me?"

"I don't think it would be a good idea for me to tag along. You have to explain to Diana that you can't stay for the fair and some stranger is going to put her and Mike on a plane when it's over this evening. It's between the three of you."

Del nodded glumly. "You're probably right." He considered just how his son would feel when he broke the news. At least he would be there to give him a hug and tell Mike he loved him.

Leah's PDA signaled incoming. Maybe a break on one of their sites? Sievers? He prayed that they'd finally gotten lucky, but he knew that would mean he'd have to send someone else to the Science Fair. *How many times do I have to fail Mike before he gives up on me?*

Leah opened the channel. "Special Agent Little here."

"What's happening?" she asked.

"Nada. Riverdale reports the same. We'll continue the surveils but I figure Sievers has made us."

Her gut agreed that they were wasting their time waiting for him to show. "Who tipped him?"

"Wish I knew. I'll be in touch if anything breaks."

The screen went blank. "Who the fuck are you, mystery man?" she muttered to herself.

On impulse, she placed a call to her grandfather. He'd seemed pretty distracted the last time they'd talked. When his face appeared on the vid, she gave him a tired smile and told him Sievers was a no-show. "It doesn't feel right, Gramps. Where the hell is he?"

"Wherever, you can bet it isn't St. Louis. John just told me they found Bob Labat's body there about half an hour ago. Shot to death in a deserted building. If the police hadn't come to collect dead and injured after a pitch-battle between two rival El-Op gangs, the scum might've lain there until the rats ate him and died of food poisoning," Adam said.

"What about Paul's man on the inside?"

"No further word. The SAC in St. Louis doesn't know if he's dead or alive."

Leah deflated. "Then the second bomb could be anywhere by now."

"I'm afraid so," the senator agreed.

"We're chasing our tails and someone in Washington knows every move we make, even the dumb ones." She stifled an oath, knowing her grandfather didn't approve.

"We could still have a chance with Paul's man in St. Louis, but that national park is a big place. The Bureau can't do anything until they know the terrorists' plans."

Leah nodded, tugging on her hair until her scalp burned. "I've been up in the Arch. It's huge."

"They discussed closing the whole park."

She shook her head. "So, the terrorists detonate at the Old Courthouse. Make a speech about Dred Scott, whatever. Won't change a thing considering the kill range."

"That's what Samson decided after John talked some sense into him."

"John must be pretty pissed at you," she said. Her grandfather was seldom wrong in his judgments about people and he believed Scarletti was innocent. She still wondered if the AG was the leak, but knew Paul had no other choice but to go to him for the surveil orders.

Adam combed his fingers through his hair. "Not pissed. Hurt would be a better word."

"And not only him but his mother," she prompted. "Why don't you call her?"

"I tried," he said quietly, then changed the subject. "You and Del get some rest?"

"Look who's talking. I bet you haven't had more than six hours sleep since last Saturday." He waved her off as she knew he would. "As a matter of fact, we checked into a hotel for a few hours." When he grinned hopefully, she added, "To sleep, Gramps, sleep." She signed off, saying, "Don't give up on Annie."

After she closed the PDA, Del said, "The Science Fair will be open by the time we catch a cab. Go with me? Mike really likes you," he cajoled.

"You just want me to protect you from Diana."

"Believe me, if Mike's safe, I'll be happy to let her beat hell out of me."

"What do you mean, they aren't here? My son is a finalist!" Delgado's voice rose, drawing stares from volunteers and parents in the crowded auditorium on the campus of New York University.

"We received a cancellation just an hour or so ago from Mrs. Shrewsbury. It seems her son was suddenly taken ill—"

"Ill!" The mousy little man wearing thick wire-rimmed bifocals shrank back in his seat as Delgado towered over him. "What hospital—"

"I'm afraid I have no idea. She only informed us they would not be able to attend. You see, the paperwork is quite in order." He shoved a form across the table quickly, glancing around as if he was just about to call security.

Leah flashed her FBI credentials, placing a calming hand on Del's back. "This is Special Agent Elliott Delgado and I'm Special Agent Leah Berglund, Mr. Hartke," she said, quickly reading his name tag. That seemed to calm both men down. "We've been trying to reach his son's mother since yesterday evening. A family emergency back in San Diego," she improvised. "It really is important that we locate them."

Del watched her work magic as Hartke began checking his PDA for registration information that might help. He tried Diana's link again. How the hell could one woman manage to buy two defective communications devices in a row! The hotel still insisted they were not registered.

When Leah turned back to him with a helpless shrug, he said, "Dammit, what if Mike's been kidnapped?"

"Chill, Del, and lower your voice," she said, pulling him into an area out of earshot of curious bystanders. "Why would they bother now? We haven't got any idea where the bomb is, Labat's dead, and Ashtray's gone to ground. There's no reason to believe Mike and Diana would be dragged into this. We know they're in New York. Have Gracie 'interrogate' upscale hotel databases and nearby hospitals. She'll find them."

9:15 A.M. CST, THURSDAY, NOVEMBER 13
ST. LOUIS, MISSOURI

Ben awakened, stiff from the cold in the unheated house and from sleeping on the floor. He had gotten very little rest and knew his nerves were on edge. "Up, Shehabi," the cell member named Banaygh said, shoving his shoulder roughly. For such a small man, the terrorist was surprisingly strong. "Here is your SIG and knife. I know you felt unclothed without them."

Ben grunted and took the weapons, concealing the sheathed blade in the small of his back. Like everyone else in the crumbling mansion, he checked the action on his gun and packed his jacket pockets with spare ammo. Armed, Shehabi had no doubt he could handle Jabbar, but first he had another task to accomplish. He watched as bin Bergi walked down the steps and entered the living room. The drapes were still closed and the light from outside cast the room in an eerie gray glow.

As his henchmen set the two nukes in the center of the floor, their leader cleared his throat for one final pep talk. The room grew absolutely silent, every eye fixed on bin Bergi's slight frame. Ben knew what the rant would be but forced himself to feign rapt attention like the rest. They squatted in a circle on the bare boards. Ben moved within arm's reach of the nukes, which gleamed dully in the half-light. He knelt behind them.

"We go out this day to destroy the Great Satan for the glory of Allah! Selim," he called for the towheaded terrorist to stand at his side. The American convert dwarfed his mentor, his bland boyish face devoid of emotion.

Selim looked like a robot whose very sophisticated programming had gone haywire. Ben knew that in his previous life as Warren Edwards, Selim had been a brilliant student from Milwaukee who had earned a degree in nuclear engineering at MIT. Then he had fallen under the influence of this perverted version of Islam and turned on his own people. Bin Bergi ranted on about the will of Allah. *As if my God has anything to do with madmen like these!*

"Selim, may the blessings of the Prophet carry you to glory! While you destroy the heart of this infidel place, I shall strike at what it considers its soul!"

What would bin Bergi consider America's soul? Ben racked his brains, trying to think like a terrorist. He'd had years of practice.

"Preprogram your bomb for two p.m. now," bin Bergi commanded.

As Selim took one of the cases and knelt, opening it up, bin Bergi continued speaking to the others. "If for any reason your mission is threatened, Selim knows how to reprogram the weapon to detonate immediately with a few strokes of the keyboard you see here. This will mean martyrdom for all of you. But do your jobs as you have been trained and you will survive to announce your triumph to the world!"

Everyone watched Selim's fingers fly over the deadly device in the case. Even Jabbar was now spellbound, ignoring Ben. Without taking his eyes from his nemesis, Ben slid one hand along the bottom of the other case and pressed the microdot in position. He could feel sweat dampening his body in the drafty room. Had this been too easy?

Then he reminded himself that if he wasn't able to make his call, the tracer wouldn't matter a damn. Nope, not easy at all. He watched Selim and bin Bergi exchange embraces. The cagey older man snapped his fingers and pointed to one of his men, who picked up the marked case. "We leave you now. God is great!" he cried in Arabic. The others echoed his shout.

Shehabi watched bin Bergi and his two men walk out the door.

Selim took charge once his mentor was gone. He was dressed in his ATS uniform. The Automatic Tram Service was an affiliate of the National Park Service. "You will arrive at the Arch and take your assigned positions in the park at ten sharp. Once you're in place, I'll go through the underground security checkpoint with no trouble. The inspection I'm supposed to carry out was arranged weeks ago by the Park Service. It's routine and I have the real inspector's ID. I'll climb the stairs to the top, pretending to do the job, hide the case, and come back down.

"After that the timing is tight. When I emerge from the Arch stairwell, we'll have less than an hour to exit the park, get our cars out of the deck, and cross Eads Bridge. If there's any delay, we won't have time to reach the airstrip where our plane waits. We'll die for the glory of Islam."

He spoke as if he were discussing nothing more than the weather. Ben watched Selim's innocent-appearing face and again wondered how a brilliant mind had become so mentally unbalanced. Shehabi had worked undercover in terrorist cells for years. Most of the members were from abroad, raised under horrific circumstances, wanting to lash out at what they perceived as the superpower behind their misery. This guy sure didn't fit the profile. Selim/Edwards creeped Ben out.

Every man on Selim's team played a backup role, disguised in street cleaner's uniforms or, in the case of the two who were to go inside the museum under the Arch with him, as tourists. They had to remain in constant contact via the special encrypted links bin Bergi had given them. That way, if any one of them spotted FBI or police, they could warn their leader. Selim would then reverse course and detonate the bomb early.

Jabbar was assigned to ride with Ben. As they drove north along Kingshighway, Ben continued mulling over bin Bergi's last cryptic remark. If the Midwest was the heart, where was the soul? Washington, D.C.? No, that might be the brain or the muscle to bin Bergi's way of thinking.

Suddenly it came to him. He knew where Ahamet bin Bergi would believe the American "soul" resided. Now all he had to do was dispose of Jabbar and make his call.

10:30 A.M. EST, THURSDAY, NOVEMBER 11
NEW YORK, NEW YORK

After the debacle at the Science Fair, Del asked Gracie to work her magic on hotel databases in Manhattan, even flights from the city. While they waited helplessly for her report and any new leads on Sievers, Leah realized they hadn't eaten in nearly twenty-four hours. "Might be a good idea to catch a bite while we have the time," she suggested more to distract a worried father than because she was hungry.

He agreed and they found a deli on Thirty-fifth that served decent pastrami. "Not New York's best, but it'll do," he said around a mouthful.

Suddenly ravenous, Leah wolfed down a mountain of lox piled on a cream cheese-slathered bagel. "Lots of capers. Good stuff."

When his link beeped, he dropped the sandwich. "Delgado here."

Leah watched the expression on his face and knew it was bad. As soon as he signed off, she said, "Talk to me, Del."

He looked around the small, cramped restaurant. Typical of New Yorkers, no one paid them the slightest attention. He said softly, "Paul heard from his undercover man. The second bomb is set for Wall Street. Guy's almost certain but that's all he knows."

"No location? How the hell are we supposed to find a bomb in a city this size?" Her fear was magnified in his eyes. His only child was somewhere in the city and he didn't have any idea where.

"NRO's working on a long shot. The agent slipped a tracer dot on the case before it left St. Louis. Think your pal Willis might be able to do something they couldn't?"

"Worth a shot," she said, not sounding as if she believed it. "Let's see if the local fibbies have any idea where scumbags like bin Bergi might hang."

"I'll put Gracie on it, too."

As they both worked their links, neither had ever felt so helpless . . . or frightened.

Just six blocks away on the twentieth story of the Marriott, Mike tried to give his mom a smile, but he just couldn't muster one. He fought back unmanly tears as he looked at the boxes filled with his papers and the display he'd brought all the way across country for the competition.

The doctor the hotel had arranged to visit him had just made his diagnosis—chicken pox! A baby's disease. And he'd caught it when he was practically a teenager! His mom and the doctor figured that her friend's three-year-old daughter had given it to him. He hated babies. Before catching himself, he'd almost called Trisha one of his dad's favorite words.

"Any contagion should run its course in a couple of days," the physician said to his mother.

"He complained of being hot and woozy when we were on our way home from the cine last night. This morning when he broke out with red spots, I was pretty concerned. I don't understand how he could contract it after being inoculated."

"Rare but not impossible. Some people simply don't respond to the routine battery of shots. We can be grateful it's a mild form of a nonthreatening disease."

"Nonthreatening! It's ruined my chance to compete at the fair," Mike said, outraged.

Dr. Walsh walked back to the boy's bedside and pulled up a chair. He was a pleasant-looking man with sandy hair going gray and warm brown eyes that crinkled at the corners when he smiled. Mike wanted to dislike him but it was difficult.

"Your mom explained how hard you've worked on your project. I'm really sorry this had to happen, but you do understand that even if you felt well enough to go, you might make some other people sick. You wouldn't want to do that, would you?"

"Naw, I guess not," Mike replied. "It'd be pretty embarrassing, having everyone know I had a baby disease, anyway," he added, trying to convince himself.

"His better nature is winning out," she said to Dr. Walsh before turning back to Mike. "Even though I've already told Geoff Wescott we couldn't be there because you were sick, I'll call him back. He is the fair director, after all. Maybe if we send your project over, he can have someone set it up for display."

He brightened slightly as his mom showed the doctor out, thanking him for the courtesy of a hotel visit. But his office was right next door, so what was the big deal? It wasn't as if he were an FBI agent on a case or a reporter breaking a big story like his dad had done. Then Mike remembered that his dad had not called and wondered about the mysterious assignment he and Leah were working on. Something so top secret that they couldn't talk about it. Now that was the real deal when it came to jobs.

Mike listened as his mother spoke on the PDA in the sitting room, trying unsuccessfully to reach Geoff Wescott. She argued and pleaded, but nothing seemed to work. He could hear the mounting frustration in her voice and knew she was doing this for him. "Don't worry, Mom," he called out when she finally broke the connection. "There's another fair next year. I'll be able to enter the high school competition then and that's a much bigger deal."

She returned to the bedroom and gave him a big hug. "You've always wanted to take that tour of the Primate Center in Seattle. Tell you what, sport. As soon as you're better, how about we do that?"

"Wow! That would really rock, Mom!"

His voice was a bit scratchy and he looked tired from the fever, although Dr. Walsh had assured her it was the normal course. "How about you get a little rest while I go out and buy some of those hot, fresh donuts from the shop you saw yesterday?"

"You're the greatest," he said softly.

Diana watched as he lay back on his pillow and drifted off to sleep. Smiling, she closed the door to his room, then crossed the sitting room and turned off the hotel PDA so it wouldn't interrupt his rest. Placing her link in her handbag, she set the security system for the suite and left. While she was out she'd hit the electronics store the concierge had recommended and buy a decent link. The one she'd picked up yesterday was a piece of junk. She had to reach Elliott, wherever he was, and let him know why they weren't at the fair.

If he even cared.

19.

Paul Oppermann let out a string of Yiddish invective that would've peeled paint from the walls of Temple El Emth where he attended services in D.C. He'd have to do some praying after this was over. Then again, he might not have the chance. His family back in Washington would say kaddish for him, he consoled himself. But what about up to a million souls in the Midwestern United States either killed outright or poisoned by radiation? Who could possibly pray or mourn for all of them? It was too monstrous to dwell on.

He squinted at the grainy pix of Warren Michael Edwards, AKA Selim. "Looks as all-American as apple pie," he said. "From Wisconsin, for crying out loud." He scanned the report from the Bureau's terrorist database on the man who was now preparing to place a bomb at the top of the Gateway Arch. Edwards had converted to Islam five years ago. Younger-looking than his thirty-four years, he was blond and blue-eyed. Smiling and wholesome.

Oppermann surveyed the room filled with grim-faced agents, then glanced over to Ben Shehabi who had just walked in the door. He motioned for Ben to come to the podium. By the time the undercover agent could subdue Jabbar the rest of the terrorists were already approaching the park by various routes. Via link he'd given them everything he knew about bin Bergi's plans. Oppermann and the St. Louis SAC had less than five hours to get their counteroperation under way and capture that bomb.

"Review everything you know with the team," the director said to Ben.

"Four cell members are staking out the park grounds near the north and south legs of the Arch. Two others will go inside the Arch shortly before Selim. Bin Bergi had his men sabotage the electrical grid nearly two weeks ago. Didn't tell the St. Louis cell about it until this morning. That gave his infiltrator a couple of minutes' window before the emergency generator kicked on. In the dark it must've been pretty chaotic. The guy got inside posing as an LEO," Ben explained. LEO stood for Law Enforcement Officer, a branch of park rangers who were armed and had police training.

Shehabi continued. "He smuggled three little Rohrbaugh R9 automatics inside and stashed them. Only Selim's two honchos, Dulghani and Banaygh, know where they're hidden. They go inside to back up Selim."

The underground mall beneath the Arch contained two movie theaters, the Westward Expansion Museum, and several shops. All the agents knew that searching for guns was useless now and would only tip off the terrorists.

"The four cell members outside are spotters, backup men, and they're armed, too. Jabbar and I were to be five and six. I called Selim and said we'd been caught in a traffic snarl because of a fender bender on Kingshighway. Told him we'd be late. God, I pray he bought it."

"If he didn't, he'll move on to the next plan—which we don't have a clue about," Oppermann told the agents in the briefing room.

"If they keep to the original scheme, the bomb's already set for two this afternoon. All Selim has to do is get it to the top of the Arch and then the whole crew will scatter like rats. If park rangers try to stall or arrest Selim, his two men inside will open fire while he recalibrates the timer for instant detonation," Shehabi said.

An agent at the back of the room raised his hand. "Why can't we nab Selim as soon as we see him approach the park, or use a sniper to take him out before he gets inside?"

"Good questions," Oppermann responded. "First, the terrain's too open this time of year for sniper concealment. Second, Selim will already have his four men scattered in the crowds. They'd start shooting civilians, create a panic. Probably one of them could reach the bomb if Selim went down. Get away with it still ticking while the others covered him."

"And if Selim's only wounded, it wouldn't take him a minute to reset. I watched him work," Shehabi added.

"Everybody dies martyrs for Holy Arabia," Oppermann said.

"You're absolutely certain they're willing to do it?" the St. Louis SAC Donnell Washington asked.

Oppermann looked at Shehabi who replied, "Absolutely certain. Selim will set off the device no matter what the cost." He remembered the calm, emotionless way the terrorist had spoken that morning and suppressed a shiver. "He's completely whacked, an ice man. And the men with him are just as crazy. Their chances of getting across Eads Bridge to the plane are slim at best. They all accepted the risk going in."

The FBI counterplan had been hastily worked out with the Chief Ranger Roger Corbett, who was in charge of security at the national park. Their first decision had been not to bring the local police into the equation. Everyone agreed there simply was not enough time. The terrorists had already familiarized themselves with all regular uniformed personnel around the park. STLPD officers flooding the place was the last thing either the Bureau or the park rangers wanted. Oppermann and Washington went over everything for their team one last time.

"As soon as Selim comes down the north stairs, Special Agent Virgil Watkins, our bomb tech, goes into action," Paul said. "He's moving into position at the door on the observation deck atop the Arch right now. He'll slip in and disarm the nuke. When Edwards or Selim, whatever the *meshugener* calls himself, walks out of the restricted stairway, Chief Corbett and I'll be there while two LEOs arrest him."

"Special Agent Shehabi will act as a spotter for Selim's men inside the mall. The pix of them won't work as well for ID in crowded close quarters. Once Ben fingers them, you have to disarm them—hopefully before they open fire," SAC Washington said, nodding to the two teams assigned that task.

"That goes down immediately after we signal we have the nuke,"

Oppermann said. He turned to the eight men and women assigned to work the outside. "You have good pix of the backup men. ID them as fast as you can, then stick with them. When I give your SAC the signal everything inside the mall is clear, he'll tell you to take them out." He turned to Ben. "Anything else you can add?"

"I'll try my best to locate the two gunmen in the crowd quickly as I can, but I have to warn you, in all probability they'll get to those hidden automatics before we can stop them." Shehabi knew as they all did how much could go wrong.

"Every step of the way, we have to prevent a hostage situation and avoid civilian casualties if at all possible," Washington emphasized.

"Selim and his men are in constant communication. If our timing on any stage is off, he could learn they've been compromised while he can still reach the bomb. End game," Oppermann said.

As all the agents left the briefing room, he shuddered, thinking about his last words.

While he and Ben Shehabi drove down Market Street, Paul watched the sidewalks teeming with people. Children were everywhere. He fought to remain calm. Maybe he should have stayed back at the FBI office and let SAC Washington handle the operation with Chief Corbett. But he couldn't let it go. He had to know he'd done everything humanly possible to stop the unthinkable. Besides, he admired Special Agent Ben Shehabi and wanted to see this through with the man who had broken bin Bergi's operation.

He and Shehabi parked on the open top tier of the Arch parking deck and walked toward the grounds. As they neared the north leg of the Arch, they pretended to be tourists, complete with cameras that were really state-of-the-art communications devices with other specialized functions such as scanning for encrypted link transmissions. The lenses of their cameras contained high-resolution monoculars.

"See any of your boys? With you and Jabbar out of the picture, they probably shifted positions," Paul said to Ben.

Shehabi was now dressed in casual slacks and a windbreaker. He sported dark glasses and an authentic-looking short beard. "No," he replied, "but they have to stay somewhere around the benches at the legs of the Arch so they can hear or see any commotion coming from the mall. Washington's people have to get a fix on all four before we nab Selim."

Paul pulled his coat collar up to ward off the wind whipping across the Mississippi as he and Ben walked along the curving path lined with bare trees. In spite of the chilly day, the sun shone brightly, mocking them. Ahead, Eero Saarinen's soaring stainless-steel masterpiece gleamed like diamond-cut sterling silver.

The city and surrounding county school administrators were hosting a Cooperating School District Conference at the St. Louis Convention Center a few blocks away. Schools were closed and many families had ventured downtown to visit the city's numerous cultural attractions—the zoo, art museum, botanical gardens, and, most famous of all, the national park that housed the Arch.

Suddenly Paul's "camera" vibrated. He pressed a button and put it up to his face, pretending to take a pix. "Units two and four have their targets sighted. One here on the north, the other on the south."

"That leaves two more." Shehabi knew they were a long way from home free. *Please God, don't let me be spotted.* He resisted the urge to touch the fake beard to see if it was securely glued on his jaw.

As they strolled down the incline leading into the mall beneath the Arch, they could feel each millisecond pass while FBI and park personnel moved into position. They bypassed the line waiting to go through the secure-scan. Two armed park rangers let them in while keeping watchful eyes on the crowd. Ben prayed none of Selim's men noticed.

Special Agent in Charge Donnell Washington observed the director and Shehabi disappear underground. Once the bomb was disarmed and the three men inside were in custody, his people had to take their targets fast and clean. The SAC knew this would be his last posting anywhere if the operation went south. When Bob Labat had escaped their trap, he'd worried about his career. That seemed like a big deal yesterday. Knowing how many people including his wife and three kids could die placed career advancements in true perspective now.

He watched as unit three, a salt-and-pepper team of female agents, walked past one of the terrorists sitting on a bench. They sent the coded signal to his communications device, then waited. He'd used every woman in his command on this assignment. Muslim extremists seldom believed a mere female could pose a threat. The agents carried pressure syringes filled with a newly enhanced version of Versed, a powerful drug that incapacitated its victim almost instantly. The trick, since the terrorists were all wearing winter clothing, was getting close enough to plunge a needle in a target's neck. Women made that easier.

One team had not located their target yet. In spite of the chilly day, Washington sweated inside his topcoat. Then he received the message that team one had their man in range. Now, all he could do was wait to hear from the inside. Since the two terrorists on each end of the Arch were in visual contact and all four could communicate via link, their takedowns had to occur simultaneously to prevent potential civilian casualties. It should work—if nobody screwed up. . . .

10:40 A.M. EST, THURSDAY, NOVEMBER 13
WASHINGTON, D.C.

Adam felt a soothing rush of contentment when Annie's face appeared on the vid. He was elated that she'd finally returned his calls, even though the situations in New York and St. Louis remained critical. He kept one eye on the incoming light on his PDA as he smiled at her. "I'm so glad to see your face, you can't know, Annie."

"You look as if you haven't slept in days, Adam. This has something to do with what you and John and the others are working on, doesn't it? Oh, I know you can't tell me about it. Neither Frank nor John ever discussed work at home . . . listen to me. I'm blathering."

"I love the sound of it, but no, you never blather, Annie. I was wrong to ask you about Frank. Or to doubt John. I apologized to him. Now I'm apologizing to you. You've raised a fine son—you and Frank," he added.

"Thank you. And no apologies are needed. I can only imagine the strain you and the others have been under while Jillie and I have been eating waffles and catching up on old times. We haven't been this close in years. It was her idea that I return your calls, Adam. And Stuart's idea that she invite me here."

"He's a good man."

She paused, smiled softly. "Yes, the sort of man our parents approved—just like you. Jillie did what was proper. I was the rebel."

"Did you ever regret it?" he asked before he could stop himself. "I'm sorry, I have no right—"

"I'm glad you asked. Shows you still care a little about me."

He could see her cheeks pinken on the vid and smiled. "Yes, I do care, a very great deal. I've thought about you over the years after my wife passed. When I heard about Frank, I almost called you."

"Why didn't you?"

He chuckled. "You're a blunt rebel still. Kept telling myself I was too old, too busy, too far away. In truth, I was a coward, I suppose. I didn't take losing you with much grace."

Now it was her turn to chuckle. "No, you exhibited that famous Manchester temper quite well. So much for the myth about taciturn, cold New Englanders!"

"I regret what I said, Annie."

"Living all those years with a volatile Italian, I grew used to emotional outbursts," she said wryly.

"John keeps his under tight control. Must be some recessive Beresford genes in him."

She agreed. They talked for nearly an hour, losing track of time, discussing their children and grandchildren, their extended families. It was a blessed relief for Adam to think about something besides nuclear catastrophe. But then Anne made an innocent comment that hummed in his mind. Surely, it meant nothing. But what if it did mean what he feared? He said good-bye as gracefully as possible, then tried to reach Gracie Kell.

He was forced to leave a message and hope that the hacker would get back to him quickly. Since this crisis began, she'd been far more available than normal, according to Del. With Paul Oppermann busy in St. Louis, Adam had agonized about calling Wade Samson as he waited, but he needed Gracie's verification first. After the longest quarter hour of his life, her waif-thin face and electric green hair appeared on his vid.

"Watcha need, Senator?" she asked. "Say, you don't look so hot. This bomb scare getting to ya?"

"More than you could ever imagine, Ms. Kell. Here's what I need you to do." He explained what he wanted.

She winked. "Piece of cake. Give me a few."

The vid went blank and he lay his head on the desk and closed his eyes, uncertain whether to pray he was wrong or that he was right.

11:03 A.M. EST, THURSDAY, NOVEMBER 13
BRONX, NEW YORK

Leonard Sievers sat in his Buick TE, drawing deeply on his Macedonian. The air inside his car was blue with smoke but he was used to it, didn't even bother cracking a window. In this neighborhood, who'd take the chance? He observed the rat-infested tenement across the street. This was a free-fire zone where more of the nineteenth-century brick buildings lay in rubble than remained standing. The gray skies cast an ugly pall over the narrow street, which was filled with junker cars interspersed with flashy Caddie and Lincoln TEs, signature vehicles for El-Op chieftains. No one in the hood messed with those prizes. All other autos were fair game.

He patted the Glock concealed inside his topcoat as he watched his rear vids. Nasty place. A big town car dripping chrome pulled up and a coterie of local thugs piled out with an array of automatic weapons in plain view as they headed toward the building he was watching. A faint hum of warning vibrated in his gut, but subsided slightly when they split up. Only two went inside. The other five ambled down the street and disappeared around the corner, laughing and shoving each other. Their reflexes were off. One stumbled over a brick. Another fell against the wall as he giggled.

Stupid kids, ride the Elevator . . . it's a long drop from that top floor.

He dismissed them, but something niggled at his subconscious. Hell, there'd been too much going on for the past week to trust even his own well-honed instincts. His target was on the top floor of the brick monstrosity. He checked his wrist unit, then opened his link and gave the voice command. His target answered impatiently in Arabic. He replied in English, their usual ritual.

"The broker still insists on meeting you. Won't deal unless you swear on the Koran that he's going to get out of this alive." He started to chuckle, then coughed.

"The greedy infidel thinks he'll escape," bin Bergi replied. "A pity he won't have time to understand the error of his ways."

The terrorist sounded anything but pitying, Sievers thought as he gave an address a dozen blocks away.

"I see no reason we should not proceed to our destination with the device now," bin Bergi argued.

Because I have to separate you from your ware. Aloud he replied, "He's your way inside. I went to a lot of trouble setting this up for you. Don't blow it. Humor him."

"It is a waste of time," bin Bergi said stubbornly.

"Look, my friend, there's no time to waste arguing. You asked for a way to place the bomb inside the New York Stock Exchange, your symbolic gesture. This creep was part of the deal."

"Very well, but as a precaution, I am going to preset the device for the appointed time before I leave. Nothing will stop jihad."

A calculated risk. But if Sievers argued any more, the bastard would get suspicious, set it anyway. "Whatever you want. It's your ass. I'm safe here in D.C.," he lied.

As soon as the terrorist agreed to the meeting, he broke the connection with a faint smile, inhaling deeply. The FBI had never been able to finger the greasy bastard. Now New York's Finest, along with all the news media, were going to break the shocking conspiracy wide open . . . with a little help from a used-up old spook. He smoked another cigarette as he waited for bin Bergi to come out of the dump. Then he would place a series of calls, beginning with the bomb squad of the NYPD. There was plenty of time, he assured himself.

That was when he heard the rat-a-tat of automatic weapons fire. *Fuck!* He considered getting out of the car, then thought better of it. The rapid bursts stopped almost as quickly as they'd begun. He ground out his cigarette and leaned back in the shadow of his visor. Cursing savagely, he realized his instincts had not been off.

Seven El-Op thugs emerged from the building and piled into the Lincoln. Before they sped away, Sievers recognized four satchels that he would bet contained a hundred million dollars in negotiable securities.

And one suitcase made of hard metallic alloy.

11:04 A.M. EST, THURSDAY, NOVEMBER 13
WASHINGTON, D.C.

Adam Manchester sat in front of his PDA scanning the damning evidence, too stunned to say anything to Gracie Kell, who had fed it directly to him as soon as she finished her computer interrogation. As he read, she talked.

"Getting in wasn't easy. He had some pretty bitch—er—tricky protocols I slipped through. Nothing like busting into BISC Central, though. I guess he never thought anybody'd try to access his private files. If you'd sent the fibbies and their techs with a court order, they'd still be picking their noses when he was grandstanding. Jeez, what an actor if he could pull that off." She shivered. "Say, Senator, you don't look so good. This creep a pal of yours or something?"

"You could say so." Manchester's tanned outdoorsman's face was white as the hacker's, numb with shock at the vicious extent of the plot. It was beyond anything he could ever have imagined. *Terrorists come in all hues.* He took a deep cleansing breath and said, "Thank you, Ms. Kell, for your help. I'll be in touch."

The senator had never used a computer as efficiently as he did then, letting go of all his old prejudices about newfangled communication. The PDA's speed and multitask capabilities might save countless lives. He considered whether or not to transmit the information to Wade Samson and decided it would only slow things down. The son of a bitch would want to closet himself with political advisors to decide how to play it to his advantage before he took action. Adam sent the address for Ahamet bin Bergi's apartment in the Bronx to John Scarletti and the SAC in New York, whom Paul Oppermann had vouched for.

When the AG came on vid, he looked as stunned as the older man. "Reed is taking half a dozen agents in under deep cover. First priority is the bomb and bin Bergi. Then Sievers."

"Could bin Bergi detonate the device if they don't get it away from him first?" Manchester asked.

"According to what Paul reports from St. Louis, yes. Reed's been apprised," Scarletti replied. "They're taking every precaution. Sievers is supposed to decoy bin Bergi away somehow. Wish we knew where, but without the bomb, he won't get far. Our biggest worry is Sievers creating a media circus before Reed and his agents can beat them there."

"That could complicate matters," Adam agreed. "I think Leah and Delgado should make the arrest." He couldn't bring himself to say the monster's name.

Scarletti seemed to understand. "Consider it authorized. Tell them to sic 'em."

11:04 A.M. EST, THURSDAY, NOVEMBER 13
NEW YORK, NEW YORK

"They're at the Marriott in Lower Manhattan where that son of a bitch told me to my face they weren't registered!"

Leah had watched Del working his PDA frantically, searching for his son. Gracie Kell had been tied up with an assignment from Adam and did not respond to his message. "How did you figure it out?"

"Took a page from Gracie and started thinking about how literal computers are. Like exact spelling, that sort of thing. Tried a series of misspellings on Shrewsbury. Threwsbury hit bingo."

As he talked, he waited to be connected to Diana's suite. The line rang and an automated voice response unit said Mrs. Threwsbury was not available to take his call. Would he like to leave a message? "Fucking robot!" He slammed down the link, then reopened it and tried the desk again. Yes, Mrs. Shrewsbury was registered and yes, the clerk again apologized for the error but it would appear she and her son had gone out for the day.

"Send someone up and check on them," he demanded.

In an officious voice the clerk said, "I'm certain if they wished to receive calls, they would open the PDA in the suite."

"The autolink's still calling her Mrs. Threwsbury. I want to know if my son is all right," he said tightly.

"It's against policy to disturb our guests when they've placed such a request with the desk . . . and Ms. Shrewsbury"—he paused to emphasize the correct pronunciation—"has done so."

Del broke the connection. "I'm wasting time arguing." He turned to Leah. "You hold down the fort while I catch a cab over there and check on Mike, okay?"

"I'm going with you," she said, thinking of the bright, brave boy whom she had found tied and gagged, held hostage last summer. What if Del's imagination wasn't running amok?

"Let's go."

They lucked out catching a freight elevator down from the seventeenth floor, flashing their badges to hop aboard as the bellman protested, then rushed outside and hailed a cab. Just as they started to climb inside Leah's link beeped. She answered immediately, recognizing her grandfather's call code, standing on the curb so the driver would not overhear anything. Del leaned out of the cab, not liking the expression on her face.

When she broke the connection, Leah knew she had to make a quick decision. "Go get your son, Del. Get him and Diana the hell out of New York."

"What's going on? A lead on bin Bergi? Sievers?"

Leah felt the holster that held her Ruger securely under her arm. "No time to talk. Get your family. Use Diana's money to hire a private jet to anywhere. FBI team's on their way to pick up the bomb but if anything goes wrong, I want Mike far away as you can get him."

Del blanched and started to climb out of the cab.

"Hey, buddy, you want this ride or not?" a fat guy with a the lifetracked face of Gene Hackman asked, his jaw working a triple wad of chewing gum big enough to strangle a rhino.

"Get them out, Del," she said, shoving him back inside.

"What are you going to do?"

She grinned but it didn't quite take. "Nothing much. Just pick up the motherfucker who started this whole nightmare. Now go. Tell Mike I love him," she whispered in a strained voice, then slammed the door.

10:05 A.M. CST, THURSDAY, NOVEMBER 13
ST. LOUIS, MISSOURI

Paul and Ben walked into the George B. Hartzog, Jr. Visitor Center beneath the Arch. The cavernous mall had a large pool in the center, surrounded by benches. To the left a long line of tourists snaked toward the ticket counters. On their right a large stuffed grizzly bear menaced those entering the Museum of Westward Expansion. Artifacts and elaborate displays from the Lewis and Clark Expedition, Native American teepees, pioneer covered wagons, and riverboat scenes with boxes of cargo were arranged in an open diorama.

The two theaters required tickets for entry and were swept clean every evening, making them unlikely places for the hidden weapons. But directly outside the entrance to the museum a stagecoach sat in easy reach of a terrorist who might have tossed a weapon through the open windows to the dark floor between the seats.

"A million places to hide guns and ammo," Oppermann muttered with a sigh. If only there weren't so many children. "You see either of your boys?"

Shehabi shook his head, his eyes continuously sweeping the crowd. "I'm going to meet the agents in the men's room like we agreed. We'll start working the crowd until we locate them."

"I'll be waiting with Chief Corbett while his men grab our 'tram inspector' when he comes down." Oppermann indicated the recessed doorway next to the incline leading to the tram cars under the north leg of the Arch. A long line of sightseers laden with cameras and kids waited patiently for their turn to take the four-minute ride to the observation deck. "As soon as you ID the targets, haul your *tokhes* inside so neither of them spots you. *Mazel,* my friend." Oppermann hoped the tension in their bodies didn't telegraph to Selim's watchdogs.

"Luck to you, too, sir. We'll stop the bastards." Shehabi's guts clenched with sheer horror. Two armed madmen were loose in a crowd of innocent civilians and Selim was placing an armed bomb at the top of the Arch. He crossed to the south side of the mall where the men's restrooms were located.

Paul punched the code he'd been given into the keypad. The door swung open and he entered a long hallway. The park ranger at the desk nodded gravely as he passed. At the end of the hall a harried Chief Corbett stood with two of his LEOs outside the steel door leading to the stairs inside the Arch.

They waited for Selim.

11:35 A.M. EST, THURSDAY, NOVEMBER 13
BRONX, NEW YORK

Stephen Reed had received his promotion to New York SAC when Paul Oppermann left the post to become director of the FBI. It was highly unusual for an insider to be given the directorship, but Oppermann had an outstanding record. The backing of Attorney General John Scarletti hadn't hurt either. Reed knew he was following a heavy hitter and didn't intend to screw up.

His men moved into their positions without a hitch. From his hidden control center in a deserted building down the street, he gave the command to break down the door of Ahamet bin Bergi's apartment. Then all hell broke loose. The terrorist was supposed to be absent and the bomb waiting for their tech to disarm.

But it did not go down that way. Instead, bin Bergi lay sprawled on the living-room floor in a widening pool of blood. When that horrifying report was relayed to him, Reed ran up the street and climbed the stairs to take charge of the scene.

"He's not dead but damn near," Special Agent Wallis Arden said to the SAC. She was a tall brunette with neatly chopped hair and nerves of steel. "I've called for an ambulance."

"The bomb?" Reed asked, dreading the answer. Three men and a woman were tearing apart the "efficiency unit," slum code for one cramped room with bath and kitchen alcove. There was damn little space to hide anything the size of the nuclear device in the sparsely furnished apartment. They'd already pulled down the Murphy bed and opened all the empty cabinets in the cooking area. The stove and mini-fridge were in the process of being disassembled and one agent was pulling the top off the ancient toilet tank in the bath cubicle. Reed knew they'd find nothing.

"Looks like an El-Op hit," he said, noting the M16 casings. The M16A1 was their weapon of choice. The walls behind the terrorist were sprayed with fresh bullet holes. "Why in hell would they come after a raggedy-looking jerk like him?"

"They thought he had something they wanted," Special Agent Bill Jefferson speculated. "Whenever somebody new moves into the hood, the Stripes check 'em out to see if they're competition. Maybe they found out he had some cash." A slender black man who'd grown up in Harlem, Jefferson had gone undercover to infiltrate a tri-state gang of El-Ops called the Stripes.

"Bin Bergi wasn't a dealer—he was a fucking terrorist!" Reed snapped.

Before he could apologize for the outburst, Arden interrupted. "He wants to talk to you, sir." She held a pressure bandage to the holes in bin Bergi's chest.

Lips bubbling blood, Ahamet bin Bergi's mouth curved in a chilling smile as SAC Reed knelt beside him. "Where's the bomb, Ahamet?" he asked.

"It does . . . not . . . matter," bin Bergi whispered, laboring for each word. "Your infidel . . . thugs came for . . . for money. Took the case. A toy for them, yes?"

His eyelids fluttered as if he were going to buy it. Arden shook her head. But then he surprised them both, raising up to look the SAC squarely in the face, spitting blood as he said, "I set the detonator for three o'clock. New York . . . has . . . not much . . . " He slumped into Arden's arms, stone dead.

Reed jumped up, pulling his link from his jacket to report the catastrophe. "Any idea where the Stripes might take their loot?" he asked Jefferson.

"I heard rumors they have a place in a deserted subway spur, one the city shut down after the budget crunch a few years ago," Jefferson replied. "Don't know exactly where. Since they're trying to muscle in on the Brown Power's action, they don't want anybody to find them."

Reed spoke into the link. "I need blueprints for Bronx mass transit—every underground line that's been discontinued in the borough! I don't care if you have to use ball bats, poison gas, call in the fucking Marines—just get it done. I want to see the info on my car's vid now!" He opened another channel to D.C. to make the call he dreaded.

John Scarletti answered on the first beep.

20.

Del jumped out of the cab. On the short ride he'd flashed his badge, then threatened the cabbie with everything from loss of license to hard time at Ithaca just for good measure. The old man swore a blood oath to wait—with the meter running. Delgado showed the security guard on the door his badge to avoid the metal detectors, mandatory across the city in places where people worth money stayed. He was waved past the lines immediately.

The lobby was big and shiny with lots of potted plants and sunken conversation pits around several classy bars. He started for the bank of elevators, then spotted Diana about twenty meters ahead of him. He yelled for her to stop.

She whirled around with a startled expression that quickly turned to chagrin as people stared at the wild man dashing toward her. "El, lower your voice. What on earth—"

He grabbed her elbow and started for an elevator that had just pinged and then began disgorging passengers. "I'll explain later. Where's Mike?"

"Asleep in our suite. I turned off the PDA so he could get some rest, poor kid."

"What's wrong? Why wasn't he at the Science Fair?"

She smiled. He looked genuinely panicked because he'd gone to the fair and they weren't there. "You know, El, sometimes I do believe there's hope for you yet. Nothing's wrong with Mike. He has chicken pox."

"Chicken pox!" He swore. The door to their floor opened and he rushed her toward the suite. "Book a private flight out of La Guardia, ready to go as soon as we get there. I don't give a damn what it costs."

She stopped before opening the door, leaning against it with her arms crossed and a stubborn look on her face. "What is going on, El? You have to tell me."

"I tried to warn you not to come, dammit, and you wouldn't listen." He grabbed the pass from her hand and swiped the door, practically shoving her inside the sitting room. "There's a bomb somewhere in the city. The Bureau may have it disarmed or not."

She blanched. "Who—"

"Holy Arabian terrorists. Now use a link that works while I get Mike." He shoved his link at her. "I don't know how much time there is and it'll take twenty at least to reach the airport."

She quit arguing and gave a voice code that connected her to a friend of her dead husband who owned a helicopter and corporate jet leasing service.

Leah promised the driver an exorbitant amount to run traffic lights, then tried to reach SAC Reed on her link while the little Puerto Rican cabbie drove like a kamikaze on uppers. She prayed like hell that the takedown was a done deal and bin Bergi's nuke was disarmed. Her face faded to the color of putty as Reed reported.

"A gang of El-Ops broke into bin Bergi's hidey-hole and took the device. Before he died, he told us he armed it."

"How long?" she asked, knowing it would not be enough.

"Zero hour is three p.m." He gave her a brief rundown on Jefferson's deserted subway lead.

She cursed. "If they go underground, the dot's useless, isn't it?"

"So says the NRO. Get your BISC pal to find it before that happens. There's a honeycomb of subway routes. Once they're underground we're fucked."

"I'll keep you posted," she said, then punched in Willis's number.

"Sweetums, you look like roadkill possum," he drawled. Her unit was too small to give the full effect of his appraising grin.

She knew he had her on some fancy wide screen vid back in Atlanta, damn the man. "Nothing ever bothers you, does it, Willie? But then you're not in New York either."

She explained the blown operation in the Bronx. "You have to pick up that dot. It's our only hope to reach the stolen device in time." She glanced at the driver who appeared absorbed playing dodge 'em cars. He couldn't hear squat over the blare of horns and shriek of brakes as he weaved in and out of traffic, cutting off everyone on the Roosevelt Expressway.

"Give me a couple," Willis said, turning away.

Leah held on to the cab's door handle with white knuckles that had nothing to do with the rough ride. In a minute that seemed like an hour, Willis reappeared on the screen.

"Got a trace," he said. "Moving in the south Bronx. I'm working on a fix now."

"Nail the exact location and your government will be eternally grateful."

"Yup, but will they pay me?" he asked cheerfully.

"Your reward will be having me alive."

"Aw, Sweetums, I never had you at all. You makin' me a promise?"

"Just pinpoint that dot, Willie, and we'll talk." Leah ended the transmission. The cab had finally slowed its breakneck pace, then pulled to a halt.

"You owe me a Bennie," the driver said.

"Good job." She practically threw him the money as she jumped out of the cab.

The flags of every nation fluttered in Technicolor array, forming a semicircle in front of the United Nations, a place dedicated to peace and harmony in the world. The irony of it did not escape Leah Berglund as she pulled out her badge for the guard waiting at the curb.

10:55 A.M. CST, THURSDAY, NOVEMBER 13
ST. LOUIS, MISSOURI

"How long's the *mamzer* been up there?" Paul asked the Chief Ranger. "This is taking too long."

Corbett, a tall man with thinning dark hair and a slight paunch, shook his head. "Riding the tram takes four minutes to reach the top. Now I don't care if this turkey's an Olympic athlete, running up and down a thousand seventy-six steps'll take him around an hour. They zigzag back and forth inside the Arch. Plus he has to stash the case somewhere. Probably behind the HVAC pipes as close to the top as he could get." Nervous perspiration beaded his scalp as he studied the blueprints again.

"Great! My bomb tech's gotta play needle in a haystack with an armed nuke," Oppermann said. "How many places to hide something big as that case?" he asked, not liking the network of heating and cooling pipes interlaced across the blueprints like spilled spaghetti.

"Depends on how high he goes. If you're right and he intends to make the symbolic gesture and place it at the top, not as many. The higher you go, the fewer the pipes."

"That's a small break. Maybe."

Directly across from them, the two LEOs fixed their attention on the service door to the stairs. When Selim walked through it, the young rangers were to seize him at all costs. Much as Paul wanted to use his own people, he knew the terrorist expected to see park rangers guarding the door. Any new faces, even in green and gray uniforms of the National Park Service, would raise Selim's suspicion. The two men assigned to take him down were fit and well trained, one a former Special Forces noncom.

Paul opened his link and spoke with the bomb tech in the other side of the Arch. "You in place?"

The tech replied, "I'm on the observation deck. Can't unlock the door here until he opens his down there. Sound echoes like a bitch inside all that steel and concrete. If he's not out first, he might hear me and turn back."

"I hope we got time for that," Paul said.

"All I need is a few seconds to remove the detonation coupler. Then we're off the clock."

11:55 A.M. EST, THURSDAY, NOVEMBER 13
BRONX, NEW YORK

Leonard Sievers followed the gang at a crawl as they took a joyride around some of the more scenic rubble in what was left of the besieged borough. During the past decade with the drug epidemic out of control, the Bronx had come to make Harlem look like paradise. Finally, they pulled the Caddie up in front of a barricaded subway entrance. The vacant lots and tumbled-down buildings were seared by winter cold. Gray skies leaden with low scudding clouds promised snow. The street was empty as they piled out of the big car.

One thug with the shoulders of a linebacker peeled back the rusted NO TRESPASSING sign covering a chain-mesh barrier and two shorter thickset guys toting the satchels of securities slipped down the stairs. Next the one carrying the suitcase followed. The others vanished one by one until the last El-Op repositioned the sign and fence so the entrance appeared impenetrable.

Not a one noticed the car parked at the far end of the block or the man observing them through a monocular. *Dumb shits.*

Sievers started to inhale the Macedonian he'd lit from the cherry of the last one, then ground it out. He couldn't afford a coughing fit that might echo underground. There were eight of them. He checked the Glock holstered under his arm and the lightweight KEL-TEC .40-caliber automatic strapped to his ankle while he waited.

His link beeped. He opened it and outlined his position, describing the firepower they would face. "We're looking at Armageddon if you don't get your people here pronto. We can all be real rich . . . or real dead."

"Rich's always better," the man on the other end of the line replied. After ending the call to Sievers, he smiled, then turned to the men sitting around him and said, "You heard him. Time's tight. We can't screw this up."

11:55 A.M. EST, THURSDAY, NOVEMBER 13
NEW YORK, NEW YORK

The head of U.N. Security escorted Leah into the General Assembly Hall as had been arranged with the president of the United States while she was en route. The American secretary of state sat beside the podium, reviewing the notes for his address to the packed semicircle representing the world's leaders. She paused in the doorway, struck with how calm and rational Stuart Kensington looked.

How presidential.

She moved down the wide aisle, flanked by two U.N. Security personnel. They carried Berettas. She was armed only with the warrant that had been waiting at the communications desk, signed by the attorney general. FBI or no, she'd been forced to turn over her weapon at the security check-in. The United Nations was its own sovereign entity on American soil.

A low murmur spread as delegates watched the armed contingent head directly to the podium where the secretary general, Rashan Suharto, of the Pacific Rim Union, was calling the session to order. A little raisin of a man who affected Mandarin collared silk suits, Suharto lost his place on the page and frowned forbiddingly at the guards.

Leah's eyes met Kensington's. He looked utterly self-possessed. She doubted he'd recognize her since she had been in grad school the last time he'd seen her with her grandfather at a social function in Washington. But his body language betrayed faint surprise when the armed men headed directly toward him. She was good at reading that. When they reached the dais, she stepped up to face him across the table. Her smile was ice cold as she held up the warrant.

"Stuart Kensington, by the authority of the attorney general of the United States, I arrest you for treason. Want me to read you your rights here or outside?"

The former general stood up and glared at her as if she were something to be scraped off the sole of his handcrafted Italian dress shoes. He was the aristocrat born and bred, utterly arrogant in his power, disbelieving that anyone would dare to challenge him. The disdainful expression on his face said it all.

Fight or run, you mother. She ached to take him down with a particularly nasty maneuver she'd learned at BISC

Kensington dismissed her, shifting his attention to the secretary general.

Suharto paled as a translator relayed Wade Samson's words via headset. His eyes flashed angrily as he turned to Kensington. "This is a member of your FBI, empowered by your government to take you into custody." The secretary general motioned for the guards to proceed as Leah handed him the warrant, which he in turn gave to an aide fluent in English. The man skimmed through it and nodded.

Voices rose in a babble of languages, waiting for some explanation on their translation units. The noise level in the room grew deafening as Kensington stood his ground. The security guards rounded the dais to physically remove him. The secretary general attempted to restore order, rapping on the podium with an ebony gavel. It did no good.

"I protest this appalling disruption by the United States," Suharto said haughtily to Leah.

She ignored him, her ice-cold gaze fixed on Stuart Kensington.

Rather than be dragged off in front of the amazed audience, the American secretary of state allowed the U.N. Security officers to escort him toward a side exit.

Leah followed. Her link beeped. The call she was expecting came through. Special Agents Plum and Wayland had just pulled up front in an armored vehicle. "Your taxi's ready," she said grimly.

"Samson can't possibly expect to silence me with some sort of insane conspiracy theory. This is ludicrous," Kensington replied.

"It *is* an insane conspiracy, not a theory, Mr. Secretary. My grandfather, Adam Manchester, accessed your computer. You laid every detail out, right down to your 'impromptu' speech before the General Assembly after a dirty bomb destroyed St. Louis and another was 'discovered' right here in New York. You were going to denounce Holy Arabia, President Samson, and Senator Manchester for allowing terrorists to contaminate the Midwest and nearly destroy the financial nerve center of the nation. You'd have been elected president in a landslide with both contenders disgraced, out of the race.

"But it isn't going down the way you intended. The Bureau had a spy in the St. Louis cell. They're on top of the Arch disarming the bomb right now. Our real problem is here. You see, Ahamet bin Bergi's merchandise has been stolen by an El-Op gang in the Bronx."

If she expected a response, she did not get one. He didn't miss a step. Visions of Del and Mike flashed through her mind. She fought for control as she continued in that same icy tone. "It's programmed to go off at three."

"If this is some attempt to frighten me, I can assure you—"

"I don't give a flying fuck if you're frightened or not," she said, letting her composure slip. "If we locate the device in time, you'll stand trial for treason and be executed. If not, you'll die with everyone else."

"If I have to give my life to expose the perfidy of this administration and destroy Holy Arabia, I'll consider my duty to my country done."

"Destroy a country to save it. Has a familiar ring. We tried that back in the twentieth century. Didn't work then either," she said as the security guard opened the door and returned her Ruger to her. At the curb, Plum and his agents watched her prod the secretary forward.

"Your interpretation of history is obviously skewed," he snapped. "I am a patriot."

"So was Benedict Arnold. My grandfather will end up in the White House and you'll end up in an unmarked grave."

That finally rattled him. "No! I will be considered a selfless patriot. You don't have proof of anything that will stand up, even in Samson's kangaroo court."

"Don't bet on it." *Or on us living long enough for your day in court.*

Before she could push him to the door of the armored vehicle, a whistling hiss disturbed the air blowing off the East River. Secretary of State Stuart Kensington crumpled to the pavement at her feet with a small red hole in the center of his forehead.

10:56 A.M. CST, THURSDAY, NOVEMBER 13
ST. LOUIS, MISSOURI

Ben Shehabi moved through the scattered clumps of people, careful to keep his movements casual, touristy, using the camera device often, more for cover than communication. Then he saw Dulghani walking past the life-sized statue of Thomas Jefferson, emerging from the Museum of Westward Expansion. He knew the terrorist must have retrieved the R9 automatic. *Probably hidden in that covered wagon or the Plains Indian teepee.*

He identified the man for the other agents on the floor. Once Special Agent Briggs was in place behind Dulghani, Ben moved on to search for Banaygh, who was Selim's most skilled gunman. Unfortunately, he was short and nondescript in appearance, melting into any crowd. Was he already armed? If not, he soon would be. The terrorists had only been able to smuggle in small compact pistols but that was all they needed to ensure that Selim could reset the bomb while they held off any resistance. Shehabi strolled into the museum, moving through the displays where a weapon could most easily be concealed.

Then he saw the little man standing beside a pile of old wooden crates next to the simulation of a nineteenth-century riverboat and its cargo on the levee. Turning his head, he focused his camera on a wall of old pix as he spoke. "Number two by riverboat display in museum. Don't know if he's picked up his hardware yet. Five six, wearing dark gray topcoat and brown boots. Lighter gray shirt, chinos. Hair dyed gray with a bald spot on top."

As soon as he saw Special Agents Morton and Andruski sight the target, he walked out of the museum, heading for the security door leading to the stairwell. Since either of the cell members might recognize him, fake beard or no, he had to drop out of sight now that they were covered. If the agents on the floor kept close without arousing suspicion, once the all-clear on the bomb was given, they stood a good chance of taking down their subjects without a gun battle.

All tram passengers were being held at the gates so that there would be no innocent civilians trapped inside the small cars for Selim to take hostage or kill if a shoot-out occurred inside the north leg, a worst-case scenario. Those on the observation deck were being brought down the south leg. Oppermann and Corbett were betting the two terrorists in the mall wouldn't detect anything amiss since the trams moved up and down at irregular intervals. This was a heavy traffic day for off season. So far, their quickly slapped together plan was working.

Shehabi punched the code into the keypad and started down the hall to where the director, the chief ranger, and the two LEOs were positioned. Suddenly the door opened and Selim appeared. He stared straight at Shehabi.

Recognition flashed in his ice-blue eyes. "Traitor," he said calmly. But he moved with blurring speed.

Selim had his Rohrbaugh in his hand before the rangers could raise their weapons. He fired point-blank at the taller officer's head, expecting the man to have on aerofoam body armor. The big ranger fell backward with a bullet in his face as Selim yanked the door shut.

"Shit!" Shehabi pulled out his SIG and ran toward the closed door as the second LEO pulled on the handle.

Oppermann called the bomb tech on the observation deck atop the Arch. "Virgil, go for the nuke now!" Then he spoke to the agents in the mall and SAC Washington outside, "Selim's on the loose. Move on all targets. Repeat, everybody move now!"

Chief Corbett seized a link, even though he knew his LEO was almost certainly beyond help. "Officer down. Security room, north leg. We need medics quick and quiet."

The second park ranger used the door for cover, squeezing off shots while Selim returned fire from inside. Oppermann drew his SIG-Sauer and flattened himself against the wall on the opposite side of the door.

"*Mamzer*'s faster than a JAP at a Bloomies sale," he muttered as Ben reached him.

"He can't get back up those stairs before we have the bomb," Shehabi said, praying it was true, realizing that he had caused the catastrophe.

The LEO made it inside the door and raced for the steps. From the narrow opening to the entrance, Ben saw the ranger take a bullet in his right arm. He dropped his piece, knelt doggedly to retrieve it.

"Fuck!" Shehabi dived through the door and rolled to the side, out of Selim's line of sight. The terrorist was already a dozen meters up the steep steel stairs, firing down.

"Virg, you reached that nuke yet?" Oppermann talked into his camera/link. "Our boy's on his way back for it."

"He must've figured someone could cross from the south leg," Special Agent Virgil Watkins said. "Slick son of a bitch's jammed the entry door to the stairwell!"

"Get it the fuck open!" Oppermann yelled as the sound of shots and screams echoed from the mall outside.

"I'm a bomb tech, sir, not a cat burglar." He swallowed so hard Oppermann could hear it over the link. "But I'll try everything I can think of."

"Do it."

Paul assessed the situation. "*Farpatshket*," he muttered. Four of Washington's agents were trying to take out two armed terrorists in the middle of a crowded mall. He could hear the chaos. Women and kids might be dying. The SAC's remaining teams had to stop the four terrorists outside. Both the LEOs were down. That left only him and Corbett to back up Shehabi. Somehow he didn't think Corbett was up to running stairs.

Neither was he.

"Right behind you, Ben," he called, slipping through the door. The woven steel stairwell seemed to go upward forever, zigzagging back and forth like a maze in the dim light. He could hear Shehabi and Selim exchanging fire overhead. To Virgil on the link Oppermann said, "Tell me how to disarm that nuke, just in case."

In the park outside, Donnell Washington listened to the takedown go sour, heard Oppermann's orders. "Move on your targets—now," he reiterated to his teams. The two terrorists on the north side of the Arch began running toward the entrance as soon as the screaming and gunfire opened up.

The SAC could not see the terrorists or his teams at the south leg but he watched north team one, a pair of female agents, work with precision. One tripped the target while the other followed him to the ground, pushing the injection into his neck. He went into paralysis almost instantly.

The second team, a man and woman, failed to stop their man. He dodged the male agent's tackle like a pro quarterback, knocked the syringe from the female's hand, and sprinted ahead, gun drawn. People screamed and ran in every direction as he waved the automatic weapon, ready to fire at anyone unlucky enough to get in his way.

"Take the shot," Washington told them.

"Civilians in our way," his link squawked back.

The SAC was positioned directly in front of the runner, the only agent with an unimpeded firing line. As he drew his SIG and knelt down, Washington regretted that he hadn't spent much time on the target range since being promoted. Bracing his weapon on one knee, he sighted in on the center of the terrorist's body, low in case he was wearing body armor. In what seemed to him agonizing slow motion he squeezed the trigger.

"We have them down, sir. Both men," Special Agent Rowland reported to Washington from the south leg of the Arch. The SAC stood looking at the dead man lying on the concrete. Over twenty years with the Bureau and he'd never killed anyone before. Pulling himself together, he said, "Good job."

The sounds of screams and gunfire poured out of the mall along with terrified civilians. A virtual stampede. He was grateful to see park rangers moving in to quell the hysteria, knowing some hapless victims would be trampled. If they were the only innocent casualties, it was the best anyone could ask now.

"Outside work's finished. One agent on each downed man. The others into the mall," he said over his link. His people had stopped the backup cold. Now to the shooting gallery below. As he issued directions for the agents converging on both north and south entries, he prayed that bomb tech had the nuke disarmed. He didn't like it that Oppermann's link had gone silent.

12:30 P.M. EST, THURSDAY, NOVEMBER 13
BRONX, NEW YORK

Leah leaned forward over the cabbie's shoulder, watching as he zigzagged crazily across the Willis Avenue Bridge cutting drivers off as he entered the Bronx. Kensington had no more than crumpled to the ground when Reed called her. A street snitch had given Special Agent Jefferson a tip on some possible locations for the Stripes' underground safe house in the subway system. They had teams en route and needed every agent assigned to the mission.

She left Plum and Wayland to handle Kensington's assassination, although the way it had gone down bothered her. Hailing a cab, she took off, after borrowing Plum's MP5. Time to worry about who'd iced the secretary if they could disarm the bomb. If not, what would it matter?

There were dozens of miles of closed subway tracks to cover and she was the agent nearest to the labyrinth. Reed transmitted the schematic onto her vid. She blessed Gracie Kell for the fancy little device. Three other insertion points were marked with agents on the way. Reed promised backup for her as soon as he could get a fourth team in place.

Her taxi exited onto Bruckner Boulevard, then twisted around back streets, approaching her destination. "Turn here." She motioned for him to head down a narrow street filled with falling down buildings and vacant lots sprinkled with junked cars. The few brick and wood structures still leaning together were covered with graffiti, as were the broken concrete sidewalks.

"Hey, I don' like this, lady," the Haitian driver said. His cab was not armored.

"I'm not paying you to like it. Just let me out there," she said, pointing to a subway entrance at the intersection. It had been barred over with a big CLOSED—NO TRESPASSING sign posted over it, barely readable through the spray-can artistry that covered it.

She paid him and hopped out in front of the subway station. Behind her the sounds of wheels screeching on the potholed street echoed as the hack driver burned rubber in a U-turn and fled. She was glad she had Plum's MP5 with extra ammo in addition to her Ruger. From the looks of the heavy steel door, she might have to blast her way in.

Shouldn't create much of a stir in this neck of the woods. She examined the lock, then grinned. No sense wasting ammo when she never traveled without her tool kit, a holdover from her BISC days. In half a minute she had the lock picked. If it hadn't been rusty, she'd have been inside in ten seconds. She looked at her wrist unit as she climbed down the stairs. Every second counted. No time to wait for Reed's team.

All she had to penetrate the inky blackness of the deserted tracks was a small electric torch from her kit. She flicked it on and checked the layout. A strong metallic taste of rusting iron blended with an acrid aroma that only came from animal waste. She could feel the icy damp penetrating her shoes and inhaled the musty stench of standing water. The tunnel dripped like an ice cave in a heat wave.

A rat bigger than her mother's cat darted by her ankle. She suppressed a shudder, glad that the threat of snow had induced her to wear boots. Not a sound echoed in either direction. According to Reed's info, these tunnels were a giant Skinner Box and went on forever. She flicked the vidlight on her link and squinted at the tiny diagram, trying to figure what her best course would be. Because the screen was so small, she had to move it in quadrants to figure out where the other insertions were taking place.

Once she was satisfied that the B team would come in from her left, she struck out to the right, moving silently, holding the narrow beam to the ground and listening for the sound of human voices. All she heard was the drip of water and the scudding of rats. As she moved quickly down the tracks, she thought of Del and Mike again. Unlike her staunchly Lutheran-Episcopal grandfather, Leah had never prayed.

Please, God, get them out of here before it's too late.

1:05 P.M. EST, THURSDAY, NOVEMBER 13
AIRSPACE OVER QUEENS, NEW YORK

"What the hell do you mean, you don't have a plane?" Delgado demanded. He sat beside the helicopter pilot. Diana and his son were behind them. Del hoped they couldn't hear over the noise of the blades as they approached La Guardia for a landing. "Fuel gauge malfunction, my ass! If it'll fly, you fly the fucker! We'll be on the ground in two minutes and it better be ready to go."

Diana leaned forward. "You'll never get them to take off if there's an equipment malfunction. It's a violation of FAA regulations."

"Fuck FAA regs!"

"You can't hold them at gunpoint, El."

"Just watch me. I'm back in the FBI, remember? I got a gun." He opened his jacket and revealed his .50-caliber Smith & Wesson.

Mike eavesdropped, forgetting the excitement of the helicopter ride from the roof of the hotel across the Manhattan skyline. His parents had refused to tell him what was wrong but he knew something very bad was happening and his dad wanted to get them out of New York. He wished they'd stop treating him like a child . . . even if he did have a baby disease. He scratched his arm, hating it that once again they were yelling at each other.

His dad only used the F-word around his mom when he was really mad. Mike remembered last summer, the day he'd met Leah. She'd explained about words grown-ups could use and kids couldn't, how it wasn't fair but life was like that. Where was she now? Working on the big, mysterious case his mom wouldn't talk about? Then why was his dad here with them and not helping her?

And why was he threatening to shoot some friend of his mom's if the guy didn't fly them away? Maybe he was a bad guy. A showdown might be pretty exciting if only he didn't feel so itchy and miserable. He pulled out the tube of cream Dr. Walsh had given him and smeared it on his face, even worked his hand under his coat sleeve so he could reach one arm, then the other. His mom spoke on the copter's radio while his dad asked the pilot, "You're sure you can't get us to Jersey?"

"Not enough gas. By the time I get a fill-up, you'd be looking at near two hours, best. This flight wasn't exactly scheduled," Beau Sinclair said, eyeing the grim man with the big gun.

Delgado shook his head, then stared at the approaching helipad, drumming his fingers on his knee. He had to get them out of the city.

Mike watched his dad who looked kinda pale. His mouth was thin and hard, the way he'd looked when he untied his son after the kidnapping last summer. *He's scared for us . . . again.*

They landed with a bump and Del jumped out of the copter, then helped Diana and Mike down. A whole airport full of planes and no way to get aboard one in time. Since the Slaughter, airport security was tight. Federal air marshals were sprinkled through La Guardia like Parmesan over spaghetti. He knew, FBI badge or not, he'd never succeed in hijacking a plane.

"Try reservations again while I talk face-to-face with that hotshot jet pilot of your pal's," he said to her.

Diana knew it was hopeless, but nodded. There was no use trying to reason with her ex-husband. At least this time she understood why he was so angry. She opened her link and tried to get them—or just her son—on any flight.

Mike felt tired and cold. He watched his dad stalk toward the fancy Learjet that sat on the runway about thirty meters away as he followed his mother toward the shelter of an all-weather booth nearby. She started calling as they walked, absorbed in what seemed a hopeless task. Discouraged, he turned and retraced his steps to the copter. It was a much neater place to wait than any dumb old plasti-booth. The chopper pilot had gone around the back of his craft and didn't see him climb inside.

Delgado had only walked a few paces when his link beeped. Before he could respond, the Lear started taxiing away. He began chasing it, then realized how hopeless that was. He opened the line and recognized Reed's voice even before he came on vid.

"Kensington's been assassinated and Berglund's in the Bronx," he said without preamble. "She needs backup and I'm short a team." He outlined the El-Op theft of the nuke and told Delgado what they knew about the Stripes' underground hideout and the last location NRO had picked up on the tracer dot. "When my team reached it, they found Leonard Sievers's body in a stripped car. Looks like a pro job. Single shot in the back of the head. I don't imagine taking out Sievers was easy."

"Bottom line?" Del asked. He felt his chest constrict.

"We don't know where the bomb is now that it's underground."

"And Leah's gone after it alone?"

"Unless you back her up. I've got every agent underground now but she went first." He gave Delgado the station number where she'd gone in.

Del turned toward the copter, desperately torn. His son and Mike's mother . . . or Leah and uncounted people in New York? No man should ever have to do what he knew he had to do. Diana stood in the doorway of a nearby plasti-rain booth. He could see she was still on her link. Mike must be inside. They had only one chance, however slim.

Del ran across the tarmac to Diana. She stepped outside into the wind as he reached her, having used up every option she had calling. "What is it?"

"FBI's located the bomb in the Bronx. Leah's gone after it. Get a cab and take the fastest route to Jersey. Keep heading west. Pay him extra to speed!" He pointed to the cab stand outside the terminal where a line of vehicles flashed vacancy lights.

"Less than two hours. It isn't good enough if the wind shifts, is it, El?"

"Yeah, I think it might be. It's the best choice left. Maybe I can reach the bomb before it detonates. Tell Mike I love him," he said, not daring to hesitate a moment more, afraid he'd lose control. He spun around and took off.

Diana's eyes filled with tears. Even if she and Mike made it to safety, she knew Del and Leah would perish with much of this great city if they failed to reach the bomb in time. She watched him run toward the chopper, then turned to get Mike. He'd been right behind her as she walked to this shelter. "Mike?" No reply. She'd been so busy on the link, she'd lost track of him!

"Michael Elliott Delgado, where are you?" she screamed. It quickly became obvious that he was not in the shadowy interior of the all-weather booth. At once she knew where he had gone!

Without a backward glance, Del climbed into the copter, yelling at the pilot to rev it up. "We're going to the Bronx. I don't care if you run out of gas and have to coast across the East River."

Sinclair looked into Special Agent Delgado's eyes. He'd seen the cannon the agent carried inside his coat. "I'll get you across somehow. Just tell me where to set her down and I hope it isn't far."

Neither of them noticed Mike crouched in the backseat or saw Diana come running across the tarmac, waving her arms frantically. The noise of the blades as they lifted off drowned out her screams.

21.

No more noodle kugel or knishes, I swear it on my mother's grave! Just let me do this. Paul Oppermann prayed, gasping for air on one switchback landing. Doggedly he kept putting one leaden foot in front of the other. How far had he come? A third of the way? That meant Selim was another third closer to detonating the bomb. Up ahead he could hear the echo of gunfire as Ben and Selim exchanged shots. He hadn't run stairs in a decade, hadn't run period since moving to Washington last summer. His breath came in labored pants. He wouldn't quit.

When he heard Shehabi curse and stumble, Oppermann felt a new burst of adrenaline. He took a gulp of stale, cold air and climbed faster. Then he saw Ben crouched behind a concrete support beam with blood streaming down his left arm. He continued firing with his right hand.

"Cover me," Shehabi hissed to Oppermann, then took off up another flight of the endless steps.

Oppermann fired blind. He couldn't see Selim, only the trail of flying concrete and lacerated steel where the terrorist's 9mm slugs smashed into the stairs and skeleton of the mammoth structure. When a hail of bullets shattered the window of a tram car, he thanked God there were no passengers inside. He fired until Shehabi reached another landing where he could flatten himself behind the piling. Then Paul followed him.

1:10 P.M. EST, THURSDAY, NOVEMBER 13
BRONX, NEW YORK

Mike listened over the noise of the blades as his father explained the awful situation to Beau Sinclair. Lots of New York City was going to be blown up by a bomb some El-Ops had stolen from terrorists if the FBI didn't find it before three o'clock. Leah was tracking them by herself in some underground subway station and his dad was coming to help her.

He had told his mom how special she was and how much he loved her that morning, but he hadn't had a chance to tell his dad or Leah. With the intuition of youth, he felt Leah needed to hear that most of all. If they all might die, he intended to be with them. But if his dad found him in the copter, he'd send him back with Mr. Sinclair, so he hid, not sure how he'd manage to get out and follow.

The copter set down on a street where most of the buildings were falling down and the cars were either junkers or fancy new TEs. Mike knew enough about the drug trade to know they were in a danger zone. He swallowed for courage and waited his chance. His dad and the pilot climbed out and Sinclair came around to where his dad was standing. As the two men held a quick conversation, he slipped out of the pilot's side and darted behind a deserted car.

Then the pilot got back in his copter and took off. His dad ran to a subway entrance. As soon as Del started down the steps, Mike darted after him, careful not to get too close. He had to reach Leah before his dad realized he was there.

It was pretty scary and smelled awful. He was glad for the warm coat, even the dorky wool scarf his mom had made him wear, as he followed the small light of his father's pencil torch through the darkness. The rats didn't scare him. Or at least he told himself they didn't. After all, he was going to be a zoologist when he grew up . . . if he grew up.

1:20 P.M. EST, THURSDAY, NOVEMBER 13
BRONX, NEW YORK

It seemed as if she'd been wandering in the dark tunnels for hours. Then Leah heard the sound of gunfire echo around the turn ahead and started to sprint. Guttural curses and screams indicated the Stripes were under attack—and righteously pissed about it. When she reached the bend she flattened herself against the slimy wall and peered around. Dim overhead light illuminated the rail tracks, accentuated by fiery flashes from automatic weapons. She could detect the sounds of pistol fire interspersed here and there as well.

The Bureau was sending agents in with full SWAT armaments. She prayed one of the teams had beaten her to the target, but given their deployment, that didn't seem possible. Who the hell was it—a rival gang? She switched off the torch and proceeded in the dark, careful not to stumble on the tracks and give away her position.

She made a quick assessment of the scene. The dim light came from overhead where recessed fixtures had been powered up, probably by a small generator that the gang used and could not now reach to turn off. While the illumination didn't exactly make them sitting ducks, it did give a slight edge to their attackers.

The Stripes' stronghold was located at the end of the deserted spur in an old subway car. They'd camouflaged it cleverly by cadging together sheets of rusted scrap metal, old car doors, hoods and fenders, even glass bricks that had tumbled from the disintegrating tunnel, all piled around the car. In the unlikely event some homeless druggie wandered down here while the lights were out, it would look like a rat-infested junk pile, not a viable shelter. It had to be their storage area for Elevator and probably excess cash. Street hoods weren't known for frequenting ATMs—even if there had been any in a zone like this.

They must have an escape exit. To survive in the cutthroat underworld of drug dealing, they had to have enough street smarts never to let themselves be backed in a corner, no matter how well concealed. Then she saw the outline of a rusted metal door at the left side of the tunnel next to the car. Inside there would be a ladder leading to an aboveground exit, the kind subway maintenance crews used. Had whoever pinned them down blocked it before the assault?

The Stripes were holding their own so far. She counted three points of return fire coming from recesses in the walls made by support beams. Not enough light to see the ID she wanted—either police or

FBI, but they definitely didn't look like El-Ops. Nor were their weapons the popular M16s or Mach 10s favored by the street gangs. They were definitely high tech—TARs and Uzis.

Leah had to make a decision. There was damn little time until ground zero. What could she lose by helping them?

Well, here you are, Berglund, an army of one.

"Leah Berglund, FBI," she yelled as she dived behind the shelter of glass brick and flattened herself in the darkness, praying these were the good guys. If they weren't, she was in big trouble. At least one had a clear shot at her.

Across the tunnel a familiar voice said, " 'Bout time, Sweetums."

"Willie, what the fuck are you doing here?" she asked after a barrage of automatic weapons fire sent glass splinters and plaster flying around them.

"Got bored in Atlanta. Heard the Big Apple was real pretty in the snow," he drawled as a burst from an M16 hit his cover.

She peered around the edge and sighted in on the flash, picked off an El-Op, whose weapon clattered through the open window of the armored car door he had crouched behind.

"Shit man, Chazz-O down. Fuckin' cops!"

"Shuddup, Jelly," a second El-Op said.

"We gonna waste your sorry asses!" another yelled, shooting wildly.

"How the hell did you find them?" she asked Willis.

"Tracer dot on the suitcase." He fired off a couple of rounds and a man screamed behind the barricade, but continued shooting. "Told you it was headed south in the Bronx, remember? When my agent here reported that it vanished near a Bronx subway entrance I followed a hunch. Talked to Reed while I was on my way. His info corroborated mine. Said he was fielding teams. When's the rest of the cavalry arrive? He promised help."

"We don't have time." She fired again. "You try explaining they have a nuke about to detonate?" She anticipated his answer.

"Yep. Think they believe it's live? They figure on selling it for serious money once they kill us. Go, Manny," he said and the man in front of him opened up as Willis moved with amazing speed for a man of his girth, crossing to her cover.

"Why'd you come in with only two men?"

"Like you said, no time." He took a shot and popped another man, who fell back, cursing. "Figgered these scum would stash the case and take off, try to cash some securities and celebrate, or maybe look for a black-market arms buyer. We'd slip in and grab the nuke."

"But you figured wrong."

"Yep. They got in a pissin' contest over who stayed to guard the hundred mil and who went out to boogie. Nobody trusted nobody." He shook his head mockingly. "Seems like old times, dudn't it, Sweet-ums?"

Over the gunfire, she asked, "See that door? We might be able to use the stairs behind it. Climb down it and catch them in a cross fire. Wonder why haven't they tried that with us? They outnumber us."

"Same reason none of the fuckers'd leave in the first place, I'd reckon. Don't trust each other with all that lovely loot. Say, where's Delgado?"

She swallowed hard. "Safe, on a flight out of New York with his son and ex."

"Wrong."

Leah heard his voice and her heart stopped beating until a barrage of shooting kick-started it again. "What the hell are you doing here?" she asked savagely.

"Too complicated." Del fired his Smith & Wesson, then dashed closer as they covered him.

With his bum knee, Del wasn't as fast as Willis but at least he made a narrower target. "We have to use that hatch and catch them in a cross fire—if they don't beat us to it."

"I'm the fastest. Cover me," Leah said. She handed the MP5 to Delgado and sprinted into the darkness.

At the curve of the tunnel she ran past Mike. He bit his lip. Calling out to her could get her killed if she stopped. He hadn't expected so much shooting. He crouched in the darkness, clutching his white wool neck scarf tightly in both fists as she ran full out, splashing through puddles and leaping over rails with only a tiny torch to guide her.

At the end of the tunnel the gunfire was deafening. The boy lost track of time, praying for Leah and for his dad.

She climbed the subway stairs two at a time. At street level she tried desperately to orient herself. "Where the fuck would that manhole cover be?" she muttered, backtracking aboveground, trying to duplicate her route through the subway. As she ran, Leah held the Ruger at her side, watching the deserted streets. A woman alone made a tempting target for punks out to have a little sexual adventure.

After three blocks she judged the distance to be about right, then turned left and looked down the lunar landscape of what had been a street. Nothing. But the next block was too far down—wasn't it? She went with her gut and turned left. Then she saw it—a round metal disk canted at an angle where the pavement had buckled. Checking to see if the area was clear, she approached, replacing the gun in its holster.

New York Metropolitan Subway System was barely legible on the dented, rust-covered top. She knelt and grabbed the pull lever with both hands, yanking upward. It did not budge.

Vinny Russo was out of breath. Damn Shaq for having legs so long he could outrun a greyhound. They'd climbed out of the subway service hatch, then stomped it down good to keep anybody else from getting through it. They cut across a vacant lot to reenter the station entrance and get behind those bastards who had invaded their turf. The two Stripes made it about halfway down the tunnel when Vinny just couldn't go any more without a break. "Shaq, my man, slow up. Ain't nobody gonna turn into a pumpkin," he panted, doubling over.

"Bamba done tol' you to quit smokin'," the tall, athletic El-Op said to his scrawny companion. "What if more them fuckin' cops show up, huh? They take the money and that gizmo. We got nothin'." He spat into a puddle of dank water and a rat scurried away.

Vinny watched the black man take off, then reluctantly trotted after Shaq. Bamba was the leader of the Stripes and he'd given them their orders. Even if Russo didn't like it, he knew better than to question Bamba. It wasn't healthy. Once they opened up on the guys from behind, Bamba and the others would bust out of the car shooting.

It'd be over in nothing flat—if he didn't get cut down by his own guys or whoever those crazy cops were.

The sounds of shooting were growing louder now. Vinny tensed, afraid, slowing down. That's when he saw something glowing in the faint light. Something white. When it moved he nearly shot before he realized it was a kid. "Hey, Shaq, lookee what we got here," he hissed.

12:20 P.M. CST, THURSDAY, NOVEMBER 13
ST. LOUIS, MISSOURI

Ben was starting to feel the blood loss. His head spun crazily as he ran, vision blurred. *Heart pumping too damned fast. Have to do something quick.* He felt the vibration from Selim's R9 as it chewed up the concrete at the side of the landing. One chunk hit him in the shin. It should've hurt like hell but he was beyond feeling pain now. He ducked behind the cover of a maze of pipes.

His reflexes were going. That had been too close. He could hear Paul coming up behind him as he yanked a handkerchief from his jeans and wrapped it around his upper arm, making a tourniquet by pulling with his teeth. He struggled to tie off the ends. Not much but it seemed to slow the bleeding.

He started running again. Selim was approaching the apex—and the bomb.

1:35 P.M. EST, THURSDAY, NOVEMBER 13
BRONX, NEW YORK

Leah pulled a small blade from its sheath and used it as leverage on the rusted pull. Just as it snapped, the grate groaned and moved. She went down the ladder so fast her shoes slipped off the rungs twice. Positioning herself beside the door into the tunnel, she pictured in her mind the layout of the scene. She visualized the locations of the El-Ops and Willis's attack squad, a skill she'd been taught by BISC.

She had spotted five still shooting after she'd iced one. Willie had hit at least one of those still standing. Not bad odds, except that she had to make it to the car door before they spotted her, a dash of six meters. She'd replaced the cover above her head before descending. No light limned her when she opened the door and slipped into the tunnel.

Del and Willis and his men were watching as she dashed to the car undetected. She was just about to pick off her first target when she heard a voice behind Del and Willie say, "Drop your guns or I shoot the kid!"

In the dim light she could see a tall black El-Op holding a struggling boy in front of him with a pistol shoved against his temple. Leah froze for an instant. It was Mike Delgado!

A smaller man stood in the shadow behind Mike and his captor, Mach 10 poised, ready to fire. "Do it, fucksticks or the kid's toast," he said in a thick Bronx accent.

"I'm sorry, Dad." Mike's voice carried down the tunnel. "Shoot 'em! Don't give up!"

Leah knew a father's indecision could cost them everything. But the El-Op scum had not seen her in the shadows. She raised her Ruger to draw their fire to her. Just then Mike aimed an awkward back kick at the tall man's knee, providing an opening when his hold on the boy slipped. *Go, Willie!*

Willis fired with blurring speed, hitting the El-Op who held Mike, a dead center head shot. In his field days Willis had been as good as she was. Through the back door of the subcar she popped her first target, then the second. The little white guy behind the tall black dude tried to scramble away but Delgado shot him. Running to his son, he knocked him to the ground as the battle inside the subcar raged.

"Let's help the little lady out," Willis said, rushing forward with his men.

Inside the car Leah shot again but missed the third target who dived behind an ancient sofa. The man Willis had winged earlier lay on the floor, betrayed by a trail of smeared blood but hidden behind a pile of boxes. She didn't know if he was still alive, but the one sprawled across the filthy rug in front of the sofa was definitely a goner.

The last man used the metal door at the opposite end of the car for cover as he let loose a burst at her. A risky choice. As she returned fire, Willis yanked open the connecting outer door behind him and put a bullet in his head before he could turn around. The security chief's men flanked the outside of the car. Through the window, one picked off the guy behind the sofa. Leah squeezed off shots at the pile of boxes, sending them flying as the wounded El-Op managed to get off a burst of fire before he died. It hit the ceiling of the car perforating it like a sieve.

"Ever'body present and accounted for?" Willis asked cheerfully as he stepped inside.

Leah emerged from the opposite door of the car and scanned the room for the case. "Where the fuck is the damned bomb?"

Willis said, "It's gotta be here."

Del checked the two dead men in the tunnel as the swift exchange of fire in the car ended abruptly. Leah could be dead or injured but he couldn't allow himself to think of that now. "You all right, Tige?" he asked his son, helping him to stand up so he could make certain Mike was really unscathed.

"I'm okay, Dad," he managed over a big lump in his throat.

"Good. Let's go find that bomb." They sprinted toward the car.

12:50 P.M. CST, THURSDAY, NOVEMBER 13
ST. LOUIS, MISSOURI

Selim had hidden the case at the very top of the big steel unit that heated and cooled the observation deck, over six hundred feet above the river. He could hear footsteps gaining on him. He recognized the traitor Shehabi, who stumbled on pieces of concrete knocked from the walls by his shots. If the bastard hadn't slipped, he'd have had him. He opened up again. Shehabi's blood-covered body jerked backward and crumpled to the steps. When he didn't move, Selim stretched his powerful arm up to grasp the case.

One-handed, it was too heavy for him. He pocketed the deadly little Rohrbaugh R9 and used both hands to lift it down, then set it on the floor and knelt to open it. The bullet took him completely by surprise, knocking him against the railing. But he was scarred by many bullet wounds already, knew the sudden impact, the creeping burn that always followed. He'd fought for Holy Arabia's mullahs from Afghanistan to Africa.

Ignoring broken ribs and torn flesh, he pulled the R9 from his pocket and sighted in on Shehabi. The traitor was crawling up the steps toward him, his SIG-Sauer clutched in a bloody fist. Selim grinned. This would be easy. He looked down the barrel of his weapon. "Get ready to die, Infidel."

For Ben the shot would not be easy. He aimed at the giant crouching like some great golden spider atop the last landing. He had only one chance. He blinked, his vision blurring as blood and sweat poured into his eyes. Just as he squeezed the trigger, the narrow door behind Selim opened with a loud clang.

Virgil Watkins rushed through. He held in his hand the plumbing pipe he'd pirated from the deck toilet to force open the lock. In the dim light, he focused on the bomb case lying on the floor before he saw the man crouched beside it. Selim pivoted and squeezed the trigger. As Virgil went down, Ben's shot plowed through the terrorist's thick yellow hair and grazed his scalp. Selim whirled around for another shot at Shehabi, but his enemy's gun dropped from his fingers and clattered down the stairs. He fell onto the steps, motionless. Selim returned his attention to the open door behind him, fearing reinforcements.

Paul Oppermann reached Ben just in time to see his shot miss and Virgil die. Shehabi might be dead as well but he had no time to find out. Selim opened the case. Paul plunged past his fallen agent, taking the steps two at a time now, not caring about the noise, wanting to distract the terrorist from his task so he would start to raise the R9 again.

Selim obliged. As he swung it down on the director, Oppermann said, "Shalom, Mr. Edwards," and fired.

Warren Michael Edwards fell backward, hit squarely in the chest. Paul stopped to steady his aim and squeezed off a second shot as the big blond man crumpled. While he heaved his way up the remaining steps, he continued firing. Every bullet hit its mark. Director

Oppermann hadn't kept up his jogging, but he practiced at the firing range twice a week.

When he reached the landing, he knelt, panting in front of the case. His hands shook. No good. He labored to get air into his oxygen-starved lungs, studying the bomb. His eye moved to the small cylinder sticking out of a mounting next to the digital time display, just as poor Virgil had described it. He reached for it, unscrewing it clumsily. When it came out of the mounting Paul fell back against the wall, numb with relief.

"Ben!" Shehabi wasn't moving and he was bled out bad. Paul opened the camera/link. "Officer down. I need paramedics up here immediately. Bomb disarmed. Repeat, bomb disarmed."

In the mall below, one of the terrorists went down after releasing a barrage of fire into the fleeing crowd. Miraculously only a couple of people were shot in the chaos. The second man seized a woman and held his R9 to her head, yelling at two male FBI agents to drop their weapons. They made a show of doing it slowly, giving Special Agent Abbie Tomaso enough time to come up behind him.

With one hand she shoved her SIG-Sauer against the back of the terrorist's head and squeezed the trigger. She calculated the angle so that when the shot passed through his skull it ended up embedded high on the wall in front of the museum entrance. The captive fainted, going down unharmed with the terrorist, who was now minus a face.

By the time the park rangers had the panicked crowd under control, Ben Shehabi was brought down by a paramedic team and rushed outside where a life-flight copter waited to fly him to Barnes-Jewish Hospital.

"You'll be all right, Ben," Oppermann had reassured the semiconscious man as they'd loaded him onto the stretcher. "After all, they have good Jewish doctors on the staff."

Shehabi managed a grin. "Jewish doctors? I feel better already."

"Hey, you're circumcised. They won't know the difference, trust me."

Ben laughed.

As Paul Oppermann watched the copter take off from beneath the glittering Arch, he only prayed Delgado and Berglund would have as much luck in New York.

2:31 P.M. EST, THURSDAY, NOVEMBER 13
BRONX, NEW YORK

As he and Mike approached the car, Delgado tried desperately to remember what his cousin Ernesto had told him about disarming the bomb. "First we gotta find the case," he muttered, seeing Leah inside, searching frantically with Willis and his men.

"Let's start out here," he said to Mike, describing what the device looked like. They began pulling apart the junk piled around the car. Willis sent his man Drago out to help them. They tossed auto body parts and brick blocks away, desperately looking for one evilly gleaming metal case.

The filthy crash pad was cluttered with old sofas, tables, and chairs. Leah, Willis, and Burke opened drawers, dumping the contents, then searching the frames for hidden spaces where a suitcase could be concealed. Burke slashed every piece of upholstery and examined the moldy contents to be sure the case hadn't been stuffed inside. The floor was littered with clothes, automatic weapons, ammo, and junk of every kind. They dug through it like starving squirrels looking for a buried acorn. Nothing.

"We pulled the crap off the outside of the car. It isn't there," Del said. Mike and Drago followed him inside.

"It's not here either," Willis said. His round face was no longer genial but beaded with sweat.

"What if the bomb isn't around the car?" Leah asked suddenly.

"Police the tunnel. No time to waste," Delgado said in a tight voice. He grabbed Mike and gave him a big hug. "Love you, Tige."

"I love you, too, Dad," Mike said. He turned to tell Leah what he'd come to say, but she was already out the door, following the fat man who seemed to be in charge.

"Spread out," Willis said. "Burke, you, Delgado, and Drago take the right side. Sweetums, you and I go left."

Everyone dispersed swiftly. Their electric torches cast eerie danc-
ing shadows across the dimly lit tunnel. They scanned the crumbling
walls, pipes, and rusty tracks. Mike followed them outside, feeling
useless and scared. He didn't want anyone to die, but what could he
do? They'd already examined the junk pile around the subway car.
Still, maybe they'd missed it. What about underneath?

Always fascinated by how mechanical things worked, he squatted
down beside the back of the car and slipped underneath an old auto
fender leaning against it. Although they'd pulled apart all the bricks
and pieces of auto salvage around the car, some of it had been tossed
back. The space between the subway car and the fender was barely
wide enough for him to get past.

One of the men with Leah had given him an extra pencil torch
earlier. He used it to scan the auto salvage. The suitcase wasn't in the
junk. Mike quickly turned his attention to the wheels beneath the car,
aiming the narrow beam of light at the rusty metal fittings. Suddenly
something gleamed dully through the levers, gears, and brake lines.
Shinnying between the wheels on the disintegrating track, he reached
up where his light bounced off a smooth new surface. A grown-up
couldn't have gotten under far enough to see it, he thought, for once
glad that he was skinny.

He held the light in his teeth and used both hands, trying to pry
the case out. It would not budge. Mike realized that it must have been
placed in hiding from inside the car. Some kind of trapdoor they had
missed. He squirmed out and yelled, "Dad! Leah! I think I found it!"

Delgado came running. Leah turned at the cry and followed but
the other men were unwilling to pay attention to a kid who'd nearly
gotten them killed.

"It's under the middle of the car but I can't get it out. Looks just
like you described it," Mike said excitedly.

"Trapdoor?" Leah asked, climbing cat-quick back into the car.
"Tell me when I'm near it, Mike," she yelled as Del tossed fenders and
other auto parts away like a madman.

"Get under there and show me where it is so I can line it up for
her," he said to his son.

Mike again squeezed under the car and pointed his pencil torch at the case. Del aligned the light with the floor of the car, then relayed to Leah, "To the right another meter . . . there—that'll do it."

She ducked down and started to root through the debris and blood-soaked securities, then rolled the big corpse over onto his face. "That sucker was covering up a hidden door cut in the floor with a butane torch," she yelled out. She gave the body another shove so she could get at the narrow door.

Willis and his men heard her call and ran after Delgado, who was the first one back into the car. Mike stood by the door, his heart pounding. Maybe this would make up for nearly getting them all killed by the El-Ops.

"Jackpot!" Leah said as she pulled the small trapdoor open. She yanked the metal case out and placed it on the rickety table against the wall. "You're on, champ," she said to Del.

"Great," he said with a silent prayer as he opened the device.

Leah stepped close to Mike, who was covered with grease and rust. "Let's give your dad some space, huh?" She gave him a hug and led him to the back door, away from the dead bodies.

Mike watched silently as his father gazed down at the mechanism inside. A nuclear bomb. He looked over at Leah and then thought of his mom. They all might die if his dad couldn't do this. "You can do it, Dad," he mouthed silently.

The arming device is a digital receiver relay switch. The diameter of a cigarette, half the length. To disarm the bomb, all you have to do is unscrew and remove the detonator coupler in the upper right corner of the device. When he'd listened to Ernesto's instructions, it had sounded so simple.

Del reached down and turned the small cylinder projecting up about two centimeters. It came out in his hand. He sagged against the wall. "My cousin was right. Piece of cake." His voice cracked as he looked at Mike who stood at the car door. The detonator slipped from his now nerveless fingers and rolled. He knelt down to pick it up.

Willis checked his wrist unit. "Three o'clock exactly." He took a deep breath. "For a fibbie turned reporter, you're not a bad bomb tech." He looked back at Leah and read her eyes. His smile faded. "You put it together, Sweetums." He sighed.

"Heads up, Del." Leah stood in the door, in front of Mike.

Delgado saw the way she held the Ruger at her side and knew something was wrong. Willis went very still, grinning like a slightly thinner version of the twentieth-century comedian Jackie Gleason. His men were both on the right side of the room. Willis was on the left. Del was caught between them. The weight of his Smith & Wesson suddenly felt good inside his coat. He knew he'd only have one chance to reach it.

"You mentioned a hundred mil in those satchels, Willie," Leah said. "Even if you had talked to Reed, he didn't know that. Didn't know the payoff was in securities either."

"I was afraid you'd tumble, Sweetums," Willis said regretfully.

"You killed Kensington. Nobody in BISC could've made that shot . . . but me or you."

"Yep, you coulda. I had to kill the sumbitch. He contracted with me to back up his spook. With Sievers out of the way, our secretary of state was the only one who knew I was involved. And, too, there was all that lovely loot—and the bomb. Know what one of these little honeys is worth on the black market? Bernal would've been dumb enough to settle for a lousy ten mil. The Rabbit wanted the hundred. Lots of Middle East types'll pay even more."

"You're just a bidnessman, right, Willie? You tried to kill me in California, didn't you?"

"Now that's an insult, Sweetums. The hit on you was strictly amateur."

"But you used a former BISC agent posing as an escaping El-Op on Delgado."

He grinned sheepishly. "That I did. It was the Rabbit's idea to get rid of you both before you could get involved. I convinced Kensington and Sievers to let you lead us to Bernal after you survived."

"You set us up in Bogotá."

"Sievers thought he had Bernal sewed up tight. We didn't need you. I figured, hell, no better way for one of us to go down than killing Cartel scum."

She shook her head. "Come on, Willie. Do I look like General Custer?"

As she talked, Delgado got ready to move, waiting for her signal or any slight indicator from Willis to his thugs.

"Kensington was always one step ahead of us," she said. "And I talked to you throughout the investigation. Stupid that I didn't put it together sooner. The hit on Del nagged at me. I should've known you used BISC freelancers in the security business. I bet these guys don't have any fingerprints either, do you, fellas?" Her eyes never left Willis.

Both men looked at their boss. Delgado reached for his gun very carefully, shielding his hand behind his open coat as he leaned forward on the floor.

"I reckon you've stalled just about as long as I can let you, Sweet-ums. Those fibbies could be just around the bend by now, you think?"

Leah smiled. "No stalling, Willie. When did the fibbies ever get anywhere on time? Way I see it, your 'bidness' is to haul ass out of here with a profit. There's a hundred mil in negotiable securities ly-ing on the floor. You can wipe off the blood later. Take 'em and run. Your govy won't give a shit as long as it has the bomb back."

"Sweetums, for you I'd do it, but your boyfriend here isn't wired like us. He only sees black and white. He'd come after me and you'd tag along to keep me from—"

Willis's gun arm raised in a blur as he spoke. That same instant Leah fired. She hit him dead center between the eyes. Delgado's .50-caliber cannon smashed into Drago's chest, knocking him against his companion whose shot at Leah went wild. Del aimed for Burke. But Burke caught his motion in peripheral and twisted around, releasing a burst of automatic fire that shredded the molting sofa. A hail of bullets passed through it and tore into Delgado's right arm and chest. When Burke opened up on Del, Leah dropped him with one shot. He fell beside Drago.

Willis lay sprawled on the rug, his corpulent body draped grotesquely over the dead El-Op. "Damn, Willie," she muttered. An-other termination. She shivered as she made certain neither of his men was alive. Then she turned to the door. "Mike, you okay?"

"Yeah, but where's my dad?"

A groan from behind the sofa answered them. Leah shoved the boy back as she knelt beside Delgado. He was bleeding badly. "Grab some of those clothes—the shirts there." She pointed to a pile of clothes tossed during the search for the bomb. Mike obeyed, bringing her a fistful of shirts. She wadded them up to use as a pressure bandage for his chest, ignoring for the minute the nasty damage to his arm.

He looked up at her, eyes glazed but still conscious in spite of the blood pouring out of him. He was white and sweaty, bad signs, she knew. "Press this tight," she instructed Mike, demonstrating by placing his hands against the packing on his father's chest. "We have to help him breathe easier." She scrambled for the pile of clothes thrown from a large box, then rolled them into a big ball that she wedged under Delgado's back so he could recline in a semi-upright position.

"Better do like she says. She gets pissed quick," he whispered to his son.

Mike nodded, swallowing hard as he applied pressure. Leah began fashioning a tourniquet for Del's arm.

Delgado recognized that shock was numbing the pain. "Damn, every time I carry an FBI badge this happens . . . last time . . . didn't have nearly . . . as pretty a nurse." He gazed at Mike, fighting to stay conscious. "Hey, Tige. You have . . . some explaining . . ."

"Dad, I'm sorry," Mike said, swallowing hard when he saw the blood soak through the bandage. He could see it on his father's lips, too, and knew that was bad. Real bad.

"Don't be . . . till your mom . . . gets a hold of you."

While they spoke, Leah opened her link and called for help, trying to describe their underground location. "I gotta go street side to direct the life-flight here. You have to hold down the fort, Mike." She hated to leave him alone with Del in this shape. But she had no choice.

"I can do it, Leah," he said solemnly.

She nodded and started for the door. He called after her, "I wanted to tell you that I loved you in case the bomb went off."

Leah didn't trust herself to turn around and look at him. "I love you, too . . . Tige."

Tears blurred her eyes as she started to run.

22.

"The bomb in the Arch has been recovered and disarmed," John Scarletti said to Adam Manchester. They were seated in the AG's office. He'd just received a full report from Paul Oppermann. Scarletti was still stunned about his uncle. How could a man like Stuart Kensington have been the mastermind behind the nightmare? He sat staring into the cup of tea on his desk, didn't trust himself to raise it to his lips. He knew he'd spill it and scald himself. "We've just come back from the abyss, Adam."

"I still can't believe he orchestrated it," Manchester said. "Your mother's with your aunt. Jillian had no idea. She just happened to mention to Annie the awful sweetish stink of tobacco on Stuart's clothing when he'd come home over the past few weeks. Even joked with her sister about Stuart having a woman on the side who wore awful perfume. They thought it was funny. But when Annie told me . . ."

"You knew it was Sievers."

"I suspected enough to have Delgado's hacker break into his files." A grim smile etched his face as he confessed to the chief law enforcement officer in the nation that he'd broken the law.

"It's a damn good thing you did. How's Delgado?"

"Holding his own so far, but he might have bled to death or died of shock in the subway if Leah hadn't been able to get paramedics to him as soon as she did."

Scarletti knew the newsman was involved with Manchester's granddaughter. "I hope he makes it. Paul credits him and Special Agent Berglund with breaking the case for us. They wiped out Lopez's crazies in Miami, even opened communication with Benito Zuloaga. She was instrumental in finding the first leads on Sievers."

"Leah called him the Ashtray before we learned his name. A mystery man who worked for Karl Banecek when he was CIA director. I wonder if the truth will ever come out about that," Manchester said carefully.

"We have a meeting at the White House in an hour. Samson's called what's left of the cast in for debriefing—Banecek, McKinney, you, and me. Paul's sitting in via a secured vid from St. Louis. It'll take him a day or so to mop up there once we decide just exactly what the public has a right to know." The bitter edge in Scarletti's voice was unmistakable.

"You think Samson will cover up Kensington's and Labat's complicity and blame low-level extremists like that kid from Wisconsin for the bomb in St. Louis." It was a suspicion that had hung unspoken between the two men since Manchester had answered the AG's request to talk before they went to the Oval Office.

"No one knows about the bomb in New York. A shoot-out between El-Op gang members where all of them end up dead—that's nothing unusual in the Bronx. Barely make a blip in the media. Neither will some ex BISC types getting killed in the fracas. Samson could make Rhys Willis and his organization go away."

"What about Kensington?" Adam played devil's advocate.

"That will put a crimp in the president's initiative for Holy Arabia. The assassination of their most bitter foe makes them look guilty as sin, but we have a report on what went on record at the U.N. this afternoon." He handed the memo to Manchester.

The senator skimmed down the page. "All that's known is that Kensington was arrested by an FBI agent and escorted outside the building where he was assassinated. Nothing was translated for General Assembly members. It wouldn't take much to get the secretary general to hush up the treason warrant."

"I hear he's infinitely bribable," the AG said. "Kensington will be a hero—but at least he's a dead one. As to Labat"—he shrugged—"he could've had a heart attack . . . or a hunting accident back in Nevada." Scarletti had a pretty fair idea about how Wade Samson and Karl Banecek would handle it. They'd arrange something nice and sanitary.

"Samson could only cover up so much last summer."

The AG nodded. He was concentrating on bringing the now tepid tea to his mouth for a drink. It tasted sour. "The failed coup was an extremely mixed blessing for him. Almost getting killed gained public sympathy, but I don't think he wants to be remembered as the president making the worst cabinet choices since Warren Harding."

"He brought me in for the wrong reasons, but I don't regret it . . . even if I can't talk about what happened publicly. I do regret what Del, Leah, and I did to you, John."

A small smile turned Scarletti's lips, softening his harsh features so that Adam could see faint traces of his mother in him. He offered his hand. "Don't worry about it. I would've done the same thing if our positions had been reversed. Anyway, who knows, we might end up related one of these days."

Adam smiled. "When the time's right, I'll ask her. Don't know if she'll have me and all the grief of the campaign trail."

"She is a Democrat," John replied as they shook hands.

"A bipartisan administration," Manchester said.

"Sounds like a win-win situation to me," Scarletti replied.

At the door the senator paused thoughtfully. "I don't know if your aunt could survive the scandal if Kensington's treason came out. All the others involved in it are dead. Bin Bergi's cells in this country have been seriously disrupted. Holy Arabia may implode. I believe keeping quiet is the best course."

"Even if it means Wade Samson gets a Nobel Peace Prize?"

Manchester shrugged wearily. "The nation needs its heroes, John. We've had a surfeit of traitors. Besides, if he makes Kensington a martyr to Holy Arabia, I doubt Samson'll be brokering peace in the Middle East anytime soon."

"Just so he doesn't get reelected."

"You're a Democrat, too, remember?" Manchester grinned.

"I've become an Independent," Scarletti said.

"I'll do my damnedest to beat the son of a bitch."

"You have my vote. My mother would make one hell of a first lady."

7:30 P.M. EST, THURSDAY, NOVEMBER 13
BRONX, NEW YORK

Waiting rooms in any hospital looked pretty much the same to those trapped inside their individual cocoons of fear and hope. At the Bronx Municipal Hospital the area was painted institutional green and the furniture was equally practical, sturdy chrome-framed chairs with dark gray cushions made of the latest stain-repellant poly fabric. The fluorescent lighting overhead bleached everyone in the tense room a shade somewhere between the colors of the walls and the chairs.

On a large vid screen high atop one wall a news anchor reported on Secretary of State Stuart Kensington's assassination. The talking heads following the news byte speculated about rumors of his arrest just before he was killed in front of the U.N. building, but the Justice Department spokeswoman refused comment. Grist for media mills, but the real drama had taken place on the St. Louis riverfront.

The screen feed switched to the Gateway Arch where a nuclear bomb had narrowly averted being detonated. Was there some connection between the Holy Arabian terrorists responsible and Kensington's death in New York? No one had any evidence yet but that never stopped the pundits.

Leah heard the voices droning on as she paced in front of a window overlooking a run-down park. El-Ops were probably conducting business beneath the bare gray trees in the darkness. It had started to snow. None of that concerned her now. Del had been rushed into surgery hours ago with multiple bullet wounds. He had a punctured lung and the blood loss was severe. The surgical team's expressions had not been encouraging when they wheeled him into the operating room.

Leah had seen that look many times over the years since entering law enforcement. *But not since I joined BISC.* There had been no survivors in the termination business.

Across the room, Mike sat with his mother, watching Leah pace. She'd been so calm during the crisis. When the medics came, she had taken Mike with her in the copter ride to the hospital, answered his questions. But now she looked lost, pale, and frightened, just like all the other people who waited for word of their loved ones.

Diana leaned over to her son and said, "Go talk to her. I think she could use a little help."

He looked at his mother, guilty because of the way he'd left her at the airport. "You sure you don't mind?"

Diana squeezed his hand. "She needs you, sweetie."

"You're really jake, Mom." He swallowed for courage, then got up and walked over to the window where Leah stared out at nothing. She didn't seem aware of him until he spoke. "I'm scared, too. I think it's okay to feel that way . . . isn't it?"

Something knotted tightly inside her loosened a bit as she realized he stood beside her and what he'd said. "Yeah, Mike, it's okay." She managed a smile. *God, he looks like Del.*

"You were awfully brave when you made those bandages for him."

"You were pretty brave yourself. You held down the fort while I went for help," she said. "Lots of guys older than you might've been afraid of blood, Mike."

"You called me Tige, you know . . . when I said I loved you. That's why I hid in the copter and followed Dad to you." He looked gravely into her eyes. "I kinda thought . . ." He cleared his throat. "I thought you might want to know that was why I did it. I had to tell you."

Leah blinked back the tears, afraid if she gave in to her emotions she'd lose it completely and terrify him. He'd already been through enough. What if Del died? Mike might have a lot worse to deal with before the day was over. So would she.

"I'm glad you did it." Then she broke down and threw her arms around him.

Mike returned her embrace, hugging her fiercely. When they finally let go of each other, both wiped away tears.

"I love you, even if I haven't shown it much these past months," she said. "I have a lot of . . . baggage from being a BISC agent. I used my work at Clean Ride to hide behind. I was afraid of letting anyone get too close."

He nodded, scrubbing at his cheeks. "That's what my mom used to say about Dad when he was an FBI agent."

"Do you want them to get back together?" *Stupid thing to ask at a time like this, Berglund!* The question surprised her as the words tumbled out, but Mike didn't seem bothered by it.

"No. For a while I thought . . . when you canceled out on us for the zoo last month I was really mad. That was just a dumb kid thing."

"I'm sorry I did that." She knew now how precious and fleeting those chances to be with loved ones were. "Guess I blew it, huh?"

"Naw. I've had time to think it over. Dad and Mom get along better when they don't live together. She likes the symphony and art museum and all kinds of society stuff that bores him. You and Dad have the same kind of jobs—well, sort of, at least when you go on secret missions like in New York."

"About that, Mike—"

"I know I'm not supposed to say anything. Special Agent in Charge Reed explained to my mom and me that it was a matter of national security," he said solemnly.

"You're a very smart guy, Tige," she said, fighting more tears.

"Did Dad tell you how he got to be called El Tigre?" he asked to distract her, sensing that displays of emotion disturbed her. After spending so much time with his father's big Mexican family, he was less bothered by it. Still, she was a government agent and he was a man . . . well, almost. He shouldn't cry either.

Leah smiled a bit. "He didn't explain. Your family in Mazatlán did."

"I bet it was Uncle Raoul, wasn't it?"

"None other."

The waiting-room door swung open and a gray-haired woman in green scrubs emerged, pulling off a surgical mask. She scanned the room of hopeful, apprehensive faces. "Mrs. Shrewsbury?"

Diana stood up as Mike and Leah quickly crossed the room to her.

"I'm Dr. Bryant. Special Agent Delgado's being taken to recovery.

We've made a graft in the pulmonary artery and reinflated the lung.
He's been given eight units of blood. He'll have tubes in his chest and
side for drainage, so don't be alarmed. The micro surgeon, Dr. Sung,
has repaired the brachial plexus as much as he could, considering the
nerve damage. It was a near thing, but I think it's safe to say the agent
is out of the woods now."

"What about the use of his arm?" Leah asked, dreading the answer.
After all the PT he went through with his leg, please not again.

"Oh, he'll require extensive physical therapy to regain partial use,"
the surgeon replied.

"How soon can we see him?" Diana asked as Mike clutched her
hand tightly.

As the doctor was explaining the time span for monitoring pa-
tients in recovery before moving them to ICU, Adam Manchester
walked into the room. Leah turned as he strode toward her. "I took a
charter as soon as I could get away," he said, giving her a hug.

"He's going to make it, Gramps," she said, burying her face against
his chest. He patted her back and held her until she raised her head.
"You look like hell."

He snorted. "Can't say you'd win any beauty prizes yourself at the
moment."

People in the room quickly recognized the senator, who had made
numerous television appearances in recent months, but no one approached him out of respect for their common concerns in this place.
Dr. Bryant's face gave a flicker of recognition, but she said nothing either, just gave them directions to the cafeteria, suggesting they all rest
and have a bite to eat while waiting to see Del.

"So it's a whitewash," Leah said. She and Adam left Mike and Diana
picking desultorily at their plates of institutional chicken and pizza,
and walked to a deserted table where he could tell her about the
meeting with Samson.

"I know how hard it was for you last summer when—"

"No, that was different, personal. I didn't work with Kensington
or Labat. Willie . . . well, that one hurt," she admitted. "At least

Kensington's supposed martyrdom should put a real crimp in Samson's bid for reelection. I can live with it—just so you win next November."

"That's what John said before the meeting."

"Smart man. What did Paul have to say about the decision?"

"I always thought your friend Lev knew how to swear in Yiddish, but he was a rank amateur compared to Paul Oppermann." He smiled grimly. "I don't think Samson caught the half of it or he might have fired him on the spot. Kicking and screaming, but the director's going along with the rest of us."

Leah could imagine how furious Paul was. "He still in St. Louis?"

"Yes. He has an agent in critical condition, the Muslim-American undercover agent who broke bin Bergi's plan. He's sticking around to make sure the guy's okay."

"It's a risky business," she said, stirring the cup of blond coffee in front of her, long gone cold.

"You and Del are out of it now, Leah-Pia. Stay out. And stay together."

"The doc says he'll need months of rehab. Dammit, he's been down that road with his leg already."

"You'll be there to help him through it."

"Mike and the whole Mulcahey clan will be there for him. I don't know if—"

"Yes, you do." His steady blue eyes held hers.

Leah felt the weight that had been squeezing her chest for months suddenly lift. She gave him a big grin. "You're so damn smart, you oughta be president."

EPILOGUE

SIX MONTHS LATER
SAN DIEGO, CALIFORNIA

"Hurts like a bitch," Delgado said as the physical therapist had him begin yet another set of exercises.

"Quit your whining. I can see the improvement every day," Leah said as she watched his sweat-drenched body move through the reps awkwardly.

The scars on his chest and arm were terrible, but new muscle was starting to rebuild, corded and powerful. The nerve damage to his right shoulder and arm had been severe. The neurologists had not been optimistic about how much use he would regain. He'd spent months in and out of hospitals and rehab centers before being allowed to return to his apartment.

"You're as merciless as he is," Del groused, glancing from where she stood in the doorway back to the therapist beside him. But he kept on moving the arm.

"I'd have never believed you'd get this much motion back, Del," Dick Helm said. Over the course of the therapy he'd become friends with the newsman and his social worker roommate.

"Neither did the doctors. I . . . knew . . . better," Delgado grunted, finishing the set.

"Arrogance is good," she said.

"Hey, whatever works," Helm replied, handing his patient a towel. As he gathered up his things, preparing to leave, Delgado dried his sweat-drenched face and upper body.

Leah let Dick out, then came back into the apartment's largest bedroom, which they'd converted into a gym. It held his weight-lifting gear and several fancy workout machines as well as her punching bag and a tatami mat where she practiced her ukemi and various katas.

"I'm hitting the showers," he said, throwing the towel over his shoulder.

She watched his backside as he walked down the hall, clad only in a pair of shorts and tennies. "Great tush for an old crip, Delgado," she said.

"That's the only part of me nobody's shot up yet," he called back cheerfully.

They had been through a real rough patch when he'd begun therapy the first of the year. This time he was the one pushing her away because he knew he might end up permanently disabled. Besides, he remembered what a bastard he'd turned into during the reconstruction of his leg. But Leah amazed him.

She just packed up her things and arrived on his doorstep one morning a few days after they'd returned to California, announcing that she'd canceled her lease and was going to commute to her job at Clean Ride. When he tried to run her off, she stuck like Velcro.

Del knew how much courage it took for Leah to make the commitment. They'd had some beauts of yelling matches. She told him it strengthened his injured lung. Once he was sure he would not end up losing the use of his right arm, he'd mellowed out. Mike and his whole family were, of course, overjoyed that she was with him. He'd become pretty damned happy himself when he recovered enough to do more than sleep in the same bed with her. Since she'd moved in, she had not had a single nightmare. Her shrink said she had finally faced her guilt and dealt with it. Del attributed it to living with him.

Grinning at his retreating backside, Leah stripped off her clothes, scattering them as she wended her way down the hall toward the bathroom. Once a neat freak, she was becoming almost as much of a slob as Delgado.

When she slipped into the steamy shower with him, he wasn't surprised. "You always like to do it wet."

"Saves water. This is southern California, remember?" she said, taking the soap from him, starting to lather up his chest. . . .

"Some jerk-offs in D.C. are starting a fund to build a memorial for that great American patriot, Stuart Kensington," Del said, glancing at a small piece in the evening newspaper.

"I called that one wrong. Told him he'd go down worse than Benedict Arnold."

"You're not bitter about it." He studied her as she moved around the kitchen, making a salad to go with the chili casserole he'd put in the oven after they finished in the shower.

Leah shrugged. "Gramps is ahead of Samson in the polls by twelve points. I told Kensington that Adam Manchester would end up in the White House, and he'd end up dead. I'll settle for getting that much right."

"More rumors about the government in Riyadh toppling. Seems the mullahs are fighting among themselves," he said. "Cohen's sending one of his aces to cover the story for us." Benjamin Z. Cohen was the editor-in-chief of Del's weekly news mag, *U.S. News-Time.*

She stopped chopping a zucchini and looked at him. "You don't want that assignment."

"I wouldn't touch it with a fork even if Ben were crazy enough to offer and I were physically up to going. You gave up risking your neck on the waterfront, I gave up risking mine for another Pulitzer."

"If you'd written the truth about Kensington and the nukes, you'd have won another one for sure."

"Maybe." He smiled that old cynical smile. "But Samson's not getting his Nobel either."

Leah grinned back at him. "As a man once said, 'I love it when a plan comes together.' "